knowledge. 知識工場

Knowledge is everything！

知識工場
Knowledge is everything！

張翔、賴素如
英語教學團隊／聯合編著

Ian Crews
／審訂

路易思
牛津英語大師／強力推薦

搶救英文失語症！

照著**學**就能**說**的超簡單**國民英語**

Let's Talk In English From Now On!

教你用APP隨手聊、脫口溜英文，英語會話，真的一本就能TALK！

👑 精華再升級！

👑 神人級應對！

👑 全方位訓練！

USER'S GUIDE

在APP邊聊邊學，掌握生活英文超簡單！

拿起你的手機，與全球接軌，談樂事、吐苦水，體驗隨身、隨時、隨地的最強英語學習法！

1 多元化的出場人物

每個單元將設計職業、性格不同的出場人物，想用英文展現真實性格？就請跟著本書的角色，學會多元的英文表達法吧！

2 隨手APP就能學英文

藉由本書教你的最實用主題，融合APP毫無侷限的便利性，就能隨時與朋友暢談生活，在閒聊中提升口說英語力！

3 強化口說的聊天TIP

在APP對話中標注慣用語和特殊語調，更快速地掌握重點字句，同時學會面對不同人時可採用的語氣！

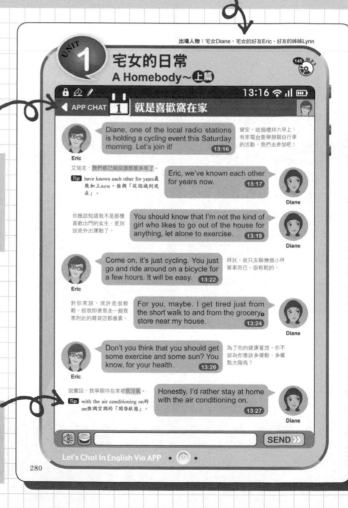

出場人物：宅女Diane、宅女的好友Eric、好友的姊姊Lynn

UNIT 1
宅女的日常
A Homebody～上篇

APP CHAT **1** 就是喜歡窩在家

13:16 🔋

Eric: Diane, one of the local radio stations is holding a cycling event this Saturday morning. Let's join it! `13:16`
黛安，這個禮拜六早上，有家電台要舉辦騎自行車的活動，我們去參加吧！

艾瑞克，我們都已經認識那麼多年了。
Tip have known each other for years最後加上now，強調「認識到現在」。
Diane: Eric, we've known each other for years now. `13:17`

你應該知道我不是那種喜歡出門的女生，更別說是出門運動了。
Diane: You should know that I'm not the kind of girl who likes to go out of the house for anything, let alone to exercise. `13:19`

Eric: Come on, it's just cycling. You just go and ride around on a bicycle for a few hours. It will be easy. `13:22`
拜託，就只是騎幾個小時單車而已，很輕鬆的。

對你來說，或許是很輕鬆，但我到即便是走一趟我家附近的雜貨店都會累。
Diane: For you, maybe. I get tired just from the short walk to and from the grocery store near my house. `13:24`

Eric: Don't you think that you should get some exercise and some sun? You know, for your health. `13:26`
為了你的健康著想，你不認為你應該多運動、多曬點太陽嗎？

說實話，我寧願待在家裡吹冷氣。
Tip with the air conditioning on的on強調空調的「開著狀態」。
Diane: Honestly, I'd rather stay at home with the air conditioning on. `13:27`

SEND »

Let's Chat In English Via APP

280

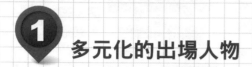

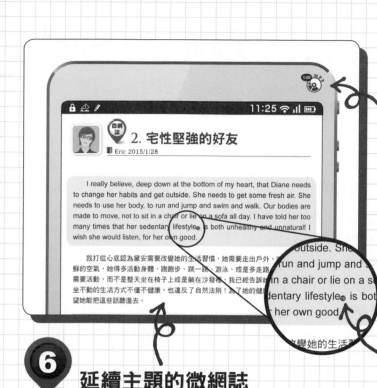

4

外師親錄MP3

隨書附贈由外籍名師親錄的MP3光碟，將隨情境呈現不同的語調。利用MP3訓練聽力、練習口說，聽與說的能力一次增進！

5

精選重點單字

從APP對話與微網誌的內容中，挑選重點單字，並於單元後的「單字動態看板」詳細解說！

6

延續主題的微網誌

延續每單元的APP對話內容，教你更深入地PO心情、談意見，跳脫基礎英語，寫出屬於你自己的「微網誌心聲」吧！

7

單字動態看板

整理單元內的重點字彙，除了基本的字義等內容，另外還會補充常見用法，一次掌握基礎單字與進階活用！

APP 單字動態看板 Vocabulary Billboard

Word 單字	Meaning 字義	Usage 常見用法
1 appointment [ə`pɔɪntmənt]	名 約會；任命；職位；委派	make an appointment 訂下約定 hold an appointment 擔任職務
2 average [`ævərɪdʒ]	名 平均；普通 形 平均的；一般的	on average 按平均值；通常 above the average 超過平均水準
3 workaholic [ˌwɝkə`hɔlɪk]	名 工作狂 形 醉心於工作的	a workaholic personality 工作狂特質 turn into a workaholic 變成工作狂
4 independent	形 獨立的；單獨的	be independent of 與⋯無關

用聊天取代教室學習，學英文也能樂在其中！

　　在英語教學的過程中，總會遇到學生向我詢問簡單、活潑的學習方式，學習外語對他們來說，固然是一個長期的過程，但若能在教學時點燃學生們的興趣，則能幫助他們持續不斷地研習，在各個階段裡精益求精，因此，「激發學習動力」一直都是我教學的目標，就是為了這樣的目的，本書才因此誕生。

　　本書在編排上，特別挑選一般大眾在生活中最常聊到的話題，並在每一個話題下，規劃內容連貫的APP對話與微網誌內容，這樣的設計就是為了能讓讀者具備進階的聊天能力。比方說，在旅遊單元裡，就從行前邀約、討論旅遊型態、一路寫到旅遊結束的心得，幫助讀者在與人聊到相關話題時，能談得更深、更廣，而不再只是淺談即止。

　　生活英語和教室裡學的英文之所以會有差異，是因為我們在實際談天時，會賦予這些英文字句更多情緒與想法，面對上司、好友、家人…等，都會產生不同的說法和語氣，為了能提供最實用的英文，本書在編排時也點出了書中人物彼此之間的關係，在這個基礎下，衍生出語氣、話題各異的聊天內容，隨著各單元的人物，讀者將能一步步跳脫以往學的基礎會話，學會多元化的表達方式。

　　學習語文的確需要長期的摸索，但它絕對不是一個枯燥的背誦過程，相反的，它應該是一個能隨著時間而越來越深入、也越來越能融入生活的一件事，如果你也希望能活用生活英語，或者想跳脫以往的學習框架，體驗更加生活化、活潑有趣的英語，就請善用這本書，從這一步開始，拓展學習語文的道路。

張翔

在APP上聊英文，生活英語就是這麼活潑！

　　近來，隨著智慧型手機聊天軟體不斷日益先進且廣受大學生和上班族的青睞，因此，編者特地結合了最夯的科技聊天軟體與英文，以幫助讀者提昇「聽」、「說」、「讀」、「寫」的能力。

　　在內容的編排上，本書囊括了五大主題：生活面面觀、人生階段、課業與職場、專長與嗜好，以及生活型態。二十三大最生活化的主題，就是希望能給學習者最實用的英文，不再害怕用英語和人交流的場合。

本書之編輯特色如下：

👍 特色一：「APP CHAT對話」

　　對話之間彼此有劇情連貫性，藉由APP CHAT，讀者可鍛鍊口語能力。

👍 特色二：「微網誌BLOG」

　　以該單元的出場人物為核心，記錄他們的心情記事，讀者可藉由這部份的內容提昇書寫能力。

👍 特色三：「單字動態看板」

　　從對話及微網誌中擷取重要單字、介紹字義，最重要的是，讀者可從「常見用法」中學到更多單字的延伸用法。

　　提昇讀者「聽」、「說」、「讀」、「寫」的英語全收錄在本書，如此簡單又生活化的學習方式，正是忙碌的現代人最需要的英文幫手！

　　本書能順利完成，歸功於整個團隊夥伴：負責撰寫對話的劉宗原老師、資深翻譯專家李江河老師與李建宸老師、以及負責全書審訂的英文主編Ian Crews，最後，再次感謝團隊齊心努力，讓本書能如期付梓。

用最生活化的方式學英文，聽說讀寫全面並進！

學習任何一種語言的第一步驟絕對是從「聽」（Listening）開始，先「聽」每個單字的發音（Pronunciation)，再藉由單字組合之片語（Phrase）或句子（Sentence）來瞭解語意（Meaning）。輸入的語言（Input）之語意「聽」懂了和「聽」通了以後，接下來的第二步驟就是意念之表達 —「說」（Speaking），也就是輸出的語言（Output）。

本書最具特色之處就是以時下最流行的智慧型手機中之「APP對話聊天軟體」為學習英文的界面，以最貼近大眾生活的主題，例如食物、醫療、求婚計畫、新婚搬家、畢業交叉口、職場菜鳥指南、喜愛文藝、電影、悠閒假日等作為「聽」與「說」的標的。透過閱「讀」這些比較輕鬆的語意內容，同學間、好友間以及同事之間就可以用APP聊天軟體聊出好英文。

本書另也介紹如何運用微網誌抒發心情，或是針對某個議題發表個人看法而不帶有任何批評的字眼；讀者們亦可藉由部落格增進自已的英文書「寫」能力。更值得一提的是作者特別將一般讀者感到十分困擾的英文單字貼心整理得更生活化，更易學、易記。

相信透過這本書在「聽」、「說」、「讀」和「寫」全方位的設計下，讀者們可以重新拾回學習英文的樂趣與成就感，學好英文，再也不是一件不可能的任務。

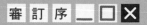

Let's Master English Through APP Chatting !

This book is a great tool for anyone interested in improving their English language ability through casual and interesting reading. This is because the conversations and blogs contained in the book attempt to simulate real-life scenarios. In other words, this book does not assume an overly pedantic tone, and it does not present the reader with dry essays while worthwhile and beneficial are also very boring. In other words, this is a fun book.

The structure of each unit in the book is two app conversations followed by two blogs. Each blog is written by one of the characters in the previous conversations. The topics of these units run the gamut of our modern lives, from college life to marriage, from exploring a night market to family gatherings. The conversations explore these topics through two fictional characters, and the blogs discuss the content of the conversations as viewed by one of the characters. Having two conversations and two blogs provides a stronger context and more detail into the topics discussed — a more complete picture.

CONTENTS

Part 1 生活面面觀~隨時與朋友分享的日常

掌握生活中的高頻率話題，學會這些英文，就能隨手傳訊聊心情！

CONTENTS

CONTENTS

Part 3 課業與職場～一步一腳印的人生藍圖

按部就班地規劃人生？盡情揮灑青春？現在就拿起手機寫你的心情記事吧！

CONTENTS

Part 4 專長與嗜好~生活中不可或缺的調劑

喜歡與同好討論相同的嗜好嗎？休閒生活不留白，大膽說出你的興趣所在！

Part 5 **生活型態**～原來每個人都不一樣

擁有特殊個性的人都聊什麼？擺脫正經八百的教科書，用英文展現性格吧！

UNIT 1 **宅女的日常** A Homebody～上篇

CONTENTS

UNIT 4 海外假期 Travel Overseas～上篇

UNIT 4 海外假期 Travel Overseas～下篇

UNIT 5 科技與人性 As Technology Develops～上篇

UNIT 5 科技與人性 As Technology Develops～下篇

Part

1

生活面面觀

隨時與朋友分享的日常

將英文融入生活的第一步，就是掌握生活中最常見的話題。
非分享不可的美食、令人滿足的血拼戰利品……
這些幾乎每天都在接觸的話題，該怎麼用英文簡單說呢？
從簡短的APP訊息，到不PO不行的心情微網誌，
本章將從飲食開始，一步步養成你的生活英語力！

Let's Chat In English
Via APP

UNIT 1

飲食人生
Enjoy The Food～上篇

001 MP3

16:30

◀ APP CHAT **1** 難以置信的食物

Bart

Can you show me around the night market? **16:30**

你可以帶我到夜市看看嗎？

沒問題，但你怎麼會突然想去夜市呢？明明我之前約你，你都說沒興趣。

Certainly. But why do you want to go to the night market all of a sudden❶? I clearly remember asking you before and you said you weren't interested. **16:36**

Alice

Bart

That's because I thought night markets were just like a kind of supermarket. **16:42**

那是因為我之前以為「夜市」就只是超市的一種。

哈哈，同樣是買東西的地方，夜市可有趣太多了，那裡最棒的是各式小吃。

Haha, they are places to go shopping, really interesting places. The best thing there is the variety of food. **16:48**

Alice

Bart

Yeah, I've heard there are some traditional snacks in Taiwan's night markets that I have to try. **16:50**

我聽說台灣的夜市裡有我一定要嚐嚐的傳統小吃。

Tip 聊到特色小吃會用到的實用片語traditional snack。

這是當然了！要不要試試豬血糕呢？

Of course! How about pig's blood cake? **16:51**

Alice

Bart

Umm...pig's blood cake? I've never heard of that before. **16:53**

嗯…豬血糕？我從來沒聽過那種食物。

  SEND »

16:30

是啊！它真的非常好吃，就像鬆軟的布丁一樣。

Yes! It's really delicious – like soft pudding. 16:54

Alice

But...blood? It sounds kind of gross. What are the other ingredients? 16:57

Bart

但是…血？聽起來有點噁心，裡面還有用到什麼材料啊？

Tip 和熟人才適合直接用gross。

其實，它就是豬血和糯米做成的。

Actually, it's only made of pig's blood and glutinous rice. 16:59

Alice

Real pig's blood? Oh, my god! That sounds horrible. 17:00

Bart

真的豬血嗎？喔，天啊！聽起來太恐怖了。

一點都不恐怖，你應該要試試看，我保證你嚐了一口之後就會愛上它的。

It really isn't. You should try it. I guarantee❷ you'll love it after taking just a bite. 17:03

Alice

All right. I'll trust you and give it a try. Are you free tonight? 17:05

Bart

好吧！我姑且相信你試試看，你晚上有空嗎？

Tip 和親近的人對話可用free詢問，語氣很口語、輕鬆。

有空啊，我們晚一點碰面，我再帶你去你家附近的夜市。

I am, yeah. Let's meet later, and I'll take you to the night market near your house. 17:08

Alice

SEND ≫

Let's Chat In English Via APP

11:45 🔋

迪恩，我的美國同學巴特是個不折不扣的甜點行家。

Dean, my American classmate, Bart, is a true connoisseur₃ of desserts. `11:45`

Alice

Wow! He must be a glutton₄ for desserts, right? `11:48`

哇！那他肯定超愛吃甜點的，對吧？

Dean

沒錯！他尤其喜歡吃巧克力蛋糕、蘋果派、以及甜甜圈。

Right! He is particularly fond of eating chocolate cake, apple pie, and donuts. `11:51`

Alice

It sounds like he is a dessert lover, just like me. `11:53`

聽起來的確是個甜食愛好者，和我差不多。

Tip 口語會話的簡短表達法。

Dean

差多了，他不只喜愛，簡直有「甜食上癮症」，一天吃好幾次甜點。

Yeah. But he doesn't just like desserts, it's almost like he has an addiction. He eats sweets several times a day. `11:56`

Alice

Was it that surprising? How often does he eat desserts? `11:59`

有那麼誇張嗎？他有多常吃甜點啊？

Tip 覺得對方說話似乎有點誇張時，才這樣問。

Dean

他告訴我的是每餐飯後都吃，早餐、午餐、以及晚餐後都會有甜點。

He told me he eats dessert after each meal – for breakfast, lunch, and dinner. `12:01`

Alice

  SEND ≫

Let's Chat In English Via APP

Dean

That's three desserts a day! I guess he can't live without them.
`12:03`

那根本是一天照三餐吃耶！我猜他沒有甜點肯定活不下去。

Tip can't live without為強調極需要某物的說法。

是啊，每當他心情不好或感到沮喪時，就會來一道他最愛的甜點：巧克力蛋糕。

Yeah. Whenever he's in a bad mood⑤ or feels frustrated, he will eat his favorite dessert – chocolate cake.
`12:05`

Alice

Dean

Oh, my god! Your classmate and I have something in common – we both love chocolate cake.
`12:07`

天啊！你同學和我有個共同點，都喜歡巧克力蛋糕。

那我介紹你們認識怎麼樣？我想你們肯定會一拍即合的。

Tip hit it off可表達出馬上成為好友的立即感。

How about I introduce you two? I think you will definitely hit it off.
`12:09`

Alice

Dean

That sounds good! I'll take him to my favorite chocolate cake store.
`12:11`

聽起來不錯喔！我要帶他去我最喜愛的巧克力蛋糕店。

喔，他也擅長做各式各樣的甜點，他做的點心簡直是人間美味。

Oh, he also excels at making a variety of desserts. The desserts he makes are out of this world.
`12:14`

Alice

Dean

Unbelievable! No wonder you call him a connoisseur of desserts.
`12:16`

真是難以置信！難怪你稱他為甜點行家。

  SEND ▸▸

微網誌

1. 那是什麼食物？！

📖 Bart 2013/8/12

Last week, I was taken to a night market to experience some of the local culture of Taiwan. As we entered the night market, I turned to my classmate, Alice, and asked, "What is that smell?" She told me, "Don't worry, I'll show you." As we walked further into the night market, the smell became stronger. We arrived at a small food stall surrounded by many people. "This is stinky tofu," she said. I could see from the size of the crowd that this was definitely a popular food in Taiwan.

上週，我被帶到夜市去體驗本地的台灣文化，當我們一走進夜市，我就轉頭問我的同學愛麗絲：「那是什麼味道啊？」她告訴我：「別擔心，我會帶你去看的。」隨著我們更往夜市裡走，那味道就越來越重，最後，我們來到一個被很多人圍住的小攤位，「這是臭豆腐。」她說，從排隊人潮的規模來看，我敢肯定，那個食物在台灣一定很夯。

Everyone seemed to be enjoying it so much, and I could not understand why. The smell was so strong. Alice convinced me to try one bite, and that one bite was all I needed to know I didn't like stinky tofu. It tasted as bad as it smelt! I asked Alice if we could continue walking around because I knew I would not want to try pig's blood cake if I saw or smelt anymore stinky tofu.

每個人看起來都吃得津津有味，但我完全無法理解，那東西的味道實在太重了，愛麗絲說服我嚐一口，我吃了，而且這一口就足以讓我確定自己不喜歡臭豆腐，它嚐起來的味道就跟聞起來一樣可怕！我問愛麗絲我們可不可以繼續逛別的攤位，因為我知道自己如果再多看一眼、或者是多聞一下臭豆腐的話，我就沒胃口吃豬血糕了。

微網誌 2. 跟著朋友品嚐甜點

Alice 2013/8/16

My American classmate, Bart, is such a dessert connoisseur and glutton. He knows and enjoys practically every kind of dessert. Yesterday, he came to class so excited and wanted to introduce a new chocolate cake store to me. He said that the cakes there are amazing. Unfortunately, I've been dieting recently. He wanted to drag me down there with him and tried very hard to persuade me. I was going to turn down his invitation, but I finally agreed to try the tempting[8] dessert. My appetite[9] outdid[10] my rationality.

我的美國同學巴特真的是個甜點行家兼饕客，他對各種甜點都瞭若指掌，而且每一種點心他都愛吃。昨天，他一臉興奮地來上課，想向我推薦一間新開的巧克力蛋糕店，他說那裡的蛋糕是難以置信的美味，不巧的是，我最近在節食。他很想拉我一起去，並費盡唇舌地說服我，我原本打算拒絕他的，但我最終還是答應去品嚐誘人的甜點，唉，我的口腹之欲戰勝了理智。

"Just one piece," I told myself. But when I took a bite, I realized Bart's insanity[11] in no time. I was like, "This is worth being fat for!" What's even worse is that I couldn't resist the temptation of some other desserts at the store and bought some brownies and donuts. Of course, my punishment came the next day when I found out I gained two kilograms. I am seriously reconsidering whether I should keep[12] hanging out with Bart or not after that day!

我告訴自己「就只吃一塊」，但當我咬了一口後，就立刻理解巴特為何會如此瘋狂地著迷了，那個時候，我腦中就只想著「為了這些美味，變胖也值得！」更糟的是，我抗拒不了店裡其他甜點的誘惑，還買了布朗尼和甜甜圈回家，當然，隔天我就受到懲罰了，我胖了兩公斤，說真的，經過那天的甜食洗禮之後，我得認真考慮是否應該繼續這樣跟巴特出去玩！

Word 單字	Meaning 字義	Usage 常見用法
1 sudden [`sʌdn]	名 突然發生的事 形 突然的；意外的	all of a sudden 突然間 on a sudden whim 因一個突然的想法
2 guarantee [ˌɡærən`ti]	名 保證；抵押品 動 保證；擔保	carry a three-year guarantee 有三年保證 offer sth. as a guarantee 拿出…作抵押品
3 connoisseur [ˌkɑnə`sɝ]	名 行家；有品味的人	a connoisseur in/of …的行家 an art connoisseur 藝術品鑑賞家
4 glutton [`ɡlʌtn]	名 貪吃的人；老饕； (口)酷愛…的人	a glutton for work 工作狂 a literary glutton 酷愛文學的人
5 mood [mud]	名 心情；生氣； 喜怒無常；氣氛	catch the mood of sb. 迎合某人的情緒 in a bad mood 心情不好
6 stall [stɔl]	名 欄，；廄；攤位； 隔間；車位	a book stall 書攤 a shower stall 淋浴的隔間
7 popular [`pɑpjələ]	形 大眾的；通俗的； 流行的	be popular among 受(團體)歡迎 sing popular songs 唱流行歌曲
8 tempting [`tɛmptɪŋ]	形 誘人的	be too tempting to resist 難抵擋的誘惑 a tempting offer 誘人的提議
9 appetite [`æpəˌtaɪt]	名 胃口；口腹之欲	an appetite for 食慾；欲望；愛好 a big appetite 胃口大增(吃很多)
10 outdo [ˌaʊt`du]	動 勝過；超越	outdo sb. in sth. 在某事中戰勝某人 not to be outdone 不甘示弱
11 insanity [ɪn`sænətɪ]	名 瘋狂；精神錯亂	a plea of insanity 辯稱案發時精神失常 certify to his insanity 證明他精神錯亂
12 keep [kip]	動 保持；維持	keep from 阻止 keep a diary 寫日記

UNIT 1

飲食人生
Enjoy The Food～下篇

🔒 📃 ✏️　　　　　　　　14:20 📶 📳

◀ APP CHAT **3** 走！請你吃飯去

Bart

Hey, I wanted to thank you for taking me to the night market. I finally experienced₁ the culture₂ of Taiwanese food and snacks. `14:20`

嘿，我要謝謝你帶我去逛夜市，我終於體驗到台灣食物與小吃的文化了。

說真的，跟你一起逛夜市還真開心呢！

Tip 口語表達，hang out的對象通常是朋友。

Frankly speaking, it was a pleasure to hang out and show you around a night market. `14:22`

Alice

Bart

Really? Why do you say that? `14:23`

真的嗎？怎麼說？

當你咬了一口臭豆腐後，愣在那裡的樣子還真夠呆的了，看到你臉上的表情，這趟夜市之旅就值回票價了。

When you were persuaded into eating a bite of stinky tofu, your face froze, and you looked so silly. The look on your face made the trip worthwhile. `14:28`

Alice

Bart

I still feel so embarrassed₃ about that. `14:29`

我到現在都還覺得很糗。

我想也是！

Tip 和朋友之間的口語英文，表達說話者能理解對方的感受。

I bet you do. `14:30`

Alice

Bart

I mean it. The taste of stinky tofu and pig's blood cake...I will never forget them. `14:33`

我是說真的，臭豆腐和豬血糕的味道…我看我這輩子都忘不掉了。

Tip 強調自己是認真的，沒有在開玩笑，就用I mean it。

 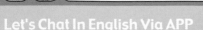 SEND ≫

對你來說應該可以列在「十大不可思議食物」的列表上了。

So for you, they should be put on the "Top Ten Weird Foods" list. `14:35`

Alice

Bart

Anyway, thanks for taking me to experience some local Taiwanese snacks. Now, it is my turn to reciprocate❹ and treat you to dinner. `14:37`

總之 謝謝你帶我去體驗台灣小吃的文化，現在輪我請你吃晚餐，當作報答。

喔，太感謝你了，你人真好。

Oh, thank you so much. That's very kind of you. `14:39`

Alice

Bart

Are you available next Saturday? `14:40`

你下週六有空嗎？

Tip available是比較有禮貌的詢問方式。

當然有空啦！我不會錯過這頓晚餐的。

Certainly! I will not miss this dinner. `14:41`

Alice

Bart

How about eating some pasta together? `14:42`

那麼一起去吃義大利麵怎麼樣？

喔，天啊！我喜歡義大利麵，那是我最喜歡的食物，真是個好主意，巴特！

Oh, my God! I love pasta. It's my favorite. What a splendid idea, Bart! `14:44`

Alice

 SEND ▶▶

22:40

上週六，我的美國同學巴特教我做義大利麵。

Last Saturday, my American classmate, Bart, taught me how to make pasta.
22:40

Alice

Wow! That sounds cool.
22:41

哇！聽起來真酷。

Dean

的確很酷，首先，我們在麵粉中加入水和蛋，攪拌後做成生麵糰，接著壓平麵糰，切成小塊，再塑型。

It was. First, we mixed flour with water and eggs to make the dough⑤. We then flattened and cut the dough into shapes.
22:45

Alice

Were there any other ingredients⑥ you used for making the pasta?
22:47

你們有加入其他材料來做義大利麵條嗎？

Dean

沒有，我們就只用了麵粉、蛋、以及水而已，醬汁的部份，我們使用了蕃茄、洋蔥、青椒、肉、起司、油跟胡椒鹽。

No, all we used were flour, eggs, and water. For the sauce, though, we used tomatoes, onions, bell peppers, meat, cheese, oil, and salt and pepper.
22:54

Alice

Was it tiring? It sounds like a lot of work.
22:55

麻不麻煩啊？聽起來好複雜。

Tip 本句英文有強調「複雜、繁複」的意思。

Dean

一點也不麻煩！巴特真的很擅長烹飪。

Tip not at all強調「一點都不、完全不會」，程度比單講no要強。

Not at all! Bart is really good at cooking.
22:56

Alice

SEND ≫

Dean

So, how did the pasta taste? Was it soft and chewy or hard and crunchy? `23:01`

那義大利麵嚐起來如何？是又軟又黏、還是又硬又脆呢？

老實說，都不是，我煮的剛剛好！而且醬汁的味道恰到好處。

Neither, actually. It was cooked perfectly! And the sauce had the perfect amount of spice. `23:05`

Alice

Dean

Stop! I am starving now. `23:06`

夠了！我現在餓死了。

Tip 關係夠親密的人，才適合用這麼強烈的stop打斷對話，否則對方會以為你生氣了。

好啦，你最好去找些好吃的，喔！但現在已經晚上十一點了。

All right. You'd better find something delicious to eat now. Oh, but it's already 11 p.m. `23:09`

Alice

Dean

Haha, don't worry. I can just go eat a late-night snack. `23:10`

哈，別擔心，我剛好可以吃個宵夜。

Tip 實用英語a late-night snack，「夜晚的點心」就是宵夜。

宵夜？你不是說要戒除吃宵夜的習慣嗎？

A late-night snack? Didn't you say you wanted to stop eating late at night? `23:13`

Alice

Dean

Last time, no one talked to me about pasta in the middle of the night! Well, keep in touch! Bye! `23:15`

上次可沒人在半夜講義大利麵的事情給我聽，再聯絡啦！掰！

  [   ] **SEND ≫**

Let's Chat In English Via APP • ⏻ •

030

3. 一個人的飲食大解放

📖 Bart 2013/8/21

Last Saturday, I had the urge❼ to eat McDonald's. I really wanted to eat some French fries. The food here in Taiwan is totally different from the food back home. On my way to the restaurant, I could not help but imagine what my mom would say to me. "Bart, you know that fast food is not good for you! How about eating an apple instead❽?"

上週六,我突然有股吃麥當勞速食的衝動,我好想吃炸薯條,台灣這裡的食物和我家鄉的完全不同。在前往速食店的途中,我忍不住想像若我媽在的話,會對我說什麼,「巴特,你知道速食對身體不好!吃個蘋果來代替如何呢?」

My mom was always the one to tell me what to eat. If I wanted a hamburger, she would make me a salad. Most families would have ice cream for dessert, but my mom would always prepare a fruit salad for me. Now that I am away from home, however, I have gone a little crazy with desserts. Alright, really crazy. I eat something sweet after every meal. I know I have started to get fat, but it is hard for me to resist when my mom isn't around. It's okay, though. Once I return home, she can resume her job helping me watch what I eat.

我媽總是那個告訴我該吃什麼東西才好的人,如果我想吃漢堡,她會準備沙拉,至於飯後甜點,大多數的家庭會吃冰淇淋,但我媽總是會為我準備水果拉沙。因為現在我沒住在家裡,所以當然免不了會多吃一點甜食,好吧,我承認是狂吃,每餐飯後我都要吃些甜的,我知道自己開始變胖了,可是我媽一不在身邊,我就很難抗拒甜食的誘惑,不過,這其實也沒關係,反正等我回家,她又可重拾監督飲食的工作了。

4. 菜式交流真有趣

📖 Alice 2013/8/22

Bart invited some of our classmates to his place yesterday. As he cooked lunch, the aroma drew me into the kitchen. I am intrigued by his passion for cooking. I never thought he would be able to cook so well. To be honest, when he said he wanted to cook, I thought he was joking! As I watched him, we began to talk about the differences between American and Chinese cuisine. He told me that Chinese food is usually healthier than Western food, but, in his opinion, American food tastes better.

巴特昨天邀請了班上的一些同學到他的住處，當他在準備午餐的時候，那香味把我引到了廚房，他對烹飪的熱情勾起了我的興趣，我從沒想過他這麼會煮菜，老實說，當他說要下廚的時候，我還以為是開玩笑的呢！當我在旁邊看他烹飪的時候，我們聊起美國食物與中國食物的不同點，他告訴我，中式食物通常比西式的更健康，但對他來說，美國食物還是比較好吃。

This time, he was making a dish of bread and meat. He showed me how to prepare the bread before he cooked it. He also showed me the correct way to cut the meat so that it cooks more evenly. Before I knew it, we were cooking together. After about thirty minutes, the dish was ready to serve. I had a great time learning and talking with Bart, but I must say the best part was eating the dish we made!

這次，他準備了麵包和肉，在烹煮之前，他示範了準備麵包的過程，同時也教我如何正確地切肉，好讓肉能在烹煮時，更均勻地受熱，在我還沒有意識到的時候，我就已經加入巴特，跟他在一起準備餐點了。大約過了三十分鐘，美食就端上桌了，我和巴特邊聊天邊做菜，度過了很愉快的時光，但說到最棒的時刻，當然還是享用美食的時候囉！

Word 單字	Meaning 字義	Usage 常見用法
1 experience [ɪk`spɪrɪəns]	名 經驗；體驗 動 經歷；感受	the teaching experience 教學經驗 widen one's experience 增長經驗/閱歷
2 culture [`kʌltʃə]	名 文化；休養	an age-old culture 古老的文化 a man of culture 有修養的人
3 embarrass [ɪm`bærəs]	動 使尷尬；使困窘	an embarrassing experience 尷尬經驗 embarrass sb. by sth. 用…使某人難堪
4 reciprocate [rɪ`sɪprə͵ket]	動 報答；交換	reciprocate one's feelings 回應某人的感情 reciprocate sth. deeply 深刻地報答
5 dough [do]	名 生麵糰	knead dough 揉麵糰 roll out the dough 桿麵糰
6 ingredient [ɪn`gridɪənt]	名 原料；材料	the ingredients of …的原料 a list of ingredients 材料清單
7 urge [ɝdʒ]	名 衝動；迫切的要求 動 催促；力勸	an urge to travel 旅行的衝動 urge sb./sth. forward 驅策；推進
8 instead [ɪn`stɛd]	副 作為替代；反而	instead of 代替；而不是 drink juice instead 改喝果汁
9 aroma [ə`romə]	名 芳香；香氣；韻味	diffuse a savory aroma 散發(食物)香味 an aroma of mystery 神秘色彩
10 intrigue [ɪn`trig]	名 陰謀；密謀 動 耍陰謀；激起好奇心	a master of intrigue 耍陰謀的高手 intrigue against 密謀陷害/反對
11 passion [`pæʃən]	名 熱情；激情	a passion for music 對音樂的熱情 passion fruit 百香果
12 evenly [`ivənlɪ]	副 平均地；平靜地； 平坦地；均衡地	breathe evenly 均勻地呼吸 be evenly matched 實力相當

逛街血拼
Go Shopping～上篇

 APP CHAT  蠢蠢欲動的週年慶

18:37

你知道這個週末遠東百貨有舉辦一場大拍賣嗎？

Did you know there's a big sale at the Far Eastern Department Store this weekend? 18:37

Laura

Of course I did. I am guessing you want to go? 18:40

當然知道，我猜你想要去吧？

Henry

拜託，那可是週年慶三折的活動，我等不及要殺過去了。

Tip …percent off為打折的實用表達。

Come on, it's the annual seventy percent off sale. I can't wait to go! 18:43

Laura

Baby, relax, okay? Every time there is an annual sale, you go a little crazy. 18:50

親愛的，冷靜點，每次一遇到週年慶活動，你就會有點失控。

Henry

因為週年慶的好康實在太多，如果不抓緊機會的話，我就又要再等一年了。

That's because these annual sales have too many good deals. And if I don't take advantage❶ of the deals, then I have to wait another year. 18:52

Laura

Okay. So, how much do you think you are going to spend this time? 18:53

好吧，那你這一次打算要「敗」多少錢呢？

Henry

哈哈，很難說耶，我只知道我一定得去，否則會錯過許多好康。

Tip 「不一定」、「沒想法」都可以用have no idea表達。

Haha, I have no idea. I just know I have to go. Otherwise, I will miss a lot of great sales. 18:55

Laura

   SEND »

18:37

Henry: But look at your closet and shoe cabinet, Laura. They are too full to put anything new in! `18:59`

可是看看你的衣櫥和鞋櫃，蘿拉，它們已滿到放不下任何新東西了！

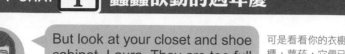

我知道，但你有看到那些東西有多舊了嗎？我得替衣櫥汰舊換新啊！

Laura: I know, I know. Have you seen how old everything is, though? I have to update₂ my wardrobe! `19:03`

Henry: Honey, remember, styles come and go quickly. `19:04`

親愛的，別忘了，流行都是很短命的。

Tip come and go quickly特別強調「變化快速」的意思。

嘿，那你呢？你不是說過想要買一件風衣外套嗎？它們也在特價喔！

Laura: Hey, what about you? Didn't you say you wanted to buy a trench coat? Well, they will be on sale, too! `19:07`

Henry: Yeah, but do you think a trench coat will look good on me? `19:09`

是啊，可是你覺得我穿風衣外套會好看嗎？

絕對好看！我保證你穿起來會非常有型。

Laura: Absolutely! You will look amazing, I promise₃. `19:10`

Henry: All right, then, let's go this Saturday. I know you can never pass on a sale. `19:13`

那好吧，我們就這星期六去，我知道你絕對不會錯過任何一場拍賣會的。

   SEND ≫

Let's Chat In English Via APP

17:15 📶 🔋

我此刻內心的滿足與興奮，是無法用言語來形容的。

Words can't describe₄ how content and excited I am at the moment. 17:15

Laura

What do you mean? Is there something you want to share? 17:17

什麼意思？你有什麼好事想和我分享吧？

Nancy

猜對了！上個週末，遠東百貨舉辦週年慶大拍賣，所有的商品都打三折耶！

Bingo! There was an annual sale at the Far Eastern Department Store last weekend and everything was seventy percent off! 17:22

Laura

Wow, I had no idea. To be honest, I haven't gone shopping at a department store in a long time. 17:25

哇！我都不知道，說真的，我很久沒去百貨公司逛街了。

Nancy

So…tell me what you got. 17:26

那快說你買了些什麼。

Tip 跟好友聊天的口語表達get，此處為「購買」之意。

Nancy

我買了好多衣物，像是上衣、裙子、牛仔褲，和圍巾之類的，另外，我還買了幾雙涼鞋和長靴。

I bought a lot of clothes: blouses, skirts, jeans, scarves, stuff like that. Also, I bought some sandals and boots. 17:29

Laura

Sounds like you bought a lot of stuff₅. 17:30

聽起來你買了很多耶。

Tip 和thing相比，用stuff更加口語化一點。

Nancy

 SEND ≫

17:15

是啊！買的東西越多，省下的錢就越多。

Well, yeah, of course. The more stuff I bought, the more money I saved. `17:32`

Laura

Nancy

Yeah, seventy percent off is too good! `17:33`

是啊，三折實在是太吸引人了！

下次有其他的大拍賣時，一起和我去血拼如何？

How about going shopping with me next time when there is another sale? `17:35`

Laura

Nancy

Sure. Actually, I have been thinking about buying a new Rolex. `17:37`

當然好，事實上，我一直想要買支新的勞力士手錶。

知道你要買什麼是很好，但我跟你保證，一旦遇到上星期那種大拍賣，你肯定會買更多。

It's good to know what you want, but I promise you that if you go to a sale like the one last week, you will buy so much more. `17:40`

Laura

我每次去就像著了魔一樣，購買清單完全被我拋在腦後。

Tip 口語會話中，or something 為「…之類的」的意思。

Every time I go, I become possessed₆ or something and any list I brought with me is forgotten in the back of my mind. `17:44`

Laura

Nancy

Haha, I understand. When you get the credit card bill in the mail later, though, you have to return to reality. `17:46`

哈哈，我明白，等信用卡帳單寄來之後，就得回到現實了。

   SEND ››

1. 買到就是賺到

Laura 2013/9/6

I had the best time shopping with my boyfriend, Henry, this weekend! Being the smart shopper I am, I waited until Far Eastern had their store-wide seventy percent off sale to go. I had some things in mind that I wanted to buy, but I totally forgot what they were the moment I walked through the entrance₀! Haha! I couldn't help myself; it was such a good sale! Because I wanted to take full advantage of the sale, I spent a long time browsing₈ each store, trying on anything I saw that I liked.

這個週末，我和我男友亨利一起去逛街，逛得實在太開心了！作為一個聰明的消費者，我一直等到遠東百貨全館打三折才去大肆採購，雖然我心裡已經想好要買的東西，但當我一跨進百貨公司的大門，我就全忘光了！哈哈！我真的無法控制自己，這次的拍賣會實在太划算了！因為想充分把握這次週年慶打折的機會，所以我好好地逛了每家店，試穿了每件我喜歡的衣服。

Henry was a great boyfriend and didn't complain once. Of course, I didn't buy everything I tried on, but I did get a lot more than I originally planned, including some items for winter. The winter items I bought were two pairs of boots, three scarves, and a jacket. The savings were just too good to ignore! I mean, really, who could resist paying thirty percent instead of one hundred?

亨利是個很棒的男友，一次也沒抱怨過，當然了，我並沒有買下我試穿的每件衣服，但我買的量的確比當初預計的還要多很多，包括一些冬季單品，有兩雙馬靴、三條圍巾、以及一件夾克，因折扣而省下的錢實在好到很難讓人忽視它！我的意思是，說真的，不需要用原價，而能用三折買到這麼多東西，這種好康誰能抵擋得住呢？

10:02

2. 女性瘋年季

Henry 2013/9/6

This Saturday, I spent an entire afternoon with my girlfriend, Laura, at the Far Eastern Department Store. From the moment we entered the store, I could see she was giddy with excitement. When I asked her why, she told me it was because of the store-wide seventy percent off sale that was going on. I imagine the sale was also why she stopped at every store, tried on every piece of clothing that caught her eye, and bought anything and everything she liked.

這個星期六，我花了一整個下午的時間，陪我的女友蘿菈在遠東百貨購物。從我們走進百貨公司的那刻起，我就看出她已經興奮得暈頭轉向，我問她為什麼會這麼興奮，她說是因為這次全館打三折的週年慶活動，我猜這也是她每家店必逛、吸引她的衣服必試穿、只要喜歡就必買的的原因吧！

She bought so many things that, if everything had been full-price, her shopping spree would have bankrupted us! She ended the day with more than seven bags of clothes, shoes, accessories, and cosmetics. I, on the other hand, bought a single trench coat. I was happy to see Laura enjoying herself, but I really don't understand the appeal of spending so much time shopping. Why do girls like to shop so much?

她買的東西很多，多到如果所有商品都是用原價購買的話，她那種瘋狂的採購行為會害我們破產！最後她以超過七袋的衣服，鞋子、配件，還有化妝品結束了那一天，相較之下，我就只買了一件風衣外套，我很高興看到蘿菈如此樂在其中，但我真的搞不懂花這麼多時間逛街購物的樂趣何在，為什麼女孩子都這麼喜歡購物呢？

Let's Chat In English Via APP

Word 單字	Meaning 字義	Usage 常見用法
1 **advantage** [əd`væntɪdʒ]	名 有利條件;利益	take advantage of 利用;趁機 buy sth. at an advantage 以優惠價買到
2 **update** [ʌp`det]	動 提供最新消息; 更新;使現代化	update one's resume 更新履歷表 update us on the date 通知我們日期
3 **promise** [`prɑmɪs]	名 承諾;前途 動 允諾;答應	keep one's promise 說話算數 a verbal promise 口頭保證
4 **describe** [dɪ`skraɪb]	動 描寫;敘述; 形容;描繪	describe sth. in words 以言語形容 describe sth. as 把某物形容為
5 **stuff** [stʌf]	名 物品;東西 動 把⋯塞滿	do one's stuff 顯身手做分內的事 kid stuff (俚)小孩的玩意兒
6 **possess** [pə`zɛs]	動 擁有;持有; 支配;控制	be possessed by 被⋯迷住、纏住 sth. possess me with anger ⋯使我憤怒
7 **entrance** [`ɛntrəns]	名 入口;門口; 進入;登場	a side entrance 側門 have free entrance to 可以自由進入
8 **browse** [braʊz]	名 瀏覽;吃草 動 瀏覽;吃葉子	browse around/about 逛 browse leaves away (牛等)把葉子吃掉
9 **giddy** [`gɪdɪ]	形 暈眩的;眼花的; 輕率的;輕浮的	be giddy with 因⋯而陶醉 act the giddy goat 胡鬧
10 **excitement** [ɪk`saɪtmənt]	名 興奮;激動	speak in excitement 激動地說 tremble with excitement 激動得發抖
11 **spree** [spri]	名 歡鬧作樂;狂飲	have a spree 狂歡作樂 a shopping spree 拼命買東西
12 **bankrupt** [`bæŋkrʌpt]	動 使破產;使枯竭 形 破產的	go bankrupt 破產 be bankrupt of feelings 毫無感情

UNIT 2 逛街血拼
Go Shopping～下篇

 APP CHAT **3** 想要什麼生日驚喜？

親愛的，你的生日就快到了，有沒有想要什麼生日禮物呢？

Tip right around the corner強調「即將到來」。

Honey, your birthday is right around the corner. What kind of present would you like? 16:30

Laura

Henry

Actually, I have been busy lately and haven't really thought about it. 16:32

事實上，我最近一直很忙，沒怎麼去想生日的事。

Henry

How about getting some food? There's a new restaurant near my office that looks good. 16:36

一起去吃頓飯如何呢？我公司附近開了一家新的餐廳。

不要改變話題，禮物或許不是一切，但卻是我想為你做的一件事。

Don't change the subject. A present might not be everything, but it's something I want to do for you. 16:39

Laura

Alright, let me think…okay, I have an idea. My nice suit is getting old and worn out. A new one would be nice. 16:43

好吧，讓我想想看…喔，我想到了，我那件高級西裝舊了，也有點磨損，一套新西裝應該不錯。

Henry

是啊，你的西裝看起來的確過時了，西裝可以列入考慮。

Yeah, your suit looks too old-fashioned now. That is something I'll think about. 16:45

Laura

那有其他想要的嗎？一隻新的智慧型手機？

Tip 較為口語的問法。

What about something else? Maybe a new smartphone? 16:46

Laura

 SEND >>

Let's Chat In English Via APP

041

Henry

That sounds okay, but the phone I bought last year is still in good condition. Besides, we should start saving more money. `16:50`

聽起來是不錯，但我去年買的手機還很好用，再說，我們應該要開始多存點錢了。

我同意，但現在就別擔心錢的問題，想想你要的生日禮物！

I agree. But don't worry about the money now. Think about what you want for your birthday! `16:54`

Laura

Henry

Okay. Well, I've been thinking about getting a new digital camera. The one I have is old and doesn't work sometimes. `16:58`

好吧，我最近有在想換台數位相機，我現在的這款舊了，而且有時候會故障。

是啊，一台新的數位相機非常實用，尤其是在旅行或開派對的時候。

Yeah, a new digital camera is very practical₃, especially for trips or parties. `17:00`

Laura

Henry

Yeah, and I only buy things that I need, not things that I want. `17:02`

沒錯，而且我向來只買需要的物品，而非想要的東西。

我真幸運，能擁有一個對金錢如此有概念的男友！

Tip with a sensible head是在誇獎他人很有概念。

I am so lucky to have a boyfriend with such a sensible head about money. `17:04`

Laura

Henry

And I am lucky to have a girlfriend as considerate₄ as you. `17:05`

而我多麼幸運能擁有一位像你這樣體貼的女朋友。

   SEND ≫

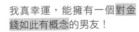

20:13 📶 🔋

Laura

Honey, do you like the grey suit I got for you? `20:13`

親愛的，你喜歡我為你買的灰色西裝嗎？

Tip 口語情境中，可用get取代buy。

那當然！非常適合我，你總是這麼體貼！但這件西裝很貴吧？

Of course! It fits me perfectly. You're always so thoughtful! But it was expensive, wasn't it? `20:16`

Henry

Laura

Don't worry. It's fall, so most of the department stores are having big sales. Everything is very cheap – that includes your suit! `20:21`

不用擔心，現在是秋季，大部份的百貨公司都有降價大拍賣，所有商品（包括你的新西裝）都很便宜。

這件西裝的質料好到令人吃驚，我真的很喜歡。

Tip 加上do之後，語氣變得更強烈。

The quality of it is amazing. I really do love it. `20:22`

Henry

Laura

Didn't you say you will have a business trip next month? Why don't you wear it then? `20:25`

你不是說下個月要出差嗎？何不在那個時候穿呢？

好主意，我知道我已經說過很多次，你挑的這件西裝真的很棒！

Tip repeat oneself意指「說了很多次」。

Good idea. I know I am repeating myself, but you did a great job picking this suit. `20:29`

Henry

Laura

I am so happy to hear you say that! `20:30`

聽到你這樣說，我真的很開心。

  SEND ▶▶

Let's Chat In English Via APP

20:13

Laura

I originally wanted to buy a black suit, but the grey one looked brighter and had better tailoring. I am positive you'll be great in it. `20:35`

本來我想買黑色的西裝，但灰色這套看起來比較亮，剪裁也比較特別，我想你穿起來一定很好看。

我也這麼覺得，寶貝，很謝謝你。

I think so, too. Thanks so much, babe. `20:36`

Henry

Laura

By the way, your dad's birthday is coming up as well. Let's buy him a new wallet, okay? `20:39`

對了，你爸爸的生日也快到了，我們送他一個新皮夾，好嗎？

那真是貼心，你實在是個很棒的女友。

Tip thoughtful有「細心、考慮周到」之意，比considerate口語。

That's so thoughtful. You really are wonderful. `20:41`

Henry

Laura

Okay. How about we go look tomorrow after you finish work? I can wait for you in front of your office building. `20:44`

好，那我們明天下班後一起去挑禮物如何？我可以在你的辦公大樓前面等你。

沒問題！那就明天見了。

Okay! See you then. `20:45`

Henry

SEND ≫

22:10

  微網誌

3. 男性禮品真難挑

Laura 2013/9/18

I always get stressed-out when buying gifts, particularly men's gifts. I never seem to be able to choose the right one. My boyfriend, Henry, is especially hard to shop for because he has very particular tastes. Recently, I heard him complain about his only nice suit. I thought a new suit would be a good birthday present. However, I had no idea where he bought it, so I took a picture of it and wrote down the brand name before going shopping. I guessed a picture of his old suit and its brand would be helpful.

買禮物總是讓我備感壓力,尤其是給男性的禮物,我好像就是挑不出適合的。我男友亨利的禮物尤其難挑,因為他的品味很獨特。最近,我聽到他抱怨唯一的好西裝舊了,所以我想一件新的西裝應該會是個好生日禮物,然而,我不清楚他之前是去哪裡買的,所以我在出門前先拍了一張他舊西裝的照片,並抄下品牌的名字,我想西裝的照片和品牌名稱應該會有幫助吧。

Because I am not confident about shopping for men, I also turned to my best friend, Nancy, for help. She has a real talent for picking the perfect present! I had her come with me to look for Henry's new suit. Without spending much time at all, she helped me find a grey suit at an expensive men's clothing store. To my delight, it was not only made of quality silk but was also fifty percent off. I can't thank Nancy enough for her help!

因為我對挑男性的禮物不太有信心,所以我向好友南西求助,她很有挑禮物的天分!我邀她陪我一起去挑選亨利的新西裝,沒多久的時間,她就在一間高檔的男裝店找到一套灰色西裝,令我喜出望外的是,這套西裝不僅是用高級絲綢製成的,而且還打五折,真是太感謝南西的鼎力相助了!

21:30

 微網誌

4. 飽含心意的禮物

Henry 2013/9/22

Believe it or not, my girlfriend Laura, who is just terrible at picking out gifts for me, bought me a beautiful grey silk suit last week for my birthday. When I opened the box it was in, I was both surprised and moved. I had no idea what to say. The suit was perfect: the color, the size, the feel, everything was just right. Without thinking, I gave Laura a big hug and thanked her for getting me such a thoughtful gift.

信不信由你，我那位超不會挑禮物的女友蘿菈，上星期竟然送我一件很棒的灰色絲質西裝當作生日禮物，當我打開包裝盒時，我真是既意外又感動，不知道該說些什麼，那件西裝真是太完美了，顏色、尺寸、觸感全都是我喜歡的，我想都沒想，就給了蘿菈一個大大的擁抱，並謝謝她為我挑了如此貼心的禮物。

I have worn the suit many times already. I have worn it to business meetings and other functions, my friend's engagement party, and out to dinner with Laura. Every time I put it on, she can see how happy I am. I always smile at her with satisfaction and tell her she chose the perfect gift for my birthday this year. Actually, I don't really care about my birthday. A nice meal with loved ones is enough for me, but Laura always surprises me with something special. She really is considerate, and I love her for that.

這件西裝我已經穿過很多次了，我穿它參加商務會議及其他場合、我朋友的訂婚派對、還有跟蘿菈一起外出享用晚餐時也會穿，每次當我穿上這套西裝，她都能看出我有多開心，我總是對她露出滿足的微笑，並告訴蘿菈，她今年為我挑的生日禮物很完美。老實說，我並不特別在意自己的生日，只要能和心愛的人在一起，就算是簡單的一頓飯，對我來說就很足夠，但蘿菈總會準備一份驚喜，她真的非常貼心，而我也愛她這一點。

Let's Chat In English Via APP

Word 單字	Meaning 字義	Usage 常見用法
1 **present** [`prɛznt]	名 禮物；贈品 形 出席的；當前的	buy sb. a present 買禮物給某人 at present 現在；當前
2 **fashion** [`fæʃən]	名 流行；時尚 動 把…塑造成	in fashion 合於時尚 fashion the clay into a vase 用黏土製花瓶
3 **practical** [`præktɪkḷ]	形 實際的；可實施的	a practical invention 實用的發明物 the practical advice 可行的建議
4 **considerate** [kən`sɪdərɪt]	形 體貼的；體諒的； 考慮周到的	be considerate of/to/toward 對…體貼 be courteously considerate 殷勤周到的
5 **thoughtful** [`θɔtfəl]	形 深思的；細心的	in a thoughtful mood 陷入沉思 be thoughtful of/about 對…考慮周到的
6 **quality** [`kwɑlətɪ]	名 品質；質量	merchandise of quality 優質商品 people of quality 達官顯貴
7 **particular** [pə`tɪkjələ]	名 細目；詳細情況 形 特別的；獨特的	be particular about 特別講究 in particular 特別；尤其
8 **shopping** [`ʃɑpɪŋ]	名 購物；買東西	the window shopping 只看不買的逛街 carry one's shopping 拿某人買的東西
9 **delight** [dɪ`laɪt]	名 欣喜；愉快 動 使高興	to one's delight 令某人高興的是 in high delight 興高采烈地
10 **pick** [pɪk]	名 選擇(權)；精華 動 挑選；選擇	get the pick of 有…的選擇權 pick out 挑選
11 **function** [`fʌŋkʃən]	名 功能；職責 動 運行；起作用	abuse one's function 濫用職權 the leading function 主要功能
12 **satisfaction** [ˌsætɪs`fækʃən]	名 滿足；滿意	find satisfaction in 對…感到滿意 a sense of satisfaction 滿足感

出場人物：醫生Allen、醫生的母親Mrs. Hill

UNIT 3 健康與醫療
Medical Treatment～上篇

 017 MP3

🔒 ✉ ✏   8:35 📶 📶 🔋

◀ APP CHAT　1　安排健康檢查

媽，幾天不見，一切都還好吧？

Mom, I haven't seen you for a few days. Is everything okay? 8:35

Allen

I haven't been feeling very well since your brother's wedding banquet❶. 8:55

Mrs. Hill

從你哥的婚宴以來，我一直都不太舒服。

真的嗎？你的血壓多高？有沒有記得多吃蔬果呢？

Oh, really? How is your blood pressure? Are you remembering to eat a lot of fruits and vegetables? 9:03

Allen

I don't know about my blood pressure, but I do eat a lot of fruits and vegetables. 9:10

Mrs. Hill

我不知道我的血壓是多少，但我吃了很多蔬果。

To tell you the truth, I have been having chest pains at night and not sleeping well. 9:20

Mrs. Hill

老實跟你說，我晚上會感到胸部疼痛，也睡不好。

Tip 意思等同於honestly，但語氣比較正經。

看起來不太好，為了安全起見，我要帶你去照一下胸部X光，還有其他症狀嗎？

That is not good. I'm going to take you to get a chest X-ray, just to be safe. Do you have any other symptoms❷? 9:24

Allen

Sometimes I feel sick and vomit in the morning. 9:31

Mrs. Hill

早上有時候會覺得不舒服，而且會嘔吐。

Tip sick表達出來的不舒服比較嚴重。

SEND ≫

Let's Chat In English Via APP

048

媽，這樣我得替你安排一下，你必須做個全身健康檢查。

Okay, Mom, I'm going to get you a full physical₃ checkup. 9:33

 Allen

Do I need to be hospitalized? Do I need to have my blood drawn? You know I'm scared of needles. 9:42

我會需要住院嗎？要抽血嗎？你知道我很怕針筒的。

 Mrs. Hill

這我不清楚，但是如果真的需要驗血，他們也只會抽一點而已。

Tip 驗血的搭配動詞用test。

Well, I don't know. But if they do need to test your blood, they will only take a little. 9:46

 Allen

Do you promise? Don't lie to your mother, now. 9:50

你確定嗎？可別欺騙你的母親。

 Mrs. Hill

我確定，媽，你別擔心，我會安排好一切的。

I promise. Don't worry, Mom. I'll arrange everything. 9:51

 Allen

All right. You are such a good boy, you know that? 9:54

好吧，就信你了，知道嗎？你真是個好兒子。

 Mrs. Hill

SEND ▶▶

Let's Chat In English Via APP

018 MP3

18:25

APP CHAT 2 營養均衡的重要性

Allen: Mom, I read your report. Everything seems to be normal❹. Your blood pressure is just a little higher than I would like, though. 18:25

媽，我看了你的檢查報告，一切正常，不過，你的血壓有點偏高。

Mrs. Hill: I've been so worried the past few days. Now I can breathe a sigh of relief❺. 18:31

這幾天我一直都在擔心這件事，現在總算可以鬆口氣了。

Tip 慣用語breathe a sigh of relief。

Allen: Seriously, Mom, you have to cut back on all the greasy❻ and salty foods. 18:38

媽，說真的，油膩和鹹的東西一定要少吃。

Mrs. Hill: I know, I know. It's easier said than done, though. 18:40

我知道、我知道，但說時容易做時難嘛！

Tip 俚語用法。

Allen: Once you get used to not eating those kinds of food, you will no longer like them. 18:44

一旦你養成不吃重鹹的習慣，就不會喜歡那些食物了。

Mrs. Hill: You know, son, sometimes I think you are more of a dietitian than a doctor. 18:48

兒子，你知道嗎？我有時候覺得你不太像醫生，反而更像一個營養師。

Allen: From now on, just cut all those foods out. For example, you could try eating oats or cereal instead of bacon for breakfast. 18:58

從現在起，別再吃那些又油又鹹的東西就是了，比方說，早餐可以用燕麥或麥片取代培根。

SEND

好吧，我是有聽人說燕麥之類的食物對降血壓有幫助。

Yeah, I heard that foods like oats are good for lowering blood pressure. 19:02

Mrs. Hill

Allen

You should also consume more vegetables and fruits daily. 19:03

你每天最好也多攝取蔬菜和水果。

這我知道，兒子，吃蔬果有益健康，從今天開始，我會盡量吃得比以前更健康的。

I know, son. A diet of fruits and vegetables will help me stay healthy. I will try my best to eat healthier, and I will start today. 19:08

Mrs. Hill

Allen

I hope you realize just how important a balanced diet is for your health. 19:11

我希望你能了解均衡的飲食對健康很重要的道理。

我很明白這一點，相信我。

Tip 和believe相比，用trust更口語，語氣也更強烈。

I do. Trust me. 19:12

Mrs. Hill

Allen

I am relieved to hear that. Okay, I have to go. I have a seminar on balanced diets later. Bye-bye! 19:16

聽你這麼說，我就放心了，喔，我該走了，我晚點要參加一個關於均衡飲食的研討會，掰掰！

去吧，兒子，媽媽愛你！

Okay. Son, I love you. 19:17

Mrs. Hill

SEND ▶▶

Let's Chat In English Via APP

微網誌

0:51

1. 急診科的挑戰

Allen 2013/9/25

I experienced something unforgettable today. A patient came into the ER I work at in cardiac arrest. I had a hard time believing the diagnosis because he was only 15! I still can't believe what happened and how I got through it. He was my first ER patient, and I almost lost him. Had it not been for Dr. Jenkins and Nurse Pattison, who both helped me as I did everything I could to get his heart pumping and his airway open again, I don't think I would have been able to save him.

今天的經歷真是令我難忘,有一位病人被推進急診室時,已經沒了心跳,我當時很難相信眼前所見的情況,因為那位病患才十五歲而已!我現在依然不敢相信,也不知道自己是怎麼熬過來的,他是我在急診室值班的第一個病人,而我差點就失去他了,在我極力救回他的心跳與打開他肺部氣道的過程中,如果少了詹金斯醫生與派蒂森護士的幫忙,我應該救不回這個年輕人。

It was an emotionally and physically draining process. The three of us took turns giving him CPR. The only thing on my mind the entire time was to get this boy back to his parents alive and healthy. I will never forget his face when he finally regained consciousness and the feeling of accomplishment and joy that came with it. I really have to thank my colleagues for being so calm. As a new physician, I would have been lost without their guidance.

急救的過程真的讓人感到身心俱疲,我們三個人輪流給他做心肺復甦術,當時的我,腦中所想的就只有把這個年輕人救活,讓他健康地回到父母身邊,我永遠都不會忘記他恢復意識時的表情,以及帶給我的成就感與歡樂,我得謝謝我的同事們如此冷靜,如果沒有他們指導我這個菜鳥醫師,我大概會手足無措吧。

微網誌

2. 偶爾也想大吃大喝

Mrs. Hill 2013/9/27

I remember when I would get up every morning full of energy. I was always busy with my career and my son, but I never felt tired. Lately, however, I have felt that my body just does not run as smoothly as it did before. I always feel fatigued and have trouble getting out of bed.

我記得以前每天早上起床，我都感到精神飽滿，雖然同時要忙工作與照顧兒子，但我從不覺得累，但是，最近我覺得身體不像以前那麼硬朗了，我總是感到疲倦，起床也變得困難。

My son has always reminded me to eat a healthy diet. He says, "Your body is only as good as the food you put into it." I suppose he is right; he is a doctor, after all. Yet I must confess that I rarely follow his advice. When I was younger, I ate whatever I wanted and still had a nice figure and lots of energy. For as long as I can remember, I have gone to fast-food restaurants to eat the occasional big, juicy hamburger or greasy pizza. I know those kinds of food are not good for my health, but they taste so good that I just can't help myself. I have never told my son because I know he would judge me for my weakness.

我兒子總是提醒我要多吃有益健康的食物，他說：「只要吃的好，身體自然就會健康。」我想他是對的，畢竟他是個醫生，但是，我必須坦承自己很少會聽他的話。年輕的時候，我想吃什麼就吃什麼，而且依然擁有曼妙的身材與充沛的體力，就我印象所及，我偶爾會去速食店大啖肉汁鮮美的大漢堡，或來份油滋滋的披薩，我知道那些食物對身體不好，但它們真的很美味，所以我實在克制不了自己，當然，我沒有告訴我兒子這件事，因為他肯定會說我意志薄弱的。

Word 單字	Meaning 字義	Usage 常見用法
1 banquet [`bæŋkwɪt]	名 宴會；款待 動 參加宴會	a state banquet 國宴 cater a banquet 承辦宴會
2 symptom [`sɪmptəm]	名 症狀；徵候	a symptom of …的症狀 a common symptom 常見症狀
3 physical [`fɪzɪkl]	形 身體的；肉體的	physical punishment 體罰 a physical therapy 物理治療
4 normal [`nɔrml]	名 標準；常態 形 正常的；平常的	back to normal 恢復正常 lead a normal life 過正常的生活
5 relief [rɪ`lif]	名 緩和；寬心； 救濟；補助	in need of relief 需要救濟 a blank wall without relief 無門窗的牆
6 greasy [`grizɪ]	形 多脂的；油膩的； 油腔滑調的	a greasy grind (俚)埋頭苦讀的學生 a greasy smile 奉承的笑容
7 consume [kən`sjum]	動 吃；喝；使憔悴； 耗盡生命	consume all food 吃光所有食物 consume away with 因…耗盡生命
8 diagnosis [ˌdaɪəg`nosɪs]	名 診斷；調查分析	make one's diagnosis 做出診斷 a presumptive diagnosis 初步診斷
9 regain [rɪ`gen]	動 取回；恢復	sb. regain consciousness 恢復知覺 regain one's balance 保持平衡
10 guidance [`gaɪdns]	名 指導；領導； 輔導；諮詢	under one's guidance 在某人的指導下 turn to…for guidance 參考
11 fatigue [fə`tig]	名 疲勞；勞累 動 使疲勞	bear the fatigue of sth. 忍受…的勞累 a fatigued journey 精疲力竭的旅行
12 remind [rɪ`maɪnd]	動 使想起；提醒	remind sb. to do sth. 提醒(人)做某事 remind sb. of sth. 使想起某事

UNIT 3

健康與醫療
Medical Treatment～下篇

◀ APP CHAT **3** 面對病患家屬的難處

我最近的心情一直都很低落。

Tip in a terrible mood的口氣比unhappy
強烈，強調「低落」。

Lately, I've been in a terrible mood.　`12:10`

Allen

Tell me about it. I'm a great listener.　`12:26`

Dana

說來聽聽吧！我是個很好的傾聽者。

昨天，一位年輕人發生了車禍，當他被送到醫院時，他的雙腳都斷了。

Yesterday, a young man was in a car accident. When he got to the hospital, I saw that both his legs were broken.　`12:34`

Allen

That sounds serious. Is the boy's condition responsible for your bad mood?　`12:36`

Dana

聽起來很嚴重，所以那男孩的傷勢是造成你情緒低落的原因嗎？

傷勢的情況也有，再加上他母親的反應，導致我心情受影響，那位母親一看到他兒子的情況，就不斷哭泣。

Well, it was actually his condition as well as his mom's reaction❶. The mom wouldn't stop crying when she saw her son and his legs.　`12:39`

Allen

她說車禍發生時是她在開車，她認為自己要為兒子的雙腳負責。

She told me that she was driving when the accident occurred, and she blames herself for her son's condition.　`12:44`

Allen

It is a normal emotional reaction. You have to pay more attention❷ to it. So, how did you comfort❸ her?　`12:47`

Dana

那是很正常的情緒反應，你就要多費心了，那你是怎麼安撫她的呢？

SEND ▸▸

我告訴她，她兒子的情況必須立即開刀，而且需要住院幾個月，配合復健療程才能康復。

I told her that her son needed an immediate operation and to be staying in the hospital for several months and could only be healed after rehabilitation. 12:52

Allen

當她聽到這件事的時候，就又開始啜泣了。

When she heard that, she started sobbing again. 12:53

Allen

Dana

I wonder whether the way you delivered the bad news affected her. How did you tell her? 12:55

有可能是你告知壞消息的方式影響到她的情緒，你當時是怎麼說的呢？

Tip I wonder 為更加委婉的詢問。

我盡量以安撫的口吻向她說明情況，但我不清楚是否有用。

I tried to tell her in a reassuring manner. I don't know if it worked, though. 12:57

Allen

Dana

You did what you could. Nobody can ask more from you. 12:59

你已經做了該做的事，沒有人能要求你做出更好的表現。

Tip 安慰的實用句，表達對方已盡力，該放寬心的意思。

我知道，但一看到那位母親的表情，我就覺得自己很失敗。

I know, but when I saw the mom's face, I still felt like I failed. 13:01

Allen

Dana

Don't worry. You tried your best. And for that, you should feel proud. 13:03

別擔心，你已經盡力了，你應該以此為傲才是。

  **SEND ▶▶**

Let's Chat In English Via APP

20:38 📶

Philip

Hey, Allen. Are you free next Saturday? 20:38

嘿，亞倫，你下星期六有空嗎？

什麼事？別告訴我你又要找人代班了。

Tip 代班的說法 work one's shift。

What is it? Don't tell me you need someone to work your shift again. 20:40

Allen

Philip

Come on! My girlfriend's birthday is next Saturday. I promised to take her to a French restaurant for dinner. 20:45

不要這樣嘛！下週六是我女友的生日，我答應要帶她到法國餐廳吃晚餐。

想當個浪漫的羅密歐啊？

Trying to be a romantic boyfriend now, huh? 20:49

Allen

Philip

Yeah, I am trying to be the good guy. Now, what do you say: can you take my shift then? 20:51

是啊，我正努力做個好男友，所以，你可以幫我嗎？

等等，我查一下行事曆，嗯，看起來我下星期六剛好有空。

Just a minute, let me check my schedule. Hmm, it looks like I will be free next Saturday. 20:56

Allen

Philip

Terrific! My girlfriend will love to hear the good news. 20:57

太棒了！聽到這個好消息，我女友會很開心的。

Philip

SEND ≫

20:38

喂，等一下！我總是幫你解決困難，而你卻連一個小小的「謝謝」都不說啊？

Tip help out不只是幫忙，還帶有「解決問題」的意思。

Hey, wait a minute! Here I am, always helping you out, and you can't even give me a simple "thank you"? `21:00`

Allen

Oh, sorry. It's very kind of you to do me such a big favor⑤. How about I buy you a beer sometime? `21:03`

Philip

呃，抱歉，你人真好，幫了我一個大忙，改天請你喝啤酒怎麼樣？

這才像話嘛！

Tip 口語用法，與朋友對話可用。

Now you're talking! `21:04`

Allen

I'll write everything down in a memo and put it on your desk. `21:06`

Philip

那我會把工作細節寫在備忘錄裡，再放到你桌上。

不用麻煩了，寄電子郵件給我就好。

Don't bother. Just send me an e-mail. `21:07`

Allen

Okay, I'll send it to you later. Thanks a lot, man. `21:08`

Philip

沒問題，我晚點寄給你，多謝了，兄弟。

祝你與女友有個美好的約會，還有，請我喝啤酒的事可別忘了。

Have a good time with your girlfriend. And don't forget about my beer. `21:11`

Allen

SEND »

微網誌

3. 終於排到的輪休

📖 Allen 2013/10/2

After a few months of non-stop working, I finally have some time to relax❻. The resort I am staying at is simply amazing. I am so happy I was able to get a room here because it is usually full and rooms need to be reserved months in advance❼. Now that I'm here though, I can finally take some time for myself and not worry about work. I think the first thing I will do tomorrow morning is get a good, long massage to ease all my aches and pains. Then, I will probably go to the golf course and play a few rounds.

經過幾個月不眠不休的工作，我終於可以好好放鬆一下了，我住的這個渡假勝地真的很棒，這次能訂到空房真讓人開心，因為這裡的房間通常很快就會被訂滿，要提前好幾個月預訂才有。來到這裡，我終於可以好好休息，把工作拋諸腦後，明天早上我要做的第一件事，就是好好地享受按摩，舒緩我所有的酸痛與疼痛，結束之後，我可能會去高爾夫球場打個幾洞。

I can't wait to have that club in my hands and just enjoy the beauty of the course. I have worked so hard for so long. And what vacation would be complete without some drinks? I will certainly be going to the resort's bar once the sun goes down for a few – or maybe more than a few – drinks. I think I deserve❽ a few beers. If I am lucky, I might meet some fellow travelers with interesting stories to share.

我等不及要握著球桿，沉浸在美麗的球場裡了。辛苦工作了這麼久之後才有的假期，沒喝個幾杯還算是渡假嗎？太陽下山後，我一定要去飯店的酒吧來個一兩杯（也許會喝更多），當作犒賞自己的辛勞，喝幾杯啤酒應該不為過，運氣好的話，或許還會碰見一些願意跟我分享有趣故事的旅客呢！

4. 我的退休計畫

Dana 2013/10/8

8:36

My job requires⑨ me to get inside and help explore⑩ the minds of my patients on a daily basis. There are times when this job feels like my whole life. The problem with this, of course, is that I am too busy with other people's lives and problems that I do not take the time to evaluate my life and my problems. After I realized this, I decided to take some time and consider my retirement plan.

　　我的工作需要花很多心思探索病患的精神狀態,並幫助他們認識自己內心的想法,有的時候,工作本身就佔滿我全部的生活,問題是,我都忙於關心別人的生活與煩惱,而沒有花時間來評估我自己的生活情況及問題,發現這一點之後,我決定花點時間來思考我的退休計畫。

Ideally, I would like to retire before I turn fifty. This would allow me to spend quality time with my loved ones and also fulfill⑪ a lifelong dream of mine: traveling around the world. In the next couple of years, I will take the time to get my finances in order so that I can make this a reality⑫. When I think of the extra work I will likely need to do, I will picture myself sitting on a sunny beach with a cocktail in my hand, and all that extra work seems like a small price to pay.

　　我的理想情況是在五十歲之前退休,這樣我才真正有時間與我所愛的人相聚,度過美好的時光,也才能實現我一直以來的夢想:環遊世界。未來幾年,我會花時間在增加收入上,如此一來,才可能實現我的退休夢,我知道工作量會增加,所以我會想像未來的畫面,我手上拿著雞尾酒,坐在陽光海灘上享受人生,一想到這個,就覺得那些辛勞根本算不了什麼。

Word 單字	Meaning 字義	Usage 常見用法
1 **reaction** [rɪˋækʃən]	名 反應；感應	a positive reaction 陽性反應 a reaction against sth. 對…的反抗
2 **attention** [əˋtɛnʃən]	名 注意；專心	pay attention to 專心在… be all attention 全神貫注
3 **comfort** [ˋkʌmfət]	名 安逸；舒適 動 安慰；慰問	the comfort of home 家居的舒適感 speak comfort for sb. 好言相慰
4 **schedule** [ˋskɛdʒʊl]	名 清單；時間表； 計畫表	have a full schedule 時間表很滿 behind the schedule 進度落後
5 **favor** [ˋfevə]	名 贊成；偏愛； 善意的行為	ask a favor of sb. 請某人幫忙 curry favor with sb. 巴結某人
6 **relax** [rɪˋlæks]	動 使放鬆；緩和	relax one's attention 鬆懈下來 relax restriction for 放鬆對…的限制
7 **advance** [ədˋvæns]	名 前進；發展 動 推進；促進	be in advance of 超越了… advance in price 物價上揚
8 **deserve** [dɪˋzɜv]	動 應受；該得	be deserving of sympathy 值得同情 sb. deserve praise 某人應受表揚
9 **require** [rɪˋkwaɪr]	動 需要；要求	be required by law 如法律所規定 sth. be required of sb. 要求某人做某事
10 **explore** [ɪkˋsplor]	動 探測；探勘	explore for oil 探勘石油 explore the possibilities 探討可能性
11 **fulfill** [fʊlˋfɪl]	動 執行；服從	fulfill one's promise 履行諾言 fulfill the requirement of 滿足…要求
12 **reality** [rɪˋælətɪ]	名 現實；真實	the virtual reality 虛擬實境 sth. become a reality 某事成為現實

UNIT 4 政治與媒體
Politics And Media～上篇

 025 MP3

Ben
Hey, did you read the article about health care in the newspaper this morning? `13:50`

嘿，你看到早上關於健康醫療的那篇新聞了嗎？

Ben
It said some Taiwanese living in foreign countries only pay a little for national health insurance, but they enjoy the same benefits❶ as Taiwanese do. `13:53`

報導說一些住在國外的台灣人只繳部分健保費，就享有和台灣人相同的福利。

既然他們繳了錢，那應該就沒關係。

I think it's fair because they are paying at least some money for it. `13:55`

Emma

Ben
No, it's not. While they do pay for national health insurance monthly, they don't pay any other taxes in Taiwan. `13:58`

當然有關係，他們每個月固然有繳健保費，但並沒有繳其他稅金給台灣政府。

Ben
Instead, they pay those taxes to the countries they are living in now. `14:00`

相反地，他們把稅金繳給他們現居的國家。

有差別嗎？你是想說他們對台灣沒有貢獻嗎？

Tip 當說話者不覺得有差別的時候才用。

What difference does it make? Are you saying that they do not contribute❷ to Taiwan? `14:02`

Emma

Ben
Exactly! Many of them fly back to Taiwan each year for a full physical checkup or something. `14:05`

沒錯！許多人每年回台灣做完整的健檢之類的。

SEND ≫

13:50 🔒 📶 ▥

這我有聽說過，但你真的認為這在台灣會成為人們關注的議題嗎？

I've heard of that. But do you really think this issue is a major concern for Taiwan? 14:07

Emma

Absolutely! We should petition the government for an immediate improvement. 14:10

那當然！我們應該向政府請願，要求立即的改善。

Ben

這主意聽起來不錯！

That sounds like a good idea. 14:11

Emma

話說回來，你對政治還真的是很狂熱。

Tip by the way 為轉換話題時的口語用法。

By the way, you really are quite a fervent[3] political activist! 14:12

Emma

Well, it concerns our nation's welfare system. These Taiwanese are using our resources at no cost. 14:15

我說，這關係到我們國家的福利制度耶！這些台灣人不計代價地在浪費我們的資源。

Ben

你說的太誇張了，不過，確實有幾分道理。

Tip 覺得對方反應過度時，可用 melodramatic（情節劇似的）。

You are being melodramatic, but you have a point. 14:17

Emma

SEND >>

Let's Chat In English Via APP • ⏻ •

19:10 🔋

Emma

There are so many different channels and diverse opinions on TV. Who can I trust?
19:10

電視頻道那麼多，評論又五花八門，我到底可以相信誰呢？

沒有可信的！雖然有些新聞是如實地報導，但大部份都是誇大其詞的內容。

No one! While some news is factual₄, too much of it gets exaggerated₅.
19:12

Ben

Emma

Why is that? The media just tries to inform us in an unbiased₆ manner, right?
19:15

為什麼會這樣？媒體不都盡量以公正的立場做報導嗎？

Tip 因為我們是單向地在接收新聞訊息，所以用inform（告知）。

你真的這麼相信嗎？你最近看了什麼新聞呢？

Do you really believe that? What news have you watched recently?
19:17

Ben

Emma

I remember I saw a terrible story on TV last week. It was about a teenager killing his grandpa...
19:21

我記得上星期在電視上看到一則駭人的新聞，關於青少年殺死爺爺…

Tip 記得要用on TV才表示「在電視的播出內容上」。

喔對！我也看到了，一位沉迷於線上遊戲的青少年逃學。

Tip 表達自己知道對方說的事，注意要用that one。

Oh, yes, that one. A teenager who was addicted₇ to playing on-line games refused to go to school.
19:24

Ben

有一天，他爺爺罵他不應該繼續這樣漫無目標地過日子，然後他做了什麼呢？他居然拿了把刀子殺死那年邁的爺爺！

One day, his grandpa scolded him for his aimless life. And what did he do? He got a knife and killed the poor old man!
19:28

Ben

🔊 😄 [   ] **SEND ≫**

Let's Chat In English Via APP • ⏻ •

Oh, my god! What a tragedy! There must be some kind of epidemic of uncontrollable youth today. `19:31`

我的天啊！好慘喔！社會上行為失控的年輕人像傳染病似地不斷擴散。

Emma

看吧，媒體讓你誤以為現在的小孩都行為失控，事實上，那則新聞只是單一事件。

See? The media has given you a false impression⑧ that all young kids are uncontrollable. The truth is, this was just an isolated case. `19:35`

Ben

Hmm, I haven't really thought about it that way. `19:36`

嗯，我的確沒想到用那樣的立場去思考這個問題。

Emma

媒體擁有龐大的影響力，能讓你相信它所播報的內容，剛剛那則新聞就讓人誤以為青少年都很危險。

The media has enormous power to make you believe almost anything. This story, for example, makes all teenagers look dangerous. `19:40`

Ben

I guess I have been too naive. I should start thinking critically, huh? `19:42`

想都沒想就全盤接受報導內容的我太天真了，我應該更嚴謹地去思考，對吧？

Emma

你當然應該這樣做了！

Of course you should! `19:43`

Ben

🔊 👄 [   ] **SEND »**

Let's Chat In English Via APP • ⏻ •

065

1. 需要解決的社會議題

📖 Ben 2013/10/11

15:28 🛜 ▪ 📶 ▫ 🔋

The abuse of our health care system must end. It is as simple as that. Too many Taiwanese emigrants live abroad and pay taxes to the countries they now call home, but they come back to Taiwan for medical issues. They abuse our system and put an increased burden on those of us Taiwanese who still live in Taiwan. Taiwanese citizens or not, if they pay no taxes here, how can they be given the same discounted medical prices as those of us who do?!

我們必須想辦法終結醫療資源的濫用情況，就是這樣。太多移居國外的台灣人付稅金給那些他們稱之為「家」的國家，卻回台灣享受醫療照顧，這些人濫用我們的醫療資源，並增加台灣居民的負擔，不管他們是不是台灣公民，若他們不付稅金，怎麼能享有納稅者的優惠醫療照顧呢？！

I wonder what, if any, opinions the current administration⑨ has on this problem and what, if any, solutions they have considered. If this problem is not addressed soon, I fear our taxes will be increased to help the government bear the cost of this abuse. I already pay almost 20% of my salary to the government. There is no way I will pay more just so a Taiwanese living in America can return to Taiwan once a year to get a physical checkup and visit the dentist. It is absurd⑩!

我想知道當前的政府對於這個議題有什麼意見，以及相關的配套解決方案（如果他們有意見及方案的話），若不盡快處理這個議題，我擔心我們將必須支付更多稅金，以幫助政府收拾這個爛攤子，作為稅金，我已經付了將近百分之二十的薪水給政府，要我幫那些住在美國的台灣人付費，讓他們每年回來做健康檢查或看牙醫，門兒都沒有，因為這實在太荒謬了！

18:03

2. 希望媒體立場更中立

Emma 2013/10/11

The goal of any professional journalist should be to tell a factual story with a neutral tone: to report the news only. Unfortunately, it has recently been brought to my attention that the current trend is to do more than just report. The trend is to sensationalize stories in order to sell newspapers, magazines, or commercial spots.

任何一個專業新聞工作者的目標,都應該是用中立的立場報導實情:只報導新聞本身就好,令人遺憾的是,我最近注意到不忠於實情的報導已變成一種趨勢,為了要讓報紙、雜誌大賣,或成為廣告的焦點,所以媒體大肆地渲染真相。

My friend helped me understand this trend by using a recent story. There was a boy who was addicted to playing on-line games and refused to go to school. When his grandfather got angry at him for this, the boy grabbed a knife and stabbed him to death! I realize now that this is a story about one boy's action and not all teenagers. But before my friend opened my eyes, the media's reporting gave me the impression that this boy was part of something bigger, something more sinister. I guess it's much more sellable to say that today's youths are more dangerous, not that one young man killed his grandfather.

我朋友用最近的一則新聞,幫助我明白這種趨勢。一個沉迷於線上遊戲的青少年拒絕上學,當他爺爺為此事罵他時,他竟然隨手抓了把刀子,殺害了他的爺爺!現在我了解這只是個人的行為,並不能代表所有的青少年都會如此,但在朋友打開我狹隘的視野之前,報導給我的感覺是,這個男孩的行為只是惡毒現象的一小部分,背後還有更嚴重的社會問題,我想,和報導「年輕人殺害爺爺」的不幸事件相比,一則強調「年輕世代危險性」的內容能賣得更好吧。

APP 單字動態看板 Vocabulary Billboard

Word 單字	Meaning 字義	Usage 常見用法
1 benefit [`bɛnəfɪt]	名 利益;好處 動 對⋯有益	bring benefits to sb. 帶給某人好處 old-age benefits 老年救濟金
2 contribute [kən`trɪbjut]	動 捐獻;提供	contribute to a magazine 向雜誌投稿 contribute to the charity 捐給慈善團體
3 fervent [`fɜvənt]	形 熱烈的;強烈的	a fervent patriot 熱情的愛國者 have a fervent desire to 有強烈的欲望
4 factual [`fæktʃuəl]	形 事實的;真實的	the factual experience 實際經驗 a factual account of sth. ⋯的如實報導
5 exaggerate [ɪg`zædʒə͵ret]	動 誇張;誇大	exaggerate excessively 過份地誇張 exaggerate about sth. 誇大某事
6 unbiased [ʌn`baɪəst]	形 無偏見的	an unbiased decision 無偏見的決定 unbiased public opinion 無偏見的輿論
7 addict [ə`dɪkt]	動 使沉溺;使醉心	be deeply addicted 深深地沉迷 be addicted to 對⋯入迷
8 impression [ɪm`prɛʃən]	名 印象;感想; 影響;效果	make a good impression on 留下好印象 be under the impression that 以為是
9 administration [əd͵mɪnə`streʃən]	名 管理;經營; 行政機構	an administration executive 行政專員 during his administration 在他執政期間
10 absurd [əb`sɝd]	形 可笑的;荒謬的	be utterly absurd 荒謬透頂 theater of the absurd 荒謬劇場
11 neutral [`njutrəl]	名 中立者(國) 形 中立的;非彩色的	a neutral report 中立的報導 a neutral color 中性色
12 sensationalize [sɛn`seʃən͵aɪz]	動 引起轟動; 帶著感情描述	sensationalize crazily 瘋狂地引起轟動 sensationalize one's life 渲染⋯的生活

UNIT 4

政治與媒體
Politics And Media～下篇

029 MP3

🔒 ✉ ✏   9:22 📶 ⬛

◀ APP CHAT **3** 我們要請願

Ben

I have formulated₁ a petition₂ that raises concern₃ about a key issue in Taiwan. `9:22`

我發起了一個請願活動，要讓大眾關注台灣的一個重要議題。

喔，你是指你上次提到的健康醫療議題嗎？

Tip 用bring up特別能表達「提出」的動作。

Oh, are you referring to the health care issue you brought up last time? `9:25`

Emma

Ben

That is a big issue₄, without a doubt, but this petition is aimed at education. `9:27`

那的確是很重要的議題，但這次的請願主要是針對教育問題。

你對公眾事務的了解程度，比我這人民公僕要高太多了。

I must say you have known much more about public affairs than a person like me, a civil servant. `9:29`

Emma

Ben

Haha, I believe every citizen should bear some responsibility and be concerned with vital issues like health care and education. `9:33`

哈哈，我們人民有責任多關心像健康醫療與教育等重大議題啊！

也對，那你們這次請願的訴求是什麼呢？

Yeah, so what is this petition about? `9:34`

Emma

Ben

I have an eighteen-year-old nephew who is taking the national college entrance exams in two months. `9:37`

我有個十八歲的外甥兩個月後就要參加大學入學考試。

SEND ▶▶

Let's Chat In English Via APP ● ⏻ ●

9:22

Ben

And for the past few semesters, his music and art classes have been replaced by math and English exams. `9:41`

過去幾個學期,學校把音樂和美術課的上課內容用數學和英語的考試取代。

真的假的?!那種作法從很久以前開始就是不合法的耶!

Seriously?! That has been illegal for a long time! `9:42`

Emma

Ben

Unfortunately, it's true. That's why I want to start this petition and bring this issue to the attention of the Ministry of Education. `9:45`

很遺憾,是真的,這就是為什麼我發起請願活動,希望教育部關注這個議題。

拜託快去做吧!學生應該有受完整教育的權利,這種權利不應該被一連串的考試給剝奪殆盡。

By all means, please do. Students are entitled to a complete education and should not be worn out by so many exams. `9:48`

Emma

Ben

I have always said that it is never too late. `9:54`

我一直認為,只要開始行動,就永遠不嫌遲。

Tip be never too late 為帶有鼓勵口吻的表達法。

Ben

We can only do our best and hope for positive results in the future. `9:56`

我們只能盡力而為,並期望未來會有好的成果。

 SEND ≫

Let's Chat In English Via APP

070

22:02 📶 🔋

Emma

The election❺ for city mayor is now over. `22:02`

市長選舉現在已經結束了。

Tip 選舉（含開票）會延續一段時間，這裡用now over強調結束的那個時間點。

快告訴我，是哪個政黨贏得市長選舉啊？

Tell me, which party won the election? `22:03`

Ben

Emma

You still don't know? I thought you would surely be planted in front of a television watching the result. `22:07`

你還不知道嗎？我以為你肯定會守在電視機前看開票的。

Tip be planted表達像植物生根般，一動也不動。

我很想，但我現在出差中，等一下還得繼續開會，不說這個，快告訴我選舉結果。

Tip on a business trip 為慣用法，記住用on做連結。

I really wanted to, but right now, I am on a business trip. Our meeting will be continuing shortly, so quick, tell me the election result. `22:10`

Ben

Emma

Well, I guess you will not be happy with it. Party A won the election. `22:12`

我猜你不會樂見於這個結果的，A政黨贏得了選舉。

什麼？！簡直無法相信，這不可能！怎麼會發生這種事？

WHAT?! I cannot believe this. That's impossible! What happened? `22:14`

Ben

Emma

Well, it is quite simple, really. Party A collected more ballots❻ than Party B. `22:17`

嗯，道理其實很簡單，A黨的選票比B黨多。

SEND ≫

Let's Chat In English Via APP • ⏻ •

22:02

這我知道！但那些蠢蛋
怎麼可能贏得這次的選
舉呢？！

I know that! But how could those fools win the election?!
22:18

Ben

B黨有能讓全體市民
受益的好政見，A黨
只想著自己的安逸舒
適而已。

Party B has a better platform that will benefit everyone. Party A just wants to make their lives easier.
22:22

Ben

Emma

Calm down. This was an open, honest, and fair election. Party A received the most votes and thus represents the will of people.
22:25

冷靜點，這可是公平、
公正、公開的選舉，A
黨的選票就代表大多數
的民意。

Emma

I am sorry that the party you supported did not win, but the election is over.
22:27

我很抱歉你支持的黨落敗了，但總之
選舉結果已經確定了。

這太荒謬了！我們完了，
整個城市都沒指望了，我
拒絕住在一個會選出這種
政黨的地方。

This is ridiculous! This is the end for us, for our city. I refuse to live in a place that elects parties like this.
22:30

Ben

Emma

Come on! It's not the end of the world. No matter who won the election, life will go on.
22:32

拜託，這又不是世界末日，無論誰贏
得選舉，日子還是得繼續下去啊！

Tip 當對方太大驚小怪，想請他冷
靜一點時用。

好啦，我知道，發洩
一下心情都不行嗎？

I know. Come on, can't a guy vent a little?
22:33

Ben

SEND ▶▶

3. 期盼有為的大政府

Ben 2013/10/15

Recently, I have noticed a certain trend in our government. People in power have been using the hard-earned tax money from the public for their own benefit. They have used this money to pay for their extravagant lifestyles. I believe that this money should be used to make Taiwan a better country for everyone, not just for those few in power. I propose that members of the current government should forfeit luxuries such as mansions, penthouses, and sports cars.

最近，我注意到我們的政府有某種傾向，手中握有權勢的人，利用民眾辛苦工作後而繳納的稅金，為自己謀福利，他們用這些錢來支付自己奢侈的生活，我認為這些錢應該用在能讓台灣人過得更好的用途上，而不是成為少數權貴的經費，我建議現任的政府官員們自動放棄奢華的生活，像是官邸、豪宅，以及高級跑車之類的享受。

This money should be used instead to improve departments like education and health care, which can benefit everyone living in Taiwan. There are many people who have been promised a better life, but I have not seen any action by the government to honor this promise. I am afraid my newest petition about school curriculum will have a similar fate. That is, they will promise to make changes, but nothing more. It's always words, empty words.

這些錢應該花在能造福台灣人的機關上，像是教育與健康醫療部門，有很多官員都承諾要帶給人民更好的生活，但我卻沒看到政府用行動來兌現他們的承諾，我擔心這次針對教育問題的請願也會遭受同樣的命運，我的意思是，政府將口頭承諾改變，之後就再也沒消息，唉，每次都只是說說，說了也沒做。

4. 我見到總統本人了！

Emma 2013/10/16

Wow, I am still trying to process what just happened. Today started as a normal day at work, a day like any other day, until I heard everyone in the office start to whisper and stand up. I did not know what was happening at first, but then I saw him. It was the president himself! My God! It was the first time I had seen the president somewhere other than on television. I was awestruck. And everyone had delayed reactions to seeing the president in our office. None of us knew what to do. It is not every day that the most powerful man in the country visits your office.

哇，我還在想著剛才發生的事，今天就像平常一樣，是一個普通的工作日，直到我聽到辦公室的大家交頭接耳，還站起身，我才發現不對勁，一開始我不知道發生了什麼事，接著我就看到了那位，是總統本人耶！天啊！這可是我第一次在電視以外的地方看到總統，我肅然起敬，而且，大家都是過了好幾秒之後才反應過來，我們全都手足無措，畢竟，可不是每天都能看到國家最高權力者來到你的辦公室。

As I watched him walk through the office and shake everyone's hand, I noticed how sincere his smile was. Everyone did their best to get a photo with him. I could not help but feel elated as he walked past me and shook my hand. He had a very natural charisma. He seemed like such a nice man that I had to remind myself that he was the president and not just a friend of mine.

當我看著他走過辦公室和每個人握手時，我注意到他臉上真誠的笑容，每個人都想盡辦法與他合照，而當他走過我身旁和我握手時，我掩藏不住內心的歡喜，他散發出一股天生的領袖魅力，看起來是個很好的人，所以我必須提醒自己，就算再有親和力，他還是總統，而不是我的朋友。

APP 單字動態看板 Vocabulary Billboard

Word 單字	Meaning 字義	Usage 常見用法
1 formulate [`fɔrmjə,let]	動 使公式化；闡述(或說明)	formulate a new idea 闡述新想法 formulate one's plan 制定計畫
2 petition [pə`tɪʃən]	名 請願書 動 向…請願；請求	a petition for divorce 離婚請願書 petition for pardon 請求赦免
3 concern [kən`sɝn]	名 關心的事 動 關於；使擔心	be no concern of mine 與我無關 be concerned about/with 對…關心
4 issue [`ɪʃjʊ]	名 問題；爭論 動 發行；發布	the environmental issue 環保議題 issue travel documents 核發旅遊證件
5 election [ɪ`lɛkʃən]	名 選舉；當選	a general election 普選 sb. stand for election 參加競選
6 ballot [`bælət]	名 選票 動 投票表決	ballot paper 選票紙 ballot for/against 投票贊成/反對
7 extravagant [ɪk`stævəgənt]	形 奢侈的；浪費的	an extravagant expense 浪費的開銷 an extravagant behavior 放肆的行為
8 forfeit [`fɔr,fɪt]	動 喪失(全力、名譽、生命等)	forfeit the right 喪失權利 forfeit one's own future 斷送前程
9 curriculum [kə`rɪkjələm]	名 (一門)課程	sth. be on the curriculum …被納入課程 a core curriculum 核心課程
10 awestruck [`ɔstrʌk]	形 震驚的	an awestruck witness 震驚的目擊者 be awestruck by 對…嘆為觀止
11 elated [ɪ`letɪd]	形 得意洋洋的	be elated at the result 對結果感到欣喜 an elated smile 得意洋洋的笑容
12 charisma [kə`rɪzmə]	名 非凡領導力；魅力	a character with charisma 性格具魅力 one's natural charisma …的天生魅力

Part 2

人生階段

從戀愛到家庭的小確幸

不管在哪一個人生階段，都有能與人分享的生活點滴。
令人臉紅心跳的戀愛經驗、婚後生活甘苦談、
有了孩子之後的父母經、與家人共同面對的老後照顧，
不管是快樂的點滴，還是不吐不快的苦水，
都可以用APP輕鬆聊不停、聰明學英文喔！

Let's Chat In English
Via APP

APP CHAT !

UNIT 1 戀愛交往
About The Romance～上篇

APP CHAT 1 好想談戀愛

8:40 🔓

喔，神啊！我那穿著一身閃耀盔甲的騎士在哪裡呢？

Oh, God! Where is my knight in shining armor? 8:40

Nina

You're not gonna find a knight in shining armor in this day and age! 8:46

Sharon

穿著盔甲的騎士什麼的，現在這個年代已經找不到囉！

Tip 使用this day and age強調對方所說的是古代的事。

拜託，我是指理想的對象，最好是能像騎士般照顧我的男性。

Please, I am talking about my ideal❶ partner, a guy who, like a knight, will take care of me. 8:49

Nina

Come on! You still believe in that fairytale nonsense? Be PRACTICAL!!! 8:51

Sharon

得了吧！你還相信那種胡扯的童話嗎？實際一點吧！

Tip 加上nonsense的語氣更強烈，較適合用在熟人身上。

我知道要實際一點啦，可是，每個女孩都需要一位白馬王子啊！

I know, I know. But come on, every girl needs an ideal man. 8:52

Nina

That's no different. You need to face reality. You're the only one who will be there for yourself. 8:54

Sharon

你那就是不實際的想法，你得面對現實，到頭來你是唯一會守候在自己身邊的人。

聽起來你好像一點也不相信真愛。

It sounds like you don't believe in true love at all. 8:55

Nina

SEND >>

Let's Chat In English Via APP

078

Sharon: It's not that. Just because I am practical doesn't mean I am cynical[2]. I just don't want to see you continue holding on to this delusion[3]. 9:02

並不是那樣，想法實際不代表我憤世嫉俗，我只是不希望你繼續抱持著這個幻想罷了。

女人是需要被疼愛、被照顧的，那是天性，也是社會的歸屬性。

Nina: Women need to be loved and taken care of. That's human nature. That's social cohesion[4]. 9:04

Sharon: Yes, and social cohesion has nothing to do with romance. 9:05

對，而且歸屬性和浪漫的幻想毫不相干。

Tip have nothing to do with 為「完全無關」的實用表達句。

你曾交過一次男朋友，不是嗎？那你應該知道戀愛的感覺。

Nina: You had a boyfriend once, didn't you? You should know what it feels like to be in love. 9:12

Sharon: I did, yes. I know what it feels like to be in love, so I don't need to pursue[5] that feeling anymore. 9:16

我是知道，就是因為明白，所以我不再需要去追求戀愛的感覺了。

你真是個怪咖，雪倫，你的內心一定缺少了什麼。

Nina: You're weird, Sharon. There must be something missing in your heart. 9:18

Sharon: Yeah, well, there must be something missing in your brain. 9:19

是啊，我看你的腦袋才一定少了點什麼吧。

🔊 😆 [_____] SEND ≫

9:14 📶 🔋

Nina

"…Starlit eyes. Oh, baby, what a pretty face." `9:14`

「…星光閃爍般的眼睛，噢，寶貝，多美麗的臉龐。」

…你是在跟我說話嗎？

Tip 不確定對方的談話對象、或者不認為在跟自己說話時，可用這句英文。

…Are you talking to me? `9:19`

Sharon

Nina

Yes. Isn't it a beautiful poem? I got so touched when I read it. Can somebody write a poem for me like this? `9:23`

是啊，很美的一首詩吧？讀的時候，我真的好感動，有沒有人能為我寫出這樣的詩呢？

你確定詩人是你的夢中情人嗎？他們通常都是窮困潦倒的。

Are you sure a poet is your dream man? Poets are usually poor. `9:25`

Sharon

Nina

Why not? Most men don't know how to please women. Poets, on the other hand, are romantic. `9:28`

有何不可？大部分的男人都不知道如何取悅女性，相較之下，詩人浪漫多了。

詩人可能沒有車可以載你到處趴趴走。

Tip 兜風實用表達drive sb. around，加上around更強調「路線」。

A poet won't have a car to drive you around. `9:29`

Sharon

Nina

That's alright. We can ride bicycles along the riverbank and watch the sunset. `9:31`

沒關係，我們可以沿著河岸騎單車、看日落。

SEND ▶▶

9:14

他可能沒辦法買鑽戒給你喔。

Tip be able to 說的是「能力上」的足夠，具體像金錢、抽象如能力都可以表達。

He might not be able to buy you a diamond ring. `9:32`

Sharon

No problem. His poems will bring me more happiness than any ring could. `9:34`

Nina

無所謂，他的詩所能帶給我的快樂遠勝於任何戒指。

知道嗎？你聽起來像是個瘋子！

Tip 口語中經常出現，無特別意義，與 well 的功用雷同。

You know, you sound like an insane person! `9:35`

Sharon

You're boring, Sharon. I don't want to be with a rich moron. Rich guys only know how to make money; they don't know how to be good lovers. `9:41`

Nina

你很無趣耶，雪倫，我不想跟有錢的白癡在一起，他們只懂得賺錢，不懂得如何當個好情人。

那你最起碼也找個有點錢的詩人吧。

Well, at the very least, you could try to find a poet with a little money. `9:42`

Sharon

Then he might not be romantic at all. All I need is his love and his beautiful poems. `9:44`

Nina

那他也許就一點都不浪漫了，我只能要能擁有他的愛和美麗的詩就夠了。

在我看來，你需要的是去看個醫生！

Tip 看醫生的慣用動詞為 see。

In my opinion, what you need is to see a doctor! `9:45`

Sharon

SEND »

微網誌

1. 夢想與現實的差距

📖 Nina 2013/10/19

Why can't I find my dream man? I don't have a long list of what I want or anything. There are just maybe nine or ten things a guy needs to be perfect for me. One guy I met last year had seven, but when he took me out for a nice dinner and ordered a steak, I dumped₈ him. I need to be with another vegetarian. I mean, I don't understand: how can someone eat dead animals? It's disgusting₉! Another guy seemed perfect, but he stood me up on my birthday. When I asked him what happened, he told me he was so busy at work that he forgot. Come on, it was my birthday! How could he forget?

為什麼就找不到我的夢中情人呢？我的要求又不是很多，成為我夢中情人的條件，大概就只有九或十項而已。我去年認識一個男人，他符合七項標準，但當他帶我出去吃晚餐，點了一客牛排後，我就甩了他，我必須和素食者交往才行，我實在搞不懂，怎麼會有人要吃動物的屍體呢？真是噁心死了！另外一個男的看似完美，但他在我生日那天放我鴿子，當我問起原因時，他告訴我，他當時忙工作忙到忘記了，拜託，那天可是我的生日耶！他怎麼可以忘記呢？

My friends all tell me I need to stop judging guys like I do. They tell me that there is no perfect guy who will have all the things I need. They say I need to be less demanding₁₀. I think they are crazy. I am a good woman, and I deserve my dream man! I won't stop looking, either. I just know he's out there, waiting for me.

我朋友都叫我不要再像這樣評斷男人了，他們告訴我，世上不會有完全符合我條件的男性，說我得降低標準才行，我倒覺得他們瘋了，我是個好女人，理應找到屬於我的夢中情人！我不會停止尋覓的，我知道他就在某處等候著我。

2. 表裡不一的男同事

Sharon 2013/10/22

If anyone asks me why I don't trust men or why I don't hold on to the fantasy⓫ of a dream man, I always tell them about my coworker. He is nice, funny, handsome, and smart. He seems like he has it all – a perfect, ideal boyfriend. But he isn't! I quickly discovered he is a terrible coworker. He is so lazy that I have to help him finish all his projects.

如果有人問我不信任男人的原因，或是好奇我為何不存有對夢中情人的幻想，我總會告訴他們我同事的例子，他人很好、風趣、英俊，又聰明，看起來好像什麼都具備，儼然是完美、理想的男友類型，但他卻不是！我很快就發現他是個很糟糕的同事，他懶惰到我得幫他完成所有的案子才行。

That's nothing compared to what his ex-girlfriend told me last week, though. She came to our office looking for my coworker, but he was out to lunch. She then told me how he used her for everything. She bought him everything – food, clothes, games; she paid his rent; she let him borrow her car; and so many other things. After only a few months, he dumped her for another girl, one he said he had been dating almost as long as her! So he may look and act like he is the perfect guy, but really he is a small and petty⓬ cheater! Be careful, ladies!

然而，那跟上週他前女友說的事根本沒得比，她來我們辦公室找我同事，但他當時出去吃午餐了，接著，她就告訴我他是如何在每件事情上利用了她，所有東西都是她買單，包括吃的、穿的和玩的；她幫他付房租；借自己的車給他，還有很多其他的事情。在交往幾個月後，他就為了另一個女孩而甩了她，一個他說交往時間幾乎跟她一樣久的女孩！所以，他的外表和舉止或許都像是個完美男人，但實際上，他只是個卑鄙又小氣的騙子而已！小心點啦，女士們！

APP 單字動態看板 Vocabulary Billboard

Word 單字	Meaning 字義	Usage 常見用法
1 ideal [aɪˋdiəl]	名 理想；典範 形 理想的；完美的	a man of high ideals 有高尚理想的人 meet one's ideal 實現理想
2 cynical [ˋsɪnɪkḷ]	形 憤世嫉俗的	be cynical about 對…感到懷疑 the cynical remarks 冷嘲熱諷的話
3 delusion [dɪˋluʒən]	名 迷惑；幻覺；欺騙	suffer from delusion 患有妄想症 be under a delusion 處於幻想中
4 cohesion [koˋhiʒən]	名 結合；凝聚	social cohesion 社會歸屬性 the cohesion of the family 家庭凝聚力
5 pursue [pɚˋsu]	動 追趕；追求	be pursued by fortune 好運連連 pursue after 追趕
6 sunset [ˋsʌn͵sɛt]	名 日落；晚年	at sunset 日落時分 be in the sunset of one's day 步入晚年
7 romantic [rəˋmæntɪk]	形 羅曼蒂克的； 不切實際的	be romantic about life 對人生充滿幻想 a romantic novel 浪漫小說
8 dump [dʌmp]	名 垃圾場 動 傾倒；拋棄	dump its load of sand 卸下沙子 dump the garbage 倒垃圾
9 disgusting [dɪsˋgʌstɪŋ]	形 令人作噁的； 十分討厭的	the disgusting food 令人作噁的食物 be in a disgusting dilemma 束手無策
10 demand [dɪˋmænd]	名 要求；請求 動 要求；需要	demand sth. from sb. 要求某人… demand the right to vote 要求選舉權
11 fantasy [ˋfæntəsɪ]	名 空想；幻想	a world of fantasy 幻想世界 indulge in fantasy 沉緬於幻想
12 petty [ˋpɛtɪ]	形 小的；瑣碎的	petty cash 小額現金 have a petty mind 心胸狹窄

戀愛交往
About The Romance～下篇

8:27 🛜 ill 🔋

◀ APP CHAT **3** 我也想成為萬人迷

哎呀，我真的好想去動整形手術。

Tip feel like表示「有那樣的想法」，語氣沒有want強烈。

Ah, I really feel like getting some plastic surgery. 8:27

Nina

Why would you say such a thing? What's wrong with your body? 8:29

怎麼這樣說？你的身材有什麼問題嗎？

Sharon

我對我的身形不滿意，我覺得這就是我一直遇不到夢中情人的原因。

I'm not satisfied with my body shape. And I think that's why I can't find my dream man. 8:34

Nina

Come on, Nina, you are just a little chubby. You don't need plastic surgery. 8:36

得了吧，妮娜，你只不過是有點豐滿而已，根本不需要整形。

Sharon

可是我每次照鏡子的時候都很自卑，真希望能像公司裡的其他女生般苗條。

But each time I look in the mirror, I feel ugly and inferior. I really hope I can look slender like the other girls at my company. 8:41

Nina

In that case, you don't need plastic surgery. A little exercise and a change in your diet are all you need. 8:45

這樣的話，你需要的不是整形，而是做運動和改變你的飲食習慣。

Sharon

那聽起來要費一番工夫，我想要的是立即的改變，不是慢慢來的那種。

Tip 用sooner rather than later強調自己喜歡快一點的改變。

That sounds like a lot of work. I want a change sooner rather than later. 8:47

Nina

SEND ≫

8:27

APP CHAT 3 我也想成為萬人迷

Sharon: Well, maybe you could pay more attention[2] to how you look: your hairstyle, make-up, things like that. 8:51

那你或許可以多留意一下外表：髮型、化妝之類的。

Nina: Oh, really? You think that would help me find my dream man? 8:52

真的嗎？你認為那會有助於找到我的夢中情人嗎？

Sharon: Maybe. I think you dress well already, but you could dye your hair brown and put on make-up every day. It can't hurt, you know? 8:55

或許吧，我覺得你的穿著已經很好了，但你可以把頭髮染成棕色、並每天化妝，那不會有壞處的，對吧？

Nina: You're such a good friend, Sharon! I can't even begin to thank you! 8:57

你真是個好朋友，雪倫！我都不知道該怎麼謝你了！

Sharon: Don't mention[3] it! For your sake, I hope you will find your dream man. 8:59

不用客氣！為了你的努力，我祝福你找到你的夢中情人。

Tip 強調「小事一樁，不用謝」。

Nina: I hope so. Sorry, but I can't talk anymore. I have a meeting in ten minutes. Good-bye! 9:01

但願如此，抱歉，我不能再聊了，我十分鐘後要開會，再見！

Sharon: Good luck! Bye-bye! 9:02

祝你好運！掰掰！

SEND

19:00

這幾天還好嗎？找到你的夢中情人了嗎？

How have you been these days? Have you met your dream man yet? **19:00**

Sharon

I did what you told me, but I still haven't found the one. I am losing hope. **19:03**

Nina

我照你說的做了，但我仍然沒找到夢中情人，我快絕望了。

Tip 進行式表示隨著時間而「漸漸」失去信心。

實際一點吧！你或許認為愛情就是一切，但並不是那樣的，你還有別的事可以做。

Be practical❹! You might think love is all there is, but it isn't. There are other things you could be doing. **19:06**

Sharon

But I feel so incomplete❺ without a partner! You know how much I would like to share my happiness, anger, sadness, and joy with someone. **19:10**

Nina

可是沒個伴我就覺得不完整！你知道我有多想跟人分享我的喜怒哀樂的。

我明白，但在單身的時候，你也必須好好過日子才對。

I understand that. But you need to enjoy your life while being alone. **19:12**

Sharon

Why are you always this rational and practical? **19:13**

Nina

你為什麼總是這麼理性和實際呢？

我只是喜歡審視自己的人生和價值觀而已。

I just like to reflect on my life and my values. **19:14**

Sharon

SEND »

Let's Chat In English Via APP

那並不代表我冷漠，我不是反對戀愛之類的，我只是相信，就算沒有愛情，女人一樣可以好好過日子。

That doesn't mean I'm emotionless. I'm not against falling in love or anything. I simply believe women can live without love. 19:19

Sharon

Nina

I guess I get what you are saying. I should try to learn how to live without love. 19:21

我想我了解你的意思，我應該試著學習沒有愛情的生活。

Tip 和朋友說話時，直接用get更口語，此處意指「了解」。

就是這樣！不要讓愛情控制你的人生，從現在起，做你自己就好。

That's the idea! Don't let love control your whole life. From now on, be yourself. 19:25

Sharon

嘿，改天下班後，要不要和我一起去做瑜伽呢？

Hey, how about going to yoga with me after work sometime? 19:27

Sharon

Nina

I'd be happy to. What time, when, and where, though? 19:28

非常樂意，時間、日期，還有地點呢？

星期三晚上七點在我辦公室前面碰面如何？我們可以一起走去瑜伽教室。

How about I meet you at 7:00 p.m. on Wednesday in front of my office? We can walk to the yoga studio together. 19:33

Sharon

Nina

Sure. See you then. And thanks for talking with me. 19:34

沒問題，那到時候見，還有謝謝你陪我聊天。

Tip 輕鬆的口語英文，也可以直接用see you。

SEND ≫

Let's Chat In English Via APP • ⏻ •

3. 新認識的律師同業

Sharon 2013/10/26

I have spent my adult life focused on my career and not on my personal life. I am not a sentimental girl. Love is nice and all, but I think it is overrated. I am not against finding a good partner, getting married and starting a family. It's just that my career will always come first.

成年之後，我都專注在職業生涯這一塊，很少注意私人生活的領域，我不是感性的女生，愛情是很好，但我覺得多數人高估了它的價值，我不反對去找一個好對象結婚，並與他建立家庭，只是，工作永遠都排在我的第一位。

If I had a dream man, he would be like me, career-minded and practical. Unfortunately, I seldom meet anyone, let alone anyone I like. Last week, however, I met another lawyer on the way to a meeting. We met by chance, actually. I was running late, and he was nice enough to hold the elevator door open for me. He saw my briefcase and asked if I was going to the meeting at the law firm on the twelfth floor. I said yes, and asked him if he worked there. He said that he was a new partner there. Then we started chatting about our respective jobs. He asked me out for coffee. I said yes. There is nothing wrong with a casual date with another professional.

如果我有夢中情人的話，他會和我一樣以工作為重，而且個性實際。不幸的是，我很少有機會認識別人，更別說喜歡的人了。然而，上個星期，我在去開會的途中認識一位律師，我們是偶然相遇的，我那時候快遲到了，而他好心地為我按住電梯的開門鈕，他看到我的公事包，問我是否要去十二樓的律師事務所開會，我說是，並問他是否在那間事務所工作，他告訴我，他是那裡的新合夥人，接著，我們就聊起各自的工作。他約我一起喝咖啡，我答應了，畢竟，與同業來個普通的約會並沒有什麼大不了的。

4. 她竟然交了男朋友！

Nina 2013/10/31

When I heard Sharon started dating a guy, I almost dropped the tea I was drinking. I still can't believe it! Sharon, Miss Practical, Miss "I Don't-Need-a-Man", is dating someone! Our mutual⑩ friend Jill – the one who told me the news – also told me that Sharon is getting serious with him. I am so surprised. I mean, she found a guy before me! How is that possible?!

當我聽到雪倫在和一個男的約會時，我手上的茶杯差一點就掉到地上了，我到現在都還無法相信！雪倫，那個實際小姐、「我不需要男人」小姐，正在與某人約會！我們共同的朋友吉兒（是她告訴我這個消息的）同時告訴我，雪倫和他是認真在交往的，我實在太訝異了，我的意思是，雪倫竟然比我早找到夢中情人，這怎麼可能呢？！

I have to say I am also a little jealous. Maybe the guy isn't her dream man, but what if he is? He certainly sounds like he is. He is a lawyer like her and has a serious personality⑪, also like her. I wonder if they will get married. You know, that would really just be too much. Here I am, looking everywhere and focusing my life on finding Mr. Right, and Sharon's falls right into her lap! Just thinking about the two of them living happily together makes me depressed⑫. I think I need a drink, or two.

我必須承認，我同時感到有點嫉妒，也許這男的不是她的夢中情人，但萬一他是呢？聽起來他肯定是的，他和雪倫一樣都是律師，而且個性嚴謹，這點也跟她相同，我很好奇他們會不會結婚，會就真的太過分了，看看我，全心全力地到處尋找白馬王子，而雪倫卻得來全不費工夫！光是想像他們兩人過著幸福快樂的日子，我就感到沮喪，我想我需要喝一杯酒，或來個兩杯。

Word 單字	Meaning 字義	Usage 常見用法
1 surgery [`sɝdʒərɪ]	名 外科；外科手術	do minor surgery on 給…動小手術 plastic surgery 整形美容手術
2 attention [ə`tɛnʃən]	名 注意；注意力； 照顧；治療	pay attention to 專注於 the focus of attention 注意的中心
3 mention [`mɛnʃən]	名 提及；說起 動 提到；說起	a mention in the newspapers 報紙提到 not to mention 更別提
4 practical [`præktɪk!]	形 實踐的；應用的； 講究實際的	in practical use 在實際的應用當中 a practical outlook on life 實際的人生觀
5 incomplete [ˌɪnkəm`plit]	形 不完整的	an incomplete report 不完整的報導 be incomplete in 在…方面不完整
6 focus [`fokəs]	名 焦點；中心 動 使聚焦；使集中	the focus of this unit 本單元的重點 focus on 集中於
7 sentimental [ˌsɛntə`mɛnt!]	形 情深的；感傷的； 多愁善感的	the sentimental parents 多愁善感的父母 out of sentimental reasons 出於感性
8 overrate [ˌovɚ`ret]	動 過高估計	overrate sth. vastly 大大地高估 overrate one's ability 高估某人的能力
9 respective [rɪ`spɛktɪv]	形 分別的；各自的	their respective jobs 他們各自的工作 take their respective seats 各自就座
10 mutual [`mjutʃuəl]	形 相互的；彼此的； 共同的；共有的	by mutual agreement 經雙方同意 a mutual friend 共同的朋友
11 personality [ˌpɝsn`ælətɪ]	名 人格；品格	have a strong personality 個性堅強 a personality cult 個人崇拜
12 depressed [dɪ`prɛst]	形 沮喪的；消沉的； 憂鬱的；貧困的	a depressed facial expression 沮喪表情 a depressed area 貧困地區

UNIT 2

求婚計畫
The Proposal～上篇

 041 MP3

🔒 ◿ ✎　　　　　14:20 📶 ▮▮▮

◀ APP CHAT　**1**　準備要求婚

Daniel

Lucy, are you busy right now? I need your recommendation❶. `14:20`

露西，你現在在忙嗎？
我需要你的建議。

Lucy

Me? Are you sure? This is the first time you've reached out to me for advice. Okay…what do you need? `14:23`

我嗎？你確定？這是你第一次徵求我的意見耶，好吧，你想問什麼呢？

Daniel

You work at a flower shop, right? So you know what kind of flowers girls like. `14:26`

你在花店工作對吧？所以你很清楚女生喜歡哪一種花。

Lucy

Don't tell me you are buying flowers for another woman. Jenny will kill you! `14:28`

別告訴我你打算買花送給別的女生喔，珍妮會殺了你的！

Daniel

Come on, Lucy. Of course they are for Jenny. She is the only love of my life. Don't worry. `14:34`

拜託，露西，花當然是要給珍妮的，她是我唯一的真命天女，放心吧！

Lucy

I thought so. Let me guess… you want to send Jenny flowers for her birthday? `14:36`

我想也是，那讓我猜猜看…你打算在珍妮生日的時候送花給她嗎？

Tip 口語說法let me guess。

Daniel

Nope, you guessed wrong. These flowers are for a very special occasion❷ : I am planning to propose! `14:40`

不，你猜錯了，這些花是為了一個特殊的場合而準備的：我要求婚了！

🔊 😀 ［　　　　　　　　　］ **SEND ≫**

Let's Chat In English Via APP ● ⏻ ●

你要向珍妮求婚了？
這是真的嗎？！

You are proposing to Jenny? Really?!
14:41

Lucy

Daniel

Yeah. You know, we've been
dating for a couple of years
now. It's about time to make a
lifetime promise to her. 14:50

是啊，我們已經交往好幾年，也該是我對
她許諾終生的時候了。

Tip make a lifetime promise為求婚的另
一種說法，強調婚姻的「承諾」。

真是太浪漫了！那你
的計畫是什麼？我能
幫你什麼呢？

That's so romantic! So, what's your
plan? How can I help you? 14:51

Lucy

Daniel

My friend recommended giving her ninety-
nine red roses when I propose to her at
our three-year anniversary❸. 14:54

我朋友建議我在慶祝三
週年的時候，買九十九
朵紅玫瑰向她求婚。

Daniel

What do you think? Can you prepare
the flowers for me? 14:55

你覺得怎麼樣？能幫
我準備花嗎？

我是可以幫你準備，但老實說，
你的招數太老套了。

Tip old-fashioned為「過時、老
套」的慣用形容。

I can, but honestly, your plan
sounds too old-fashioned.
14:58

Lucy

SEND ▸▸

Let's Chat In English Via APP

15:01 📶

如果你希望珍妮被你感動，答應求婚，你就需要一個更周到的計畫。

If you want Jenny to be moved by your proposal and say yes, you will need a more thoughtful₄ plan.　15:01

Lucy

Ok, so what should I do, Miss "Love Expert"?　15:02

好吧，那我該怎麼做呢？「愛情專家」小姐。

Daniel

拜託別那樣，說真的，珍妮是我最好的朋友，我當然希望你的求婚能讓她印象深刻。

Come on. Don't be like that. Seriously, Jenny is my best friend. I truly want your proposal to be impressive₅.　15:07

Lucy

I know you really are a good friend. Well then, do you have any ideas?　15:08

我知道你真的是個很棒的朋友，那你有什麼想法嗎？

Daniel

在我看來，送女人玫瑰當下是能讓她們開心，但花很快就會凋謝，就沒意義了。

In my opinion, sending women roses will make them happy at that moment, but the flowers will die and mean nothing.　15:11

Lucy

How about setting off fireworks at the beach? That's romantic, right?　15:13

那在海灘放煙火怎麼樣？那樣很浪漫，對吧？

Tip set off有「使爆炸」之意，強調煙火爆開的那一瞬間。

Daniel

這個主意是好多了，但卻不是我在想的。

Tip 口語表達，think後方省略了about。

Much better, but that's not what I'm thinking.　15:14

Lucy

  SEND ≫

15:01 📶

我會給你的建議是：去做一些更有意義的事情。

My recommendation would be for you to do something more meaningful. `15:16`

Lucy

或許你可以再度造訪那些對你和珍妮都很重要的地方，像是初識、第一次約會的地點，類似這樣的場所。

Maybe you could revisit places that are important to you and Jenny, like where you first met, where you went on your first date, places like that. `15:19`

Lucy

帶一張寫著「嫁給我」、並簽滿你們親友名字的海報，在每個地點拍下你跟海報的合照。

Bring a "Marry-Me" poster with you, one that your friends and family have signed. Take pictures with the poster at each place. `15:22`

Lucy

然後用這些照片製作成投影片，類似這樣的舉動會很浪漫、感人。

Then, take all the pictures and make a slideshow for her. Something like that would be so romantic and touching! `15:24`

Lucy

Daniel

Wow, excellent idea! I will start making the poster right away. `15:25`

哇，這主意太棒了！我要馬上著手做海報。

Tip 意思雖與immediately相同，但right away更加口語。

Hopefully, you will hear some good news from me soon! `15:26`

Daniel

希望你很快就可以聽到我的好消息！

SEND ≫

🔒 ⚠ ✏   0:17 📶 📊 🔋

1. 五花八門的意見

📖 Daniel 2013/11/01

Phew. I just got back from a night out with the guys, and I am exhausted! Tonight, I finally told them about my plan to propose to Jenny, and man, I was totally unprepared for their reactions❼. I thought they would congratulate❽ me and quickly move on to talking about sports, cars, or another one of our usual topics. But as soon as they heard it, they all started offering me different suggestions!

呼！我晚上和朋友在外面聚會，現在才回到家，真是累死人了！今晚，我終於告訴他們我準備向珍妮求婚的事情，天啊！完全沒預料到他們的反應會是這樣，我以為在簡單的祝賀後，大家就會把話題轉回運動、汽車，或其他我們常聊的事情上，但他們一聽到求婚的事，就開始提供各種不同的建議！

Tom agreed with my original plan and told me I should keep it simple and classy: get down on one knee and propose in a nice restaurant. John suggested making it memorable❾ by surprising Jenny on a trip. Maybe propose to her while in Penghu. Jeremy agreed with John that I should surprise her, but he told me I should do it more casually❿. I feel like each guy had a great idea, and hearing them all has made it harder for me to decide just what to do. Maybe I should ask someone else, though, someone who really understands girls and, more importantly, someone who understands Jenny.

湯姆贊成我原先的計畫，認為應該維持簡單又別緻的風格：在一家不錯的餐廳跪地求婚；約翰則建議來一趟令珍妮永難忘懷的驚喜旅程，也許在澎湖求婚；傑瑞米同意約翰的想法，認為我應該給珍妮一個驚喜，但他覺得可以做得更若無其事一點，我覺得每個人的主意都很棒，聽了這些反倒讓我更無所適從了，也許我應該徵詢別人的意見，一個懂得女生想法，更重要的是，真正了解珍妮的人。

17:30

2. 準備求婚的友人

Lucy 2013/11/03

My good friend, Daniel, told me he couldn't sleep because he was thinking about how to propose to Jenny. I was flabbergasted! I didn't expect a guy my age to be so romantically-inclined – to think so much about proposing that he loses sleep! I have heard too many stories of guys proposing at home watching a movie, or at a cheap restaurant, or even in bed before going to sleep!

我的好友丹尼爾告訴我，他因為在思考該如何向珍妮求婚而無法入睡，這件事讓我大吃一驚！我沒想到和我同年齡的男性之中，竟然有人會這麼浪漫，為了求婚的事而失眠！我聽過太多男生無趣的求婚方式，比方說在家裡看電影時，或是在便宜的餐廳裡，甚至在就寢前，就躺在床上求婚！

So, even though I felt bad that Daniel wasn't feeling well, I was too interested in his proposal plan to care about that! When he told me he planned to propose with flowers during dinner at a restaurant, I was not surprised. It's totally something a guy would think is romantic. Daniel is a good friend of mine, so I helped him by suggesting a proposal Jenny would like. After all, I am a girl! He said it was perfect and he would definitely do it. I can't wait to hear how it works out for him!

所以，即便我為丹尼爾的不舒服感到難過，我對他的求婚計畫還是更有興趣一些！當他告訴我，他準備在餐廳用晚餐時，捧著鮮花求婚，我完全不驚訝，這就是一般男人會覺得浪漫的方式，丹尼爾是我的好朋友，所以我給了他另外的建議，一個珍妮會喜歡的求婚，畢竟，我和珍妮一樣是女生，他說這個計畫很完美，他一定會照做，我等不及想知道結果如何了！

APP 單字動態看板 Vocabulary Billboard

Word 單字	Meaning 字義	Usage 常見用法
1 recommendation [ˌrɛkəmɛnˋdeʃən]	名 推薦；建議	act on one's recommendation 依建議 a recommendation letter 推薦信
2 occasion [əˋkeʒən]	名 場合；時機； 起因；理由	on numerous occasions 無數次 give occasion to anxiety 引起不安
3 anniversary [ˌænəˋvɜsərɪ]	名 紀念日	on the anniversary of 在…紀念日 the anniversary sale 週年慶
4 thoughtful [ˋθɔtfəl]	形 深思的；細心的	in a thoughtful mood 陷入深思 be thoughtful of/about 對…很體貼
5 impressive [ɪmˋprɛsɪv]	形 留下深刻印象的	live to an impressive age 活很久 be far from impressive in 表現平平
6 revisit [riˋvɪzɪt]	動 再訪；重遊	revisit a crime scene 重回犯罪現場 revisit the issue 重提舊事
7 reaction [rɪˋækʃən]	名 反應；感應	produce an evil reaction 產生副作用 the reaction shot 臉部特寫鏡頭
8 congratulate [kənˋgrætʃəˌlet]	動 祝賀；恭禧	congratulate sb. on/upon 祝賀 congratulate sb. heartily 衷心祝賀
9 memorable [ˋmɛmərəbḷ]	形 難忘的	a memorable honeymoon 難忘的蜜月 make sth. memorable 使…令人難忘
10 casually [ˋkæʒjuəlɪ]	副 偶然地；無意地	sth. casually happen 偶然發生 be dressed casually in 隨便穿著…
11 flabbergasted [ˋflæbəˌgæstɪd]	形 (口)大吃一驚的	look flabbergasted 看起來大吃一驚 be flabbergasted at 對…感到吃驚
12 proposal [prəˋpozḷ]	名 建議；求婚	accept one's proposal 接受求婚/建議 a proposal ring 求婚戒指

UNIT 2 求婚計畫
The Proposal～下篇

出場人物：男性Daniel、花店女Lucy、花店女的姊姊Claire

 045 MP3

9:50

 Lucy

I don't think I need to ask you how your proposal went. I saw the pictures on your Facebook. **9:50**

我想我不用問你的求婚結果了，我已經看到你臉書上放的照片。

 Lucy

That big smile you've got, it looks like somebody put a hanger in your mouth. **9:52**

你臉上的笑容活像有人放了個衣架在你嘴裡似的。

Tip 形容他人的笑容極度燦爛，和朋友聊天時可用。

露西，你的計畫太完美了！珍妮一看到我製作的影片，以及簽滿親友名字的海報，就高興得哭了。

Lucy, your plan worked perfectly! Jenny cried with happiness when she saw the slideshow I made and the poster with all our loved ones' signatures. **10:00**

 Daniel

 Lucy

Of course! If I were Jenny, I would have cried, too. **10:01**

那當然，如果我是珍妮的話，我也一定會哭的。

奇怪的是，珍妮馬上就知道那是你的主意了。

The strange thing was that Jenny knew it was your idea right away. **10:03**

 Daniel

 Lucy

Haha, well, that's because we have discussed our ideal proposals before. **10:05**

哈哈，那是因為我們之前就討論過彼此心中理想的求婚。

難怪！那我問你，你們是怎麼聊到這個話題的啊？

Tip 和朋友聊天可用的口語英文。

No wonder! Let me ask you, how did this topic come up? **10:06**

 Daniel

  SEND

Let's Chat In English Via APP

099

Lucy

I don't know. Maybe it was my female sixth sense. 10:07

我也不清楚，也許是我女性的第六感吧！

Tip 表達「直覺、第六感」的實用片語 the sixth sense。

Lucy

I just had a feeling that you might be planning to propose to Jenny, so I brought it up at lunch one day. 10:10

我只是感覺你可能計劃向珍妮求婚，所以有一天吃午餐時，我就提起了這個話題。

等一下，你們是最近討論這個話題的嗎？

Wait a minute. Did you discuss this recently? 10:11

Daniel

Lucy

Yeah, it must have been about a month or so ago. 10:12

是啊，是一個月左右之前的事情吧。

哇！真是靈異的可以了。

Tip eerily意指「怪異地、恐怖地」。

Wow, that's eerily psychic. 10:13

Daniel

Lucy

Anyway, congratulations, Daniel! 10:14

無論如何，恭喜你了，丹尼爾！

Tip 注意congratulations的複數s，和人聊天講「恭喜你」時，必須用複數型。

再次謝謝你，露西，想當初也是你介紹我跟珍妮認識的，你真是我們的最佳媒人呢！

Thanks again, Lucy. You originally introduced Jenny and me, and for that, we both think you are the best matchmaker. 10:17

Daniel

SEND ⟫

16:13

Claire

Lucy, I passed by your flower shop today and saw you. You seemed a little depressed. What's up? `16:13`

露西，我今天經過你的花店有看到你，你看起來有點沮喪，怎麼了嗎？

沮喪？不可能啊！丹尼爾告訴我他的求婚（那是我出的主意）結果很成功。

Depressed? No way! Daniel just told me that his proposal, which was my idea, was a success. `16:15`

Lucy

他跟珍妮都是我的好朋友，所以我很替他們高興。

Both he and Jenny are good friends of mine, so I'm happy for them. `16:17`

Lucy

Claire

Oh, I know what this is all about. You envy❹ your friend, Jenny, don't you? `16:19`

噢，我知道這是怎麼回事了，你羨慕你的朋友珍妮，對不對？

克萊兒，我不希望你提起那些關於我前未婚夫的不好回憶。

Claire, I don't want you bringing up the bad memories about my ex-fiancé. `16:21`

Lucy

Claire

I'm your sister. I can tell that you are just pretending that you don't care about your friends' engagement❺. `16:25`

我是你姊姊，我看得出來你只是假裝不在乎你朋友的訂婚。

克萊兒，你必須了解，在婚禮前被未婚夫給甩了這種事，是真的很難釋懷的。

Claire, you have to understand that it's really hard to get over something like getting dumped by your fiancé right before the wedding. `16:28`

Lucy

SEND >>

16:13

Claire

Yes, but it's time to let it go and move on. 16:29

是很難，但你也該放下了，好好過日子。
Tip let it go、move on都表達出「該放下過去」的意思，口語上很實用。

Claire

Just think, he was not the right one for you, and he did you a favor by not marrying you. You'll find someone better. 16:32

你就這麼想，他並不適合你，他沒娶你算是幫了你一個大忙，你會找到更好的對象。

謝了，克萊兒，我真的很高興珍妮就要嫁給這麼好的男人了。

Thanks, Claire. I'm really happy that Jenny is going to marry such an amazing guy. 16:34

Lucy

Claire

Oh, my god! Did you fall in love with Daniel, Lucy? 16:35

噢，天啊！露西，你愛上丹尼爾了嗎？

饒了我吧！克萊兒，他只是我的朋友，就像珍妮一樣。

Tip 和朋友聊天時的實用英文。

Give me a break, Claire. He is my friend, just like Jenny. 16:38

Lucy

Claire

I'm only joking. Don't take everything so seriously⑥. 16:40

我只是開個玩笑，別什麼事都那麼嚴肅看待嘛！

那我告訴你，不好笑，所以別鬧了。

Well, it's not funny, so stop it. 16:41

Lucy

 SEND ≫

🔒 ✉ ✏   10:08 📶 ▮▮▮ 🔋

  3. 感謝朋友們的幫忙

📖 Daniel 2013/11/9

Success! I am engaged to the love of my life, and I couldn't be happier! I have to thank my friends, Tom, John, and Jeremy, for their ideas. I almost followed John's advice and proposed to Jenny on a trip to Penghu. But before I reserved seats on a flight and a room at a nice hotel, I asked a mutual friend of ours, Lucy. Thank God I did, because she gave me the best idea, the one I ended up using.

　　成功了！我跟我的真命天女訂婚了，真的是開心到不行！我必須感謝我的朋友湯姆、約翰，和傑瑞米所提供的主意，我幾乎就要採用約翰的建議，在澎湖之旅時向珍妮求婚，但就在我預訂機位以及高檔飯店的房間之前，我問了我和珍妮共同的好友露西，感謝老天！讓我想到去問露西，因為她提供了最棒的主意，一個我最後採用的求婚方式。

The poster with all our loved ones' signatures and well-wishes was amazing, but the slideshow of me traveling to all the important locations in our relationship was what really moved Jenny to tears. She gave me the biggest hug and barely managed to say yes through her tears of joy. It turns out that Lucy got the idea from my fiancée, but I didn't know that when she told me. I am elated that my proposal turned out so well. Jenny often complains that I am not original enough. I guess this time it was for the best!

　　一張寫滿親友簽名與祝福的海報很棒，但真正讓珍妮感動落淚的是我走訪所有交往的紀念地點後，所製成的投影片，她給了我一個大大的擁抱，哭到幾乎無法開口答應我的求婚。後來我才知道，露西的想法是從我未婚妻那裡得來的，但當她給我建議時，我並不知道這一點，真高興求婚的結果能這麼成功，珍妮總是抱怨我沒什麼創意，我想這次的求婚應該讓她大為改觀了吧！

4. 植物園一日遊

📖 Lucy 2013/11/10

Anyone who knows me knows how much I love plants and flowers. And even someone who doesn't know me at all can probably guess. I do own a flower shop, after all. I have been having mixed feelings about my friends' engagement lately. I am happy for them, but their engagement has forced me to remember my failed one and the ex-fiancé who left me only a month before our wedding.

認識我的人都知道，我有多麼喜歡植物和花卉，就算是不認識我的人，大概也猜得到，畢竟我擁有一家花店。最近我一直對我朋友的訂婚，有種很複雜的情緒，我替他們感到高興，但他們讓我想起自己失敗的那次訂婚，還有那個在婚禮前一個月離開我的未婚夫。

Whenever I feel sad or unhappy, I always take a day and go to the botanical⓫ garden outside the city. The colors and smell make me feel so much better. I would also find inspirations⓬ for my shop. Sometimes I even discover new plants in places I had never thought of before. On the trip I took last week, for example, I found a beautiful orchid and, after some research, ordered some for my shop. I think I am lucky to have found a place that not only helps me relax but also gives me ideas for my business.

每當我感到悲傷或不開心時，我總會找一天到市郊的植物園走走，繽紛的色彩和植物的味道能讓我感覺好些，我也會為了自己的花店，去看看有沒有能激發新想法的東西，有的時候，甚至會在想都沒想過的地方發現新品種呢！例如上週去的那一趟，我就發現了一種美麗的蘭花，經過一番研究後，我為店裡訂購了一些。我覺得自己很幸運，能擁有這樣的一個地方，不僅幫助我放鬆身心，同時還能為我帶來一些生意上的想法。

Word 單字	Meaning 字義	Usage 常見用法
1 **signature** [ˋsɪɡnətʃɚ]	名 簽名;簽署	withhold one's signature 拒絕簽字 a ballot without signature 無記名投票
2 **psychic** [ˋsaɪkɪk]	形 精神的;心靈的; 超自然的	a psychic shock 精神打擊 a psychic medium 靈媒
3 **matchmaker** [ˋmætʃ͵mekɚ]	名 媒人	impress the matchmaker 給媒人留印象 be one's matchmaker 給…作媒
4 **envy** [ˋɛnvɪ]	名 妒忌;羨慕 動 妒忌;羨慕	out of envy 出於妒忌 envy at/with 對…感到忌妒
5 **engagement** [ɪnˋgedʒmənt]	名 訂婚;婚約; 雇用;諾言	an engagement party 訂婚派對 keep to one's engagement 遵守約定
6 **seriously** [ˋsɪrɪəslɪ]	副 認真地;嚴肅地; 嚴重地	take sth. seriously 認真對待 be seriously damaged 嚴重受損
7 **advice** [ədˋvaɪs]	名 勸告;忠告	keep one's own advice 不發表看法 be deaf to all advice 聽不進一點意見
8 **relationship** [rɪˋleʃənˋʃɪp]	名 關係;關聯	love-hate relationship 愛恨交織的關係 have a relationship with 與…有關係
9 **hug** [hʌg]	名 緊抱;擁抱 動 擁抱;抱有	hug oneself at (為…而)沾沾自喜 give sb. a big hug 緊緊擁抱某人
10 **original** [əˋrɪdʒənḷ]	名 原物;原著 形 原作的;最初的	refer to the original 參考原文 be original in design 構思新穎
11 **botanical** [boˋtænɪkḷ]	名 植物性藥物 形 植物學的;植物的	a botanical garden 植物園 a botanical specimen 植物的標本
12 **inspiration** [͵ɪnspəˋreʃən]	名 靈感;妙計; 鼓舞人心的人或事	draw an inspiration from 從…獲得靈感 a brilliant inspiration 絕妙的主意

出場人物：新婚都市女Carol、大學教授Hugo

3 新婚與搬家
Marry And Move～上篇

🔒 ✉ ✏   16:30 📶 ▫️

◀ APP CHAT **1** 恭喜你結婚了！

Carol

I've got some good news to tell you, Professor Hugo. 16:30

雨果教授，我有好消息要跟您説。

喔？是什麼好消息？是在工作上獲得升職之類的嗎？

Oh, what's that? You got a promotion or something? 16:38

Hugo

Carol

Not that. Do you remember Jack, the guy who always wears black glasses? 16:40

不是，您記得總是帶著黑框眼鏡的傑克嗎？

當然記得，你們兩個一直都很登對。
Tip make a good couple爲口語聊天的實用表達，稱讚情侶用。

Of course I do. You two seem to make a good couple. 16:44

Hugo

Carol

Well, guess what? We're getting married in November! 16:46

您知道嗎？我們要結婚了，婚禮將在十一月舉行。

這真是天大的好消息！祝福你們！
Tip 加上all the best之後，祝福的語氣就更加強烈。

That is certainly good news. I wish you two all the best. 16:48

Hugo

Carol

Thanks a lot. I am telling you because we would like to invite you. 16:50

謝謝教授，跟您説這個消息，主要是想邀請您參加我們的婚宴。

                    SEND ≫

Let's Chat In English Via APP • ⏻ •

106

16:30

謝謝你們的邀請，我很樂意參加。

Tip 客氣的說法，用 would be my pleasure 表達委婉的語氣。

> That is very thoughtful of you. It would be my pleasure to attend. 16:52

Hugo

Carol

> Really? Jack will be glad to hear that. 16:53

真的嗎？傑克聽到一定會很高興的。

哈哈，我以為他會害怕看到我，他以前一上課就打瞌睡呢！

> Haha, I thought he would be afraid to see me. He was always falling asleep in my class! 16:57

Hugo

Carol

> Yeah, but we both liked your class. In fact, Jack was the one who said we should invite you! 17:00

是啊，但我們都很喜歡上您的課，這次其實是傑克說要邀請教授的呢！

坦白說，能娶到你是他的福氣，對了，你們打算去哪裡度蜜月呢？

> Honestly, he's lucky to have found a girl like you. By the way, where are you going on your honeymoon? 17:03

Hugo

Carol

> We're going to Italy for three weeks. Extravagant, right? 17:05

我們打算到義大利度蜜月三個星期，很奢侈對吧？

是啊，同時也會很浪漫的，要記住時常保持愉悅的心情，才能保有幸福美滿的婚姻。

> Yes, sounds romantic, too. Remember to always try to be happy. Happiness is the key to a successful marriage. 17:09

Hugo

SEND ≫

8:22 🔼 ⏹

Hugo

How have you been since your wedding, Carol? 8:22

卡蘿，結婚以後一切都還好嗎？

不瞞您說，我現在完全是累垮了的狀態。

I'm totally exhausted₃, to be honest. 8:36

Carol

Hugo

Why? Is the marriage dragging you down? 8:37

為什麼呢？是婚後生活造成你這樣筋疲力盡嗎？

Tip drag down強調被某事拖垮，同樣是在講累，但更強調累垮的「過程」。

是有點，嗯…但不完全是，主要的問題是：我懷孕了。

Kind of. Well…not the marriage exactly. I have a big problem: I am pregnant. 8:39

Carol

Hugo

Congratulations! Why would that be a problem? 8:40

恭喜了！那怎麼會是個問題呢？

因為傑克和我都還沒有享受夠兩人世界的生活，兩個月前，我們才剛從義大利度蜜月回來而已。

Because Jack and I haven't enjoyed our married life enough. We just came back from our honeymoon in Italy two months ago! 8:44

Carol

Hugo

Well, try to look on the bright side. You're going to be a mom soon! 8:46

試著往好的方面想，你就要成為母親啦！

Tip look on the bright side有「鼓勵他人往好的方面想」之意。

   SEND ≫

8:22

But I always planned to have a career[4] before becoming a mom. Besides, I'm not positive[5] that I can take care of a baby. I am too young. `8:50`

但是，我一直計劃要在成為母親之前，先去工作，而且，我沒把握能照顧孩子，我還太年輕了。

Carol

Hugo

Don't worry so much. You have a partner for life in Jack, and you can ask him for help. `8:53`

別太擔心，你現在身邊多了一個人生伴侶傑克，你可以請他幫忙。

You would think so, right? But it's so hard to get him to do anything. `8:55`

您這麼想嗎？但要他做事可難了。

Carol

He's so absorbed[6] in online games that he doesn't even do the chores he has now. `8:59`

他只專注在他的線上遊戲，家事好像跟他完全無關似的。

Carol

I can't imagine he will be much help with the baby. `9:00`

要他幫忙帶小孩，我想就更難了。

Carol

Hugo

Sounds like a bad situation. Maybe I can talk to Jack and encourage[7] him to take more responsibility[8]. `9:02`

聽起來不太妙，或許我可以找傑克聊聊，鼓勵他承擔更多的家庭責任。

I don't know if it will work. After all, a leopard never changes its spots. `9:05`

我不知道他會不會聽您的，畢竟，牛牽到北京還是牛。

Tip 實用俚語，口語、書寫皆可用。

Carol

   SEND >>

Let's Chat In English Via APP

109

1. 結婚賀禮真不好挑

Hugo 2013/11/10

I always have the hardest time picking out gifts. No matter what the occasion is, a friend's birthday, my anniversary, Valentine's Day, a wedding, I can never find the perfect gift. I had a particularly difficult time finding a gift for my student's wedding. She was the first student to ever invite me to a wedding. I started to worry immediately① after she invited me because I didn't know what kind of gift would be appropriate.

我對挑選禮物這件事完全沒輒,無論是什麼場合,朋友生日、結婚週年紀念、情人節、婚禮,我都找不到最合適的禮物,這次要送給學生的結婚禮物尤其讓我傷腦筋,她是第一個邀我參加婚禮的學生,接受邀請之後,我馬上就開始擔心了,因為我不知道要送她什麼結婚禮物才合適。

It didn't feel right to ask her what I should buy, so I spent an hour or two thinking about the right gift. Finally, I remembered she told me how much she likes religious② artwork. I went to the local bookstore and found a dozen books on the subject. It took me an entire afternoon to find the right one, but, at last, I found a book full of paintings of Jesus that I thought she would like. For her husband, I got a spy novel. I honestly have no idea if he will like it. It was a real challenge for me to pick out gifts for these newlyweds.

我總覺得去問她該買什麼禮物並不得體,所以我花了一兩個小時思考該送什麼禮物,最後,我想起她非常喜歡宗教藝術品,所以我到當地書局找了許多關於這方面的書,並花了整個下午的時間挑選適合送給她的結婚禮物,不過,最後我反而買了一本充滿耶穌畫像的書籍,我想她應該會喜歡,至於她先生,我準備送他間諜小說,但我實在不確定他會不會喜歡,對我來說,幫這對新婚夫妻挑禮物還真是一大挑戰。

2. 蟲鳴鳥叫的鄉下生活

📖 Carol 2013/12/26

Moving to the countryside has turned out to be a huge mistake. I have already been here for almost two months, and every day I still find myself wishing I was back in the city. There is nothing to do here: no malls, no department stores, no bookstores, not even a nice restaurant. The nearest grocery⊚ store is a thirty minute drive away. My husband and I sometimes go to the old-fashioned movie theater in town, but it is not enough.

　　搬到鄉下來真是個錯誤至極的決定，我在這裡住了快兩個月，每天都還希望能搬回都市，因為這裡什麼都沒有：沒有購物中心、百貨公司、書局、甚至連間像樣的餐廳都沒有，離家最近的雜貨店，開車還要三十分鐘，有時候，我老公和我會去鎮上的老式電影院看電影，但光是看電影根本就不足夠。

I guess after two months of trying, I can finally say I am not a country girl. And it's not just because it is boring here. For one, I never get enough sleep because the rooster in our neighbor's yard always starts crowing before dawn. I never feel comfortable⊚ because there is no air conditioner for the summer heat and only a wooden stove to keep the house warm in the winter. The bugs are so big here, too! Worst of all, I have no friends. It's just me and my husband. I really want to move back to the city!

　　試了兩個月後，我可以確定一件事，我無法適應鄉下生活，這不光是因為這裡很無聊，另外的原因之一是，我從來都睡不飽，因為天還沒亮，隔壁鄰居庭院裡的公雞就開始啼叫。這裡夏天沒有冷氣，冬天又只有木製火爐來維持室內的溫暖，所以我從來沒有感到舒適過。另外，這裡的蟲子也好大隻！最糟糕的是，我在這裡沒有朋友，就只有老公和我兩個人而已，真的好想搬回都市喔！

Let's Chat In English Via APP

APP 單字動態看板 Vocabulary Billboard

Word 單字	Meaning 字義	Usage 常見用法
1 pleasure [ˋplɛʒɚ]	名 愉快；高興；娛樂；消遣	cloud one's pleasure 使某人掃興 with beaming pleasure 面帶喜色地
2 honeymoon [ˋhʌnɪˏmun]	名 短暫的和諧期；蜜月旅行	the honeymoon between A and B 和諧期 be on one's honeymoon 在度蜜月
3 exhaust [ɪgˋzɔst]	動 抽完；汲乾；使精疲力盡	exhaust air from a tube 抽光管中的空氣 be exhausted by disease 因病衰竭
4 career [kəˋrɪr]	名 職業；經歷 形 職業的；專業的	start on one's career 開始⋯的事業 make a career 出人頭地
5 positive [ˋpɑzətɪv]	形 確定的；積極的	have positive proof 證據確鑿 keep a positive attitude 保持積極態度
6 absorb [əbˋsɔrb]	動 吸收；汲取；吸引(注意等)	absorb sweat 吸汗 be absorbed in 全神貫注在⋯
7 encourage [ɪnˋkɝɪdʒ]	動 鼓勵；促進	encourage sb. to do sth. 鼓勵某人做 encourage one's laziness 助長⋯的懶惰
8 responsibility [rɪˏspɑnsəˋbɪlətɪ]	名 責任；義務	take full responsibility 負全責 be lack in responsibility 沒有責任感
9 grocery [ˋgrosərɪ]	名 食品雜貨	a local grocery store 當地的雜貨店 groceries in stock 現存的雜貨
10 comfortable [ˋkʌmfətəbl̩]	形 舒適的；自在的	a comfortable climate 宜人的氣候 make sb. comfortable 使某人感到舒適
11 immediately [ɪˋmidɪɪtlɪ]	副 立刻；馬上	be immediately involved in 直接牽連進 rescue sb. immediately 立刻援救某人
12 religious [rɪˋlɪdʒəs]	形 宗教的；虔誠的	a religious ceremony 宗教儀式 be deeply religious 極度虔誠

UNIT 3
新婚與搬家
Marry And Move～下篇

 053 MP3

🔒 📂 ✏️   16:30 📶 ▮▮ 🔋

◀ APP CHAT **3** 習慣鄉下生活了

Carol

Professor, I think I finally got used to life in the countryside. `16:30`

教授，我想我終於習慣鄉下的生活了。

我早說過你一定會適應的。

I told you that you would get used to it. `16:34`

Hugo

Carol

Now, I look forward to being woken up by that rooster before dawn because it means I can see the sun rising on the horizon❶. `16:43`

我現在會期待在天亮前被那隻公雞叫醒，因為那樣我就可以看到太陽從地平線升起的景色。

很動人對吧？在城市裡，你就只能看到由一排排建築物所構成的天際線。

Tip 同樣是講建築物很多，用a row of buildings生動許多。

Astonishing❷, isn't it? In the city, the only skyline you get is a row of buildings. `16:45`

Hugo

Carol

Also, when dusk falls, I sometimes sit beside the river and dabble❸ my feet in the water, watching the sunset. `16:48`

黃昏的時候，我有時會坐在河邊，把腳伸進水中拍打，邊欣賞日落的景色。

所以你漸漸變成一個鄉村女孩了，是嗎？

So you are gradually turning into a country girl, then? `16:50`

Hugo

Carol

I guess so, yeah. Oh, I almost forgot: I finally made some new friends in the area. `16:53`

我想應該是，對了，差點忘了說，我終於交到幾個住在我家附近的新朋友。

Tip 「交朋友」的實用表達make new friends，注意用make這個動詞。

  [_____] **SEND »**

16:30

那真是好消息，是跟你年紀差不多的女性嗎？跟她們談過你懷孕的事了嗎？

That's good to hear. Are they women your age? Have you had a chance to talk about your pregnancy with them? `16:57`

Hugo

Carol

Yes. I don't think I will suffer from prenatal depression now that I have their company and support. `16:59`

談過了，而且有了她們的陪伴與支持，我應該不會得到產前憂鬱症。

你不會的，我保證，我太太在懷孕時，身邊就有就好朋友陪伴。

You won't, I promise. My wife used to spend time with her best friends during her pregnancy. `17:02`

Hugo

結果她根本沒得到產前或產後憂鬱症的機會。

Tip 講病症時，可以用suffer，「受苦」之意會更明確。

And, as a result, she didn't suffer prenatal or postnatal[4] depression. `17:03`

Hugo

Carol

That's reassuring. Now, I'm super excited about my new life here in the country and the baby inside me! `17:07`

那我就放心了，現在我對鄉下的新生活與肚子裡的寶寶都感到很興奮呢！

最後送你一句話：小心點，嬰兒有時就像是惡魔的化身呢！

A final word of advice: be careful, babies can be the devil incarnate[5]! `17:09`

Hugo

SEND ≫

8:09 📶 🔋

教授，我剛剛得知一個壞消息。

Professor, I've just heard some bad news. 8:09

Carol

我老公被調回在市區的辦公室了，我們下個月就得搬回去。

My husband's been transferred back to his company's office in the city. We have to move next month. 8:12

Carol

How is that bad news? You always said you wanted to move back. 8:15

Hugo

那怎麼會是壞消息呢？你不是一直都想搬回市區嗎？

Tip 口語英文，表達說話者的不解。

之前是這樣沒錯，但現在我也不確定，我已經適應這裡的生活，也交了些很棒的新朋友。

Before, yes, but now I don't know. I am used to my life here now and have made some great new friends. 8:18

Carol

That's really sentimental. What can you do, though? 8:19

Hugo

真是令人感傷，那你打算怎麼做呢？

我有想到讓傑克通勤上班，但他說光是到市區的新辦公室，就要開兩個小時的車。

Well, I was thinking about asking Jack to commute₆ to work. He said it would take him two hours to drive to his new city office. 8:23

Carol

You can't be that selfish. Imagine how tiresome it would be for him to spend four hours every day driving to and from work! 8:27

Hugo

你不能那麼自私，一天花四個小時來回通勤上班，實在太累人了！

Tip 善用介係詞to and from表達「來回」的動作。

SEND ≫

Let's Chat In English Via APP

115

也許會有折衷的辦法？

Maybe there is a compromise?
8:28

Carol

I'm not sure there is one. There is a job waiting for Jack in the city.
8:30

Hugo

這我不敢說，傑克在市區的工作等著他回去接。

Anyway, just think: you can reconnect with your friends in the city now.
8:32

Hugo

既然如此，不妨這麼想：你可以趁這個機會和在城市裡的朋友敘舊。

那我在這邊交的新朋友怎麼辦呢？天啊，我真討厭這種進退兩難的情況。

What will I do about all my new friends? Oh, I really hate dilemmas like this.
8:34

Carol

Don't be so negative. You can still stay in touch with your new friends.
8:37

Hugo

別往壞處想，你還是可以和你的新朋友保持聯絡的。

Tip 口語實用表達stay in touch。

怎麼保持聯絡呢？他們都是科技白痴，不用智慧型手機，甚至連電子郵件是什麼都不知道。

How? They are technologically handicapped. None of them use smart phones, and they barely know what e-mail is!
8:41

Carol

Then you can write letters to them. Listen, if you want to stay in touch, you will find a way.
8:44

Hugo

那你可以寫信，聽著，只要你有心要與他們保持聯絡，總會找到辦法的。

🔊 😶 [   ] **SEND** ≫

Let's Chat In English Via APP • ⏻ •

116

3. 我也去找份工作吧！

Carol 2014/1/3

I am worried about moving back to the city. Life out here in the country is great now, it really is. Whereas before I would have loved to get out of here, thinking about leaving now makes me feel reluctant. However, I know myself, and I know I am a city girl at heart. I am worried, though, about my husband's job. Living in the city is expensive. Here in the country, he makes enough money for the both of us, but I am afraid that won't be true when we move back to the city.

我很擔心要搬回都市這件事，現在鄉下這裡的生活真的很棒，之前我的確很想搬離鄉下，但現在真的要搬走，反倒讓我覺得捨不得，不過，我很了解自己，我原本就是個都市女孩，真正讓我擔心的，其實是我老公的工作，住在城市，什麼都比較貴，在鄉下，他的薪水足以負擔我們的日常花費，但是，當我們搬回都市生活，那他賺的錢恐怕就不夠了。

Our financial burdens are something that must be considered. That's why I think I need to get a job when we move back. I haven't told Jack yet. I will probably wait until I find one because I know he doesn't want me to work. He wants me to stay at home and rest while I am pregnant. But I really don't think his job can support the two of us. And after the baby is born, what then?

經濟負擔也是需要好好考慮的一件事，因此，我覺得自己需要去找份工作，我還沒有告訴傑克這件事，或許我會等找到工作後再跟他說，因我知道他並不希望我去工作，他希望我懷孕期間待在家裡休息，但我真的不認為他的收入足以支撐我們兩人的生活，尤其在嬰兒出生以後，該怎麼辦呢？

10:46

微網誌 4. 鄉村景點大推薦

Hugo 2014/1/4

I felt a little disappointed when I heard my student was moving back to the city with her husband. I know she had a difficult time adjusting to her new life. Although she recently told me she feels that she has finally adjusted, I think she still hasn't experienced some of the best parts about life in the countryside. I don't think she is moving for a few months, so I will try to write a long list of things she should do and see before moving and e-mail it to her.

得知我學生和她老公要搬回都市時，我感到有點失望，我知道她在適應鄉下生活的那段期間很不好過，雖然最近她跟我說她終於適應了，但我覺得她還沒有體驗到鄉下生活中最棒的部分。我想她應該過幾個月才會搬回都市，所以，我準備列一張長清單，寫下她搬離鄉下前應該去做、以及該去看的事物，再把清單用電子郵件寄給她。

The top of the list has to be Green Point Waterfall. It is the one thing people travel from all over the country to see. The waterfall is over one hundred meters tall, and the pool at the bottom is perfect for relaxing in. There are three other landmarks I will probably include: a grove of trees that are all almost a thousand years old, a huge lake with perfect, crystal-blue water, and an area in the nearby forest that is great for bird watching.

清單上的首站是綠點瀑布，這個景點是全國觀光客必造訪之地，瀑布超過百米高，下方的水池是放鬆身心的絕佳地點，除此之外，還有三個我想納入清單的地標，包括：樹齡近千年歷史的小樹林、閃耀著水晶般湛藍色光澤的巨大湖泊，以及附近森林裡的絕佳賞鳥地點。

APP 單字動態看板 Vocabulary Billboard

Word 單字	Meaning 字義	Usage 常見用法
1 **horizon** [hə`raɪzn]	名 地平線；眼界；視野	on the horizon 在地平線 broaden one's horizon 開某人的眼界
2 **astonishing** [ə`stɑnɪʃɪŋ]	形 令人驚訝的	an astonishing verdict 令人驚訝的裁決 an astonishing performance 驚人的表演
3 **dabble** [`dæbl]	動 (把手腳)放入水中；涉獵；淺嘗	dabble in art 涉獵藝術 dabble with the text 竄改原文
4 **postnatal** [post`netl]	形 產後的；出生後的	postnatal depression 產後憂鬱症 one's postnatal efforts 後天的努力
5 **incarnate** [ɪn`kɑr,net]	動 賦於形體；代表 形 化身的；肉色的	be incarnated in 被賦予…形體 a demon incarnate 魔鬼的化身
6 **commute** [kə`mjut]	名 通勤 動 減輕(刑罰)；通勤	commute from A to B 往來於 AB 之間 commute pain for pleasure 化苦為樂
7 **dilemma** [də`lɛmə]	名 困境；進退兩難	face the dilemma 左右為難 be in a dilemma 處於進退兩難的境地
8 **reluctant** [rɪ`lʌktənt]	形 不情願的；勉強的	be reluctant to give up 捨不得放棄 a reluctant feeling 不情願的感覺
9 **burden** [`bɝdn]	名 重擔；負擔 動 加負擔於	bear the burden 承擔責任 be burdened with worries 憂心忡忡
10 **pregnant** [`prɛgnənt]	形 懷孕的；多產的	be 5 months pregnant 懷孕五個月 a pregnant year of rice 稻米豐產年
11 **adjust** [ə`dʒʌst]	動 改變…以適應；調整；解決	adjust the speed 調整速度 adjust oneself in the chair 在椅子裡挪動
12 **perfect** [`pɝfɪkt]	動 使完美；做完 形 完美的；精通的	perfect oneself in 熟練；精通 Practice makes perfect. 熟能生巧

出場人物：媽媽Mia、好友Laurel

UNIT 4 家庭生活
Family Life～上篇

057 MP3

🔒 ✏️ 17:24 📶 ▂▄▆

◀ APP CHAT **1** 孩子的夢想

Mia

My little girl just said she wanted to be a dancer when she grows up. Isn't she adorable? `17:24`

我小女兒剛剛說她長大後想當一名舞者，很可愛吧？

她現在這樣是可愛，但如果她二十歲了，卻還想當舞者，你就不會覺得她可愛了。

Now she is. You won't think so when she is twenty years old and still trying to be a dancer, though. `17:29`

Laurel

Mia

That's true. Even professional₀ dancers make very little money. `17:32`

那倒是真的，即使是職業舞者，收入也很少。

說起我大兒子布萊恩，我就頭痛。

Tip be such a pain的pain隱含「讓人極度憂心」的意思。

My oldest son, Brian, is such a pain. `17:35`

Laurel

他只想創業，而不想找份正職的工作，說什麼找工作與他的計畫會有所衝突。

Tip 實用英語work a real job。

All he ever talks about is starting his own company and how he can't work a real job because it conflicts with his plan. `17:40`

Laurel

Mia

Oh, he sounds ambitious₂. That's a trait all entrepreneurs₃ need. What's the problem? `17:43`

聽起來很有企圖心啊！這是所有企業家必備的特質，有什麼不妥嗎？

問題是，他對創業的內容完全沒有一點頭緒。

The problem is, he has no clue what kind of business he wants to create. `17:45`

Laurel

     SEND ≫

Let's Chat In English Via APP ● ⏻ ●

120

Mia

It sounds like he lacks focus.
`17:46`

感覺他缺乏明確的目標。

要我說的話，史蒂夫·賈伯斯的成功不是偶然，而是努力的結果。

If you ask me, people like Steve Jobs are not successful by chance but by hard work.
`17:48`

Laurel

但是，很多年輕人只看到他的成功，而沒有看見努力的過程。

Tip 此處 yet 的意思與 but 相同，但較適用在口語會話上。

Yet, many young people only see the success, not the work.
`17:50`

Laurel

Mia

Yeah. Focusing on these results gives our youth the mistaken idea and neglects₄ the fact that you must work hard to achieve that kind of success.
`17:54`

是啊，只強調成功讓年輕人產生錯誤的印象，忽略了成功之前所必需付出的努力。

沒錯！就跟我兒子一樣，他們只想著要成功。

Yes! Like my son, they only know that they want success.
`17:56`

Laurel

Mia

I agree. If you ask them how they plan to be successful, they wouldn't be able to answer.
`17:59`

我同意，如果你問他們要怎麼做才能成功，他們也答不出來。

真希望布萊恩能夠明白找工作與創業不能混為一談的道理。

Tip 用 do not mix 就可表達兩者不可混淆之意。

I really hope Brian can know that finding a job and entrepreneurship do not mix!
`18:02`

Laurel

SEND ▶▶

Laurel

My oldest son, Brian, worries me more every day. He can't even hold a part-time job. `16:30`

我那大兒子布萊恩，每天都讓我擔心，他連打工都做不久。

Tip 實用講法，用hold可表示持續一份工作的狀態。

他還年輕，也許你可以把這個看作一個暫時的階段。

He's still young. Maybe you can see it as a temporary stage. `16:41`

Mia

他現正吸收各式各樣的工作經驗，之後對於想要從事的工作就會有概念。

He is gaining a variety of work experience now and will have a better idea of what kind of career he wants later. `16:44`

Mia

Laurel

But he's already graduated from the university and he claims to be starting his own business! `16:47`

但他都已經大學畢業了，還老說著要自己創業！

Laurel

He should at least be looking for a full-time job. `16:48`

我認為他至少要先找份正職的工作來做。

你不覺得他正處於摸索的階段，在尋找真正適合的工作嗎？

Tip true calling有「天職」之意。

Don't you think he could be going through a stage, looking for his true calling? `16:50`

Mia

Laurel

I agree, in theory, but he's had ten jobs in only six months! `16:52`

理論上是如此沒錯，但也不應該在六個月內就換了十份工作吧！

  SEND ≫

Let's Chat In English Via APP • ⏻ •

122

16:30

十份工作！那我得收回剛剛說的話，十份工作的確是太誇張了。

Tip 實用口語表達way too much，加上way更強調程度。

TEN JOBS!!! Wow, I take back what I said. That's way too much! `16:53`

Mia

Laurel

I keep telling him that he should stick with a job for three months before quitting. `16:57`

我一直告訴他，一份工作至少要做滿三個月。

是啊，三個月差不多才能讓他評估自己是否喜歡那份工作。

That seems like a reasonable amount of time for him to decide whether or not he likes a job. `17:00`

Mia

Laurel

Honestly, I wonder how he will answer the interviewers if they ask him why he changes jobs so frequently. `17:06`

老實說，如果面試官問他換工作的頻率為何這麼高，我真的不知道他會怎麼回答。

我想布萊恩也許就會瞭解短時間換這麼多份工作是不恰當的。

Well, my guess is that Brian might finally realize that it's inappropriate₀ to change jobs in such a short time. `17:10`

Mia

Laurel

I hope it doesn't come to that. But, as we speak, he's out looking for job number eleven! `17:13`

希望不要等到那個時候，喔，我們在談話的此刻，他正要出門找第十一份工作了。

Tip 也有「不希望會那樣」的意思。

像他這種換工作的頻率，可能導致他不被錄用呢。

Because of the number of his jobs, he very well might not be hired. `17:15`

Mia

  SEND »

Let's Chat In English Via APP ● ● ●

123

微網誌 **1. 教養的難處**

Laurel 2014/1/8

I did everything I could to raise a responsible, hardworking boy, and so far all my son has done is continue to live at home and work a string of part-time jobs. I worry about him all the time. Sometimes, I wonder if his laziness and lack of motivation is my fault. He graduated from the university already. Why hasn't he taken control of his life yet? What can I do?

為了將兒子養成一個有責任感、腳踏實地努力的人，我什麼都試過了，遺憾的是，他依然只知道待在家裡，然後到處打些零工，我真的很擔心他，有時候，我會懷疑，他之所以會這麼懶散又缺乏上進心，是不是我的錯？他都已經大學畢業了，卻還不能打理自己的生活，唉，我該怎麼做才好呢？

Really, what can I do? Along with my husband, I did everything I could. We both gave our son so much love and affection, a good education, and a stable home environment. I really believe we did the best we could. Of course, we weren't perfect; but then again, no one is. We still love our son and want to see him succeed, but we are losing patience. Maybe it is time to give him some tough love and make him start paying us rent to live with us or – and I hope it doesn't come to this – ask him to move out.

真的，我到底應該怎麼辦呢？能做的事情，我和我先生都做了，給他很多的愛和關心、提供良好的教育以及穩定的家庭環境，我們真的都盡力了，當然，我們並非完美的父母，但話又說回來，沒有人是完美的。我們當然還是很愛他，也希望看到他成功，但我們漸漸失去耐心了，也許，我們得採取嚴厲一點的方式，同住的時候，讓他付給我們租金，又或是要求他搬出去自立，不過，我是希望不用做到搬出去的程度就是了。

2. 帶女兒去動物園

📖 Mia 2014/1/10

I took my daughter to the zoo last weekend. I have only two words to say about our trip: never again! She has told me many times how disgusting she thinks animals are. It was silly of me, but I thought a trip to the zoo and a chance to see big elephants, exotic⑪ penguins, and other animals would change her mind. After all, the only animals she has seen in the city are rats and stray⑫ dogs and cats. Unfortunately, the zoo had the opposite effect.

上個週末，我帶女兒去動物園，只有一句話能形容這次的旅程：絕不再來動物園了！她和我說過很多次，她覺得動物很噁心，我太傻了，以為來一趟動物園之旅，讓她看看大象、異國的企鵝，以及其他動物之後，她就會改變想法，畢竟，她在城市裡可以看到的動物就只有老鼠、流浪狗及流浪貓，可惜的是，去動物園反而造成了反效果。

I say that because, from the moment we went inside, I could see she wasn't happy. Nothing excited her, not even the pandas, Siberian tigers, or flamingos. In fact, she took one look at most of the animals and kept walking. She spent most of the time complaining about how stupid and boring the zoo was. I don't know if it is because she is too old or just hates animals, but I do know we won't be going back ever again.

我會這樣說是因為，從我們踏進動物園的那一刻起，我就看出她並不開心，沒有能讓她感到開心的事物，甚至連貓熊、西伯利亞虎，還有紅鶴都吸引不了她，事實上，大部分的動物她都只瞄了一眼，就繼續往前走，大多數的時間，她都在抱怨去動物園有多愚蠢和無聊，真不知道是因為她長大了，還是單純因為她討厭動物才會這樣，但有件事我倒是很確定，我們以後不會再去動物園了。

Word 單字	Meaning 字義	Usage 常見用法
1 **professional** [prə`fɛʃənļ]	形 內行的	a professional pianist 專業的鋼琴家 the professional ethics 職業道德
2 **ambitious** [æm`bɪʃəs]	形 野心勃勃的	be ambitious of 渴望 ambitious after wealth 熱中於追求財富
3 **entrepreneur** [ˌɑntrəprə`nɜ]	名 企業家	an entrepreneur in …的企業家 a construction entrepreneur 承包商
4 **neglect** [nɪg`lɛkt]	名 忽略;疏忽 動 忽視;忽略	treat sb. with neglect 怠慢某人 neglect one's duty 玩忽職守
5 **gain** [gen]	名 獲得;利潤 動 得到;增添	be greedy of gain 貪得無厭 gain sb. over 把某人爭取過來
6 **graduate** [`grædʒʊˌet]	動 畢業	be graduated in law 法律系畢業 graduate from 從…畢業
7 **inappropriate** [ˌɪnə`proprɪɪt]	形 不合適的	an inappropriate example 不合適的例子 be inappropriate for 不適於…
8 **motivation** [ˌmotə`veʃən]	名 刺激;推動	without motivation 沒有動機 motivation of one's success 成功的動力
9 **affection** [ə`fɛkʃən]	名 做作;假裝; 感情;鍾愛	an affection of indifference 無動於衷 one's unrequited affection 單相思
10 **stable** [`stebļ]	動 穩定的;可靠的	a stable income 穩定的收入 sth. remain stable 維持穩定的狀態
11 **exotic** [ɛg`zɑtɪk]	形 異國的	wear exotic clothes 穿奇裝異服 the exotic culture 異國文化
12 **stray** [stre]	動 流浪;偏離 形 迷路的;走失的	stray off the path 偏離路徑 a stray heart 迷失的心

UNIT 4

家庭生活
Family Life〜下篇

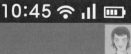

◀ APP CHAT **3** 做家事也不容易

親愛的，你在忙工作嗎？

Tip 實用表達 be busy at work，注意介系詞 at，有限定busy範圍的作用。

Honey, are you busy at work? 10:45

Mia

Richard

Not really. Is there something you want to talk about? 10:47

還好，你有什麼事要跟我說嗎？

Tip 這裡用not really回應，表示自己 能跟對方聊天。

我只是要跟你說，我很感 謝你昨天幫我做家事。

I wanted to thank you and let you know I appreciated① your help with the chores② yesterday. 10:50

Mia

Richard

Why would you say that? We are a team, you know that. You don't need to thank me. 10:52

幹麻這麼客氣呢？我們 是夫妻，你不用特別謝 我的。

嗯，無論如何，都很謝謝你幫 我清洗浴室。

Well, thanks anyway for cleaning the bathroom. 10:53

Mia

Richard

It looks cleaner than before, right? 10:55

現在浴室看起來比之前更乾淨 了，對吧？

這是毫無疑問的，浴室真 的乾淨許多，聞起來也很 香，但是…

Without a doubt. It's much cleaner and smells much better. But... 10:57

Mia

  **SEND ≫**

10:45

Richard

But what? What's the matter?
10:58

但是？怎麼了嗎？

你忘了把垃圾拿出去倒。

It's just that you forgot to take out the trash.
10:59

Mia

Richard

Did I? Oh, sorry. My mistake. When I get home tonight, I'll be sure to take it out.
11:02

真的嗎？喔，對不起，是我的錯，晚上回家後，我一定會記得把垃圾拿去倒。

不用了，我剛剛已經把垃圾拿出去丟了，還有，你又忘了應該把拖把放在哪裡。

It doesn't matter now. I just took it out. Also, you forgot where we put the mop again.
11:04

Mia

你把它放在書房裡耶，你知道拖把要放在外面的陽台上的，對吧？

Tip go outside表示「拿著拖把移動」的過程，後面的on表最終的地點。

You put it in the study room. You know it goes outside on the balcony③, don't you?
11:07

Mia

Richard

Oh, darling, I'm so sorry. I totally forgot.
11:09

喔，親愛的，我真的很抱歉，我完全忘了注意。

Richard

I'll be sure to take out the trash and put the mop on the balcony next time. Don't be angry, okay?
11:12

下次我會記得倒垃圾，也會把拖把放在陽台上，不要生氣，好嗎？

SEND ≫

Let's Chat In English Via APP

🔒 ✏️ 13:15 📶 🔋

◀ APP CHAT **4** 不要跟我說經商！

嘿，你這個星期三下午有空嗎？要不要一起喝個下午茶呢？

Hey, do you have free time this Wednesday afternoon? Want to join me for afternoon tea? `13:15`

 Laurel

 Mia

I need to check my schedule, but I think I am free. `13:16`

我得看一下我的時間，但我應該有空。

Tip 注意同樣是「看」，本句有「查看」時間表之意，所以用check。

那太好了，噢，跟你說，我老公下星期要從大陸回來了。

Great. Oh, I wanted to tell you that my husband is coming back to Taiwan from Mainland China next week. `13:20`

 Laurel

 Mia

That's great news! You two can finally reunite④ after, what, a year apart? `13:22`

真是個好消息！你們終於可以團聚了，分隔兩地有…一年了吧？

Tip 中間加what停頓，「向對方確認」的作用，只適用於口語表達。

實際上是十個月，他這五年多來都在大陸做生意，這你也知道對吧？

Actually, it's been ten months. You know that he's been doing business in China for more than five years, right? `13:25`

 Laurel

 Mia

Of course. How could I forget about him, the successful businessman? `13:27`

當然，我怎麼可能忘記你那位成功的商人老公呢？

即使有一波台商鮭魚返鄉潮，他還是堅持要在大陸做生意。

Even though there is a trend of Taiwanese entrepreneurs coming back and staying in Taiwan, he insists⑤ on doing business there. `13:33`

 Laurel

 [_____] **SEND »**

 Let's Chat In English Via APP ● ⏻ ●

Mia

Your husband must have a goal or a reason for that, then. 13:35

你老公一定有他的目標或其他待在大陸的原因。

是的，他想要蓋一間製作手機處理器的工廠。

Yes. He wants to build a factory that manufactures cell-phone processors❻. 13:38

Laurel

Mia

And he wants to be the plant's owner? That will cost him a fortune! 13:41

他要當工廠的老闆嗎？那得花一大筆錢耶！

Tip 實用表達，cost後面加上a fortune強調「鉅款」。

他說大陸的市場值得投資，因為將來還有許多成長潛力。

He says that it's a good area to invest in with lots of potential for future growth. 13:44

Laurel

他還跟我說已經有不少資本家有興趣投資他的企劃了。

He also told me there were a number of capitalists interested in investing in the business. 13:48

Laurel

Honestly, I know so little about business. Whenever you mention it to me, my head feels dizzy. Let's talk about something else. 13:52

説真的，我對商業所知不多，每次一聽你提起，我就感到頭暈，我們聊點別的吧！

Mia

SEND ≫

Let's Chat In English Via APP

3. 幫忙做家事又錯了？

📖 Richard 2014/1/12

I don't know how much more I can take. I have tried my best to make Mia happy, but she is never satisfied. I wish today was an isolated❼ incident, but, unfortunately, this happens every week, over and over. Every time I help with the housework, my wife manages to find something I have done wrong or forgotten to do, and she never hesitates❽ to call me or tell me about it. Of course, I understand she just wants to remind me, but I really feel frustrated.

我不知道我還能忍多久，我已經盡力使米亞開心，但她永遠都不滿意，真希望今天的事情只是單一的偶發事件，不幸的是，這種事情每週都會發生，一遍又一遍地重演，每次我幫忙做家事時，我老婆都會找出我做錯或忘記的地方，並毫不猶豫地打電話給我，告訴我哪裡沒做好，當然，我理解她只是想要提醒我，但這樣一項一項提出來實在讓人感到很挫折。

We have been married a long time now, and I still feel like she doesn't appreciate anything that I do! I mean, I am the one who works a full-time job. She only works in the mornings at a kindergarten. She has much more time than me to do the chores. But because I want our marriage to be equal, I try my best to help around the house. Without fail, every time I do the chores, she will find something to complain about. My God, what can I do to satisfy this woman?

我們結婚已經很久了，但我總覺得她依然不會感激我為她做的事，我的意思是，我是個有全職工作的人，而她只有早上的時間在一所幼稚園工作，她有更多的時間做家事，但是，因為我希望我們的婚姻關係是平等的，所以還是盡力幫忙，只不過，我每次幫忙做家事，她都能找到可以拿來抱怨的事情，屢試不爽，天啊，我到底要怎麼做，她才會滿意呢？

🔒 ⚠ ✏   18:55 📶 ▮▮▮

微網誌 4. 老婆也有本難唸的經

📖 Mia 2014/1/15

I really think Laurel is lucky to have me as her friend. Of all our mutual friends, I am the only one who still listens to her talk on and on about her husband and his Chinese business ventures⑨. I am not happy or excited when she brings up the topic. In fact, I can only take a few minutes of her droning⑩ before I get a headache. However, I am her friend, so I try to listen. It's just really, really, really hard.

我真的認為勞蕾爾能有我這個朋友是很幸運的,在我們所有共同的朋友當中,我是唯一一還願意聽她談她老公,以及他在中國的投資事業的人,每當她談起這個話題,我都不是很開心或興奮,老實說,聽她滔滔不絕地說了幾分鐘後,我就感到頭痛,但我們是朋友嘛,所以我會努力去聽,只是,這對我來說真的非常、非常、非常辛苦。

I think the problem is that neither of us are business people. Laurel's husband is, of course, but she is not. She is a housewife, whose highlight⑪ each day is taking care of her two children and doing chores around the house. As for me, I teach at a kindergarten in the mornings. I know Laurel wants to feel involved⑫ in her husband's life. If listening to her talk on and on about things she knows nothing about helps her feel involved, then I am happy to do it. After all, what are friends for?

我想這當中的問題在於,我們兩個都不是生意人,勞蕾爾的老公是商人,這點毫無疑問,但勞蕾爾不是,她只是個家庭主婦,每天的生活重心就是照顧她的兩個孩子和做家事,至於我的話,則有一份早上在幼稚園教書的工作。我知道勞蕾爾想要多參與她老公的生活,如果這樣聽她講一些她也不很懂的事,能讓她有參與感的話,我還是很樂意聽她說,不然,朋友是做什麼用的呢?

Word 單字	Meaning 字義	Usage 常見用法
1 appreciate [ə`priʃ͵et]	動 增值(土地、貨幣)；欣賞；賞識	deeply appreciate sth. 深深地感謝 appreciate his integrity 讚賞他的正直
2 chore [tʃor]	名 家務；例行工作	do one's daily chores 做日常雜務 a laborious chore 繁瑣的工作
3 balcony [`bælkənɪ]	名 陽台；露臺	stand at a balcony 站在陽台上 the first balcony 戲院的第一層樓廳
4 reunite [͵riju`naɪt]	動 再結合；重聚	to reunite eventually 最終重聚 be reunited with 與…重聚
5 insist [ɪn`sɪst]	動 堅持；強調	insist on an opinion 堅持一項主張 insist on one's innocence 堅持無罪
6 processor [`prɑsɛsɚ]	名 加工者；製造者；(電腦)信息處理機	a word processor 文字處理軟體 the food processor 食物處理機
7 isolate [`aɪs͵et]	動 孤立；隔離	isolate oneself from others 孤立自己 an isolated incident 個別事件
8 hesitate [`hɛzə͵tet]	動 躊躇；猶豫	hesitate about 對…感到猶豫 hesitate between A and B 無法決定
9 venture [`vɛntʃɚ]	名 冒險；投機活動 動 冒險；大膽行動	at a venture 冒險地；胡亂地 a joint venture 一家合資企業
10 drone [dron]	名 嗡嗡聲 動 嗡嗡聲；單調地說	a boring drone 令人討厭、嘮叨的人 drone on and on 無聊地進行
11 highlight [`haɪ͵laɪt]	名 強光；最重要的事 動 用強光照射	the highlight of sth. 最精彩的部分 highlight one's face 照亮面孔
12 involve [ɪn`vɑlv]	動 使捲入；連累；牽涉	be involved in 使專注；使忙於 get involved with 被…纏住了

UNIT 5 父母的老後
When We Get Older～上篇

◀ APP CHAT **1** 必須買間新房子

Allison： I am beginning to think I need a real estate agent. `13:52`

我想我可能需要找一家房屋仲介。

Greg： Why? Are you planning on moving? I thought you liked your apartment. `14:00`

為什麼？你在計劃搬家嗎？我以為你很喜歡你現在住的公寓。

Allison： I do. It's because my parents are getting older. I want to find a bigger place so they can live with me and I can take care of them. `14:19`

我是喜歡啊！但因為我父母的年紀越來越大，所以我想找間大一點的房子，這樣他們就可以跟我一起住，我也方便照顧他們。

Greg： That's so sweet of you! Are you looking for an apartment or a house? `14:20`

你真貼心！你想找公寓還是一般平房啊？

Tip 常用句型，依句意不同，sweet可用kind等形容詞替換。

Allison： I think I want to buy an apartment. It should be cheaper and more convenient。 than a house. `14:22`

我想買公寓，公寓應該會比一般平房便宜，也比較方便。

Greg： What kinds of things are you looking for in your new place? `14:23`

那你想找的公寓有什麼條件嗎？

Allison： One thing my parents need is an elevator. It's not easy for them to climb stairs anymore. `14:26`

第一要件是要有電梯，我父母的年紀大了，爬樓梯對他們來說很吃力。

Tip 慣用片語climb stairs，要注意「爬」所採用的動詞climb。

SEND ≫

Let's Chat In English Via APP

還有其他的要求嗎？比方說你需要幾房？希望附近有便捷的大眾交通工具可搭乘嗎？

Anything else? Like, have you thought about how many bedrooms you need, and whether you want to live near public transportation₂?　14:30

Greg

Allison

We will need more space with my parents moving in. And it would be great if we are near public transportation.　14:33

跟父母同住，我會需要大一點的空間，如果附近有大眾交通工具當然最好。

明白了，對了，你要我跟在房屋仲介公司上班的朋友聯絡嗎？

Okay. Hey! Would you like me to contact my friend who works in real estate?　14:35

Greg

Allison

You have a friend in real estate?! Why didn't you say so?　14:37

你有朋友在房屋仲介公司上班？！你怎麼不早點說呢？

所以你不覺得我剛剛問的很詳細嗎？

So you don't feel like what I just asked was a little too specific?　14:38

Greg

Allison

Not at all. Could you tell your friend my case is urgent₃?　14:41

不覺得，那能告訴你的朋友說我很急嗎？

Tip 口語常用，表示「一點都不」的否定。

沒問題！他一有消息，我就會盡快讓你知道的。

Tip as soon as possible在口語、書寫都常用，打字為求簡短時，會直接用ASAP取代。

No problem! I will let you know what he says as soon as possible.　14:42

Greg

 [_____] SEND »

21:28

Greg

Hey! What did you think of the places? My friend said he took you to see a few last week. `21:28`

嘿！房子看得還好嗎？我朋友說他上星期帶你去看了幾個地方。

是看了一些，他先帶我去看了一間公寓，附近就有公車可搭，也有一些商店。

Yeah, we saw a few. The first place he took me to see was an apartment with a bus stop and some stores nearby. `21:33`

Allison

Greg

So…was that apartment perfect for you and your family or what? `21:35`

所以…那間公寓適合你和你的家人嗎？

公寓是很棒，但是我不確定那間是否適合。

It was really nice, but I'm not sure whether it's the right one or not. `21:37`

Allison

Greg

Why do you say that? Weren't you satisfied with it? `21:38`

為什麼這麼說？你不滿意嗎？

Tip 在BE動詞上加否定(weren't)，表示說話者自己覺得對方應該會滿意。

嗯，我擔心的是，他帶我去看的那間公寓空間不夠大。

Well, I'm afraid the one he showed me just won't give us enough space. `21:40`

Allison

Greg

Did you tell my friend? I'm sure he can help you find other, larger places. `21:42`

你有告訴我朋友這個問題嗎？我相信他會幫你找其他空間較大的房子的。

SEND ▶▶

Let's Chat In English Via APP

21:28

當然有，我告訴你朋友後，他帶我去看那棟公寓附近的一棟大廈。

Of course I did. After I told him, he took me to see a mansion close to the first building. 21:44

Allison

Well...did you like that one? 21:45

那…你喜歡那一間嗎？

Greg

怎麼可能不喜歡？！房子很大，而且有視野絕佳的陽台，能俯瞰這座城市。

Tip with接上a great view of the city描述特色。

How could I not?! It was huge, and it had a balcony with a great view of the city. 21:48

Allison

So it suits your family? 21:49

所以它很適合你們家的需求囉？

Greg

那是當然，但是價位實在太高了，我負擔不起。

Absolutely it does. But the price is way too high. I can't afford⑤ it. 21:51

Allison

Have you thought about public housing? It's cheaper. 21:52

你有沒有考慮買國宅啊？那比較便宜。

Tip 慣用片語public housing，談到建築物樣式時很實用。

Greg

國宅嗎？那也是一個選擇，為了我的家人，我會繼續尋找理想的公寓。

Public housing? I guess that's a possibility. For now, I will continue looking for the ideal apartment for my family. 21:55

Allison

SEND ▶▶

Let's Chat In English Via APP

137

微網誌

1. 買房子的考量

📖 Allison 2014/1/18

I can't think of anything more stressful than buying a house! I am literally having trouble sleeping. I was lucky enough to get a real estate agent from Greg's recommendation. Still, it's like I have to consider so many things. Too many things, if you ask me! The price might be the most important, but there are so many other things like location, size, parking spaces, apartment-style or traditional house, and whether the house is furnished or not that I have to consider. And then I have to make sure my parents like the house, too!

　　我想不出一件比買房子更有壓力的事！我最近連覺都睡不好，我很幸運的是，葛瑞格推薦了一位他在做房屋仲介的朋友給我，不過，我依然要考慮很多事情，如果你問我的話，實在有太多東西要考慮了！價格可能是最重要的考量，但也要顧慮許多其他的細節，例如地點、大小、停車位、公寓式或傳統的房子、有沒有附家具等等，這些我都要考慮，而且，我還得確定我父母也喜歡才行！

Everyone tells me that buying a house is a great investment, though. They also say that it is never a bad idea to invest in real estate of any kind. I believe them, I do. It's just that it's such a pain finding the right house for my family, and I know I will have to wait years before the value of the house goes up. With all the stress I am under, it's too hard to think about the future!

　　每個人都跟我說買房子是一項很棒的投資，他們也說投資房地產這個主意絕對不會錯，他們的說法我都相信，但是，為家人找間合適的房子實在是件苦差事，而且在房價上漲之前，我還得等好幾年才行，在目前這種壓力之下，我實在很難去思考那些未來才會發生的事！

🔒 ✉ ✏   13:48 📶 📶 🔋

  微網誌

2. 租房子也不錯

📖 Greg 2014/1/19

As I have gotten older, I have seen so many of my friends getting married and buying houses. They all tell me that real estate is a great investment for the future. They say that when they get older, they can sell their house for much more than they bought it. I believe them, I guess, but my wife and I still haven't bought a house. We have been married almost five years, and we feel that renting⑩ is the right choice.

當我年歲漸長，我看到許多朋友結婚、買房子，他們都告訴我就長遠來看，房地產會是絕佳的投資，說以後年老時，賣房子的錢會遠遠超過他們當初買的價格，這一點我相信，但是到目前為止，我太太和我都沒有買房子，我們結婚快五年了，始終覺得租房子是正確的選擇。

We came to this decision a couple of years ago after I told her I wanted to buy a house. All of our friends were buying houses, I told her, so why shouldn't we? Surprisingly, she told me that renting might actually be a better idea. After carefully thinking about it for awhile, I agreed that renting would let us save a lot more money than buying a house. Also, with renting, we wouldn't have to worry about loans, mortgages⑪, or any other headaches that come with buying a house. I must say she made a compelling⑫ case for renting!

幾年前，在我告訴她我想買房子後，我們做出了這個決定，那個時候，我告訴她，我們的朋友都在買房子，為什麼我們不買呢？讓我驚訝的是，她說租房子會是個更好的主意，後來我仔細想了一下，比起買房子，租房子的確可以讓我們存更多的錢，此外，租屋可以不用擔心貸款、抵押品、或任何其他買房子時會遇到的頭痛問題，我必須說，她主張租屋的這件事，實在令我信服！

Word 單字	Meaning 字義	Usage 常見用法
1 convenient [kən`vinjənt]	形 合宜的；方便的	a convenient memory 只記對己有利的 a convenience store 便利商店
2 transportation [ˌtrænspə`teʃən]	名 運輸；輸送	give free transportation to 免收運費 public transportation 大眾交通工具
3 urgent [`ɜdʒənt]	形 緊急的；急迫的	in urgent need of relief 急需救濟 an urgent meeting 緊急會議
4 satisfied [`sætɪsˌfaɪd]	形 感到滿意的	be satisfied with 對…感到滿意 give a satisfied smile 露出滿意的笑容
5 afford [ə`ford]	動 負擔；買得起	afford upon one's income 依收入負擔 barely afford to 勉強負擔
6 literally [`lɪtərəlɪ]	副 逐字地；實在地	translate sth. literally 逐字翻譯 be understood literally 按字面理解
7 agent [`edʒənt]	名 代理人；特工	an agent for sth. 某物的代理人 make sb. my agent 讓…做我的代理人
8 traditional [trə`dɪʃənl]	形 傳統的；慣例的	traditional Chinese medicine 中藥 a traditional custom 傳統習俗
9 investment [ɪn`vɛstmənt]	名 投資	foreign investment 外國投資 make a large investment 大量投資
10 rent [rɛnt]	名 租金；租費 動 租用	raise/lower the rent 提高/降低租金 for rent 出租的
11 mortgage [`mɔrgɪdʒ]	名 抵押；抵押借款 動 以…作擔保	mortgage loan 抵押借款 pay off the mortgage 還清貸款
12 compelling [kəm`pɛlɪŋ]	形 令人注目的； 令人信服的	the compelling evidence 有力證據 a compelling argument 有力的辯詞

UNIT 5

父母的老後
When We Get Older～下篇

你找到適合你父母住的房子了嗎？

Have you found the perfect house for your parents yet? 17:57

Greg

Not yet. It really is becoming too much! 17:58

還沒有耶，找房子實在很累人啊！

Tip 英文表達「隨著時間過去，心理壓力越來越大」的漸進感。

Allison

我妹妹去年買了一間公寓，找房子的甘苦談，我可聽得太多了。

Tip 用完成式have heard it才能表達「過去那段時間聽得很多」。

My sister bought an apartment last year, so I have heard it all before. 18:02

Greg

對了，你覺得買二手屋這個想法怎麼樣？

By the way, how do you feel about buying an older apartment? 18:03

Greg

Well, I am not against it. Brand new apartments can be really expensive. 18:05

我不反對，全新的公寓真的是太貴了。

Allison

聽到你這樣說真是太好了！我有個同事，最近買了新公寓，因此正打算賣掉舊房子。

That's great to hear! One of my colleagues bought a new apartment and is looking to sell his old one. 18:08

Greg

為了吸引買家，他留下了全部的家俱。

As an incentive① to buyers, he is leaving all his furniture there. 18:10

Greg

  SEND ▶▶

Let's Chat In English Via APP • •

141

Allison

Sounds promising⊘, but I have lots of questions. How old is the apartment, and how many rooms does it have? Is it situated⊙ in a good location? `18:14`

聽起來很有希望，但我還是有很多問題，公寓的屋齡幾年？有幾房？地點好嗎？

那是棟屋齡十年的舊公寓，有四房，附近有醫院和小公園。

It is a ten-year-old apartment. It has four rooms. Nearby, there is a hospital and a small park. `18:20`

Greg

Allison

That sounds almost perfect! Tell your colleague that I am interested in seeing his apartment. `18:23`

聽起來完全符合我的需求！告訴你同事，我有興趣去看他的公寓。

沒問題！那你是準備自己去看房子，還是跟你父母一起呢？

Tip 完整表達為 do sth. by yourself，但口語用 do sth. yourself 即可。

No problem! Will you check the apartment yourself or with your parents? `18:25`

Greg

Allison

I think I will go alone. My parents' health is too poor. `18:26`

我父母的身體狀況不好，我想我還是自己去看吧！

好，我再告訴你他何時有空，如果需要人陪，我可以跟你一起去看房子。

Okay. I'll let you know when he is available⊙. If you want some company, I can join you. `18:30`

Greg

Allison

That's so nice of you. I would love some company. Thanks! `18:32`

你人真好，我很樂意有人陪我一起去，謝謝你！

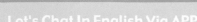

SEND ≫

Let's Chat In English Via APP

142

就我個人而言，完全看
不出你朋友的公寓已經
有十年了。

Personally, I can't believe that your friend's apartment was ten years old. 8:15

Allison

室內的裝潢與家俱都還
很新。

The interior⑤ design and the furniture were so modern. 8:16

Allison

I noticed that the lighting inside the apartment was very good and not so dim, like most old apartments. 8:18

Greg

我有注意到，它不像大部
分的老舊公寓那樣昏暗，
室內的光線很充足。

是啊！我父母的視力不好，所以他
們會害怕撞到東西。

Tip 如果bump into後面加上人的
話，有「巧遇」的意思。

Yep! My parents no longer see well, and they're afraid of bumping into things. 8:20

Allison

如果室內有充足的採光，
絕對會是加分要素。

It is definitely a plus if there is enough lighting inside. 8:21

Allison

Also, the apartment was on a high floor with a great view! I wasn't expecting that. 8:23

Greg

而且，因為樓層位置高，所以視野
很棒！我沒想到視野會那麼好。

Tip 隱含「比原本想的好」之意，
基本上表示正面的肯定。

只有一個問題：我爸有輛休
旅車，他有時會開車去親戚
家，所以一個車位對我們而
言是不夠的。

One thing, though: my dad has a van that he sometimes drives to visit relatives, so one parking space is not enough for us. 8:26

Allison

Greg

That shouldn't be a problem. My friend said the building rents additional parking spaces for $2,000NTD a month. 8:29

那沒問題，我朋友說，大樓裡另外租個車位，一個月只要兩千元。

那太好了！醫院和附近的公園也是很棒的優點。

That's great! The hospital and the nearby park are huge bonuses, too. 8:30

Allison

Greg

It's important – and convenient – that a hospital is nearby while living with parents. 8:32

與父母同住，附近有家醫院很重要，而且也很方便。

而且公園離公寓很近，如此一來，我下班後就可以陪他們到公園散步。

And with a park so close to the apartment, I can walk with them after work. 8:34

Allison

Greg

Everything seems perfect. But what about the price? Is it in your budget? 8:36

每個細節看起來都很完美，那麼價位呢？有在你的預算之內嗎？

Tip 注意「在預算之內」的介係詞可用in/within，in更口語一些。

事實上，價格也有在我的預算之內，但在買之前，我還是讓我父母看一下比較好。

Actually, it is. It's just now I am thinking I really should let my parents see the apartment before I buy it. 8:39

Allison

   SEND

10:36

 3. 找房子甘苦談

Allison 2014/1/22

I am really starting to question my desire to buy a house. Every day is more stressful than the day before, and every house or apartment I see that does not fit my needs makes me lose a little more hope. Some are too small, some are too expensive, and some are too far away from the city. I am honestly about ready to give up. Maybe I will just buy the next one I see that is within my budget. Just forget my needs and my family's needs and buy whatever I find.

我真的開始質疑我買房子的動機了,每天的壓力變得越來越大,多看一間不符合我需求的房子或公寓,我就變得更加失落,有的空間太小、有的太貴、有的又離市區太遠,老實說,我準備要放棄了,也許,無論下一間房子怎樣,只要它在我的預算之內,我就會買下來,不管我或家人的需求,買了就好。

I can't wait much longer. My parents seem to be getting worse, and they really need me to help them. Last week, I drove to their house four times to help them with simple things like washing clothes or mopping! My mom had slipped and fell in the bathroom recently. Even though I immediately bought a mat for the bathroom, I am still worried about her – or my father – having another accident. Knowing that they are alone in their house stresses me out almost as much as looking for a new house.

我不能等太久,爸媽的健康每況愈下,他們真的很需要我的幫忙,上週,我開車到他們家四次,就為了去幫忙做些簡單的家事,像是洗衣服及拖地之類的。之前我媽才在浴室滑了一跤,我雖然馬上去幫他們買了防滑墊,但心裡還是會擔心我爸媽又發生類似的意外,他們兩人獨自在家這件事帶給我極大的壓力,幾乎和找房子的壓力一樣大了。

🔒 ⚠ ✏   22:36 📶 📶 🔋

4. 朋友的那棟二手屋

📖 Greg 2014/1/26

I have noticed Allison has been in poor spirits⑨ for a long time. I know she has been looking for a house for her parents and has had no luck. I watched my sister go through the same thing last year, so I can relate⑩. I think Allison is worse off, though, because she has to find an apartment that is suitable for others, and my sister only had to find one for herself.

我注意到艾莉森的精神狀況一直不是很好，我知道她在為她的父母找房子，但是目前為止都沒找到適合他們的，我妹妹去年也經歷過同樣的事，所以我很能理解，不過，我覺得艾莉森的情況更難辦，因為她必須找一間適合其他人住的公寓，而我妹妹只需要為她自己找房子就好。

Fortunately, my colleague told me that he recently bought a new apartment and was looking to sell his old one. I immediately told Allison and helped her schedule a meeting to see it. I went with her to see the apartment and try to lift her spirits. The apartment was old, but it was furnished⑪ and decorated in a very modern⑫ style. When my colleague told Allison the price, I could see she was very interested. I don't know if she will end up buying the apartment, but it makes me happy to see her less stressed and more excited for a change.

幸運的是，我同事告訴我，他最近買了一間新公寓，所以準備出售舊的那間房子，我馬上告訴艾莉森這件事，並幫她安排看房子的時間，我陪她一起去看了那間房子，並試著為她打氣。那是棟舊公寓，但它內附家俱，而且裝潢得很現代，當我同事說出他想賣的價格時，我看得出艾莉森很感興趣，雖然不知道她最後是否會買下那間公寓，但看到她的壓力稍稍減輕以及終於開朗起來的表情，我就替她感到高興。

Word 單字	Meaning 字義	Usage 常見用法
1 incentive [ɪnˋsɛntɪv]	名 刺激；鼓勵 形 刺激的；鼓勵的	an incentive to exertion 努力的動機 the incentive payment 獎金
2 promising [ˋprɑmɪsɪŋ]	形 有希望的； 有前途的	a promising leader 有前途的領導者 of great promise 大有希望的
3 situate [ˋsɪtʃʊˌet]	動 使位於；使處於	be situated at/in/on 坐落於 be awkwardly situated 處境困難
4 available [əˋveləbl]	形 可用的；可得的； 有空的；有效的	available space 可使用的空間 be available for spending 可供花費
5 interior [ɪnˋtɪrɪə]	名 內部；內陸 形 室內的；國內的	in the interior 內陸 an interior designer 室內設計師
6 bonus [ˋbonəs]	名 獎金；額外津貼； 額外好處	an added bonus 紅利 an annual bonus 年終獎金
7 budget [ˋbʌdʒɪt]	名 預算；經費	reduce/cut a budget 削減預算 on a budget 精打細算的
8 stress [strɛs]	名 壓力；緊張 動 強調；著重	the stress of sth. 某事帶來的壓力 stress the importance of 強調重要性
9 spirit [ˋspɪrɪt]	名 精神；心靈；特質 動 拐走；鼓舞	a man of spirit 精神飽滿的人 spirit away 拐走
10 relate [rɪˋlet]	動 認同；有關； 涉及；敘述	relate with the fact 與事實相符 relate a story vividly 生動地講故事
11 furnish [ˋfɝnɪʃ]	動 給房間配置；裝備	furnish sth. with/to 提供某物給… a furnished apartment 附傢俱的公寓
12 modern [ˋmɑdən]	形 現代的；時髦的	modern society 現代社會 a course on modern art 現代藝術的課程

課業與職場

一步一腳印的人生藍圖

你所規劃的人生藍圖都有些什麼內容呢？
學生時期，會遇到主修以及畢業後的選擇，
進入職場後，將逐步接觸到更廣泛的交友圈，
從懵懂的新鮮人到經驗豐富的老手，
這些人都在聊些什麼，本章通通教給你！

Let's Chat In English
Via APP

APP CHAT !

UNIT 1

課業本份
School Work～上篇

073 MP3

15:22 📶

嘿，蘇西，要不要出門找點樂子呢？

Hey Susie, want to go out and have some fun? 15:22

Rick

Sure! The past three weeks have been exhausting. I need to chill out. 15:24

好啊！這三個禮拜真是累死我了，我需要放鬆一下。

Tip 實用表達chill out，表示「放鬆一下」。

Susie

我也是，這就是我之所以想約你出門玩的原因，我這學期修的課真的很難。

Me too. That's why I thought it would be fun to go out and do something fun together. My classes this semester are so difficult. 15:27

Rick

我修了生物學101、化學101與數學202之統計學。

I'm taking Biology 101, Chemistry 101, and Math 202: Statistics. 15:28

Rick

Wow. To be honest, I have no idea what those classes are even about! 15:30

哇，說真的，你說的那些課程，我一點概念都沒有！

Susie

生物學101在講生物的特性，化學101則在探討物體的成分，例如碳與氧。

Well, Biology 101 is all about the characteristics[1] of living things. Chemistry 101 is about the component[2] parts like carbon and oxygen. 15:33

Rick

That seems way above my level. Hey, have you read "The Odyssey" before? 15:35

那些聽起來都超出我的理解範圍，對了，你有讀過《奧德賽》嗎？

Tip 聊天若講到「配不上某人」，也可以用above one's level表達。

Susie

🔊 😆 [   ] SEND »

15:22

有啊，我高中讀過，是關於一個人拯救世界的希臘史詩嘛。

Yep, I read it back in high school. It's an epic poem from Greece about a man who saves the world. `15:38`

Rick

No, it's not! It's about a warrior who is punished by the sea god Poseidon with a decade-long exodus. `15:41`

才不是！那是關於一個戰士被海神波塞頓懲罰，在外漂流十年的故事。

Susie

嗯，是啊，那也是，算了，我們就別再談科目的事了。

Tip that's enough talking about 表達「已經說得夠多」之意。

Well, yeah, that too. Anyway, that's enough talking about our classes. `15:43`

Rick

I agree. Since we major in different areas, our classes have nothing in common. `15:46`

我同意，我們的主修不同，所以沒有一堂課是相同的。

Susie

那這個週末一起去打羽毛球怎麼樣？

How about playing badminton this weekend? `15:47`

Rick

Okay. That will be a great way to relax. `15:48`

好啊，那感覺是個紓解壓力的好方法。

Susie

SEND »

Rick

I doubt whether my math professor really knows how to teach. All he does is teach things straight out of the textbook. `14:00`

真的很懷疑我的數學教授到底會不會教書,他都只照著教科書的內容講課。

你是說他只是重複書上的公式而已嗎?那太令人失望了吧!

You mean he only repeats the formulas from the book? That must be frustrating! `14:02`

Susie

Rick

Yeah, he never explains anything. So now I have no idea how to do this week's homework. `14:05`

對啊,他從來不講解,所以這個禮拜的作業我都不會做。

這就是為什麼我要唸文學,記公式不是我的強項。

Tip not a strength of mine 會比not good at更強烈、活潑。

That's why I study literature. Memorizing formulas isn't a strength of mine. `14:07`

Susie

不過,文學的問題在於,在談論個人意見的時候,有時候必須做出讓步。

The problem with literature, though, is that you sometimes need to compromise③ on your views. `14:10`

Susie

Rick

Why? Every reader's personal perception④ of a book should be valid. `14:14`

為什麼要讓步呢?每個讀者的看法都會有自己的道理。

這點我同意,遺憾的是,據我所知,學生最好不要與教授意見相左比較好。

I agree! Unfortunately, I have learned that students shouldn't disagree with their professors. `14:20`

Susie

SEND »

14:00

Rick

What will happen if you do? You won't pass the class or what? `14:22`

意見相左會怎麼樣？這一科就會被當之類的嗎？

對啊，聽起來很專制，對吧？

Yeah. It sounds like a dictatorship⑤, right? `14:23`

Susie

Rick

Yeah, it does! I think you should be able to challenge your professors. They should like it when their students propose different ideas. `14:30`

是啊！我覺得你可以挑戰你的教授，有學生提出不同的想法，他們應該會喜歡的。

但還是有風險，瑞克，我不想因為自己不認同教授的想法，就被當掉。

> **Tip** 實用表達fail a class，還有flunk 可表示「當掉」之意。

But it's risky⑤, Rick. I don't want to fail a class just because I disagreed. `14:32`

Susie

Rick

If you do, then at least you are thinking for yourself. `14:33`

如果你這麼做，至少你提出了自己的想法。

好吧，也許我會試試，但可不保證一定會。

> **Tip** fine通常是在對方講了很多之後，才勉強答應，與OK這種爽快的答應不同。

Fine. Maybe I will try. No promises, though. `14:34`

Susie

 SEND ≫

Let's Chat In English Via APP ● ●

153

1. 選修課真有趣！

📖 Rick 2014/1/23

It's been one week now in my first semester as a pre-medicine student. It's pretty challenging already though, especially Biology 101 and Chemistry 101. They are very complicated subjects, and the textbooks are gigantic! After the first week, I can see that I will have to concentrate and study hard if I want to pass both.

上醫科先修後的第一個星期已經過去了，所有課程都相當有挑戰性，尤其是生物學101與化學101，它們的上課內容很複雜，而且這兩門課的教科書都超厚重的！上完第一個星期的課之後，我就知道如果要順利修過這兩門課，就得集中精神、用功唸書才行。

Biology is a very interesting subject. We began the course learning about how some animals can grow back their limbs if they lose them. The professor asked us if this had any practical applications❼ for humans. I told him I thought scientists might someday be able to mimic❽ these animals and provide replacement limbs for people. Chemistry is challenging as well. In our first class, the professor showed us a few basic chemical reactions. I found out that the element carbon is in everything that is alive! I can't wait to see what else I will learn this semester.

生物學是一門非常有趣的科目，一開始上課，我們就學到某些動物具備失去四肢後再生的能力，教授問我們，這樣的特性是否有可能應用在人類身上，我的回應是，也許有一天，科學家們會仿照這些動物，提供四肢的替代品給那些需要的人。化學也滿有挑戰性的，第一堂課，教授向我們展示了基本的化學反應，而且我現在才知道，原來所有的生物體都有碳元素！我等不及要看這學期還能學到什麼其他的知識了。

2. 吸引我的人文課程

Susie 2014/1/24

This semester at university, I decided to take a few humanities[9] courses. I have wanted to take Psychology 101 and Sociology 101 for awhile, but they were always full. I think psychology is engrossing[10]. Our brains are so complicated, and learning about why people do the things they do fascinates me. My interest started when I learned about Munchausen syndrome[11] after a girl at my high school pretended to have cancer for two years. As a bonus, if I learn more about people's behavior, maybe I can figure out why my sister is always getting mad at me!

這學期我決定要修一些人文學科課程，我一直很想修心理學101以及社會學101這兩門課，但它們的選課人數總是額滿。我覺得心理學很引人入勝，我們的大腦很複雜，去學習人類行為背後的原因真的很吸引我，我想我對這門課的興趣，是從高中時學到孟喬森症候群（一種幻想自己得病的精神疾病）時就開始的，當時學校裡有個女孩，在兩年間都幻想自己得了癌症，此外，如果我了解更多關於人類行為背後的原因，也許就能弄清楚我姐姐為什麼總是生我的氣了！

Sociology is another subject[12] that seems intriguing to me. It's important to know how our society works, and what we can do to improve it. Sociology 101 is a very broad course. It talks about everything from religion, to politics, to law. I want to be challenged by these classes, and to work really hard. I just hope that I will still have time to hang out with my friends on the weekends!

社會學是另一門吸引我的課程，了解社會是如何運作，以及我們能做些什麼來改善生活，這些都很重要，社會學101的內容非常廣泛，它從宗教談到政治、及法律的一切，我想要將這些課程看作挑戰，努力地去研讀，當然，我還是希望週末能有時間和我朋友玩！

Word 單字	Meaning 字義	Usage 常見用法
1 characteristic [ˌkærəktə`rɪstɪk]	名 特性；特徵；特色 形 特有的；獨特的	a distinguishing characteristic 突出特徵 a characteristic taste 獨特的味道
2 component [kəm`ponənt]	名 構成要素；成分 形 組成的；構成的	a key component of ⋯的關鍵要素 the component parts 零組件
3 compromise [`kɑmprə͵maɪz]	名 妥協；和解 動 危及；讓步	compromise with sb. 與某人妥協 compromise one's reputation 損害名譽
4 perception [pə`sɛpʃən]	名 感知；認識； 觀察力	a man of great perception 有洞察力的人 extra-sensory perception 第六感
5 dictatorship [dɪk`tetə͵ʃɪp]	名 獨裁；專政	establish a dictatorship 建立獨裁政府 under a dictatorship 在獨裁政治之下
6 risky [`rɪskɪ]	形 危險的；冒險的	be bold and risky 大膽且危險 run the risk of 冒⋯的風險
7 application [ˌæplə`keʃən]	名 應用；申請	an application for a loan 貸款申請 be of wide application 應用範圍很廣
8 mimic [`mɪmɪk]	動 模仿；學⋯的樣子 形 模仿的；模擬的	mimic one's voice 模仿某人的聲音 a mimicked battle 一場模擬戰爭
9 humanity [hju`mænətɪ]	名 人性；人道； 人文科學	treat sb. with humanity 人道地對待 out of one's humanity 沒有人性
10 engrossing [ɛn`grosɪŋ]	形 使人全神貫注的； 引人入勝的	an engrossing story 引人入勝的故事 be engrossed in 全神貫注於
11 syndrome [`sɪn͵drom]	名 (醫)併發症狀； 綜合症狀	menopausal syndrome 更年期症候群 survivor syndrome 倖存者症候群
12 subject [`sʌbdʒɪkt]	名 主題；科目 形 易受⋯的	cram up a subject 死記某門課 be aside from the subject 偏離主題

UNIT 1

課業本份
School Work～下篇

15:22 📶

嘿，蘇西，你在忙嗎？

Hey, Susie! Are you busy?
15:22

Rick

I am just trying to finish reading this chapter. It's from a book we're reading in my study group.
15:33

Susie

我正在努力讀完這個章節，是我們讀書會要讀的一本書。

讀書會？你是從什麼時候開始參加讀書會的啊？

Tip 用 since when 的完成式去問，強調「持續的過程」。

A study group? Since when have you been going to a study group?
15:35

Rick

Since a couple of weeks ago. Some of my classmates talked me into it. They said it would really help a lot.
15:38

Susie

幾個星期前，我的同學說服我參加的，他們說讀書會的幫助很大。

是喔，那結果有幫助嗎？

Well, has it?
15:39

Rick

I think so, yeah. Everyone must contribute a summary on the assigned part and give feedback₀ to others.
15:42

Susie

我認為有，每個人都必須對自己負責的內容提出摘要，並分享自己的感想。

但我自己唸書，考試就可以考得很好了。

Tip 實用表達 do well on，後面放上擅長、拿手的事物即可。

But I can just read the book by myself and do well on the exams.
15:44

Rick

SEND ▶▶

15:22

Susie

It's not just about preparing for exams. You learn so much more as a part of the group. `15:46`

參加讀書會不只是為了考試而已，加入讀書會之後，你會學到很多。

嗯，比方說像是什麼樣的好處呢？

Yeah, like what kind of benefits? `15:47`

Rick

Susie

By discussing the class books with each other, we all get a chance to understand others' ideas. `15:50`

透過彼此對書的討論，我們就有機會了解其他人的想法。

Susie

This really stimulates₂ our critical₃ thinking skills. `15:51`

這樣討論真的能刺激我們批判思維的能力。

聽起來不賴，也許我下學期會參加，這學期實在沒時間。

Tip 實用片語be tied up，表示「忙到沒時間」。

That doesn't sound too bad. Maybe I will try one next semester. This semester, I am too tied up. `15:53`

Rick

Susie

And just think: you might even meet a hot girl! `15:54`

而且你可以這麼想：去了還有可能認識正妹呢！

SEND »

10:28 📶 🔋

我的天啊！我兩天後有十頁的報告要交，而我現在才開始寫。

Tip due表達「到期」之意。

Jesus Christ! I have a 10-page paper due two days from now, and I am only starting on it.
10:28

Susie

Rick

Calm down. You need a hand?
10:29

冷靜點，你需要幫忙嗎？

Tip 實用片語，注意只有在口語用法中才能省略助動詞do。

需要，上一次交報告，教授說我的報告寫得不好，結果我重寫了兩次，他才終於收下報告。

I do. Last time, my professor told me my paper wasn't acceptable, and I had to rewrite it twice before he accepted it.
10:32

Susie

我真的很擔心他這次不會再那麼仁慈了。

This time, I am really worried he won't be so lenient.
10:33

Susie

Rick

What's the course?
10:34

是什麼課啊？

Tip 雖然有些時候可用class替換，但詢問特定課程要用course。

歷史270：古羅馬時代，修起來頗吃力的一堂課。

History 270: Ancient Rome. It's pretty demanding.
10:35

Susie

Rick

Are you having trouble finding sources for your research?
10:38

你是在找資料的時候有困難嗎？

SEND ≫

159

那也是問題之一，我去圖書館查了一大堆的書，但卻沒找到什麼實用的資料。

That's one of my problems. I've been to the library and checked out a pile of books, but I am having a hard time finding anything useful. **10:42**

Susie

Rick

Have you ever tried our library's electronic databases and e-journals? They are really excellent sources of information. **10:45**

你有找過圖書館的電子資料庫和電子期刊嗎？那些會是很好的資料來源。

沒有耶，要怎麼使用你說的資料庫啊？

No, how do I use them? **10:46**

Susie

Rick

Well, the databases are accessible through our library's website. You can ask the librarians for help. **10:49**

嗯，資料庫可以從圖書館的網站連結過去，你可以詢問館員。

Rick

I always get more than half of my sources from these online databases. You should give it a try. **10:52**

我總是可以從這些線上資料庫中，獲得一半以上的資料，你不妨試試。

好，我會試試，謝謝你的幫忙，還有什麼其他的建議嗎？

Ok, I will. Thanks for your help. Any other suggestions? **10:53**

Susie

Rick

How about next time not waiting so late to start writing your essay? **10:55**

下次別這麼晚才開始寫報告怎麼樣？

SEND »

3. 讀書會的分工閱讀

📖 Susie 2014/1/27

I just finished this week's study group session⊙. Once again, I found it more interesting than the actual class! Don't get me wrong, the professor is brilliant and his lectures⊙ reflect that. It's just that he can be a little boring and, more importantly, he focuses only on his area of research. Naturally, there are a number of other research areas out there, and it is only in my study group where I learn about them.

我剛結束這週的讀書會,再一次讓我覺得它比上課有趣多了!不要誤會我的意思,教授很優秀,上課的內容也充分反映出這一點,只是偶爾會有點無聊,更重要的是,教授只專注在他自己的研究領域,但是,值得研究的事物其實有很多,而這些我都只能在讀書會學到。

The next paper is due in a few weeks, so for our most recent meeting, we discussed the paper topics. Listening to others' topics and areas of research opened my eyes to the different interpretations⊙ people have of the class material. One member said she is focusing on feminist interpretations; another is interested in economic issues; and another wants to look at religion. Our professor never mentioned any of these! Needless to say, I am looking forward to reading their final drafts.

我們下一份報告再過幾星期就要交了,所以,在最近一次的讀書會上,我們討論了報告的題目,聽大家討論真的讓我大開眼界,因為每個人想做的主題都不同,對課堂上的內容也各有詮釋的觀點,有位同學說她會專注在女權主義方面的詮釋;有一位則對經濟議題感興趣;還有人想以宗教的觀點去分析,這些我們的教授都從未提過!不用說,我很期待能讀到他們最終完成的報告。

微網誌

4. 寫報告與上台報告

📖 Rick 2014/1/28

If I am honest with myself, the reason why I haven't joined a study group or taken a class in the humanities department is because I am very uncomfortable with the idea of sharing my thoughts with others. I am introspective⑪ with my thoughts. It is probably because I am deathly worried people will disagree with me, point out exactly why I am wrong, and even think I am stupid. I am much more comfortable in the sciences, working with facts, data, and equations⑫.

老實說，我不加入讀書會，也沒修人文學系課程的真正原因是，與他人分享想法這件事會讓我很不自在，我習慣把想法放在心裡反思，這可能是因為我非常擔心其他人不同意我的看法，怕他們指出我的錯誤，甚至擔心他們會認為我很笨，我還是覺得和事實、數據與方程式相處自在多了。

The reason I am a pre-medicine student on the way to becoming a doctor is because I want to help people. That's all. Later in my career, I may need to give lectures in front of large groups of people. I can accept that for two reasons: one, I know it will be something I only have to do a few times a year; and two, I will be presenting facts, not opinions or ideas. And I am not afraid of sharing facts with a large audience.

我之所以選擇醫科先修，決定往醫生這條路走，只是因為我想幫助別人而已，當然，成為醫生以後，我可能要在很多人面前發表演說，而我能接受這個的原因有兩個：第一，一年當中，我大概只需要發表個幾次而已；第二，那時候我只需要根據事實做報告就好，不需要分享意見或想法，如果是和大眾分享一些事實數據的話，我一點都不會感到害怕。

Word 單字	Meaning 字義	Usage 常見用法
1 **feedback** [`fid,bæk]	名 反饋	give feedback on 針對…提供意見 receive feedback from 從…得到意見
2 **stimulate** [`stɪmjə,let]	動 刺激；促進…的功能	stimulate economic growth 促進經濟 stimulate sb. into efforts 鼓勵…努力
3 **critical** [`krɪtɪk!]	形 緊要的；關鍵性的；批評的；批判的	the critical time 關鍵時刻 be critical of 對…表示不滿
4 **due** [dju]	名 應得之物；應付款 形 應支付的；到期的	due to 由於；歸因於 be due for promotion 應該要升職
5 **lenient** [`linjənt]	形 寬大的；仁慈的	be lenient towards 對…寬厚 the lenient disposal 寬大的處置
6 **database** [`detə,bes]	名 資料庫；數據庫	build an database 建立資料庫 a multimedia database 多媒體數據庫
7 **accessible** [æk`sɛsəb!]	形 可接近的；受到讚賞的	be accessible to pity 有同情心 an accessible novel 受歡迎的小説
8 **session** [`sɛʃən]	名 開會；會議；開庭期間；學期	in session 開會；開庭；上課 a bull session (美/俚)自由討論
9 **lecture** [`lɛktʃɚ]	名 演講；告誡 動 演講；講課	appear at lectures 出席講座 a lecture upon history 歷史講座
10 **interpretation** [ɪn,tɜprɪ`teʃən]	名 解釋；闡明；翻譯；口譯	to back one's interpretation 支持論述 an one-sided interpretation 片面解釋
11 **introspective** [,ɪntrə`spɛktɪv]	形 內省的；反思的；自省的	in an introspective mood 在自省中 be introspective about 自我反省
12 **equation** [ɪ`kweʃən]	名 方程式；相等；平衡；均衡	solve/work an equation 解方程式 the military equation 軍事上的均衡

出場人物：理科男Rick、文科女Susie

UNIT 2 課餘生活
Leisure Time ～上篇

11:39 🎈 📶 🔋

Susie

The student I tutor in English has great comprehension. `11:39`

我英文家教的學生理解力很強。

Tip have great comprehension是在強調「理解力卓越」的意思。

那麼你教的時候就不用解釋太多了，這種學生教起來肯定很容易。

Then you don't need to explain much to him. Must be an easy student to teach. `11:41`

Rick

Yeah, but the downside is that he loves to learn colloquial₀ language, and it's not easy to explain why that kind of language is not suitable for English class. `11:47`

是啊，缺點是他喜歡學口語英文，要解釋那為什麼不適合拿來做教材，不是件簡單的事。

Susie

嗯，我知道有些人喜歡學髒話的說法。

I know some people love to learn dirty words. `11:48`

Rick

It's not just that; it's vernacular₀ language in general. Think about Taiwan: students often write in Chinese vernacular. `11:51`

不僅如此，他們還會學方言，拿台灣來說，學生在寫文章的時候，也時常用到方言用字。

Susie

我懂你的意思，學生容易把他上課所學的與日常生活的用法混在一起。

Tip 生活化用法，朋友之間常用。

Ah, I get your point. Students tend to mix the information they learn with their daily life. `11:53`

Rick

Yeah, and that's not good for a beginner to learn a language. `11:54`

沒錯，而且這對初學者來說是不好的。

Susie

SEND ≫

Let's Chat In English Via APP • ⏻ •

11:39

還好我在教數學時，不會發生這種情形，數學公式沒有方言可用。

Fortunately, this never happens when I tutor in mathematics. There is no vernacular in math formulas. `11:57`

Rick

Lucky you! I need to make sure what he learns complies₃ with English grammar. `11:59`

Susie

你真幸運！我都得先確定他學到的符不符合英文文法。

Tip 口語用法，語氣較活潑。

And it's hard to clearly explain why a grammatically wrong phrase is used by so many people. `12:02`

Susie

而且，要解釋為什麼不合文法的片語還是繼續被使用，也很不容易。

你可以跟他說，這些文法不通的話之所以還被使用，是因為沒有人改正。

I think you can tell him it's something incorrect that no one has fixed. `12:04`

Rick

I tried to. But then he asked why people still use it, and I had no idea how to answer him. `12:07`

Susie

我試過了，接著他就問，那為什麼大家還是要用它呢？我完全不曉得該如何回答他。

這個嘛，就跟他說，有些人的英文不是在教室學，而是從家裡聽來的，這兩種英語本來就不同。

Well, just tell him because some people don't learn English in a classroom but at their homes. It's just different. `12:11`

Rick

SEND ≫

Let's Chat In English Via APP

165

21:15 📶 🔋

瑞克，聽說你又找了一份兼職工作，這是真的嗎？

Rick, I heard that you got another part-time job. Is that true? `21:15`

Susie

Rick

Yeah, I did. I work the night shift at a convenience store. `21:16`

沒錯，我在便利商店值大夜班。

Tip 舉凡商店、醫院…只要是值夜班，都可以用 work the night shift。

什麼？！你是不是瘋了？你整晚都在工作的話，怎麼有時間睡覺呢？

Tip 因為 insane 有「精神病」之意，所以較適合對熟人用。

What?! Are you insane④? How do you have time to sleep if you work all night long? `21:18`

Susie

Rick

I finish my tutoring⑤ job at 9:00 p.m., and my convenience store job starts at 11:00 p.m. That gives me two hours between the two jobs for a nap. `21:22`

我家教到晚上九點，十一點開始便利商店的工作，所以在那之前，我有兩個小時的時間小睡一下。

那點睡眠時間根本不夠，如果我是你，我就會把其中一個工作給辭掉。

That is way too little sleep. If I were you, I would quit one of those jobs. `21:24`

Susie

Rick

Honestly, I have no choice. I need to pay all my tuition by myself. `21:25`

坦白說，我沒有別的選擇，我得自己負擔學費。

你不知道可以申請助學貸款嗎？如果申請到的話，你就不用工作得這麼拼命了。

Don't you know you can apply for a student loan? If you got one, you wouldn't have to work so hard. `21:27`

Susie

SEND ▶▶

Rick

I know. I think it's a bad idea, though. What if I cannot find a job immediately after I graduate? How will I pay it off? `21:30`

這我知道，但我覺得助學貸款不是個好辦法，畢業後如果沒有馬上找到工作，那我要如何還貸款呢？

Rick

No, I would rather work hard now and have no debt when I graduate. `21:31`

我寧願現在辛苦一點，而不要一畢業就負債。

也是，現在失業率那麼高，助學貸款又只提供前兩年的免利息優惠。

Yeah. The unemployment rate is so high, and now student loans only have two years of free interest. `21:33`

Susie

Rick

Exactly. Alright, Susie, I'll talk to you later. I need to get some sleep before I go to work. `21:35`

沒錯，好了，蘇西，晚點再聊吧，工作前我得先去小睡一下。

好吧，好好照顧自己，記得有機會就好好睡一覺。

Tip get some real sleep是要對方好好睡，而不只是小睡一下。

Okay, take care of yourself. And get some real sleep! `21:36`

Susie

Rick

Thanks, but at the moment, I think that's impossible. `21:37`

謝了，但目前看起來，我是不可能有好好睡覺的機會了。

   SEND ≫

Let's Chat In English Via APP

167

1. 申請實習工作

📖 Rick 2014/2/1

A few days ago, my advisor told me that it would be a great idea to intern❼ this summer. He said an internship at a good company is the best way to get a head-start before graduating. When I went to the student services office, I saw so many other students who were also applying for summer internships. I guess it is general knowledge that if you gain experience now before you finish university, you will have a better chance of getting a good job.

前幾天我的指導教授跟我說，這個夏天去實習會是個很好的作法，他說，如果能取得在好公司實習的經驗，畢業後就有搶在起跑線上的優勢，當我去學生服務處時，看到很多學生都在申請暑期實習的機會，我想這大概是一般人共同的想法，大家都覺得，如果能在畢業前取得工作經驗，就比較有機會找到一份好工作。

I applied to a few different internships. One will be at a laboratory doing stem cell research. Another one will be at a media company that educates the public about how chemistry affects the world. I'm not so sure that I want this one, but it is the only paid internship I found. The last internship I applied for was another lab assistant❽ position. This one will be at a pharmaceutical❾ company, though. I hope I get the position at the stem cell lab, but they all seem interesting, so I'll probably be happy with whichever I get offered.

我申請了幾個不同的實習工作，一個是在實驗室裡做幹細胞研究；另一個是在媒體公司實習，教導大眾化學是如何影響這個世界，我不確定自己是否想要這一個，但它是我所找的實習工作當中，唯一有薪水的；我最後申請的是另一間實驗室的助理，那是一家製藥公司的職缺。我比較喜歡幹細胞實驗室的工作，但這些實習看起來都很有趣，所以無論哪一家願意錄用我，我都會很開心的。

9:40

 微網誌

2. 學校舉辦的大型餐會

Susie 2014/2/6

Last Saturday, I went to a big feast hosted by the university. It was great! I met students from the Art, Mathematics, and Communications departments. I met two students in particular whom I got along really well with. One was a guy named Dave, who told me he is on the debate team. He invited me to go watch a debate. I think I'll check it out. The other person I met was a boy named Kyle, who is in my Shakespeare class. Kyle seemed funny and nice. He said that maybe we could have coffee some time. I still can't believe it now. He asked me out on a date!

上個星期六,我去參加學校主辦的大型宴會,超棒的!我認識了藝術系、數學系、以及傳播系的學生,其中,有兩位學生和我處得特別好,一個是參加了辯論隊的男生,名叫戴夫,他邀請我去看辯論比賽,我想我應該會去看看。另一個是名叫凱爾的男生,他和我修同一堂莎士比亞課,凱爾風趣又善良,他說改天我們可以一起喝杯咖啡,我到現在都還不敢相信,他居然邀我去約會耶!

They had a massive spread at the feast. If you ask me, there was too much food. But that's not really a complaint, is it? The highlights were the sushi, caviar, and crab legs. I ate so much sushi that my stomach started to hurt. All in all, I had a fantastic time with some great food and new friends. And best of all, I got asked out on a date!

他們真的是準備了一場盛宴,如果你問我的話,吃的食物實在太多了,但這話並不能算是抱怨,對吧?最值得一提的是壽司、魚子醬,以及蟹腳,我吃了超多壽司,吃到胃都痛了,總之,我度過了很愉快的時光,享受了美食,也交到一些新朋友,最棒的是,有男生約我去約會呢!

APP 單字動態看板 Vocabulary Billboard

Word 單字	Meaning 字義	Usage 常見用法
1 colloquial [kə`lokwɪəl]	形 口語的；會話的；用於口語的	a colloquial expression 口語表達 in colloquial usage 以口語用法
2 vernacular [və`nækjələ]	名 方言；白話 形 方言的；白話的	in vernacular writing 以白話文寫作 a vernacular poet 方言詩人
3 comply [kəm`plaɪ]	動 依從；順從	comply with the law 遵守法律 refuse to comply 拒絕遵從
4 insane [ɪn`sen]	形 精神錯亂的；荒唐的；瘋狂的	go insane from sth. 因某事發瘋 be insane on 在…上是荒謬的
5 tutor [`tjutɚ]	名 家庭教師 動 指導；輔導	study under a tutor 在指導下學習 tutor for one's living 當家教謀生
6 debt [dɛt]	名 負債；借款	leave debts behind one 死後留債 the active debt 有息借款
7 intern [ɪn`tɝn]	名 實習生 動 做實習生	work as an intern 以實習身分工作 with intern experience 具實習經驗
8 assistant [ə`sɪstənt]	名 助理；助手 形 助理的；有幫助的	a teaching assistant 助教 an assistant to …的助手
9 pharmaceutical [ˌfɑrmə`sjutɪkl̩]	形 藥的；配藥的；製藥的	pharmaceutical safety 藥品安全 a pharmaceutical formula 藥劑配方
10 communication [kəˌmjunə`keʃən]	名 傳達；交流；通信；傳染	hold communication with 保持聯繫 a communication satellite 通訊衛星
11 debate [dɪ`bet]	名 辯論；爭論 動 爭論；與…辯論	be beyond debate 無可爭議 close a debate 終止辯論
12 massive [`mæsɪv]	形 巨大的；大量的；厚實的	make massive efforts 極為努力 on a massive scale 大規模的

UNIT 2 課餘生活
Leisure Time～下篇

085 MP3

🔒 ✏️ 22:45 📶 ▮▮▮

◀ APP CHAT **3** 餐會過後

Susie

Hey, I just got back from the feast❶. `22:45`

嘿，我從學校舉辦的餐會回來了。

餐會怎麼樣？有認識你喜歡的人嗎？
Tip 使用go詢問事情進展是比較生活化的口語用法。

Oh, how did it go? Did you meet anyone you like? `22:48`

Rick

Susie

I saw this boy Kyle from my Shakespeare class. I was surprised when he started talking to me, and he even asked me out for coffee. `22:54`

我遇見跟我一起上莎士比亞課的一個男生，凱爾，當他開口跟我說話時，我嚇了一跳，而且他還邀我喝咖啡耶！

真的嗎？！他約你出去？
Tip ask out是邀請約會的意思，更完整的說法會加上on a date，口語上常省略。

Really?! He asked you out? `22:55`

Rick

Susie

Yeah. I think it's hard to believe, too. I was so intimidated❷ by him that I never made eye contact❸ with him once in class. And he asked me out! `22:58`

是啊，我也不敢相信，我看到他就會緊張，所以在課堂上從來沒跟他有眼神接觸，結果他竟然約我出去！

哇！真替你高興耶。
Tip good for you帶有祝賀之意，肯定他人作爲時也會用到。

Wow. Good for you. `22:59`

Rick

Susie

Thanks. To tell you the truth, I am a bit worried about the date. `23:01`

謝謝你，老實説，我有點擔心這次的約會。

SEND ▶▶

Let's Chat In English Via APP ● ⏻ ●

171

22:45

Rick

你就這樣想：他可能只是想跟你討論莎士比亞課的事情！

Just think of it this way: he probably wants to talk about the Shakespeare class you two are in together! `23:04`

Susie

Thanks for ruining my expectations. Some friend you are... `23:06`

是喔，感謝你澆我冷水，真是我的好朋友…

Tip 帶有反諷的意味，適合用在好友身上。

開個玩笑嘛！你可以問你姊啊，她不是對打扮很有一套嗎？

Hey, I am just kidding. You can ask your sister to help you with your make-up. She is really good at it, right? `23:09`

Rick

Susie

Can I not ask? She will do nothing but mock. me. `23:10`

可以不要嗎？在那之前我一定會先被她調侃到不行。

哈哈，也是啦，但她才了解什麼打扮最適合你。

Haha, that's probably true. However, she does know the kind of make-up that suits you best. `23:12`

Rick

Susie

I know, so I will still go ask her to help me. Anyway, how about next time you go to the feast with me? `23:15`

我知道，所以我還是會請她幫忙的，先不說我姊，下次我們一起去參加餐會怎麼樣？

聽起來滿有趣的，下次也讓我知道吧，我會再看看是否有空參加。

Tip 口語適合的說法。

That sounds like something. Let me know next time, and I will see if I am free. `23:17`

Rick

SEND »

Let's Chat In English Via APP

172

◀ APP CHAT **4** 討論寒假計畫

12:15 🛜 ‖ ▥▥

嘿，瑞克，你期末考結束了嗎？

Tip 口語用法，be done with 表達「完成、結束」之意。

Hey, Rick, are you done with your finals? `12:15`

Susie

Rick

Almost, I still have an exam next Monday. Then I will be all done. What about you? `12:17`

差不多了，我下週一還有一科考試，然後就結束了，你呢？

我最後一份報告下週二交，結束之後，我就會直奔機場。

The deadline for my last paper is next Tuesday. After that, I am heading straight to the airport. `12:19`

Susie

Rick

Where are you going? `12:20`

你打算要去哪裡啊？

香港，我家人和我準備到香港渡假。

Hong Kong. My family and I are spending the holidays there. `12:22`

Susie

Rick

Cool, how many days are you gonna stay there? `12:23`

真酷！你們會在那裡待幾天？

Tip gonna 是 going to 的口語用法，正式書寫文章不要這麼用。

大約十天左右，你呢？寒假有什麼計畫嗎？

Tip 實用片語 the winter break，和 vacation 相比，用 break 更加生活化。

About ten days. What about you? Any plans for the winter break? `12:26`

Susie

   SEND ≫

12:15

Rick

Nothing much really. I will go back to Kaohsiung and enjoy some time with my family and maybe catch up with some friends. `12:30`

沒什麼確切的計畫，我會回高雄，花點時間陪家人，也許還會和一些朋友聯絡吧。

Rick

I have been looking forward to sleeping late since the second week of school! `12:33`

從開學的第二週開始，我就一直待著每天可以睡到很晚的日子來臨。

聽起來很棒啊，我們偶爾也需要充充電。

Tip pamper oneself 有「善待自己」之意。

That sounds good. We all need to pamper₆ ourselves once in a while. `12:35`

Susie

有時懶散一下，不用擔心作業的繳交日、約會之類的，這樣也不錯啊。

It's nice to be lazy and not have to worry about deadlines, appointments, and stuff like that. `12:38`

Susie

Rick

Tell me about it! Too bad winter break is only three weeks. `12:39`

說得對極了！可惜寒假只有三個星期而已。

Tip 很多情境下都可以使用，表示「同意、附和對方的話」，不能從字面去理解。

三星期夠長了，你不會想要休息太久的，否則之後就又要重新調整作息時間了。

Three weeks is a long time. You don't want to take too long of a break. If you do, you will have to readjust all over again. `12:42`

Susie

Rick

Yeah, you're right. But when I think about it, three weeks just doesn't feel like enough. Oh, well. I'll see you next semester. `12:48`

你說的是沒錯，但每次想到寒假，就覺得三個星期好短，喔，那就下學期見了。

SEND »

Let's Chat In English Via APP

174

微網誌

🔒 ✏️

10:36 📶 ▮▮

3. 寒假出國旅遊

📖 Susie 2014/2/20

I just got back from my trip to Hong Kong with the family. It was my first time there, and I have to say, I was quite impressed. There were so many people, but everything was clean. I heard English being spoken everywhere. Indians, Americans, Chinese: everyone was conversing₀ in English. I was surprised at first, but I quickly started taking advantage of the situation and practiced English every chance I got.

我剛和家人從香港渡假回來,這是我第一次去那裡,我必須說,香港給我很深的印象,雖然人潮很多,但所到之處都很乾淨。而且,無論到哪裡,都可以聽到英文,印度人、美國人、以及中國人,每個人都用英語交談,起初我感到很訝異,但我很快就開始善用這個情境,把握每個練習講英語的機會。

One complaint I had – in fact, my entire family had – was the customer service in some areas. One server at the restaurant we went to was incredibly rude. He didn't care a bit about making our experience enjoyable. It was all grunts₀ and head-shaking when we ordered, and, if we asked a question, he acted like we were imposing₀ on him, like it wasn't his job to serve us! Other than that, I had a great time exploring the city and taking in the sights and sounds.

但是,我要抱怨一件事(事實上,我家人也都和我一樣不滿),那就是部分地方的服務態度不佳,我們去的餐廳裡,有一位侍者的態度真是難以置信的無禮,他一點都不在意我們是否會有愉快的用餐經驗,我們點菜時,他不是嘀咕個不停,就是搖頭,如果我們問了問題,他就表現出一副我們要求過多的態度,好像服務並非他的工作似的!不過,除了這點之外,我度過很愉快的時光,探索了這個城市,也體驗到許多視覺與聽覺上的享受。

🔒 ✍️ 📝　　　　　　　　　　　　13:27 📶 📊 🔋

  微網誌 **4. 與家族共度春節**

📖 Rick 2014/2/21

Spending my break at home was just what I needed. The first few days, I was practically comatose⑩. I was so exhausted from final exams. I slept all day and all night, only getting out of bed to eat something or go to the bathroom. After I caught up on sleep, I was finally able to spend some time playing video games, watching movies, reading manga, and spending time with my family.

寒假待在家休息正是我需要的，假期開始的前幾天，我都在昏睡，準備期末考真的很累人，所以我簡直是不分日夜地昏睡，只有下床吃東西或是上洗手間而已，在補了睡眠後，我才終於有精神玩電動、看電影、看漫畫、以及陪家人。

I was a little disappointed, though, that many of my high school friends did not come back for Chinese New Year. Most decided to travel to Thailand, Vietnam, or the Philippines. After seeing the pictures they posted on FACEBOOK, I can't say I blame⑪ them. It looked like they spent the entire time at the beach, swimming, snorkelling, and sunbathing. I am a little jealous⑫, of course, but I still think coming home was the right thing to do. I hadn't been home the entire semester, and my family would have been upset if I had chosen to spend my break abroad with my friends instead of at home with them.

然而，令我有點落寞的是，我許多高中的朋友都沒有回來過春節，大部分的人都去了泰國、越南，以及菲律賓渡假，看到他們把渡假的照片貼在臉書上，我也不能說什麼，看起來他們大部分的時間都在海邊游泳、浮潛，以及做日光浴，我當然有點嫉妒，但我還是覺得回家是正確的，我整個學期都沒回家，如果我連寒假都選擇與朋友出國，沒有和家人一起過，他們一定會不高興的。

Word 單字	Meaning 字義	Usage 常見用法
1 feast [fist]	名 盛宴；筵席 動 盛宴款待	a feast for the eyes 賞心悅目的事 hold a feast 舉行宴會
2 intimidate [ɪnˋtɪmə͵det]	動 威嚇；脅迫	be intimidated into silence 嚇得不敢出聲 intimidate sb. with sth. 以⋯使某人懾服
3 contact [ˋkɑntækt]	名 接觸；聯繫 形 接觸的	break into contact 突然接觸 wear contact lenses 戴隱形眼鏡
4 mock [mɑk]	動 嘲弄；嘲笑 形 假裝的	mock at sb./sth. 嘲笑 with mock severity 故作嚴厲
5 straight [stret]	形 筆直的；純粹的 副 直接地；坦率地	be straight with me 對我說實話 be straight in one's dealings 待人老實
6 pamper [ˋpæmpɚ]	動 縱容；姑息	pamper a child 縱容小孩 pamper one's appetite 吃個痛快
7 converse [kənˋvɜs]	動 交談；講話	converse with sb. in English 以英文交談 converse with ease 毫無拘束地聊天
8 grunt [grʌnt]	名 嘀咕聲 動 咕噥著說	give/utter a grunt 咕噥一聲 do sth. with a grunt 咕噥地去做
9 impose [ɪmˋpoz]	動 把⋯強加於； 利用；欺騙	impose oneself as 自稱為 impose oneself upon sb. 硬纏著某人
10 comatose [ˋkɑmə͵tos]	形 昏睡狀態的	feel comatose 感覺昏昏欲睡的 be in a comatose state 處於昏迷狀態
11 blame [blem]	名 指責；責任 動 責備；指責	blame sth. on me 把某事歸咎於我 be blamed for sth. 對某事負責
12 jealous [ˋdʒɛləs]	形 妒忌的；吃醋的	be jealous of sth./sb. 忌妒某事或某人 be insanely jealous 忌妒得發瘋

UNIT 3

畢業交叉口
The Graduation～上篇

 23:12 📶

◀ APP CHAT **1** 進修還是就職？

時間過得真快，真不敢相信我們就要畢業了。

Tip 講述「時間快到」的接近感，可用be about to表達。

> Time has gone by so fast. I can't believe we're about to graduate. `23:12`
>
> **Susie**

 Rick

> Me either. Did you know the current unemployment rate has risen to its highest point in decades? `23:15`

我也不敢相信，你知道目前的失業率是數十年來最高的嗎？

是啊，我聽說了，我不確定自己要繼續深造還是立即就業，你呢？

> Yeah, I heard. I am not sure whether I should pursue my education further or begin working. How about you? `23:18`
>
> **Susie**

 Rick

> I am still planning on becoming a doctor. After all, I did get a degree in pre-medicine. `23:20`

我依然準備當醫生，畢竟，我已經拿到醫科先修的學位了。

這我知道，真不曉得你的成績怎麼能這麼好，大家都知道醫科先修很難唸。

> I know that. I just don't know how you got such good grades. Everyone knows pre-medicine is really hard. `23:23`
>
> **Susie**

 Rick

> Because it's what I want to do. You know I have always wanted to help people. `23:25`

因為那是我想做的事，你知道我一直都想幫助別人的。

決定就業方向真的讓我很頭痛。

Tip 口語表達give sb. a headache，這裡的headache為抽象的「傷腦筋」。

> Making a career choice is really giving me a headache. `23:27`
>
> **Susie**

  SEND ≫

23:12

APP CHAT 1

進修還是就職？

Rick: How about becoming an English teacher? You were majoring in foreign languages, right? 23:30

當英文老師怎麼樣？你是唸外文系的，不是嗎？

Susie: Before, yeah, but I changed my major to Philosophy❷, remember? 23:32

之前是，但後來我轉唸哲學系了，記得嗎？

Tip 轉系的動詞可直接用change，後面加上to與轉入的學系，意思更完整。

Rick: Oh, right. Sorry, I forgot for a minute. So what did you study in your classes? 23:34

喔對，抱歉，一時間忘了你轉過系，那你在哲學系都學了些什麼呢？

Susie: I learned a lot about the ideas of individual❸ philosophers like Plato and Kant. 23:36

我學到很多哲學家的思想，像是柏拉圖和康德等等。

Susie: And I also developed my critical thinking abilities. I loved it. 23:38

而且，哲學還增進了我批判思維的能力，我很喜歡這一點。

Susie: My worry now is that a degree in Philosophy will not be useful in the job market. 23:40

我現在只擔心哲學系的文憑對找工作沒幫助。

Rick: I have no idea about that. All I know is what I want to do, and that is to help people get better. 23:42

這我就不清楚了，我只知道我想做的事，就是幫助別人過得更好。

SEND

20:46 📶 📶 🔋

嘿，蘇西，我今天去參加一個關於心血管疾病的座談會。

Hey, Susie, I went to a seminar₄ on cardiovascular₅ diseases today. `20:46`

Rick

Yeah? How did it go? `20:47`

是嗎？那座談會怎麼樣？

Susie

這一次的座談會很棒！有我們學校著名學者的兩場精彩演講。

It was an awesome event, with two wonderful presentations by distinguished₆ scholars from our university. `20:51`

Rick

參加座談會的還包括一些醫學院學生，以及其他來自著名機構的教授。

The full panel also had medical students and professors from other famous institutions. `20:53`

Rick

Sounds terrific. You must have learned a lot. `20:54`

聽起來超棒的，你一定學到不少東西。

Tip 口語用法中，常省略主詞it，但正式的書寫英文最好不要省略。

Susie

的確如此，其實我能參加真的很幸運，因為我忘了回覆邀請函，而且，這場座談會並沒有對外開放。

Indeed. I was lucky to get in, though, because I forgot to RSVP to the event. And it wasn't open to the public. `20:59`

Rick

Really? Well, how were you able to get in, then? `21:00`

真的嗎？那你是怎麼入場的啊？

Susie

SEND ≫

還好，我的朋友趕不上參加的時間，他人很好，把他的邀請函讓給我。

Tip can't make it表示「來不及」，通常隱含一個到期時限。

Luckily, my friend couldn't make it. He was nice enough to give his invitation letter to me. `21:03`

Rick

I see. Was it more like a lecture or a seminar? `21:04`

Susie

原來如此，所以這場座談是講座的形式？還是正式的研討會呢？

Tip 口語英文，比understand更常使用。

是一場互動式研討會，講者會與聽眾對話，討論一些罕見的心血管疾病。

It was an interactive seminar. The speakers conversed with the audience on some rare cardiovascular diseases. `21:07`

Rick

然後他們會留時間給聽眾發問，我聽到很多深刻的見解。

Then, they gave the audience time to ask them questions. There were a lot of insightful ideas. `21:09`

Rick

Cool, I wish the School of Liberal Arts would have events like this. `21:10`

Susie

酷，真希望文學院也能舉辦類似的研討會。

我相信他們會辦的，也許你應該問一下你的教授。

I am sure they do. Maybe you should ask one of your professors. `21:12`

Rick

Ah, of course. I'll also try to check the bulletin board in the Liberal Arts Building more often. `21:14`

Susie

那當然，我也會常去查看文學院大樓的公佈欄的。

  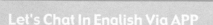 SEND ≫

Let's Chat In English Via APP • ⏻ •

181

1. 參觀就業博覽會

Susie 2014/3/22

I spent several hours last weekend speaking with various company representatives at my college's summer job fair. At the beginning of the day, I felt a bit nervous. Seeing the number of booths that had been set up was overwhelming[9]. However, seeing how friendly everyone was made me relax. I was able to work up enough courage to go up to a few booths and introduce myself. The representatives were all very nice and cordial[10], answering all of my questions with a lot of enthusiasm. If they were pretending to be interested in me and in promoting their companies, then they were doing a good job because they all seemed so genuine.

　上週末我去了學校舉辦的暑期就業博覽會，並花了幾個小時的時間與各家公司的代表談話，剛到的時候，看到那麼多公司攤位，讓我很緊張，但因為每個人都很友善，所以讓我的心情放鬆了不少，也因此能鼓起勇氣到幾個攤位做自我介紹，攤位的代表都很友善、充滿熱忱，熱心地回答我所提出的問題，如果說他們對我的興趣與宣傳公司的行為都是裝出來的，那麼他們真的是箇中高手，因為表現得實在太自然了。

I'm happy to say that, upon leaving the job fair, I had scheduled three interviews and given two other companies my e-mail address. If all goes well, one of these three interviews will land me a job after graduation. Since the job fair, I have been feeling much more positive about my post-graduation life!

　我能很高興地說，離開就業博覽會後，有三家公司找我去面試，我也留了電子信箱給另外兩家公司，如果一切順利，三場面試中，就會有一家公司要我畢業後去上班，在參觀了就業博覽會之後，我對畢業後的出路有了更正面的期待！

16:28

 2. 短期出國進修

Rick 2014/3/29

I never considered studying abroad before my academic advisor suggested it. He told me I have been too focused on my schoolwork and my future career and needed to have some other experiences. So I passed on the internship and came to California on a student exchange program. Although my time here is short, it has been amazing so far. In fact, the past weeks have been the most amazing experience of my life!

在教授給我建議之前,我從來沒想過出國進修的事,他認為我太專注於課業與未來的出路,需要增加其他的經驗,因此,我放棄實習機會,來到美國加州做短期的交換學生,雖然我在加州的時間還不長,但到目前為止,這裡的一切都很棒,老實說,過去幾個星期的生活已經成為我人生中最美好的經歷了!

California is beautiful! The people are kind and the beaches are breathtaking. Every day I learn some new words, which I practice by walking around the town and finding friendly people to have conversations with. Talking with them has given me a chance to learn some slang words. Learning slang is fun, but the most important thing for me is using every opportunity I can to become fluent. As an aspiring doctor, I must be able to communicate in English as it is essential for treating foreign patients in Taiwan.

加州是個美麗的地方!這裡的人很友善,海灘的美令人嘆為觀止,我每天都能學到新單字,我會到鎮上走走,找些友善的人對話,練習學到的單字,另外,跟當地人聊天可以學到英文俚語,學俚語很有趣,但對我來說,最重要的是把握每一個能讓我英文變流利的機會,既然我這麼想做醫生,就必須能用英文與人溝通,這樣才能替在台灣的外國患者看診。

Let's Chat In English Via APP

183

Word 單字	Meaning 字義	Usage 常見用法
1 decade [`dɛked]	名 十；十年	in the present decade 在這十年內 for decades on end 數十年如一日
2 philosophy [fə`lɑsəfɪ]	名 哲學；原理；人生觀	a moral philosophy 倫理學 a philosophy of life 人生哲學觀
3 individual [ˌɪndə`vɪdʒʊəl]	名 個人；個體 形 個體的；單獨的	an individual's behavior 個人行為 give sb. individual help 給…個別幫助
4 seminar [`sɛməˌnɑr]	名 研究班；研討班； 專題討論會	a seminar schedule 研討會時程表 a seminar on 關於…的討論會
5 cardiovascular [ˌkɑrdɪo`væskjʊlə]	形 (病等)心血管的； 侵襲心血管的	cardiovascular disease 心血管疾病 cardiovascular efficiency 心肺功能
6 distinguish [dɪ`stɪŋgwɪʃ]	動 區別；識別； 使顯出特色	distinguish A from B 區分 A 與 B be distinguished for 以…著稱
7 interactive [ˌɪntə`æktɪv]	形 相互作用的	interactive teaching 互動式教學 be closely interactive with 密切互動
8 insightful [`ɪnˌsaɪtfəl]	形 具洞察力的； 有深刻見解的	an insightful critic 具洞察力的評論家 be acutely insightful 有敏銳的觀察力
9 overwhelming [ˌovə`hwɛlmɪŋ]	形 壓倒的；勢不可擋的	an overwhelming majority 絕大多數 an overwhelming defeat 壓倒性勝利
10 cordial [`kɔrdʒəl]	名 甘露酒 形 熱忱的；衷心的	a cordial reception 熱忱的招待 be cordial to everyone 真誠待人
11 aspiring [ə`spaɪrɪŋ]	形 高聳的；有志氣的； 有強烈願望的	be aspiring to become 有抱負成為 an aspiring scholar 有抱負的學者
12 essential [ɪ`sɛnʃəl]	名 要素；要點；必需品 形 必要的；本質的	essentials to health 健康的要素 the essential features 基本特徵

UNIT 3

畢業交叉口
The Graduation～下篇

093 MP3

Susie

It's been two months since you went to study in California. Is everything ok? `10:30`

你去加州唸書已經兩個月了，一切都還好吧？

Tip 不管對親近的朋友或長輩都可用的一句話。

超棒的！這裡的天氣、食物、以及文化，所有的一切對我而言都很新鮮、有趣。

It's great. The climate, food, and the culture here are all new and exciting. `10:32`

Rick

Susie

Wow, so it must be difficult to concentrate on your studies. `10:34`

哇！如此一來，要專心唸書肯定很難了。

Tip 實用片語concentrate on one's studies，為比較正經的說法。

那還用說！光拿食物來說，就很令人吃驚了，到處都有壽司餐廳以及道地的墨西哥美食。

Tell me about it. The food, for example, is amazing. There are sushi restaurants and authentic① Mexican food everywhere. `10:36`

Rick

還有超棒的漢堡餐廳、牛排餐廳以及義大利麵餐廳，一應俱全！

Also, there are great hamburger restaurants, steak restaurants, pasta restaurants, everything! `10:38`

Rick

Susie

That sounds awesome②. If I were you, I would definitely go to a new restaurant every day. `10:43`

聽起來真棒，如果我是你，肯定會忍不住每天換餐廳的。

我同意，但天天吃美食導致我的成績退步、荷包大失血，這就是為什麼我從上個月開始較常在學校自助餐廳吃飯的原因。

I agree. But it is hurting my grades as well as my wallet. That's why last month I started eating at the school cafeteria more. `10:47`

Rick

　　　　　　　　　　　SEND »

Let's Chat In English Via APP　•　　•

10:30

Susie

It must be hard going from fancy restaurant food to cafeteria food. 10:49

從高級餐廳變成到自助餐店用餐，這種落差肯定教人很難適應。

那還用說，在學校的自助餐廳，我有時都吃不下飯，因為所有的食物看起來都很倒胃口。

Oh, god yes. I sometimes don't eat anything at the cafeteria because everything looks so unappetizing. 10:51

Rick

Susie

You mentioned the culture, too. What's different? 10:52

你剛剛有提到文化，和我們這裡有什麼不一樣嗎？

這邊大多數的商店在晚上六七點左右就打烊，而酒吧在凌晨兩點停止營業。

Tip 對時間不確定的時候，就加上 around，表「大概」之意。

Well, most stores close around 6 or 7 p.m., and bars all close at 2 a.m. 10:54

Rick

Susie

2 a.m.? That's so early! 10:55

凌晨兩點就打烊嗎？這也太早了吧！

是啊，所以我朋友跟我都會提早出門（大概八或九點），以便在打烊前有更多的時間待在酒吧。

Yeah. My friends and I have started to go out early – like 8 or 9 – in order to spend more time at the bars before we are forced to go home. 10:58

Rick

  SEND »

Let's Chat In English Via APP

186

8:00

Rick

Hey Susie, you know what? Today's discussion in class really shocked me. 8:00

嘿，蘇西，你知道嗎？今天課堂上的討論真的嚇到我了。

> **Tip** 注意class前面不加冠詞，in class 才能表示「上課時」。

Rick

Several students challenged the professor, expressing₃ their doubts about his lecture. 8:02

有幾個學生竟然挑戰起教授，表達他們對上課內容的質疑。

哇，那真是令人驚訝…這種事情在台灣可沒怎麼聽說過。

Wow, that's surprising...and pretty much unheard of in Taiwan. 8:03

Susie

Rick

Unheard of? I don't think so. I think it does happen in Taiwan, but not so much. 8:05

沒聽說過？我不這麼認為，我覺得台灣也有同樣的情景，只是沒有那麼多而已。

> **Tip** 語氣較直接，表達「不認同」。

是啊，我們有時候會擔心如果去挑戰教授，就可能會被當掉。

Yeah, we sometimes are afraid of failing the class if we challenge the professor. 8:06

Susie

Rick

Actually, I think universities in Taiwan have atmospheres that encourage independent thinking. For instance, many have group discussions. 8:09

事實上，台灣的大學裡已經有鼓勵學生獨立思考的氣氛，比方說，很多課程都有小組討論這樣的設計。

當學生開始獨立思考的時候，上課就會變得更有趣。

Class is more interesting when students get to think for themselves. 8:11

Susie

 SEND ▶▶

Let's Chat In English Via APP

187

不過，大多數的台灣學生還是依賴教授的指導，跟你那裡的風氣還是不同吧？

However, most students in Taiwan still look to their professors for guidance. That is still different from where you are, right? 8:14

Susie

Yeah. Also, in addition to disagreeing with the professors, the students here will also have disputes④ among themselves. 8:17

是啊，除了不同意教授的想法外，這裡的學生們之間也會辯論。

Rick

所以，那裡的每個人都靜不下來囉？

So everyone is really boisterous⑤ over there? 8:18

Susie

Most are. Oh, and professors will sometimes try to spark⑥ debates among their students. 8:20

大部分學生是，而且教授有時還會試著去挑起學生之間的辯論。

Tip spark表達「激發」之意。

Rick

為什麼？那樣他們就不用教得那麼辛苦，上起課來比較輕鬆？

Why? So that they don't need to teach or something? And it's less work for them? 8:23

Susie

It's completely the opposite of that. They work hard to get their students thinking for themselves. 8:27

正好相反，教授會認真地引導學生們獨立思考。

Rick

我明白了，和我們這裡的風格很不一樣呢！

I see. That seems so different from the style here. 8:29

Susie

 [   ] SEND »

3. 國外的溫馨節慶

📖 Rick 2014/4/3

One of my American friends, John, invited me to his home and church for Easter. I learned about Christmas and Thanksgiving and why Americans celebrate₇ them when I was younger, but I am not really familiar with Easter. John told me it is the day Jesus Christ rose from the dead. It is apparently₈ the most important day for Christians. Christmas is important, too, but Easter is the most important day of the year.

　　我美國朋友當中一位叫約翰的同學邀請我到他家及教會過復活節,小時候,我就學到聖誕節和感恩節的故事,所以了解美國人之所以會在這兩個節日大肆慶祝的原因,但我對復活節就不是很熟悉了。約翰告訴我,復活節是耶穌基督復活的日子,對基督徒來說,那很顯然是最重要的一個日子,聖誕節當然也重要,但復活節才是一年當中最重要的一天。

I met John on the Saturday before Easter. He took me to his house, and I shared a huge meal with him and his family. Sunday morning, we all went to church. It was my first time in a church, and I have got to say I was both impressed and intimidated. It was a huge, beautiful building, packed full of people! The one thing I could not understand about Easter was the Easter bunny and the candy. What does a big bunny and candy have to do with Jesus' death and resurrection₉?

　　我在復活節前的那個星期六與約翰碰面,他帶我去他家,我和他及他的家人吃了頓大餐,星期日早上,我們一起去了教堂。這是我第一次上教堂,我必須說,教堂令我印象深刻,讓人肅然起敬,那座教堂是一座巨大、出色的建築,而且裡面還擠滿了人!有件關於復活節的事,我一直想不明白,就是復活節兔子及糖果,大兔子和糖果與耶穌的死亡和復活究竟有什麼關連呢?

4. 所學與應用

📖 Susie 2014/4/8

I know majoring in philosophy isn't the most practical choice. I could have studied law, economics, business, or a number of other majors with clear job paths after graduation. Even now, looking back, I would still major in philosophy. I believe education should be about learning and growing as a person and not just making you employable. From my studies, I gained a great understanding of the world of ideas, became a much better critical thinker, and challenged my preconceptions. Only in the liberal arts would I have been able to do this.

　　我明白哲學並不是最實用的主修，我可以唸法律、經濟、商業，或對畢業後找工作比較有幫助的科系，但是，即便回到過去，我仍然會選擇唸哲學系，我始終相信教育應該涉及一個人的學習和成長，而不只是就業的工具而已。藉由哲學系的課程，我理解更多哲學界的知識、也成為一個更懂得獨立思考的人、挑戰了自己原有的偏見，這些都只有在文科的領域中才能做到。

I am confident that what I learned will be helpful in whatever job I find. Being able to think and write clearly are things that jobs can't teach. Potential employers should be able to recognize that and see me as a good employee. Then, they can train me in whatever skills I need for the job. I am confident specific skills like photoshopping are much easier to teach than something general like critical thinking.

　　我相信不管日後我找到什麼工作，所學的知識必定能有所幫助，清楚的思考邏輯與條理分明的寫作能力並非工作能教的，那些可能雇用我的老闆應該能賞識這份能力，並視我為好員工，再針對我工作所需的技術加以培訓，和抽象如批判思維的能力相比，我相信圖像處理之類的特定技術教起來會容易得多。

Word 單字	Meaning 字義	Usage 常見用法
1 **authentic** [ɔ`θɛntɪk]	形 可信的；真正的；可靠的	an authentic report 可靠的報告 an authentic manuscript 真正的手稿
2 **awesome** [`ɔsəm]	形 有威嚴的；可怕的；令人敬畏的	face an awesome task 面臨驚人挑戰 look awesome in 穿…很好看
3 **express** [ɪk`sprɛs]	名 快遞；快車 動 表達；快遞	air express 航空快運的包裹 express oneself freely 暢所欲言
4 **dispute** [dɪ`spjut]	名 爭論；爭執 動 爭論；對…質疑	under dispute 在爭論中 an industrial dispute 勞資糾紛
5 **boisterous** [`bɔɪstərəs]	形 喧鬧的；愛鬧的；猛烈的；狂暴的	a boisterous student 愛鬧的學生 a boisterous wind 暴風
6 **spark** [spɑrk]	動 發動；點燃；發出火花	spark a revolt 策劃發起反叛 spark off 導致
7 **celebrate** [`sɛlə͵bret]	動 慶祝；頌揚	celebrate sth. for 因…讚頌某物 celebrate sth. pompously 盛大地慶祝
8 **apparently** [ə`pærəntlɪ]	副 顯然地；表面上；似乎	be apparently essential 顯然必要 be apparently unharmed 顯然沒受傷
9 **resurrection** [͵rɛzə`rɛkʃən]	名 復活；復興；重新啟用	the resurrection of sth. …的重建 beyond resurrection 無法挽救
10 **preconception** [͵prikən`sɛpʃən]	名 預料；先入之見；偏見	without preconceptions 沒有偏見 an effect of preconception 偏見影響
11 **potential** [pə`tɛnʃəl]	名 可能性；潛力；潛能 形 潛在的；可能的	commercial potential 商業潛力 show one's potential 展現潛能
12 **recognize** [`rɛkəg͵naɪz]	動 承認；確認；識別；認識	recognize A as B 承認 A 是 B be recognized for 因…而得到承認

UNIT 4 職場新鮮人
Find A Job～上篇

 097 MP3

16:30 📶

🔒 ⬆ ✏

◀ APP CHAT **1** 五花八門的求職管道

蘇西，你最近都在忙些什麼事情呢？

Susie, what have you been doing recently? 16:30

 Rick

Well, I've been busy looking for a job. 16:31

 Susie

我一直在忙著找工作。

Tip 「忙著找工作」的英語：用完成式能表達「最近一直」之意。

喔，那工作找得怎麼樣了？

Tip 口語用法，注意本句採用的動詞 hunt（找）與go（找得如何）。

Oh, how's the job hunting going? 16:32

 Rick

I haven't found a job that I'm qualified[1] for yet. I am beginning to get worried. 16:35

 Susie

目前為止，我還沒找到可以勝任的工作，我開始在擔心了。

試過網路上的求職網站嗎？你可以上傳履歷，然後舒服地在家瀏覽工作機會。

Have you tried any job sites on the Internet? You can post your resume and browse for a job from the comfort[2] of your home. 16:39

 Rick

I'm too afraid of scams and frauds[3] to use those websites. 16:40

 Susie

我很害怕網路上的求職陷阱以及詐騙事件。

I have heard too many horror stories. And you? Have you applied to any medical schools? 16:42

 Susie

我聽過太多可怕的事了，你呢？申請醫學院了嗎？

 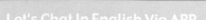 SEND ▶▶

16:30

當然，我們一畢業，我就向醫學院提出申請，我的錄取信一星期前才剛寄到。

Yes, I applied to the medical schools right after we graduated. My acceptance letter came just a week ago. 16:44

Rick

Susie

Congratulations! That's awesome. As for myself, I am beginning to think a headhunter might help. 16:47

恭喜！那真是太棒了，至於我嘛，我在想人力仲介或許會有幫助。

那倒不是個壞主意，我家附近有家人力仲介公司。

That's actually not a bad idea. There is a headhunting agency near my house. 16:49

Rick

我不知道他們好不好，但你可以試試看。

Tip 和單用try相比，give sb. a try這種表達法更加口語、活潑。

I don't know how good they are, but maybe you can give them a try. 16:51

Rick

Susie

Okay, I will see what their office hours are and stop by tomorrow to fill out an application. 16:54

好的，我會查清楚他們的營業時間，明天再過去填個申請書。

祝你好運！我對你有信心。

Best of luck! I believe in you. 16:55

Rick

Susie

Thanks a bunch. Talk to you later. 16:56

謝了，那就晚點再聊。

SEND >>

17:50 🔽 ▐▐ 🔋

Rick

Susie, I am a little curious as to what exactly you can do with that Philosophy degree of yours? `17:50`

蘇西，我有點好奇，想知道你的哲學系文憑能做什麼工作。

有很多工作都用得到哲學的思考方式，為什麼這麼問？

Well, it has a lot of general applications for a number of jobs. Why do you ask? `17:53`

Susie

Rick

I am worried about you! I believe we are living in a time when your major determines₄ your career. `17:56`

我是在擔心你！我相信我們活在一個由主修決定職涯的時代。

Rick

If you choose the wrong major, then you are doomed. `17:57`

如果你選錯了主修科目，你就會失敗。

Tip 注意be doomed這種隱含「注定失敗」的用法，只適合用在熟人身上。

有那麼嚴重嗎？那你告訴我，什麼才能算是「正確的主修」呢？

Is it really that bad? And tell me, what is the "right major" in your opinion? `17:59`

Susie

Rick

Anything that gives you satisfaction and pays your bills. Take medicine for example. `18:01`

任何可以帶給你成就感，並能付你薪水的科目，以醫學系為例好了。

Tip 當必須點出特定項目為例時，可以用take sth. for example。

Rick

I love helping people, so it satisfies me; and a doctor is paid well, so it provides for me! `18:03`

我喜愛幫助別人，因此這門科系滿足我；而醫生的薪水相當豐厚，所以它足以支持我的生活水準！

   SEND ▶▶

但我只想找一份我喜歡的工作，然後時時刻刻享受在其中。

Tip 強調自己會享受每分每秒的英文enjoy every minute of sth.。

But I just want to find a job I love and enjoy every minute of it. 18:05

Susie

Rick

The thing is, you might regret this attitude if you keep having trouble finding a job. 18:08

問題是當你一直找不到工作的時候，也許就會為這樣的態度感到後悔了。

Rick

I will find a job easily after I finish medical school. What about you? 18:10

我讀完醫學院之後，很快就能找到工作，而你呢？

Rick

I mean, what can you do with philosophy besides staying in academia₅? 18:13

我的意思是，除了留在學術界做研究，你唸哲學還能做什麼呢？

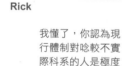

我懂了，你認為現行體制對唸較不實際科系的人是極度不公平的。

I get it. You think that the system is extremely₆ unfair for people who major in less practical subjects. 18:17

Susie

Rick

Yes. That's why I am worried about you. 18:18

是的，那就是我替你感到擔心的原因。

別擔心，哲學能應用的範圍比你想的多！我只是需要多一點時間而已。

Don't worry. Philosophy has more applications than you think! I just need some more time. 18:22

Susie

  SEND »

1. 與父母的爭執

📖 Rick 2014/4/15

I got into an argument again with my parents last week over my decision to become a doctor. They have never supported me and are always trying to convince me to join the family business and manage one or two of our bicycle factories. This time was particularly bad, probably because I am preparing to go to medical school. They must have seen it as the last chance to get me to change my mind.

我上禮拜再次為了當醫生的事與我父母起了爭執,他們從來沒有支持過我,總是試圖說服我加入家族企業,去管理一或兩家自行車工廠,也許是因為我準備要去醫學院的關係,所以這次爭執的情況特別嚴重,他們肯定把這當作是最後一次能改變我心意的機會。

Every time they ask me to change my mind, I tell them the same thing: I want to help people. I thought the fact that I will make good money would make my mom and dad happy, but it hasn't. They have always wanted me to inherit their business once they retire. Maybe they feel offended that I don't want to, like I am rejecting them or something. It's not that at all, though. I just want to be a doctor and help sick people. I wish my parents could understand that. Unfortunately, I'm not sure they ever will.

每次他們要求我改變心意時,我告訴他們的回應都一樣:我想幫助人。我一直以為,成為醫生後的薪水會很優渥這個事實會讓我爸媽開心,但並非如此,他們還是一直希望我能在他們退休後繼承事業,也許我不想繼承的態度讓他們覺得被冒犯,好像我在拒絕他們之類的,但根本不是這樣的,我只是想成為能幫助病人的醫生而已,真希望我的父母能理解,不幸的是,我不確定他們這輩子是否會有了解我想法的一天。

微網誌

2. 父親給我的求職建議

Susie 2014/4/21

I am lucky to have such a supportive father. When I changed my major to philosophy, he didn't complain or yell at me. He told me I should study what I want and enjoy college. Now that I am preparing to enter the working world, he has once again been there to encourage me. When I told him that I was worried about not being able to find the perfect job after graduation, he sat me down and told me not to worry. "Daughter," he said, "There are no perfect jobs. Remember that. You should find something you are interested in and just try it. If it doesn't work, then it doesn't work."

我很幸運有這麼支持我的父親，當我轉到哲學系時，他沒有抱怨或責罵我，只說我應該唸自己想唸的科系，並好好地享受大學生活。而現在，我準備要進入職場，他又再次從旁鼓勵我，當我告訴他，我擔心畢業後找不到一份適合自己的完美工作時，他讓我坐下來，要我別擔心，「女兒，」他說，「沒有所謂完美的職業，記住這一點，你該做的，是去找一份你有興趣的工作，並放膽去嘗試，如果行不通的話，就不要勉強。」

I really think that was exactly what I needed to hear. I have been putting too much pressure on myself, mistakenly thinking that my first job after graduation will be the only job I will ever have, and, if I quit that job, I will be a failure and a disappointment. Thanks to my dad, I know that this is not the case.

我打從心底覺得那就是我需要聽到的話，我一直都給自己太大的壓力了，誤以為我畢業後的第一份工作將會是我唯一的工作，如果到時候辭職的話，我就是個失敗者和令人失望的人，感謝我的爸爸，讓我知道情況並不是我想的這樣。

Word 單字	Meaning 字義	Usage 常見用法
1 qualify [`kwɑlə,faɪ]	動 使具有資格； 使合格；限定	be qualified as/to be 具有…的資格 qualify oneself for 證明自己能勝任
2 comfort [`kʌmfət]	名 舒適；安慰 動 慰問，使安逸	live in ease and comfort 生活安逸舒適 speak comfort to sb. 好言安慰某人
3 fraud [frɔd]	名 欺騙；詭計； 騙局；騙子	see through the fraud 識破騙局 a fraud on the people 對人民的欺騙
4 determine [dɪ`tɜmɪn]	動 決定；使下決心； 確定；判決	be determined about 下定決心 determine sth. beforehand 事先決定
5 academia [,ækə`dimɪə]	名 學術界	an issue in academia 學術界的議題 the academic world 學術界
6 extremely [ɪk`strimlɪ]	副 極端地；非常	be extremely sorry 非常抱歉 carry sth. into extremes 把…引向極端
7 convince [kən`vɪns]	動 使確信；說服	be convinced of 相信 be convinced beyond a doubt 深信不疑
8 inherit [ɪn`hɛrɪt]	動 繼承	to inherit genes 承襲基因 inherit a fortune from 從…繼承財產
9 offend [ə`fɛnd]	動 冒犯；觸怒	offend against the law 違法 be offended at my joke 被我的笑話觸怒
10 supportive [sə`pɔrtɪv]	形 支援的；贊助的	one's supportive family 支持…的家人 be supportive of the idea 支持這個想法
11 mistakenly [mɪ`stekənlɪ]	副 錯誤地；被誤解地	mistakenly think that 誤以為… be mistakenly killed 被誤殺
12 failure [`feljə]	名 失敗；疏忽； 衰退；不及格	repeat a failure 重蹈覆轍 can't survive a failure 承受不了失敗

職場新鮮人
Find A Job～下篇

101 MP3

Rick: Susie, what would you do if your parents tried to interfere① with your future?　16:30

蘇西，如果你的父母試著要干涉你的未來，你會怎麼做啊？

Susie: I don't know because my parents are pretty hands-off. If they acted like hands-on② parents, I would probably move out.　16:35

我不知道，因為我爸媽不太干涉的，如果他們管東管西的話，我可能搬出去住吧。

Rick: That's not a bad idea, actually. I think it might be time for me to move out.　16:38

説真的，這主意還不錯，也許該是我搬離家裡的時候了。

Susie: Are your parents still trying to get you to take over the family business?　16:40

你父母仍然試著要你接管家族事業嗎？

Rick: Yeah. They have only gotten worse since I got accepted to the medical school.　16:43

是啊，自從我被醫學院錄取後，他們就更變本加厲了。

Susie: Ouch. You told them you don't want to be a businessman, right?　16:45

哇，你有向他們表明不想當個生意人吧？

Rick: All the time. I feel like every day I have to remind them my dream has always been to be a doctor.　16:48

一直都有，感覺好像每天都必需提醒他們，我的夢想是當醫生。

Tip 加強語氣的all the time，強調「一直、從早到晚」的時間延續感。

SEND ▶▶

16:30

他們不能接受還真是奇怪，
幫助別人是多高尚的事啊！

It's strange they don't accept that. Helping others is such a noble₃ thing to do. `16:50`

Susie

Rick

Noble is a strong word. I think I am doing a right thing by becoming a doctor, not a noble thing. `16:53`

講高尚太沉重了，我只是
覺得當醫生是對的選擇，
跟高不高尚沒什麼關係。

嘿，如果你真的需要的話，
我可以問我哥，看你是不是
可以暫時住在他的公寓。

Hey, if you really needed to, I can ask my brother if you can stay at his apartment for a while. `16:56`

Susie

先遠離你的父母，好好把事情理出個頭緒。

Tip over有「從頭至尾」的意思，所以think over表示「徹底想清楚」之意。

You know, to get away from your parents and think everything over. `16:58`

Susie

Rick

Thanks. That's really nice of you. I will definitely think about it. `16:59`

謝啦，你人真是太好了，我
一定會好好考慮這件事。

小意思，不過，別忘了，你最終還是
得和你父母溝通才行。

Tip reconnect with表達「重新聯繫、溝通」之意，語氣較正經。

No problem. Just don't forget that you have to reconnect with your parents afterward. `17:02`

Susie

Rick

God! I spent all four years of college communicating with them. Isn't that enough? `17:04`

天啊！我大學四年
都在跟他們溝通，
這還不夠嗎？

SEND ▶▶

Let's Chat In English Via APP

200

12:48

Susie

Hey, Rick, how did your last talk with your parents about your future go? `12:48`

嘿，瑞克，關於未來的出路，你上次和你父母談得怎麼樣？

不太好，我父母說我得先和他們一起工作兩年。

Tip 此句為 It didn't go well 的省略，口語會話才適合用。

Not well. My parents said I must work with them for two years. `12:50`

Rick

如果兩年後我想當醫生的決心依然沒有動搖，他們就願意支持我。

If my determination to be a doctor has not waivered after two years, then they will support me. `12:52`

Rick

Susie

That doesn't sound like a problem. Two years isn't such a long time. `12:53`

那聽起來不會是個問題，兩年並不算是很長的時間。

是啊，但我不想浪費時間在我不感興趣的事物上，他們真的很奇怪，居然不希望我成為醫生。

Yeah, but I don't want to waste any time doing something I have no interest in. It's bizarre that they don't want me to be a doctor. `12:56`

Rick

Susie

Do they have a negative perception of the medical industry? `12:58`

你父母對醫療產業是不是有什麼負面的印象啊？

上星期我問過他們這個問題，他們認為醫生就只會推銷藥品、開開藥方而已。

I asked them last week about that, and they said they think doctors are pill pushers and do nothing but prescribe medicine. `13:00`

Rick

 SEND ≫

Let's Chat In English Via APP

201

12:48

Susie

That sucks. Well, so what now? 13:01

真慘，那你現在打算怎麼辦呢？

Tip suck在俚語中為「爛」的意思，所以不要隨便使用在不熟的人身上。

我想我得接受你的提議，借住在你哥的公寓幾天。

I think I need to take you up on your offer and spend a few days at your brother's place. 13:03

Rick

Susie

You seriously want to move out, huh? 13:04

你真的想搬離家裡喔？

Tip 「搬出」的片語move out；搬進某地方則用move in。

我需要出走個幾天冷靜一下，然後也許我就能接受他們的提議了。

I need to get out for a few days and calm down. Then, maybe I will be able to accept their proposal. 13:08

Rick

Susie

Yeah, or they might even be able to understand how serious you are about becoming a doctor. So, when do you want to move out? 13:11

是啊，或是他們有可能理解你有多認真地看待成為醫生的事，那你什麼時候要搬出家裡呢？

Susie

My brother said it would be cool if you stayed with him, but he needs some notice first. 13:13

我哥說暫住沒問題，但得提前跟他說。

我會收拾一些東西，下星期過去，可以嗎？

I'll pack some of my things and move next week. Okay? 13:14

Rick

 SEND ≫

Let's Chat In English Via APP ● 🔘 ●

3. 教授勸說的結果

📖 Rick 2014/4/29

I had a long talk with my academic advisor, Professor Lin, last Friday about my future. I told her I felt my parents were trying to sabotage my plan of becoming a doctor. After listening to me ramble for what must have been an hour, she offered to call my mom and dad. Needless to say, I was surprised! I did not expect her to take such a personal interest in me.

上週五,我和學術顧問林教授針對我未來的出路,促膝長談了一番,我跟她說,對於我想成為醫生的這件事,我的父母一直試圖阻止,聽了我一小時的臆測之後,教授提議由她打電話給我的父母,不用說,我感到很驚訝!我沒料到她會對我的事這麼親力親為。

Well, fast forward to earlier this afternoon. My parents told me that over the weekend, they had been thinking of ways to compromise with me. They said they had finished talking to Professor Lin and that she had reinforced how strong my desire to be a doctor was. She helped them understand that two years is too long. So, they have finally changed their mind and said they will be happy if I work with them for six months. Even though that is still not ideal for me, it will have to do. I have to thank Professor Lin for supporting me and talking some sense into my parents!

好了,快轉到今天下午稍早的時刻,我父母跟我說,他們花了一整個週末的時間思考各種妥協的方式,他們和林教授談過,教授也向他們強調我想成為醫生的心願有多強烈,她讓我父母了解到兩年的時間太長,因此,他們終於改變心意,並且說,如果我能和他們一起工作六個月,他們就會很滿意了,儘管這個結果對我來說仍然不是很理想,但還是不得不接受,我得謝謝林教授這樣地支持我,也感激她向我父母說明事理!

Let's Chat In English Via APP • •

203

4. 我被錄取了！

📖 Susie 2014/5/9

My prayers have been answered! I got a job working as an administrative assistant for an electronics company just outside the city. Because I have no experience, the salary isn't very good and the hours are long. But with the job market being so bad, I am just happy I was hired. My only concern is that I will be too bored. Going from reading books on metaphysics⑩ to making Microsoft Excel spreadsheets and filing paperwork probably won't be an easy transition.

我的祈禱得到回應了！我找到一份在外縣市電子公司當行政助理的工作，因為我沒有工作經驗，所以薪水不是很高，上班的時間也很長，但在就業市場這麼低迷的情況下，能被錄取我就已經很開心了。我唯一擔心的是，這份工作可能會過於無聊，從閱讀形上學的書籍到寫微軟試算表和文書整理，這或許不會是個容易的轉變呢！

The job starts at the beginning of June, but first, there is a mandatory⑪ two-week training program at the company's headquarters⑫ in Singapore. The program is mandatory for all new employees. I am more excited about the training program than the job itself because they are paying for my flight to Singapore, my hotel, and they are even giving me money for food and shopping! I am going to treat the trip to Singapore like a small vacation before I start my job.

我會從六月初開始工作，但在那之前，位於新加坡的總公司有一場為期兩週的培訓計畫，所有的新進人員都必須參加，我對於培訓計畫的期待更甚於工作本身，因為公司會支付到新加坡的機票、飯店費用，甚至還會補助飲食與購物的花費，在正式上班之前，我會將這趟新加坡之旅視為一趟小小的渡假。

Word 單字	Meaning 字義	Usage 常見用法
1 **interfere** [ˌɪntəˈfɪr]	動 妨礙；衝突；抵觸	interfere in private concerns 干涉私事 interfere with 干涉；妨礙
2 **hands-on** [ˈhændzˈɑn]	形 親自動手的；躬親的	a hands-on manager 事必躬親的管理者 have hands-on experience 有實踐經驗
3 **noble** [ˈnobl̩]	形 高貴的；高尚的	a man of noble mind 思想高尚的人 die for a noble cause 為崇高理由犧牲
4 **perception** [pəˈsɛpʃən]	名 感知；察覺	one's perception of 某人對…的看法 a man of keen perception 敏銳的人
5 **prescribe** [prɪˈskraɪb]	動 規定；指定；開藥方；囑咐	do as the law prescribes 依法辦事 prescribe for the disease 為病症開藥
6 **sabotage** [ˈsæbəˌtɑʒ]	名 破壞；妨礙 動 從事破壞活動	a sabotage mission 破壞的任務 sabotage on 對…進行破壞
7 **ramble** [ˈræmbl̩]	名 閒逛；漫步 動 閒逛；漫談	a literary ramble 文學隨筆 ramble about the streets 漫步於街頭
8 **forward** [ˈfɔrwəd]	動 轉交；遞送 副 向前；今後	forward sth. to sb. 轉交某物給某人 look forward to seeing you 期待見你
9 **reinforce** [ˌriɪnˈfɔrs]	動 增強；補充；添加	reinforce one's argument 強化論證 reinforced concrete 鋼筋混凝土
10 **metaphysics** [ˌmɛtəˈfɪzɪks]	名 形上學；空談；抽象論	weary with metaphysics 厭倦空談 metaphysical poetry 形上學派的詩
11 **mandatory** [ˈmændəˌtorɪ]	形 命令的；指令的；義務的；強制的	mandatory military service 義務兵役 with mandatory pat-downs 強制搜身
12 **headquarters** [ˈhɛdˈkwɔrtəz]	名 (軍警)司令部；總部；總署	the headquarters of …的總部 the general headquarters 總司令部

UNIT 5 職場菜鳥指南
A Guide For Newbie～上篇

105 MP3

11:10

◀ APP CHAT 1 忙碌又充實的菜鳥

Susie: My God! I'm absolutely exhausted after the first few weeks at my new job. 11:10

我的天啊！新工作才做了幾個禮拜，我就快累趴了。

Rick: Pull yourself together. You have a long, long way to go before retirement❶. 11:12

振作一點，你離退休還有很長一段時間呢！

> **Tip** 口語用法pull oneself together，通常用在叫人「打起精神撐下去」的時候。

Susie: I know, but it's harder than I thought. I have to deal with piles of documents, make copies, mail letters, and even brew❷ coffee for the entire office. 11:15

我知道，可是這份工作比我當初想的還難，我要處理堆積成山的文件、影印、寄信、甚至還要泡咖啡給全辦公室的人。

Rick: No wonder you feel so tired. Do you think you will stay at this job much longer? Or will you quit soon? 11:17

難怪你會覺得那麼累，你會再待下去嗎？還是很快就準備辭職了？

Susie: No, I'll stay. I would rather be busy and engaged❸ than bored. 11:18

不，我要繼續待下去，我寧願忙到沒有時間，也不要無聊到沒事做。

Rick: Okay, but I think you will want to quit soon. People who enjoy their jobs don't complain all the time like you do. 11:21

好吧，但我覺得你很快就會辭職，真正樂在工作的人，才不會像你這樣老是抱怨。

Susie: How do you not know that complaining is a way to relieve stress? 11:22

你怎麼會不知道抱怨也是一種抒壓的方式呢？

SEND ▶▶

Let's Chat In English Via APP

我知道每個人都需要發洩情緒，只是你似乎<u>宣洩</u>得太超過了。

Tip a lot of基本上沒有負面意思，只是隨著情境而引伸出「過多」之意。

I know everyone needs to vent. It just seems like you are doing a lot of venting. 11:24
Rick

 Susie
Alright, I will try not to complain so much. Honestly though, I like being busy at work. 11:26

好啦，我儘量少抱怨一點就是了，老實說，我喜歡工作忙碌一些。

 Susie
It not only helps speed up time and makes the work day go by quicker, but it also challenges me to learn and grow. 11:29

它不僅能使上班的時間過得快一點，還能刺激我學習成長。

對啊，忙碌的時候，日子總是<u>過得特別快</u>！

Tip go by quicker因為有比較級，所以會帶出「更快、比較快」之意。

Yeah, busy days always go by quicker! 11:30
Rick

 Susie
By the way, there will be a welcome party for new employees next Saturday. Do you want to come? My boss said everyone could bring a guest. 11:35

對了，我們下星期六有一場迎新派對，你要來嗎？我老闆說每個人都能帶一位客人。

好啊，我要去，那聽起來很吸引人。
Yeah, that sounds like something. 11:36
 Rick

  SEND >>

18:10

嘿，這個星期六的晚宴你會來的吧？

Hey, you're still coming to the dinner party this Saturday, right? `18:10`

Susie

Yeah, of course! Where is it going to be? `18:11`

是啊，我當然會去，晚宴的地點在哪裡呢？

Rick

我的同事瑪莉告訴我，晚宴辦在我們公司附近的一家知名牛排館。

My colleague, Mary, told me that it will be at a famous steak house near our office. `18:14`

Susie

Sounds great. I love a good steak. Is everyone in your company going? `18:16`

聽起來很棒！我愛美味的牛排，你們公司的所有人都會去嗎？

Rick

不會，這是「菜鳥限定」的晚宴，我聽說每年的新人都會利用這個機會來抒壓。

No, it's a dinner party for new employees only. I heard every year the newcomers use the party as a chance to release some stress. `18:20`

Susie

I'm curious to see if the other newcomers have a manager as tough as yours. `18:22`

真好奇其他新人是否有像你一樣的強勢經理。

Rick

是啊，我也想知道，對了，我還聽說晚宴上會有很多其他部門的漂亮女生來喔。

Yeah, me too. Hey, I heard there will be a lot of pretty girls from other departments at the party. `18:24`

Susie

SEND ▶▶

18:10

搞不好你會要到一些電話號碼，很難說的…

Tip 常補在句子最後，表示「世事難預料、一切都很難說」之意。

You might be able to get a few phone numbers. You never know… 18:25

Susie

Now I definitely am going! 18:26

Rick

這下我肯定要去了！

Tip 除了definitely之外，還用現在式強化語氣，表達「一定要去」的決心。

等等，你得答應我不會喝得太超過，也不做傻事，有女孩子在的場合，你有時會失控。

Wait a minute. Promise me you will drink responsibly and not do anything stupid. I know you sometimes go a little crazy around girls. 18:29

Susie

Are you kidding me? I can control what I drink, and I am not crazy around girls. 18:31

Rick

別開玩笑了！我當然會控制喝的量，而且我才不會因為有女孩子在就失控。

Tip be crazy around表示「有…在周圍時會失控」，口語常用。

拜託！你難道忘了我們大一的時候，你和我朋友跳舞，結果吐在她身上的事了嗎？

Come on! Don't you remember first year of university when you threw up on my friend while dancing? 18:33

Susie

That was one time. Can't you let it go? I promise I'll be on my best behavior◎. 18:35

Rick

就那麼一次而已，你就不能別提了嗎？我保證會好好表現的。

Tip 實用片語on one's best behavior，加上I promise是強調。

 SEND ≫

Let's Chat In English Via APP • •

209

🔒 ✉ ✏   11:06 📶 ▤

1. 難以相處的同事

📖 Susie 2014/6/18

I have been enjoying my new job a lot. The hours are long and it is very demanding❼, but I go home every night feeling satisfied, and that's what is important. My manager has already noticed and complimented❽ me. Unfortunately, so has one of the other new employees. This guy, George, has already been written up for being late twice, and we have only been working for three weeks! He clearly does not take the job seriously. He has noticed how much effort I am putting into my job, and he must be getting jealous because he is trying to undermine❾ me whenever he can.

我一直非常喜愛我的新工作，這份工作的上班時間很長，要求也頗高，但我每天晚上都心滿意足地回家，這點對我來說才是重要的。我的經理已注意到我的表現並稱讚我，不幸的是，還有另一個新員工也注意到了，喬治這傢伙，已經被登記兩次遲到，但我們才工作了三個星期耶！他顯然不把工作當一回事，他注意到我投注在工作中的心力，肯定是因此而嫉妒我，因為只要一有機會，他就會試圖妨礙我工作。

For example, he saw me going to make copies this week and jumped out of his desk to use the machine before me. I waited more than five minutes for him to finish, only to find out he was making copies of a flyer for a party at his house this weekend! I really want to tell our manager, but I am afraid of being seen as a tattler.

例如，這星期他一看到我要影印，就馬上從他的位子跳出來，趕在我之前用影印機，我等他印完等了超過五分鐘，卻發現他是在印這個週末在他家辦的派對傳單！真的很想跟我們經理舉發，但我害怕被看作是一個愛打小報告的人。

22:08

  微網誌

2. 初次去高檔牛排店

📖 Rick 2014/6/22

Susie's company's recent dinner party turned out to be quite a shock for me. I have never eaten at a formal Western restaurant before, only Taiwanese imitations⑩. There is nothing special at Taiwanese imitations. Of course I have had steak before, but nothing like the kind of steak I had at the dinner party. It was, in a word, amazing!

蘇西公司最近的晚宴帶給我相當大的震憾,我以前從來沒有在正式的西餐廳用過餐,只有試過台灣人仿效的,台灣人仿效的西餐廳沒什麼特別的地方。當然,我之前是有吃過牛排,但跟我在晚宴上吃的那種完全不一樣,簡單的說,這次的晚宴實在太棒了!

The entire⑪ meal was definitely a new experience for me. For one thing, I had never seen so many utensils⑫ in my life! Each person had two forks, three spoons, and two knives. I had to ask the waiter why there were so many. He told me that each one was for a different course: one knife for steak, one for butter; one fork for steak, one for salad; and one spoon for soup, one for dessert, and one for coffee. Having the entire table served at the same time with the waiters serving everyone on their right side was another new experience. Overall, the experience was enjoyable.

對我來說,整個用餐過程是全新的體驗,首先,我這一生從未見過這麼多的餐具!每個人有兩支叉子、三支湯匙,和兩把刀子,我還得問服務生為什麼有那麼多餐具,他告訴我每道菜都會使用不同的餐具:一支刀子用來切牛排,一支用來塗奶油;一支叉子用來吃牛排,一支吃沙拉;一支湯匙用來喝湯,一支吃甜點,還有一支是喝咖啡用的,其次,服務生同時在同一桌客人的右側上菜,對我來說又是一項新體驗,總的來說,這次的用餐經驗很享受。

Word 單字	Meaning 字義	Usage 常見用法
1 retirement [rɪˋtaɪrmənt]	名 退休；退職	go into retirement 退休 retirement benefits 退休金
2 brew [bru]	動 泡(茶)；釀造	be brewed from 由⋯所釀造 brew you some tea 幫您沏茶
3 engaged [ɪnˋgedʒd]	形 從事⋯的；忙於⋯的	be engaged in 忙於某事；投入某事 one's time be engaged 時間被佔用
4 colleague [ˋkɑlig]	名 同事；同僚	work as one's colleague 與某人共事 a former colleague 以前的同事
5 tough [tʌf]	名 暴徒；惡棍 形 堅韌的；剛強的	a gang of toughs 一群暴徒 be tough with sb. 對某人強硬起來
6 behavior [bɪˋhevjɚ]	名 行為；舉止； 反應；變化	the decent behavior 舉止得體 be of good behavior (律)表現良好
7 demand [dɪˋmænd]	名 要求；需求 動 要求；請求	be in great demand 需求量很大 demand an apology from 要求道歉
8 compliment [ˋkɑmpləmənt]	名 讚美的話 動 讚美；恭維；祝賀	return a compliment 回報 compliment sb. on 誇獎某人⋯
9 undermine [ˏʌndɚˋmaɪn]	動 在⋯下挖坑道； 暗中破壞	undermine one's authority 破壞威信 undermine one's worth 貶低⋯的價值
10 imitation [ˏɪməˋteʃən]	名 模仿；仿製品 形 人造的；偽造的	in imitation of 為了仿效 imitation leather 人造革
11 entire [ɪnˋtaɪr]	名 全部；整體 形 全部的；整個的	the entire of the night 通宵 waste an entire day on 浪費整天時間
12 utensil [juˋtɛnsḷ]	名 器皿；用具	nonstick cooking utensil 不沾鍋廚具 the flower watering utensil 澆花器

UNIT 5

職場菜鳥指南
A Guide For Newbie～下篇

🔒 ⚐ ✎   22:48 📶 ▊▊

◀ APP CHAT **3** 我的古怪主管

Susie

> I can't stand my manager anymore. I thought he was okay before, but now I just can't stand him! `22:48`

我再也無法忍受我的經理了，以前我覺得他還滿好的，但現在我實在受不了他！

Susie

> He gives orders tentatively❶ and changes his mind all the time. He is just being a pain. `22:51`

他在下達指令時很猶豫不決，一直改變心意，實在很讓人受不了。

我討厭反覆無常的人，所以我懂你的意思，他有多嚴重啊？

Tip 要記得bad隱含你對所講的對象有負面評價。

> I hate fickle people so I understand what you mean. How bad is he? `22:52`

Rick

Susie

> He's the worst! I never know when he will suddenly tell me to stop whatever task I'm currently doing to work on something totally unrelated. `22:56`

最嚴重的那種！我永遠不知道他何時會突然打斷我手邊的工作，派我去處理完全不相干的事。

那就先把新的工作放一旁，等他改變心意後再著手呢？

Tip 實用片語put sth. aside，sth.可以是具體物品，也可以是抽象事物。

> How about putting the new assignments❷ aside and waiting for him to change his mind? `22:58`

Rick

Susie

> Impossible. He is very impatient and checks my progress every half-hour. `23:00`

不可能的，他非常沒耐心，每隔半小時就檢查我的工作進度。

Tip 用「every+時間」表達「每隔多久時間就…」的意思。

喔，我的天啊！讓我猜猜看：他的性格同時很陰晴不定？

> Oh my! Let me guess: he is also moody? `23:01`

Rick

   SEND ≫

Let's Chat In English Via APP • ⏻ •

213

22:48

Susie

Of course. It fits perfectly with his fickleness₃ and impatience, right?
23:03

那當然，跟猶豫不決和沒耐心還真是絕配，對吧？

我真的很佩服你在那邊替他做事做了三個月還沒辭職。

I'm impressed that you have worked there for three months and not quit.
23:05

Rick

Susie

I have to. I need to work here for at least a few years. Otherwise, future employers might think I am irresponsible.
23:08

我不得不如此，我至少要在這裡工作個幾年，否則下個老闆可能會認為我是個不負責任的人。

聽起來很合理，那麼你打算兩年後辭職還是怎麼樣？

That sounds reasonable. So are you going to quit after two years or what?
23:10

Rick

Susie

Three years, I think. That should be long enough to satisfy other companies. I just pray I can survive that long with my current manager.
23:13

三年吧，那應該符合其他公司的任用標準，我只祈禱能在經理底下存活那麼久。

我也會為你祈禱的。

I'll pray for you, too.
23:14

Rick

  SEND ▶▶

12:30 🔋

I just read that the unemployment rate has gone up to 8%.
`12:30`

Susie

我剛看到失業率已攀升到百分之八了。

That's no surprise. I heard the hospital where I work part-time has recently started to give unpaid vacation leave to some employees.
`12:33`

那沒什麼好大驚小怪的，我兼差的那家醫院最近已經開始對部分員工實施無薪假了。

Rick

What?! They have already started doing that? Are you afraid that they might start firing people?
`12:35`

Susie

什麼？！他們已經開始那樣做了嗎？你會害怕他們裁員嗎？

Of course I am!
`12:36`

當然會啊！

Rick

That really sucks. Are you worried you might get laid off?
`12:37`

Susie

真是太慘了，你會擔心被資遣嗎？

Tip get laid off為「被資遣」之意，語氣比get fired要正式。

Absolutely! This job is the only one that fits into my work schedule at my parents' office.
`12:41`

當然！考慮到我在我父母公司上班的時間，這是唯一能配合我時間的工作了。

Rick

Well, here's something that might cheer you up: if you do get laid off, you can apply for unemployment benefits. `12:44`

Susie

這或許會讓你開心一點：如果你被資遣了，你可以向政府申請失業津貼。

SEND »

Let's Chat In English Via APP

215

可以領到你原來薪資百分之六十的金額，連續領六個月。

And you will receive 60% of your salary from the government for six consecutive◦ months. `12:46`

Susie

Rick

I think that only applies to full-time employees. Besides, I am interested in the experience of working at a hospital, not the money. `12:50`

我記得那只適用於正職員工，況且，我感興趣的是在醫院工作的經驗，不是錢。

你不能去上與醫學相關的職訓課程嗎？在你等待深造的期間，那個應該也會有幫助吧？

Can't you go take some medical-related training courses? That could also help while you are waiting to go study again. `12:53`

Susie

Rick

That's a good idea. If I really do get laid off, I will look into training courses. `12:55`

那倒是個好主意，如果我真的被裁員的話，我會去找找職訓課程的。

Tip 片語look into有「查找」之意。

是啊，我不擔心你，你會沒事的。

Yeah. I wouldn't worry too much. You will be okay. `12:56`

Susie

Rick

Thanks. I appreciate it. `12:57`

多謝啦，感激不盡。

Tip appreciate在表達謝意的程度上比thank深。

[_____]
SEND ≫

Let's Chat In English Via APP · ⏻ ·

216

18:54

3. 也許該找份新兼職

Rick 2014/8/26

I finally found a part-time job working at a hospital near my house, and it looks like I might get fired. Many of my coworkers have told me that some non-essential employees will lose their jobs. Apparently, the hospital is struggling because of the poor economy right now. My job is the definition of non-essential – it's administrative work – so I am extremely worried that I may be fired soon.

我終於在我家附近的一家醫院找到兼職工作，但現在看起來，我很有可能會被解雇，許多同事告訴我，一些非必要的員工將失去工作，很顯然，由於現在的經濟不景氣，醫院正在苦撐著，我完全符合「非必要員工」的定義，我負責的都是些行政工作，所以，我真的很擔心自己可能很快就會被解雇。

Meanwhile, thanks to Susie's suggestion, I am looking into training courses or anything else I can do to get some experience in medicine. I have recently been thinking that volunteering might be worthwhile. In fact, it may even be better than my current job because the volunteering would allow me to comfort patients or assist nurses. It will give me some real hospital experience. My current job has me sitting at a desk typing out data sheets every Saturday and Sunday. Hmm, maybe I should just quit my boring desk job and start volunteering.

同時，感謝蘇西的建議，我正在尋找職訓課程，以及其他能讓我獲得醫療經驗的工作，我最近在想，義工或許滿值得做的，事實上，它可能比我現在的工作還要好，因為做義工可以讓我有安撫病患或協助護士的機會，給我實質的醫院經驗，我現在的工作就是讓我在每週六、日的時候，坐在桌子前輸入資料表而已，嗯，也許我真該放棄這份枯燥的案頭工作，轉而投向義工這塊領域。

4. 什麼樣的同事都有

Susie 2014/9/18

As I get to know my coworkers more and more, I am discovering who is nice and helpful and who is hostile and difficult. George is still the worst of the bunch. He is always a huge pain in my side, constantly interrupting me while I work. Some of my other coworkers are also hard to get along with. Two older women, Sara and Michelle, like to leave passive-aggressive⓵ notes on my desk when I am out to lunch. The notes are usually petty⓫ things, like improper stapling or taking up too much space in the refrigerator. It is annoying, but I don't think I will confront⓬ them about it.

　　隨著我對同事的了解越來越深，我漸漸發現誰樂於助人，誰則對我充滿敵意又處處刁難。喬治依然是所有同事中最難搞的那個，他對我來說一直都是個大麻煩，經常在我工作時打擾我，除了他以外，也有其他難相處的同事，有兩位年齡較大的女同事，莎拉和米雪兒，喜歡在我中午外出用餐時，留下隱含惡意的字條在我桌上，字條上面寫的通常都是些雞毛蒜皮的小事，像是不當的裝訂或佔用冰箱太多空間之類的事，這很惱人，但我應該不會為此跟她們衝突。

Fortunately, there are just as many good coworkers as bad. There is a newly-married couple who met at the office, Leo and Grace, and they are super helpful. I usually go to them with any questions I have. Brandon is another great coworker as well. He has given me a lot of tips for being more efficient at work.

　　幸好，好同事也很多，公司裡有一對新婚夫婦，里歐和葛瑞絲，他們這一對是在公司認識的，他們兩個人都很樂於幫忙，每當我有問題的時候，通常都是去問他們，布蘭登也是個很棒的同事，他教給我許多能增進工作效率的訣竅。

Word 單字	Meaning 字義	Usage 常見用法
1 tentatively [`tɛntətɪvlɪ]	副 試驗性地；暫時地；不確定地	do sth. tentatively 不確定會不會做 one's tentative idea 初步的想法
2 assignment [ə`saɪnmənt]	名 指派；功課；分派的任務	the assignment in English 英文作業 the country of assignment 派駐國
3 fickleness [`fɪkəlnəs]	名 舉棋不定；浮躁；變化無常	accuse sb. of fickleness 責備…反覆 the fickleness of fate 命運的無常
4 unemployment [ˌʌnɪm`plɔɪmənt]	名 失業；失業人數	rising unemployment 失業人口增加 an unemployment benefit 失業津貼
5 lay [le]	動 下蛋；放；擱；賭錢；安排	lay sb. off 把某人解雇 lay money on sth. 下賭注
6 consecutive [kən`sɛkjʊtɪv]	形 連續不斷的；連貫的	the consecutive rain 連續不斷的雨勢 in consecutive order 按順序
7 struggle [`strʌɡl]	動 奮鬥；掙扎；競爭；對抗	struggle on 繼續努力 struggle for liberty 為自由而奮鬥
8 administrative [əd`mɪnəˌstretɪv]	形 管理的；行政的	one's administrative talent 管理才能 administrative district 行政區
9 medicine [`mɛdəsn]	名 藥物；醫學	take the medicine 服藥 a medicine for fever 退燒藥
10 aggressive [ə`ɡrɛsɪv]	形 侵犯的；侵略的；有進取精神的	an aggressive war 侵略性戰爭 be aggressive in doing sth. 積極做
11 petty [`pɛtɪ]	形 小的；瑣碎的；心胸狹窄的	the petty cash 小額現金 bug sb. with petty things 拿小事煩人
12 confront [kən`frʌnt]	動 迎面遇到；遭遇；勇敢面對；對抗	confront one's emotion 面對…的感情 confront sth. with optimism 樂觀面對

Part 4

專長與嗜好

生活中不可或缺的調劑

認真生活之餘，總有屬於自己的消遣時光。
你是喜愛文藝的文青派？有運動習慣的健康一族？
還是對電影與電視瞭若指掌的影視喜好者？
不管興趣為何，當然都找得到同好圈分享，
想聊自己的休閒生活，就用本章的英語談天說地吧！

Let's Chat In English
Via APP

APP CHAT!

UNIT 1

藝術工作者
Performing Artist～上篇

113 MP3

22:10

◀ APP CHAT **1** 學生的音樂比賽

凱倫，明天的比賽你準備好了嗎？

Karen, are you ready for tomorrow's competition①? 22:10

Sean

別忘了檢查小提琴、琴弦、琴弓以及其他比賽會用到的用品。

Don't forget to check your violin, violin strings, your bow, and anything else you will need. 22:12

Sean

Karen

Mr. Field, although we've rehearsed the competition repertoire② for months, I still have no confidence in myself. 22:15

菲爾德老師，雖然比賽曲目我們已經練了好幾個月，我仍然沒自信。

Karen

I know I'll mess it up, I just know it! 22:16

我知道我會搞砸這次比賽的，我就是知道！

Tip know並非真的知道，只是表達一種臆測，但語氣很強烈。

放輕鬆，你一直都很努力練習，我確信只要你盡力去表現，就一定沒問題。

Take it easy. You've been working really hard. I'm convinced that as long as you do your best, you'll be fine. 22:19

Sean

Karen

Thanks. Hearing that from you means a lot. 22:20

謝謝，你的鼓勵對我來說，有很大的意義。

Tip mean a lot是比thank更深的感激之情；主詞若換成sb.，則表示某人對我很重要。

對自己要有信心，你明天的演出將會是最精彩的，等著看吧！

Have confidence in yourself. Your performance will be the most marvelous③ one tomorrow, just wait and see. 22:23

Sean

SEND ≫

Let's Chat In English Via APP

Karen

Alright, like you always say, "Faith can move mountains." I only need to believe in myself, and I will win the grand prize. Believe and achieve! `22:26`

好吧，就像你常說的：「信念可移山」，我只需要相信自己，就能贏得大獎，堅守信念、達成目標！

沒錯！只要拿出你平時練習的表現，就一定能令人驚呼連連的。

That's right! Just play like you've been practicing and you'll give an amazing performance. `22:30`

Sean

Karen

You really think performing like I do in practice will be enough? `22:31`

你真的認為我練習時的表現就可以了嗎？

絕對可以，就用你的音樂打動觀眾的心，不用害怕任何事情！

Absolutely. Let your melodies move the audiences' hearts, and don't be afraid of anything! `22:33`

Sean

記得我的另一句話：「恐懼是心靈的殺手。」

Remember my other saying: "Fear is the mind-killer." `22:34`

Sean

Karen

I feel much more courageous₄ now! Mr. Field, thanks for your words of encouragement. `22:36`

我現在覺得勇氣十足了！菲爾德先生，謝謝你一番鼓勵的話！

 [_____] **SEND ≫**

21:30

Rocky

I just saw your student, you know, the one who performed that amazing piece and won the competition. What was her name again? 21:30

我剛剛看到你的學生，就是演出令人讚嘆、贏得比賽的那一位，她叫什麼名字來著？

她的名字叫做凱倫，她演奏得怎麼樣？相當不錯，對吧？

Her name is Karen. What did you think of her performance? Pretty good, huh? 21:32

Sean

她很認真地準備這次的比賽，你呢？最近還好吧？

She practiced so hard for this competition. Anyway, how is everything with you? 21:35

Sean

Rocky

I'm doing pretty good. I'm now an owner of a pub in high repute. 21:37

我最近過得很不錯，我現在可是一間名氣響亮酒吧的老闆呢！

Tip in high repute表示「名氣響亮」。

你是在跟我開玩笑的吧？上次我們碰面的時候，你看起來慘極了。

You're joking, right? Last time we saw each other, you looked miserable. 21:39

Sean

現在你竟然跟我說你開了一間酒吧？總之，先恭喜你了。

Tip be in order有「要好好好恭喜」之意。

Now you're telling me that you own a pub? I guess congratulations are in order. 21:42

Sean

Rocky

Thanks, Sean. You know, you should stop by for a drink sometime. The name of my bar is "Rocky's House". 21:46

謝了，西恩，改天過來店裡坐坐吧，店名是「洛基之家」。

 　　　　　　　　　　　　　　SEND ≫

21:30

謝謝邀請！我改天一定會過去看看。

Tip stop by是輕鬆的「順道去」，若是正式的拜訪建議用visit。

Thanks for the invitation. I will definitely stop by for a visit soon. 21:47

Sean

Rocky

Excellent. And you know what? I was so impressed by Karen that I'd like to invite her to my pub to perform. 21:50

太好了！你知道嗎？我對凱倫印象深刻，想邀請她到店裡表演。

Rocky

Do you think she would be interested? I would pay her, of course. 21:52

你想她會感興趣嗎？當然，我會付給她演出酬勞的。

真的嗎？那可是天大的好消息！我會馬上告訴她，之後再回覆你。

Tip get back to有「再聯絡」之意。

Really? That's great news! I will tell her right away and then get back to you. 21:54

Sean

Rocky

Ok! Let's stay in touch. Oh, and remember to tell Karen she did an amazing job! 21:57

好啊！保持聯絡，喔對，記得跟凱倫說，她的演出真的很棒！

那當然，我一定會將這句話轉達給她的！

Of course I will. 21:58

Sean

SEND ▶▶

1. 比賽當天的老師

Karen 2014/9/24

I am truly blessed to have a teacher like Mr. Field. I thank God every day for bringing him into my life. It is because of Mr. Field that I won the university's annual violin competition. Every day, he worked tirelessly with me, helping me prepare for the competition by correcting my mistakes and encouraging me. If it wasn't for his attentive guidance, I wouldn't have been able to perform my Paganini piece so well.

我打從心裡感謝能有像菲爾德先生這樣好的老師，我每天都感謝上帝把老師帶進我的生活，因為有他，我才能贏得大學年度小提琴比賽。他每天都不辭辛勞地陪我練習比賽的曲目，指出我演奏中的錯誤並鼓勵我，如果沒有他細心的指導，我不可能這麼成功地演奏出帕格尼尼的作品。

After winning the competition, though, I couldn't find him anywhere. I was worried something had happened. Then, the announcer called his name and said Mr. Field would be giving a performance to end the evening's competition. This was my first chance to listen to him perform. And, my goodness, he was amazing! He played a piece by Mozart brilliantly. After listening to his performance, I know I still have a lot to improve on. But with Mr. Field's help, I will work hard to do just that!

然而在贏了比賽後，我到處都找不到菲爾德老師，正當我擔心他是否出了什麼事時，就聽見廣播員報出菲爾德老師的名字，說他將演奏一曲，為今晚的比賽畫下句點，這是我第一次有機會欣賞老師的正式演奏，天啊！他真的好厲害喔！老師完美地演奏了莫扎特的作品，聽完他的演出後，我才明白自己還有很多需要改進的地方，不過，有菲爾德老師的指導，我一定會努力改善自己的不足的！

2. 到酒吧演奏小提琴

📖 Sean 2014/9/28

After I congratulated Karen on her performance, I gave her the good news that my friend, Rocky, invited her to perform at his bar. I could see Karen was a little hesitant at first. I can't say I blame her. How many violin performances have you heard at a bar? Besides, Karen doesn't drink, and my guess is she has never been to a bar before. However, with some good encouragement and positive thinking, I convinced her to give it a go.

向凱倫祝賀她成功的演出後，我告訴她一個好消息，就是我朋友洛基想邀請她到酒吧表演，我看出凱倫一開始有點猶豫，這一點我不能怪她，你有聽過在酒吧裡演奏小提琴的嗎？此外，凱倫不喝酒，我猜她之前從來沒有去過酒吧這樣的場所，然而，在給了她一些鼓勵和正面的想法後，我成功地說服她去試試看。

Despite the strangeness of playing violin in a bar and Karen's awkward appearance on stage, from the second she started playing, she had everyone's full attention. Everyone in the bar stopped talking immediately. They all turned and watched her play. She is a true virtuoso with the violin. Every note she plays is full of emotion. That emotion, combined with how technically skilled she is, makes her an amazing, one-of-a-kind violinist. I think I might have seen people crying at the bar.

儘管在酒吧演奏小提琴的感覺有點奇怪，凱倫對舞台也很陌生，但她一開始演奏的那瞬間，就立刻取得所有人的注意，酒吧裡的每個人都突然停止交談，轉過頭欣賞她的演出。凱倫的確是小提琴演奏的箇中高手，她所彈奏出的每個音符都充滿了感情，那種感情與熟練的技巧結合，造就她成為獨一無二的小提琴家，我想我當時還看到一些觀眾當場落淚呢！

Word 單字	Meaning 字義	Usage 常見用法
1 competition [ˌkɑmpəˋtɪʃən]	名 競爭；比賽	be/stand in competition with 和…競爭 the competition in armament 軍備競賽
2 repertoire [ˋrɛpəˌtwɑr]	名 曲目	the competition repertoire 比賽曲目 a wide-ranging repertoire 豐富的曲目
3 marvelous [ˋmɑrvələs]	形 了不起；妙極的； 令人驚嘆的	a marvelous gift for …的非凡天賦 a marvelous view 了不起的見解
4 courageous [kəˋredʒəs]	形 英勇的；勇敢的	be courageous enough to 夠勇敢去做 a courageous action 英勇的行動
5 piece [pis]	名 作品；(商品)單位 動 拼湊；修補	play a piece of Chopin 演奏蕭邦的作品 be paid by the piece 按件計酬
6 repute [rɪˋpjut]	名 名氣；聲望	of international repute 享有國際聲譽 a man of solid repute 信譽可靠的人
7 annual [ˋænjʊəl]	形 一年的；每年的； 全年的	the annual turnover 年銷售量 one's annual leave 某人的年假
8 attentive [əˋtɛntɪv]	形 注意的；留意的； 殷勤的；體貼的	be attentive to sb. 對某人體貼周到 an attentive listener 專心的聆聽者
9 announcer [əˋnaʊnsɚ]	名 宣告者；廣播員	a sports announcer 體育播報員 an announcer in …的廣播員、主持人
10 hesitant [ˋhɛzətənt]	形 遲疑的；躊躇的	take a hesitant step 遲疑地邁開步伐 be hesitant about 對…猶豫不決
11 virtuoso [ˌvɜtʃʊˋoso]	名 藝術愛好者；行家 形 藝術愛好者的	a well-known virtuoso 知名藝術愛好者 be a virtuoso at sth. 某領域的行家
12 combine [kəmˋbaɪn]	動 使結合；使聯合； 兼有；兼備	combine A with B 兼具；結合 …and…don't readily combine 不易混合

UNIT 1

藝術工作者
Performing Artist～下篇

Sean

Erin, I went to see your exhibition① last week. It's a pity that I didn't see you in the gallery. `22:10`

艾琳，我上星期去看了你的個展，可惜沒有在畫廊碰到你。

你應該先給我個電話的，這樣的話，我一定會到場。

Tip sb. be around有「在附近」的意思。

You should've called me before you came. That way, I could have made sure I was around. `22:13`

Erin

Sean

Anyway, I liked your paintings. In fact, I thought a lot of them were astonishing②. `22:16`

總之，我喜歡你的畫，說真的，很多作品都令人讚嘆。

令人讚嘆？這也未免太輕描淡寫了吧，老實說，你真正的感想是什麼？

Astonishing? Come on, that's too simplistic. How did you really feel? `22:18`

Erin

Sean

Well, I felt there was something beyond the paintings. They felt different from those you used to paint, more open and more mature. `22:22`

在畫作之外，我感受到更深層的東西，跟你以往的作品不同，更開放、也更成熟。

這還差不多，不愧是我最好的朋友！

That's better. No wonder you are my best friend! `22:23`

Erin

Sean

Did you perceive③ something new or different in your everyday life that made you change your style? `22:25`

你是不是從日常生活中領悟到不一樣的東西，才因此改變了風格啊？

 SEND >>

Let's Chat In English Via APP

229

22:10

事實上，的確有，去年我開始接觸攝影。

Tip 意思與in fact相同，但相較之下，語氣更強烈一點。

As a matter of fact, I did. Last year, I started studying photography. `22:28`

Erin

在新創作的畫作中，我試著將一些攝影概念融入進去。

In my new pieces, I tried to merge the perception of some photographs into a painting. `22:31`

Erin

Sean

Yeah, I noticed that. They were all quite moving. `22:32`

這我有注意到，很感動人心的畫。

聽到你這麼說真是榮幸，那你過得怎麼樣？

Tip honor是很正式的字，可以藉此感受到說話者的正經態度。

It's an honor to hear that coming from you. How about you? `22:34`

Erin

Sean

Excellent! Actually, a producer invited me to her studio to record a demo. `22:37`

很不錯啊！事實上，有個製作人邀請我到她的錄音室錄試聽帶。

那真是太棒了！如果你拿到唱片合約，記得告訴我第一張專輯的發行日啊！

That's awesome! If you get a record deal, don't forget to tell me when your first album will debut. `22:40`

Erin

SEND ≫

9:49 🛜 📶 🔋

Erin

Sean, what was the producer's reaction to your demo? `9:49`

西恩,製作人對你錄的試聽帶反應怎麼樣?

她非常喜歡!我剛簽了合約,她要我用接下來的幾個月錄製整張專輯。

She loved it! I just signed a contract, and she wants me to record a full album in the next few months. `9:55`

Sean

Erin

Wow, so you're going to be famous then, huh? Remember not to let stardom change you. `9:58`

哇,那麼你就快要出名了,是吧?記得千萬不要被名利沖昏了頭。

Erin

Oh, and remember to autograph a copy of your album for me. `10:01`

喔,還要記得給我一張你的簽名專輯。

拜託,別鬧了,我還不知道除了製作人之外,還有誰會喜歡呢!

Tip knock it off是在叫對方認真點,別調侃自己。

Come on, knock it off. I don't even know if anyone other than the producer will like it. `10:04`

Sean

Erin

You need to have a little faith in yourself. You're about to become a big star. `10:06`

你得對自己有點信心,你就要成為大明星了耶。

我不知道,這一切都太不真實了,這些年來我一直都只是個音樂老師。

I don't know. Everything is so unreal. I've been a teacher for years. `10:10`

Sean

   SEND ▶▶

Let's Chat In English Via APP

231

9:49

而現在，<u>突然間</u>，我就要錄專輯了。

Tip 本句now與all of a sudden的連用，會增加「突然」的強度。

> And now, all of a sudden, I have been asked to record a full album. 10:11

Sean

Erin

> That's what's interesting about life: you never know what will happen next. 10:13

這就是人生有趣的地方：你永遠不知道接下來會發生什麼事。

Tip 冒號後面說明「有趣之處」，可視狀況省略。

是那樣沒錯，但我還是覺得這一切都太令人難以相信了。

> That's true, but it's still hard to believe. 10:14

Sean

Erin

> You're an avant-garde⑦ musician that nobody appreciated before. Now, the time has come for you to be recognized as the great musician you are. 10:20

你是個擁有卓越天份的音樂家，只是以前沒人欣賞而已，現在，讓大家理解你實力的時刻終於到了。

謝啦，真的很感謝你的鼓勵。

> Thanks. I really appreciate your support. 10:21

Sean

Erin

> Oh, you will be performing a concert for the release of the album, right? 10:23

對了，你發行唱片時會舉辦演奏會吧？

抱歉，我完全忘了要告訴你這件事，要來嗎？我可以送你幾張免費的門票。

> Yes, sorry, I totally forgot to mention that. Want to come? I can get you some free tickets, no problem. 10:27

Sean

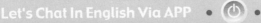 SEND ≫

Let's Chat In English Via APP • •

微網誌

3. 畫作的靈感來源

📖 Erin 2014/10/1

My newest exhibition contains the first paintings I can say are my own. My work before this has been interpretations of other artists. I was always excellent at mimicking⑧, but I always felt I lacked a real voice. Only now, after finishing the pieces in this exhibition do I feel comfortable calling myself an artist and a creator.

在我最新的展覽中,我終於創作出第一批可以稱得上原創的作品,在此之前,我的畫作都只是在詮釋其他藝術家的東西,我一直都很擅長模仿,但我總覺得那些作品都傳達不出我的聲音與想法,直到完成這次展覽的作品後,我才開始覺得自己是個真正的藝術家與創作者。

I actually found my voice only after studying another area of art, photography. I was unhappy with my artwork and wanted to take a break from painting, so I went to a local exhibit on scenic photography. The pictures were so direct and lacked all pretension⑨, yet, when I looked at them, they had a surprising depth. It didn't seem to be anything the photographers intended, either. No, the pictures themselves spoke to me. I bought a few replica⑩ photos and went back to my art studio. I studied the pictures, determined to paint in a similarly simple style.

真的能在畫作中融入自己的聲音,是在我遇見另一個創作領域之後的事,那就是攝影。那個時候,我不滿意自己的作品,想休息一陣子,就去參觀本地的風景攝影展,那些相片所傳達的訊息很直接,沒有絲毫的做作,但當我細看時,其中所蘊含的深度又令人驚訝,而且看起來不像攝影師刻意為之的成果,不,照片本身就在向我訴說,我買了幾幅複製品,拿回工作室研究,並決定以同樣簡單的風格作畫。

Let's Chat In English Via APP

233

4. 在海外的見聞

📖 Sean 2014/12/10

My worldwide concert tour has been going well. I have spent the last few months in North America, playing everywhere from San Francisco to Toronto. What has struck me the most is how big everything is. The people, the food, the houses, the cars, everything is larger in North America!

　　我在海外的巡迴演奏會進行得很順利，過去幾個月，我都在北美洲演出，一路從舊金山到多倫多，最讓我吃驚的是，這邊的東西都很大，人、食物、房子，以及汽車，在北美洲，一切東西都是大尺寸！

I know I am not tall at 172cm, but I am still average[1] in Taiwan. In America, though, I feel tiny. I am the same height as most of the women I have met, and the men are all taller than me. I have to look up to talk to my North American tour manager. Having said that, I think he is a great guy. When I played in New York, he offered[2] to let me stay at his house. His wife cooked cheeseburgers one night that must have been twice the size of the ones we have in Taiwan! There was no way I could finish mine. It has been an interesting trip to say the least, but I am looking forward to going back to Taiwan, where everything is the right size for me.

　　我知道我個子不高，只有172公分，不過，在台灣，我的身高也還在平均值之內，但在美國，我覺得自己變得很矮小，我所遇見的女性中，大多數都和我一樣高，男性則都比我高，我必須要抬頭，才能和我的北美巡演經理人說話，說到我的經理人，他人實在很好，我在紐約演出的時候，他邀請我住他家，有天晚上，他太太做了起司漢堡，那份量足足有台灣的兩倍大！我根本不可能吃完的，總之，這次的巡演還滿有趣的，但是我依然期待回台灣，因為在那裡，所有東西的大小對我來說才剛剛好。

Word 單字	Meaning 字義	Usage 常見用法
1 **exhibition** [ˌɛksəˋbɪʃən]	名 展覽；展覽會； 展示；陳列品	a photographic exhibition 攝影展 on exhibition 展出中
2 **astonishing** [əˋstɑnɪʃɪŋ]	形 令人驚艷的； 使人讚嘆的	the astonishing scenery 令人讚嘆的景色 be astonished at 對⋯感到讚嘆
3 **perceive** [pəˋsiv]	動 領悟；瞭解	perceive a difference between 看出區別 perceive one's error 察覺到錯誤
4 **merge** [mɝdʒ]	動 合併；結合；融入	merge A with B 合併A 與B merge into/with 融入
5 **debut** [dɪˋbju]	名 出道；首演 動 出道	make one's debut 做某人的出道表演 one's debut in a movie 首次出演電影
6 **stardom** [ˋstɑrdəm]	名 非常有名氣的地位	be destined for stardom 註定成名 shoot to stardom 一舉成名
7 **avant-garde** [ɑvɑnˋgɑrd]	名 (藝術界)前衛派 形 跨時代的；新穎的	an avant-garde painting 跨時代的畫作 an avant-garde author 標新立異的作家
8 **mimic** [ˋmɪmɪk]	動 學⋯的樣子 形 模仿的	to accurately mimic sb. 精準地模仿某人 a mimicked smile 假裝微笑
9 **pretension** [prɪˋtɛnʃən]	名 藉口；自稱； 假裝；做作	make pretension to beauty 自詡為美人 with great pretension 神氣活現地
10 **replica** [ˋrɛplɪkə]	名 複製品；複製； 酷似	the exact replica of ⋯的精確複製品 a replica in bronze 青銅複製品
11 **average** [ˋævərɪdʒ]	名 平均；中等 形 平均的；一般的	work out an average 算出平均數 above the average 在一般水準之上
12 **offer** [ˋɔfə]	名 提供；報價 動 給予；提供	goods on offer 供出售的貨品 offer oneself for a position 自薦任某職

UNIT 2 文藝生活
Literature And Art～上篇

121 MP3

15:22 📶

◀ APP CHAT 1 一起去看展覽吧！

瓊，我現在覺得好寂寞喔！

Tip lonely形容「寂寞感」，如果想說「單獨」則用alone。

I feel so lonely now, Joan.
15:22

Sophia

How come? You're still with your boyfriend, aren't you? 15:24

Joan

怎麼會呢？你還跟你男友在一起，不是嗎？

Tip 意思同why，但how come更強調問話者的不解與疑惑。

是還在一起，但老實說，我跟他根本就沒有共通點，沒錯，他人是很好，也很體貼。

I am, yes. But, honestly, I have nothing in common with him. Yeah, he is sweet and considerate①. 15:26

Sophia

譬如我們去逛街時，一袋袋的戰利品都是他負責拿，一起外出吃晚餐的時候，錢也都是由他付。

Like when we go shopping, he will hold my bags. Or when we go to dinner, he will always pay the bill. 15:30

Sophia

He sounds so sweet! What is the problem? 15:31

Joan

他聽起來很貼心啊！問題出在哪裡呢？

是這樣子的，每次我們去看展覽時，他都只會默默站在我旁邊玩他的手機。

Well, every time we go to exhibitions, he stands silently beside me, playing with his phone. 15:33

Sophia

It must be discouraging② to go to an exhibition with someone who doesn't share their feelings and ideas. 15:36

Joan

跟不分享感想和心得的人一起看展覽，感覺好掃興喔！

  SEND ≫

Let's Chat In English Via APP ●

236

就是說啊！你知道我有多麼喜歡看展覽，妳結婚之前一直都是我看展覽的伴，但是現在…

Exactly! You know how much I love exhibitions, and you used to accompany me before you got married. But now...　15:39

Sophia

我無法忍受跟一個像我男友那樣木訥寡言的人一起去看展覽。

I can't stand going there with such a slow and inarticulate₃ partner as my boyfriend.　15:41

Sophia

Joan

Don't be upset. My husband has been pretty busy recently. Maybe we can go to an exhibition together soon.　15:44

別心煩了，我老公最近非常忙碌，說不定我們很快就又能一起去看展覽了。

Joan

Are there any upcoming ones that you are interested in?　15:45

最近有沒有哪個展覽是你想去看的呢？

聽到你這麼說，我太高興了！我現在就上網查資料，真的好期待喔！

I am so glad to hear you say that! Let me check online right now for some information. I am so excited!　15:48

Sophia

Joan

Let me know if you find something interesting.　15:50

如果你看到什麼有趣的展覽，再跟我說吧。

Tip let me know是「請對方告知」的口語表達，正式的情境可用inform。

　　SEND ≫

Let's Chat In English Via APP ● ● ⏻ ● ●

237

23:16 📶 🔋

你找到想去看的展覽了嗎？我差不多要睡了。

Have you found anything yet? It's almost my bedtime. 23:16

Joan

Here, I found this website: www.npm.gov.tw. Check it out and let me know what you think. 23:20

Sophia

我找到這個網站：www.npm.gov.tw，你看一下裡面的資訊，再告訴我你的想法吧。

好，我看看，「中國歷代銅器展」、「明清雕刻展」…

Ok, let me take a look…"Chinese Bronze Through the Ages"…"The Carvings of Ming and Qing Dynasties"… 23:27

Joan

等等，我喜歡這個，「巧雕玉石展」，在第二頁第五項。

Wait, I like this one: "Jade Carvings and Precious Stones". It's the fifth item on page two. 23:29

Joan

Ah. It's an exhibition about Chinese jade artwork. 23:30

Sophia

這是有關於中國玉石工藝的展覽。

The well-known "Jadeite Cabbage with Insects" is supposed to be a great piece that is representative[4] of the general style. 23:33

Sophia

著名的「翠玉白菜」應該是最具代表性的作品。

沒錯，用石頭做的看起來居然能這麼精緻！

Tip too…to…在此有讚嘆的效果，注意「石頭」與delicate（精緻）的反差。

That's right. And it looks too delicate[5] to be made of stone! 23:34

Joan

   SEND »

Let's Chat In English Via APP ●

238

23:16

Sophia

Yes! When I first saw it, I thought it was incredible! 23:35

是啊！我第一次看到它的時候，就覺得太不可思議了！

聽說有很多參觀故宮博物院的觀光客都是衝著它去的。

Tip 用that one piece更強調「那一個」的獨一無二性。

I heard a lot of the tourists that visit the National Palace Museum go there just to see that one piece. 23:37

Joan

Sophia

Yeah, it is quite famous. Okay, let me check when the exhibition starts. 23:39

是啊，「翠玉白菜」真的很有名，我來確認一下展覽日期。

Sophia

Oh, here. "December 25th to the 30th, 8:00 a.m. to 4:00 p.m." How about going the first day? 23:41

有了，十二月二十五日到三十日，開放時間是上午八點到下午四點，我們第一天去怎麼樣？

十二月二十五日嗎？我想想看…噢，糟糕！我那天要參加家族聚會。

December 25th? Let me think… Oh no, I have a family gathering that day. 23:43

Joan

Sophia

You don't say! Ok, let's go the next day then, the 26th. 23:45

不會吧！好吧，那我們就約隔天，十二月二十六日再去好了。

Tip 朋友之間可用，語氣類似Oh no，但意思上指翻譯的「不會吧！」

  SEND »

Let's Chat In English Via APP

9:12

  # 1. 新的藝文中心

📖 Sophia 2014/12/13

I am so excited to have made plans with Joan to go see the jade exhibition at the National Palace Museum. We haven't been to an exhibition together in ages. I think the last time we went together was last year, before she got married. I am happiest when I go to exhibitions with Joan. Our tastes❼ are quite different, and that makes it a pleasure to share my impressions with her.

　　我很高興能與珍妮計劃一起去故宮博物院看玉器展,我們已經很久沒一起看展覽了,我們最後一次一起去看展覽,應該是在她去年結婚以前的事了,對我來說,和瓊一起看展覽是最開心的,因為我們的喜好很不一樣,所以分享心得的時候也特別有樂趣。

But what I might be even more excited about is the almost-finished culture center near my house. It won't be able to compete with the National Palace Museum in terms of size and scope❽, but it is only a five minute walk from my house. I have already glanced at the first month's schedule. There are a number of exhibitions planned, and I am anticipating every one of them, except maybe the contemporary❾ art one. I am not a fan of contemporary art – it is all too abstract for me. But, because the culture center is so close, I might go take a look anyway!

　　但更令我興奮的是,我家附近的文化中心快落成了,就規模和展覽的範圍而言,文化中心當然不能與故宮博物院相提並論,但它離我家只有五分鐘的路程。我瞄了一下第一個月的展覽安排,有許多已經排定的展覽,除了當代藝術展之外,我想每一個我都會去看,我不是當代藝術的愛好者,它對我來說太過抽象了,但是,既然文化中心離我家這麼近,我可能還是會過去看看的!

19:54

  2. 家族聚會的準備

Joan 2014/12/18

Every month or two, my family⑩ and my husband's family get together for a huge, home-cooked meal at our house. I enjoy it a lot. I love getting up early and going to the market to buy all the food. I love coming home and cooking all the food. I love eating with all of my nephews and nieces. And I love seeing the look on everyone's face after we finish eating. That look of contentment⑪ makes all the preparation much more enjoyable.

每隔一到二個月,我家人和我老公的家人會在我們家舉辦盛大的家常菜聚會,我非常喜歡每次的聚會時光,我喜歡早起上市場買食材,並回家烹煮的感覺;喜愛和我外甥、外甥女一起吃飯;更喜歡看到每個人用完餐後的表情,他們臉上的滿足感,讓所有的準備工作都變得很有樂趣。

I think my favorite part of the day has to be the cooking. Normally, I am too tired from work to cook a big dinner, so what usually happens is my husband or I get dinner on the way home and we eat while we watch television. I don't like it, but it is my daily life. If I had the energy, I would cook every day. That's why I try to cherish⑫ the chance these big family meals give me to not only enjoy everyone's company but also to simply cook.

家族聚會那天,我覺得我最愛的還是做菜的時刻,平常下班後,因為太累,沒精神煮頓豐盛的晚餐,所以,通常都是我老公或我在回家的路上,順道買晚餐回家,兩個人邊看電視邊吃晚餐,雖然我不喜歡這種感覺,但這就是我的日常生活。如果我有精神的話,我會每天做飯的,這就是為什麼我很珍惜與家族的大家聚餐的機會,因為,在聚餐的時候,我不僅能享受家人的陪伴,而且也可以好好地煮一頓飯。

Word 單字	Meaning 字義	Usage 常見用法
1 **considerate** [kənˋsɪdərɪt]	形 體貼的;體諒的;考慮周到的	be considerate of 對⋯體貼 in a considerate manner 以體貼態度
2 **discouraging** [dɪsˋkɝɪdʒɪŋ]	形 令人沮喪的;令人洩氣的	be awfully discouraging 太掃興了 a discouraging result 洩氣的結果
3 **inarticulate** [ˏɪnɑrˋtɪkjəlɪt]	形 口齒不清的;不善辭令的	the inarticulate passion 內心的激情 be slow and inarticulate 木訥寡言
4 **representative** [ˏrɛprɪˋzɛntətɪv]	名 代表;代理人 形 代表的;典型的	a legal representative 法定代理人 be representative of 代表⋯
5 **delicate** [ˋdɛləkət]	形 脆的;精美的;嬌弱的;纖細的	in delicate health 體弱多病 handle a delicate matter 處理棘手事
6 **gather** [ˋgæðɚ]	名 聚集;積聚 動 集合;收集	gather up 收集;拾起 gather oneself together 振作
7 **taste** [test]	名 味覺;味道;愛好 動 嚐;體驗	lose one's taste for 對⋯失去興趣 a mild taste 清淡的味道
8 **scope** [skop]	名 範圍;領域;機會;見識	beyond one's scope 超出能力範圍 have scope for 有施展⋯的機會
9 **contemporary** [kənˋtɛmpəˏrɛrɪ]	名 同時代的人 形 當代的;同時代的	a contemporary novelist 當代小說家 be contemporary with sb. 與⋯同輩
10 **family** [ˋfæməlɪ]	名 家庭;家人;家族	an extended family 大家庭 a family portrait 全家福照片
11 **contentment** [kənˋtɛntmənt]	名 滿足;知足;滿意	bathe in contentment 沉浸在滿足中 a smile of contentment 滿足的笑容
12 **cherish** [ˋtʃɛrɪʃ]	動 珍愛;愛護;懷有(感情等)	cherish a hope that 懷有⋯的希望 cherish a grudge against 耿耿於懷

文藝生活
Literature And Art～下篇

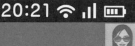

🔒 ◇ ✏   20:21 🛜 ▂▃▅ 🔋

◀ APP CHAT **3** 家庭聚會的邀約

Joan

Family gatherings are exhausting but are also so much fun. If you have time, you should join one of mine. `20:21`

參加家庭聚餐很累人，但也很有趣，如果你有空，一定要來參加我的家族聚會。

謝啦，但我不太喜歡非得社交閒聊的場合。

Thanks, but I don't like to be in situations where I am forced to mingle and make small talk. `20:24`

Sophia

Joan

Don't worry! My family is full of nice people. They won't bite. `20:25`

別擔心，我的家人都很善良，他們不會對你怎麼樣的。

Tip 字面上的意思是「他們不會咬人。」常用來鼓勵對方嘗試。

這和你的家人無關，瓊，是我自己的問題。

Tip It's not about sth. 意指「無關」，在對方推測不正確時，可用來解釋。

It's not about your family, Joan. It's about me. `20:26`

Sophia

Joan

Oh, don't say that. I really hope you change your mind and come meet my family sometime. `20:29`

噢，別這樣說，我真的希望你哪天能改變主意，跟我的家人見面。

嗯，我不是那種喜歡社交場合的人，說真的，我不懂為什麼有人會喜歡參加派對。

Well, I am not the kind of person who likes social events. In fact, I don't get why people enjoy parties at all. `20:31`

Sophia

Joan

It's not the party that matters; it's the ambiance❶ of it all. `20:32`

派對並不是重點，大家聚在一起的氣氛才重要。

Tip 虛主詞it之後的名詞，往往才是說話者的重點。

 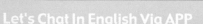 SEND »

我比較喜歡展覽會裡充滿藝術品的氛圍，氣氛比到處都是叫囂聲的派對好多了。

I prefer the ambiance of an exhibition hall, surrounded by artwork, over the ambiance of a party full of people yelling over each other. `20:35`

Sophia

Joan

Sophia, I really think you should get out and interact₂ with others more. `20:37`

蘇菲亞，我真的覺得你應該要多出門走走，和人交流、互動。

我有啊，我透過作品和藝術家們交流。

I do. I interact with artists through their works. `20:38`

Sophia

人很複雜，但藝術作品本身卻能很直接、純粹地傳遞出人們想要表達的訊息。

People are complicated, but their work conveys₃ what they want to express with a purity they don't have. `20:40`

Sophia

Joan

Life is not only about art. You occasionally need to keep in contact with other people. `20:43`

人生不是只有藝術，你有時候也需要跟其他人接觸。

老實說，跟我爭論這個是沒用的，因為我就是這樣，不會改變，對了，別忘了我們這個週末的約會喔！

Seriously, there is no use discussing this because I know I won't change. Oh, by the way, don't forget our date this weekend. `20:48`

Sophia

 [_____] **SEND »**

昨天參觀完故宮博物院後，我整個人就累趴了。

I am totally exhausted after our trip to the National Palace Museum yesterday. 11:37

Joan

Yeah, the museum was huge, and they had so many collections. All the walking we did really wore me out. 11:41

Sophia

是啊，故宮實在很大，裡面有好多收藏品，走那麼多路，真的把我累壞了。

不過所有的展覽品都很棒，我覺得「翠玉白菜」真是一項傑作。

But all the exhibitions were great! I thought the exquisite₄ piece "Jadeite Cabbage with Insects" was a masterpiece. 11:44

Joan

I agree! Those artists really had a meticulous₅ approach to their crafts₆. 11:46

Sophia

我同意！當時的藝術家真的擁有非常精細的工法。

是啊，我好喜歡那些精細的雕刻細節。

Yeah, I appreciated the detail in all the jade carvings. 11:47

Joan

Me too. Tragically, the skill hasn't been passed down. It's a lost art. 11:49

Sophia

我也是，可惜這種技藝沒有傳承下來，成為失傳的藝術。

Tip a lost art裡的lost是失傳的結果，和輸贏無關。

但話說回來，就是因為手藝已失傳，留下的這些作品才更彌足珍貴。

If you think about it, though, being a lost art makes the pieces we have much more precious. 11:52

Joan

SEND ≫

Let's Chat In English Via APP

245

11:37

Sophia

Good point. Although I liked all the jade pieces, I thought the paintings we saw were not very interesting. 11:55

説得好！不過，雖然我喜歡所有的玉石雕刻作品，但對畫作卻不感興趣。

你在説什麼啊？那些畫作既精細又栩栩如生耶！

Tip 口語常用，表達説話者的驚訝。

What are you talking about? The paintings were very detailed and vivid. 11:57

Joan

Sophia

That's the problem. Most painters from that period focused on their skills and failed to render any essence into their paintings. 12:00

那正是問題所在，那個時期大部分的畫家都只著重於繪畫技巧，未能表現出畫的精髓。

這我就不懂了，我就相信你説的吧。

Tip take one's word for it裡的word指的是聊天内容，而非單字。

Umm, I have no idea what you mean. I guess I'll have to take your word for it. 12:02

Joan

Sophia

You'll understand if you spend some time and study it out. 12:03

如果你花點時間研究的話，你就會理解的。

Tip study out意指「研究出」，其中帶有研究後的「結果」。

我沒有太多時間研究藝術，不過，以後有了小孩，我倒是很樂意你教他如何鑑賞。

I don't think I have enough time to study it out. However, after I have a baby, I would love it if you taught him or her how to appreciate art. 12:06

Joan

SEND ⟫

3. 家族聚會全記錄

Joan 2014/12/25

13:18

Our family gatherings are always a delightful mix⑧ of chatting, eating lots of food, and just relaxing in the company of family. This time, people began arriving around 11 a.m. and didn't stop arriving until almost 3 p.m. I didn't count how many relatives came, but it must have been close to twenty-five. Even my younger sister, who has been working in America for the last few years, came. When I saw her walk through the door, I burst into tears. I was so happy! We began eating at around 1 p.m., and, much to my delight⑨, all the food was gone by 4 p.m. Also, I noticed a lot of the children have been growing like weeds!

我們的家族聚會一直以來都讓人很開心，大家聚在一起聊天、吃東西、並享受有家人陪伴的靜謐時光。這一次，大家從上午十一點開始紛紛抵達，直到將近下午三點才到齊，我沒有算實際的人數，但一定接近二十五位左右，連過去幾年在美國工作的妹妹也回來了，當我看到她走進門，我的眼淚便奪眶而出，我實在太高興了！我們大約下午一點開始吃午餐，讓我高興的是，所有食物在下午四點時就都被吃完了，另外，我還注意到孩子們就像植物抽芽一般，長得很快呢！

People began leaving at dusk. By 8 p.m., the house was empty. The end of each family gathering is always the worst part. Not only do I have to wait another month or two for the next one, but I also have to clean up the mess everyone left.

黃昏時，親戚陸續離開，到了晚上八點，客人們就都走光了，聚會結束的這一刻總是最令我感傷的，這不僅是因為下次聚會還得再等一、兩個月，同時也因為我得面對聚會後的髒亂景象，並收拾乾淨。

10:36

4. 必看不可的展覽

Sophia 2014/12/26

After viewing the "Jade Carvings and Precious Stones" exhibition, Joan and I had some extra time and decided to go look at the Qing Dynasty paintings that were also on display. As an art lover, I thought both exhibitions on the art were perfect representations of the style. Before, it was enough for me to go to view the artwork and be satisfied. This time, however, I feel compelled⑩ to push my friends and colleagues to all go see for themselves.

那天與瓊去故宮看完「巧雕玉石展」後，由於還有一些時間，所以我們決定去看同時間展出的清朝畫作展覽。身為一名藝術愛好者，我覺得兩個展覽的作品都足以代表當時的風格，在此之前，只要能參觀展覽，對我來說就很足夠且滿足，但這一次，我覺得自己有義務要鼓勵朋友和同事親身走一趟才行。

I think it might be because so much of the artwork is irreplaceable. The techniques⑩ the artists who worked with jade are now lost to us, so there will never be new pieces in the same style. Another reason might be my recent talks with Joan. She has helped me rediscover⑫ my passion for art. I had been spending too much time with my boyfriend, whose reaction to any piece of art is a grunt or, if I am lucky, a "cool" or a "neat". And, of course, the beauty of every piece was also a major reason.

我想這可能是因為其中有很多藝術品是無可取代的，那些雕玉工藝現在都已經失傳，因此，未來也不可能再有相同風格的新作品；另一個原因可能來自於我最近與瓊的談話，她幫助我重新找回對藝術的熱愛，我花了太多時間和我的男友一起，他對藝術作品的反應通常就是咕噥一聲，運氣好的話，會聽到他回應「酷」或「很棒」，當然囉，想推薦給其他人的主要原因，還是因為每件作品都很吸引人。

APP 單字動態看板 Vocabulary Billboard

Word 單字	Meaning 字義	Usage 常見用法
1 ambiance [`æmbɪəns]	名 氣氛；格調；周圍環境	a comfortable ambiance 輕鬆的氛圍 the ambiance of sth. …的氣氛、環境
2 interact [ˌɪntəˈrækt]	動 互動；互相影響	interact with sb. 與某人互動 interact in price setting 互相影響定價
3 convey [kənˈve]	動 傳遞；傳達	convey one's appreciation 傳達感謝 convey goods by express 快遞運送貨物
4 exquisite [ˈɛkskwɪzɪt]	形 精美的；劇烈的	have exquisite taste in 對…極為講究 a pang of exquisite suffering 一陣劇痛
5 meticulous [məˈtɪkjələs]	形 縝密的；周詳的；完整而詳細的	handle…with meticulous care 謹慎處理 be meticulous in one's planning 計畫周密
6 craft [kræft]	名 技藝；工藝；手腕；奸計	master a craft 掌握一門手藝 a man full of craft 詭計多端的人
7 render [ˈrɛndə]	動 表達；翻譯；以…回報；提出	render a play into English 劇本譯成英文 render good for evil 以德報怨
8 mix [mɪks]	名 混和；結合 動 使混和；混淆	be mixed up in a quarrel 捲入爭吵 mix one thing with another 搞混兩件事
9 delight [dɪˈlaɪt]	名 愉快；樂趣 動 使高興	find delight in sth. 以…為樂 in high delight 興高采烈地
10 compel [kəmˈpɛl]	名 強迫；使不得不；強使發生	compel sb. to do sth. 強迫某人做某事 compel obedience from me 逼我服從
11 technique [tɛkˈnik]	名 技巧；技術；技法	adopt advanced techniques 採先進技術 a statistic technique 一種統計方法
12 rediscover [ˌridɪsˈkʌvə]	動 重新發現；再發現	to rediscover one's youth 找回青春 rediscover oneself 重新找回自我

UNIT 3

運動與健身
Doing Exercise～上篇

129 MP3

🔒 ◻ ✏️　　　　　　　　　　　10:20 📶 ▯▯▯ 🔋

◀ APP CHAT　**1**　**體育比賽LIVE直播**

Kevin

The Heat and Rocket game this morning was awesome! 10:20

今早熱火對火箭的比賽真是太精采了！

Tip 口語簡潔表達the A and B game，直接用and表示這兩隊之間的比賽。

我還在想你怎麼會在中午之前傳訊息給我，原來是早起看NBA球賽了。

I was trying to think of why you sent me a message before noon. Now I see you got up early to watch an NBA game. 10:25

Ralph

Kevin

Did you see it? Lebron James was amazing! It's hard to believe anyone can play basketball like that! 10:29

你有看嗎？「小皇帝」詹姆斯太了不起了！很難相信有人可以那樣打籃球。

你知道他高中時期從事兩種運動嗎？

Tip 表達「高中就學時期」，high school前面不加冠詞。

Did you know he was a two-sport athlete when he was in high school? 10:31

Ralph

Kevin

Yeah, I remember he played basketball and football, right? 10:32

知道啊，我記得他同時參加籃球和橄欖球這兩種運動，對吧？

沒錯，那正是他比其他籃球選手還要強壯的原因之一。

Yep. That's one of the reasons he is stronger than other basketball players. 10:34

Ralph

Kevin

I think "strong" isn't enough to describe him. He's like a monster on the court! 10:37

我覺得「強壯」不足以形容他，他在球場上的表現簡直就是個怪物。

🔊 😊 ｜　　　　　　　　　　　　｜ **SEND ≫**

我同意，他很擅長在被犯規後得分。

Tip get fouled意指對方犯規，常見用語還有foul out（犯滿離場）等等。

I agree. He is really good at scoring after he gets fouled₂. 10:38

Ralph

Kevin

On the other hand, Jeremy Lin is good, but nowhere near as good as Lebron. 10:40

另一方面來講，林書豪是打得很好，但還不及詹姆斯。

他還需要一些時間去適應，畢竟，他在成為尼克隊的先發球員之前，一直坐冷板凳呢！

He still needs time to adjust to the NBA. After all, before he was made a starter for the Knicks, he was always a substitute₃. 10:43

Ralph

Kevin

Yeah, his story has inspired so many people to continue to chase their dreams. 10:46

是啊，他的故事激勵了許多人繼續去追逐他們的夢想。

可惜的是，他並沒有帶動一般大眾的運動風氣。

Too bad that he didn't affect the general public's exercise frequency. 10:48

Ralph

Kevin

Well, it is much easier and enjoyable to watch others exercise than to do it yourself. 10:51

這個嘛，看別人運動還是比親力親為要簡單且有趣得多。

是啊，那就是我擔心的事。

Yeah, that's something I worry about. 10:52

Ralph

  **SEND ≫**

 Let's Chat In English Via APP ● ⏻ ●

251

9:25 🔋 📶 🔋

Ralph

Hey, Kevin, I'm going out to play basketball right now. Do you want to join me? `9:25`

嘿，凱文，我現在要出門打籃球，你想跟我一起去嗎？

Ralph

We can get lunch together after we finish playing. `9:26`

打完球之後，我們可以一起吃午餐。

不了，我今天起了個大早看籃球比賽，我現在想小睡一下。

Nah, I woke up really early this morning to watch basketball. I think I'm going to take a nap right now. `9:29`

Kevin

Ralph

You'd rather wake up early and watch TV than exercise? That's not healthy. `9:32`

你寧願早起看電視，也不願意運動嗎？那樣並不健康。

拜託，外面太陽那麼大又熱得要死，在這種天氣打球很容易中暑的，我們可以晚一點再出門吧！

Come on, it's so sunny and bloody₄ hot outside. It's easy to get heatstroke in weather like this. We can go out later. `9:35`

Kevin

Ralph

Okay, then, how about we go play basketball around three? `9:36`

好吧，那麼下午三點左右去打籃球怎麼樣？

那個時間也不太好，剛好是我的午睡時間。

That's not a good time, either. It's my siesta₅ time. `9:37`

Kevin

SEND ≫

Let's Chat In English Via APP

252

Ralph

You're going to take a nap right now and you will still take a siesta this afternoon?! `9:39`

你現在要去小睡，下午還要再睡午覺？！

Tip take a nap意指「打盹、瞇一下」，通常不會很久。

嘿，我也沒辦法啊，吃過中飯後，我就是會想睡覺。

Tip can't help it爲「不由自主」之意。

Hey, I can't help it. I always feel sleepy after lunch. `9:40`

Kevin

Ralph

Fine! Then how about 4 o'clock? You'll be awake by then, won't you? `9:42`

好！那改成四點可以嗎？你那時應該已經醒了吧？

是醒了，但我計劃和朋友去喝下午茶。

Yes, but I have plans to have afternoon tea with some friends. `9:44`

Kevin

Ralph

At the rate you are going, you'll die of laziness and obesity⑥. Fine, I'll go play alone. `9:46`

照你現在的生活步調，你遲早會因懶惰和過胖而死，算了，我自己去。

好啦！好啦！我現在不睡就是了，我去準備一下，三十分鐘後球場見。

Alright! Alright! I won't take a nap now. I'll get my things and see you at the court in thirty minutes. `9:49`

Kevin

 　　　　　　　　　　　　　　　 SEND >>

Let's Chat In English Via APP ● ●

253

1. 戶外運動全記錄

Ralph 2014/12/28

　　I love exercising so much that I made it my career! I spend most of my time in the gym teaching people how to stretch, lift weights, run, box, and just generally stay healthy and active. Even though I enjoy my job, I don't like spending all my time indoors. I love being outside, feeling the sun on my face and the wind in my hair. So, when I am not working, I try to get outside and exercise.

　　我熱愛運動，所以讓它成為我的職業！大部分的時間，我都在健身房教人伸展四肢、舉重、跑步、練拳擊，以及一些能保持健康和活力的普通運動，儘管我樂在工作，卻不喜歡整天待在室內，我喜歡戶外，感受陽光灑在我臉上，以及風吹拂髮梢的感覺，因此，當我沒在工作時，我會盡量出門運動。

　　Most of the time, I go to the park and play basketball. If I am alone, I try to join a team; and if I go with friends, we make our own team and challenge others. For a long time, I have been looking to try some other, more adventurous sports. So last month, I went out and bought some hiking gear and started doing day-long hikes in the mountains on my days off. It's been so much fun that I regret waiting until recently to start. It is the perfect way for me to stay active and be outdoors in my free time.

　　大部分的時間，我會去公園打籃球，如果只有我一個人，我就試著加入別人；若是和朋友一起去，我們就組隊和其他隊鬥牛。有很長一段時間，我都想要嘗試更具冒險性的運動，所以，我上個月去買了一些登山裝備，休假的時候，開始到山上做一整天的登山健行，那真的很有趣，我真後悔自己到最近才決定這麼做，對我來說，這項活動實在很完美，不僅能訓練體能，還能讓我在空閒時享受戶外的感覺。

🔒 ✏️   16:27 📶 ▂▄▆

微網誌 🔖 2. 下定決心來運動

📖 Kevin 2014/12/30

Everyone says I need to exercise more. My girlfriend tells me, my parents tell me, and even my friends tell me that I am way too fat. I used to be fit⑩ in college. I ran every day and played basketball and badminton. Once I graduated and got a job, everything changed. I no longer have time to exercise. I wake up, go to work, come home around eight or nine and eat dinner, watch some television and go to sleep. The only time I have for exercising is on the weekends, but that time is for my girlfriend. She insists we spend every Saturday and Sunday together.

每個人都說我需要多運動,我女朋友這樣說,我爸媽也唸,甚至連我的朋友們都說我真的太胖了,我在大學的時候,身材很標準,每天會去跑步、打籃球和羽毛球,但當我畢業找到工作之後,一切就變了,我不再有時間運動,我一覺醒來就去上班,大約八、九點回到家,接著吃晚飯,看些電視節目,然後就上床睡覺,唯一有空運動的時間是在週末,但那兩天的時間要空下來給我女朋友,她堅持我們週六和週日要一起共度。

I know I need to start exercising, I really do. I can see my belly getting bigger. I have less and less energy⑪ and feel more and more tired as the months pass. I talked to my trainer friend, Ralph, and we are going to play basketball once a week. I am also going to sign⑫ up at his gym. I promised him I will go twice a week before work.

我知道自己必需開始運動,我真的很清楚這件事,我可以看到我的肚子越來越大,幾個月下來,我的精神越來越差,也越來越容易感到疲倦,我跟做健身教練的朋友羅夫談過,我們約好每週去打一次籃球,我也打算報名他的健身房課程,我答應他,我每週會選兩天,在上班前到健身房運動。

Word 單字	Meaning 字義	Usage 常見用法
1 athlete [`æθlɪt]	名 運動員	an all-around athlete 全能運動員 be a natural athlete 天生的運動健將
2 foul [faʊl]	名 比賽犯規 形 骯髒的；惡劣的	through foul and fair 不管順利或困難 fall foul of the employer 觸犯老闆
3 substitute [`sʌbstə‚tjut]	動 代替；作代替者 形 代替的；替補的	substitute A for B 用A代替B a substitute teacher 代課老師
4 bloody [`blʌdɪ]	形 流血的；殘忍的 副 很；非常	a bloody battle 血流成河的惡戰 get a bloody nose 流鼻血
5 siesta [sɪ`ɛstə]	名 (西)午睡	one's siesta time 某人的午睡時間 be in siesta 在睡午覺
6 obesity [o`bisətɪ]	名 肥胖；過胖	widespread obesity 普遍肥胖的現象 be prone to obesity 容易變胖
7 stretch [strɛtʃ]	名 伸展；伸縮性 動 伸直；展開；延伸	give a stretch 伸懶腰 stretch out a helping hand 提供援助
8 generally [`dʒɛnərəlɪ]	副 通常；一般地； 大體而言	generally speaking 一般來說 in general 通常；一般
9 regret [rɪ`grɛt]	名 懊悔；後悔 動 感到後悔	with regret 遺憾地 express regret for 對…表示遺憾
10 fit [fɪt]	名 合身；(感情)突發 動 適合；安裝	by fits and starts 一陣一陣地 fit in with the facts 和事實相符
11 energy [`ɛnədʒɪ]	名 活力；幹勁	be full of energy 生氣勃勃；精力充沛 conserve one's energy 保存精力
12 sign [saɪn]	名 符號；標誌；暗號 動 簽名；作手勢通知	give me a sign to withdraw 示意我退下 sign for a registered letter 簽收掛號信

UNIT 3

運動與健身
Doing Exercise～下篇

🔒 ✉ ✏   8:45 📶 ▁▂▃ 🔋

◀ APP CHAT **3** **腰酸背痛的運動體驗**

天啊！我全身肌肉酸痛，它們在哭喊著叫救命。

Tip cry for help的主詞通常是人，本句強調肌肉酸痛的程度，增加口語的活潑度。

> Oh, man! My muscles ache; they are crying for help. `8:45`
> — Kevin

Ralph

> That's because you haven't exercised in so long that your muscles have atrophied❶. `8:47`

那是因為你太久沒運動，所以你的肌肉都萎縮了。

再次運動之前，我得好好休息一陣子，不過，我必需說，偶爾這樣揮汗運動，感覺很不錯。

> I think I need to take a long break before I exercise again. However, I must say that I liked sweating profusely❷ for a change. `8:51`
> — Kevin

Ralph

> You really shouldn't stop now. Otherwise, you won't see an effect. Exercising once isn't enough. `8:54`

你真的不該現在停下來休息，否則會看不到效果，只運動一次是不夠的。

你是說，就算全身酸痛，我還是應該運動嗎？

Tip are you saying that有確認對方意思的涵義。

> Are you saying that I should exercise even with aching muscles? `8:56`
> — Kevin

Ralph

> Yes. Right now, your muscles lack strength and stamina❸, so every time you exercise, they will ache. `8:59`

沒錯，現在你的肌肉缺乏力量和耐力，所以你每次運動，肌肉都會酸痛。

Ralph

> You need to continue exercising in order to build them up. `9:00`

你必須持續地運動，才能鍛鍊出肌肉的耐力。

Tip 實用片語build up，因為在講肌肉，所以有「使…健康或強壯」之意。

     SEND »

Let's Chat In English Via APP ● 🔘 ●

257

8:45

But it's hard to move now. How can I exercise when my muscles ache like this? Shouldn't I rest and let them recover? 9:03

Kevin

可是我現在運動都很困難了，怎麼可能在這種狀態下運動？難道不應該先休息一陣子，讓肌肉復原嗎？

No, that's actually not correct. Instead of doing nothing, you should do some easy, less intense exercises. 9:05

Ralph

不，那樣子其實不好，你可以做一些輕鬆、不那麼激烈的運動，而不是什麼都不做。

That will help your recovery more than no exercise. 9:06

Ralph

以緩和的運動取代，會比停止運動更能幫助你復原。

聽起來實在太累人了，難道就沒有消除肌肉酸痛的捷徑嗎？

That sounds like too much work. Isn't there a shortcut to diminish₄ my aches? 9:08

Kevin

Stop being lazy. There is no shortcut. 9:09

Ralph

不要再懶下去了，沒有捷徑這種事。

你還真是個嚴格的教練，羅夫，那我接下來該做什麼呢？

You're really a tough trainer, Ralph. So, what should I do next? 9:10

Kevin

How about jogging at least once every few days and playing basketball with me every weekend? 9:13

Ralph

那至少每幾天慢跑一次，然後每個週末和我去打籃球怎麼樣？

SEND ≫

Let's Chat In English Via APP

258

10:20

嘿，凱文，我那天在街上看到你，你好像變胖了。

Hey, Kevin, I saw you the other day on the street. You seem to be getting bigger. 10:20

Ralph

你沒照我的指示做，對不對？

You haven't been following my instructions, have you? 10:21

Ralph

Kevin

It's been really chilly recently. I'm afraid that I'll catch a cold if I go out jogging. 10:24

最近天氣一直都很冷，我怕出門跑步會感冒。

Tip catch a cold意指「著涼、感冒」。

那就是你的藉口嗎？你最好想個更好的理由，讓我相信你的懶惰是不可避免的結果。

So that's your excuse? You'd better come up with a better one that will convince me that your laziness was inevitable⑤. 10:27

Ralph

Kevin

Well…I did sprain my ankle last week. 10:28

那…其實我上個星期扭傷腳踝了。

怎麼回事？你該不會是模仿馬拉松選手，結果跑太多了吧？哈哈！

What happened? Did you try to emulate⑥ a marathon runner and do too much? Haha! 10:30

Ralph

Kevin

That's mean, Ralph. Not everybody is as fit as you. 10:31

這話太刻薄了，羅夫，不是每個人都像你一樣健康。

Tip mean在此指「說話很毒」，若想委婉一點，可用That's harsh（嚴厲）。

SEND ≫

10:20

I know. Sorry, man. But you know that jogging is good for your health. `10:33`

Ralph

我知道，抱歉，兄弟，但你知道慢跑對你的健康有益。

Kevin

I agree. But how can I keep jogging if I don't like it? To be honest, I hate jogging! `10:35`

這我同意，但是如果我不喜歡慢跑，怎麼有辦法堅持下去呢？老實說，我討厭慢跑。

如果你真的那麼討厭慢跑的話，那麼試試別的運動怎麼樣？游泳呢？

If you really hate jogging that much, then how about something else? Swimming? `10:38`

Ralph

Kevin

Swimming, hmm...that sounds okay. It will be a lot easier on my ankles than jogging. `10:40`

游泳，嗯…聽起來還不賴，那對我腳踝造成的負擔會比慢跑要少得多。

是啊，而且你也不用擔心流汗，那是件好事，對吧？

Yeah. You don't have to worry about sweating, either. That's a good thing, right? `10:43`

Ralph

Kevin

Absolutely, it is. What are you, a mind reader, Ralph? `10:44`

絕對是的，羅夫，你是怎麼樣，會讀心術嗎？

Tip what are you要依情境理解（本句有「你是做什麼的？」意思），最好對熟人使用。

SEND ≫

Let's Chat In English Via APP

260

3. 吸引人的音響廣告

📖 Kevin 2015/1/2

I am terrible at finding discounts❼, deals, or sales. Everyone I know tells me I am a bad shopper. I will buy whatever it is I need from the first store I go to that has it. I decided last month that my house needed a new stereo system. I was planning on going to the electronics store after I got my paycheck. However, as luck would have it, I saw an advertisement❽ for a discounted stereo system while jogging.

對於找折扣、交易、拍賣這些事情，我真的很不擅長，每個我認識的人都說我很不會買東西，就算只是第一家走進的商店，只要有賣我需要的產品，我就會當場買下它。上個月，我決定要替家裡添購一台新的立體音響系統，我本來計劃在拿到薪水後，到電器行看看，幸運的是，我在慢跑時看到了一則立體音響打折的廣告。

I usually don't pay attention to ads when I jog. I would put my MP3 player in its arm strap, put my headphones on, and listen to some loud rock music. That night, however, I forgot to charge my MP3 player and had to run with no music. It was a nice change at first, looking at the scenery❾ as I jogged. It became even better when I saw the billboard advertising such an inexpensive stereo system! It was such a good deal that I went the next day after work and bought one.

我慢跑的時候，通常不會注意廣告，我會把MP3播放器放到專用的上臂帶裡，綁在手臂上，戴上耳機，聽些熱鬧的搖滾音樂，然而，那天晚上，我忘了幫播放器充電，所以必須在沒有音樂的情形下跑步，起初，這是個不錯的體驗，可以邊跑步邊欣賞風景，而當我看見佈告欄上的廣告，發現這台價格低廉的立體音響時，那感覺更棒，價格實在太划算，所以我隔天下班後就跑去買了。

🔒 ✏️   14:30 📶 ▁▃▅ 🔋

微網誌

4. 學生的運動傷害

📖 Ralph 2015/1/6

A common problem my students have is their propensity⑩ to injure themselves. And it is usually the newer students that have the highest number of injuries. It seems like after only a week or two, most sprain an ankle or pull a muscle and have to rest for at least a month. It doesn't matter what they are doing, either. I have seen injuries from lifting weights, running, playing basketball, or even just walking up stairs.

我的學生們有個常見的問題，就是很容易受傷，通常越是新來的學生，受傷的人數就會越多，似乎在一、兩週之後，大多數的人就會扭傷腳踝或拉傷肌肉，必需休息至少一個月，他們受傷和做的運動沒有絕對的關聯性，我有見過練舉重而受傷的，跑步、打籃球的也有，甚至見過連上個樓梯都會受傷的學生。

My theory is that these students are trying to do too much and too fast. They take a class or two with me, and they think they know enough about their bodies to begin exercising alone. I always tell my new students to go slow when they first start exercising. Their bodies aren't used to the intensity⑪ and, as a result, get injured easily. For example, my good friend, Kevin, sprained his ankle jogging last weekend. He didn't tell me how it happened, but I can guess he either jogged too much or with improper⑫ form.

對於這種情況，我的推測是這些學生在運動時做得太多、也一下做得太急了，跟我上了一、兩堂課，就以為自己夠了解身體狀態，可以自行鍛鍊，我總會告訴新來的學生，剛開始一定要慢慢來，因為他們的身體還不習慣激烈的運動，所以很容易受傷，像我的好友凱文，他上週末慢跑時就扭傷了腳踝，他沒有告訴我發生的原因，但我大致猜得到，不是一下子跑太多，就是跑的方法不對。

Word 單字	Meaning 字義	Usage 常見用法
1 **atrophy** [`ætrəfɪ]	名 (醫)萎縮 動 萎縮；虛脫	cause atrophy of the liver 導致肝萎縮 an atrophied muscle 萎縮的肌肉
2 **profuse** [prə`fjus]	形 毫不吝惜的； 充沛的；過多的	profuse with one's money 揮金如土 profuse in one's apologies 一再道歉
3 **stamina** [`stæmənə]	名 精力；耐力	a great test of stamina 耐力的考驗 get enormous stamina 精力旺盛
4 **diminish** [də`mɪnɪʃ]	動 變小；減少；減弱	diminish one's strength 損傷元氣 diminish in size 縮小尺寸
5 **inevitable** [ɪn`ɛvətəbl]	形 無法避免的	bow to the inevitable 聽天由命 the inevitable hour 死期
6 **emulate** [`ɛmjə,let]	動 同…競爭；仿效	emulate one's success 仿效…的成功 in a spirit of emulation 以競爭的精神
7 **discount** [`dɪskaʊnt]	名 折扣；不全信 動 打折扣	be at 25% discount 打七五折 a discount on air fares 飛機票優惠價
8 **advertisement** [,ædvə`taɪzmənt]	名 廣告；宣傳	paste up an advertisement 張貼廣告 a classified advertisement 分類廣告
9 **scenery** [`sinərɪ]	名 風景；景色	the rustic scenery 鄉村風光 melt into the scenery (美/俚)隱沒
10 **propensity** [prə`pɛnsətɪ]	名 傾向；習性； 癖好；偏愛	one's propensity for evil 生性喜作惡 a propensity for 對…的偏愛
11 **intensity** [ɪn`tɛnsətɪ]	名 (思想等的)強烈； (電、熱等的)強度	grow in intensity 日益加劇 the intensity of feeling 強烈的感情
12 **improper** [ɪm`prɑpə]	形 不適合的；錯誤的； 不成體統的	make an improper diagnosis 誤診 an improper joke 不合時宜的笑話

UNIT 4

影視娛樂
TV And Movies～上篇

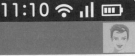

11:10 📶 🔋

◀ APP CHAT **1** 全新電視音響設備

Kevin

Guess what? I just bought a new stereo. The sound is so good that I don't need to go to the theater anymore! `11:10`

你猜怎麼著？我剛買了一套新音響，音效好到我不再需要去電影院了。

聽起來不賴，可惜還是比不上現場觀看比賽的感覺。

That sounds alright. It's a pity❶ that it can't compare to going to see a sports game. `11:12`

Ralph

Kevin

Well, the sound quality does make you feel a bit like you are courtside. `11:14`

說實話，這套音響的聲音品質會讓人感覺像在場邊一樣。

真的嗎？真令人難以相信。

Tip 如果改用unbelievable，驚訝的程度則更高。

Really? That's hard to believe. `11:15`

Ralph

Kevin

It does, really! Besides, TV is my favorite creature❷ comfort because, as you know, I love spending my free time on the couch. `11:20`

是真的！而且，看電視是我最享受的事，你知道的，我有空就喜歡窩在沙發上。

沒錯，你就是個沙發上的馬鈴薯。

Tip a couch potato意指極度沉迷於電視節目的人。

Yep, you're definitely a couch potato. `11:21`

Ralph

Kevin

You know it. I wonder why there isn't a furniture company asking me to make a commercial for them. `11:23`

你真了解我，我還納悶怎麼沒有傢俱公司請我幫他們拍廣告呢！

SEND ≫

Let's Chat In English Via APP ● ●

264

11:10

哈哈，說真的，那套音響只會助長你成天久坐的壞習慣。

Haha. Seriously though, that stereo will exacerbate③ your sedentary④ behavior.
11:25

Ralph

Kevin

Don't be so serious. I just want to enjoy my free time more. I will still continue exercising.
11:28

別那麼嚴肅嘛，我只是想多享受閒暇時光，我還是會持續運動的。

是嗎？你之前也是這麼說，聽著，要你運動已經有難度了，現在…

Tip 直譯為「像第一次聽到這話似的」，表達說話者的不信任感。

Really? Like I haven't heard that before. Listen, it's already hard enough to get you to exercise, and now…
11:32

Ralph

Kevin

Hey! Have a little confidence in me, okay, man?
11:33

嘿！兄弟，你也對我有點信心好不好？

你知道的，我只希望你能多注意一下身體健康。

You know I just want you to pay more attention to your health.
11:34

Ralph

Kevin

You know what? I think you should get a stereo, too.
11:35

你知道嗎？我覺得你也應該買套音響。

Tip 口語中的常見用法，這句話沒有特別意義，主要是為了引起注意而已。

不了，我不需要，我花在運動的時間比看電視的時間還多。

Nah, I don't need one. I spend more time exercising than watching TV.
11:37

Ralph

  SEND ≫

21:18 🛜 📶 🔋

羅夫，這禮拜三晚上我們來看場電影吧！我去租DVD，你帶一些洋芋片來我家。

Ralph, let's have a movie night this Wednesday. I'll rent a DVD and you bring some chips to my place. `21:18`

Kevin

Ralph

Wednesday night? I usually stay late at the gym and lift weights on Wednesday. I'll think about it. `21:21`

禮拜三晚上嗎？星期三我通常會在健身房待到很晚，練舉重，我考慮一下。

拜託，休息一天吧，你很久沒看電影了，不是嗎？

Tip take a day off 表「請假、休息」之意。

Come on, take a day off. It's been awhile since you saw a movie, hasn't it? `21:23`

Kevin

Ralph

Well, yeah. I mostly watch sports, not movies. Sports are more exciting. `21:25`

是啊，和電影比起來，我通常會選體育節目，那比較刺激。

看電影是不一樣的，你會看到忘我，並沉浸在劇情裡。

Watching a movie is different, though. You can get lost and find yourself absorbed in the story. `21:28`

Kevin

你花那麼多時間在運動上，都不覺得生活失衡了嗎？

Don't you feel your life will be unbalanced if you spend so much time exercising? `21:31`

Kevin

Ralph

I think someone like you, who is quickly getting a big beer belly, leads a more imbalanced life. `21:34`

我倒覺得，像你那樣的驚人啤酒肚才失衡了吧。

SEND ▶▶

Let's Chat In English Via APP • •

266

21:18

你別岔開話題，我是在說你的生活需要各種調劑。

Tip change the subject表示「改變話題」之意。

Don't change the subject. I am trying to tell you that you need variety in your life. 21:37

Kevin

Ralph

Alright, alright. I'll go. But I'll bring some vegetables and cheese dip. Chips are unhealthy. 21:39

好啦，我去就是，但我會帶一些蔬菜和奶酪沾醬，洋芋片不健康。

聽起來真噁心，你帶些洋芋片就好了啦。

That sounds gross. Just bring some chips. 21:40

Kevin

Ralph

Watching the movie is the point, right? Who cares what we eat? 21:42

看電影才是重點，對吧？誰在乎我們吃什麼啊？

當我沒說，我來準備洋芋片，你帶些喝的總可以吧？

Tip forget it意指「當我沒說、算了」，通常會在說話者有點受不了時使用。

Forget it. I'll get some chips. How about you bring some drinks? 21:44

Kevin

Ralph

Fine, whatever. I'll bring a case of beer. Are you happy now? 21:46

好吧，服了你了，我會帶一箱啤酒，這樣你高興了吧？

  SEND ▶▶

Let's Chat In English Via APP ● ⏻ ●

1. 朋友家的新電視音響

Ralph 2015/1/13

I am starting to really worry about my friend, Kevin. I have watched him gain a lot of weight over the past few years. Now, he told me he bought a new stereo for his TV. The more money he spends on improving his entertainment system, the less money he has to spend on things like running shoes and a gym membership. Also, he loved watching TV enough already. I think that with a new stereo, he will have even less incentive to get off the couch and go exercise.

我真的開始擔心我的朋友凱文了，過去幾年來，我看他胖了不少，而現在，他告訴我他買了一套新的電視音響，他花在娛樂設備上的錢越多，花在慢跑鞋和健身房會員上的錢就會越少，而且，他已經很愛看電視了，我猜有了這套新音響，他就更沒有離開沙發去鍛鍊身體的動力了。

I can't deny how awesome the new stereo is, though. It is a surround-sound system, so the sound comes at you from all directions$_8$. It really immerses$_9$ you in what you are watching. I thought it would be a nice, small improvement, but it totally changes the experience. I know he will enjoy the hell out of it. I just hope he finds a way to stay active and doesn't continue to get fat.

然而，我不否認這套新電視音響真的很棒，它有環繞音效系統，所以聲音會從四面八方傳來，真的會讓你沉浸在所觀賞的節目內容當中，我原本以為這套音響大概就是提升一點聲音效果而已，沒想到它帶來完全不同的影音體驗，凱文絕對會沉迷其中的，我只希望他能找到一個能激勵他持續運動的動力，而不是一直這樣發胖下去。

2. 陪女友上電影院

📖 Kevin 2015/1/16

I thought after buying a big TV and a nice stereo, I could say goodbye to movie theaters. I thought I would enjoy watching movies at home just as much as at the theater. These past few months, I have done just that. The other day, however, my girlfriend asked me to take her to see the new 3-D movie. If I had a 3-D TV, I would have told her to wait for the movie to come out on DVD. Unfortunately, I don't. So, I reluctantly① agreed to take her.

　　我原以為買了寬螢幕電視和不錯的立體音響之後，我就可以跟電影院說再見了，在家看電影將會變得像在電影院一樣享受，過去這幾個月，我的確都在家裡觀賞電影，然而，就在前幾天，我女朋友要我帶她去看新上映的3-D電影，如果我有3-D電視的話，我就會告訴她，等DVD出來之後再看就好了，可惜我沒有，所以，我只好勉強同意，帶她去電影院。

Now I know: even with my nice entertainment system, watching a movie at home cannot compete① with watching it at a movie theater. Everything at the theater is louder, clearer, and just better. Watching a movie at home is also not as enjoyable② as watching it with a group of people at the theater. Of course, I am still going to continue to watch movies at home, but I must thank my girlfriend for reminding me how different – and fun – going to the movies is!

　　現在我知道了，即使有完善的娛樂設備，在家看電影的效果和到電影院觀賞根本沒得比，在戲院裡，所有東西都更大聲、更清晰，效果就是比較好，而且，在家看電影也不像在電影院那樣享受，因為在電影院裡，有其他人和你一同觀賞，當然了，我仍然會繼續在家看電影，但我必須謝謝我女友，讓我想起到戲院看電影有多不一樣、多有趣！

Let's Chat In English Via APP　•　　•

Word 單字	Meaning 字義	Usage 常見用法
1 pity [ˋpɪtɪ]	名 憐憫；可惜的事 動 憐憫；同情	feel pity for 對⋯感到同情 do sth. out of pity 出於同情而去做
2 creature [ˋkritʃɚ]	名 生物；創造物； 傢伙	the living creatures 生物 creature comforts 物質享受
3 exacerbate [ɪgˋzæsɚˏbet]	動 使惡化；使加重	exacerbate a condition 使狀況惡化 be exacerbated by stress 受壓力而惡化
4 sedentary [ˋsɛdnˏtɛrɪ]	形 坐著的；久坐的	a sedentary lifestyle 久坐的生活型態 to remain sedentary 保持久坐不動
5 lead [lid]	名 指導；領先地位 動 引導；致使	give sb. a lead 以身作則 lead up to a conclusion 導出結論
6 variety [vəˋraɪətɪ]	名 多樣性；變化； 種種；種類	be rich in variety 富於變化 a variety of uses 種種用途
7 unhealthy [ʌnˋhɛlθɪ]	形 不健康的；有病的； 對身心有害的	an unhealthy diet 不健康的飲食習慣 find sth. unhealthy 發現某物有害
8 direction [dəˋrɛkʃən]	名 方向；方位； 指導；指示	a good sense of direction 方向感很好 take a new direction 有新趨勢
9 immerse [ɪˋmɝs]	動 使浸沒；使埋首於	immerse oneself in pleasure 耽於享樂 be immersed in debts 陷入債務之中
10 reluctant [rɪˋlʌktənt]	形 不情願的；勉強的	be reluctant to step in 不願意插手 a reluctant nod 遲疑的點頭
11 compete [kəmˋpit]	動 競爭；對抗； 比賽；比得上	compete with/against 與⋯競爭 compete in price 在價格上競爭
12 enjoyable [ɪnˋdʒɔɪəbl]	形 愉快的；有樂趣的	an enjoyable vacation 愉快的假期 be enjoyable for everyone 皆大歡喜

UNIT 4 影視娛樂
TV And Movies ～下篇

🔒 ⚷ ✎   9:58 📶 ⯈ 🔋

◀ APP CHAT **3** 要看什麼電影？

What kinds of movies do you like? And don't say romances❶...I am not watching a romance movie with you. **9:58**

你喜歡哪一類的電影啊？可別說愛情劇…我才不跟你一起看愛情片。

Kevin

Ralph

I'm not gay, okay? Besides, I only watch romance movies if they have a hottie like Angelina Jolie in them. **10:01**

我又不是同性戀，更何況，我只看有出現安潔莉娜裘莉那種辣妹的愛情片。

Ralph

I watch them so I can imagine I am the guy hugging her tightly, and, at the end of the movie, kissing her affectionately❷... **10:04**

邊看邊幻想自己是那個緊抱著她，並在電影結束時，深情地吻她的那個…

夠了，羅夫！太噁心了！你害我都快吐了。

Tip 指對方的言行太過肉麻，對有交情的朋友才適合這麼說。

Stop it, Ralph! That's disgusting! You're making me feel sick. **10:05**

Kevin

Ralph

All right. How about a science fiction❸ movie? "Transformers 3" looks good. It did great at the box-office. **10:08**

好啦，科幻片怎麼樣？《變形金剛3》應該不錯，票房成績很亮眼。

聽起來不錯，但是我沒看過前兩集，我會不知道它在演什麼。

Sounds good, but I haven't seen the first two. I won't understand what's going on. **10:10**

Kevin

Ralph

Yeah, probably not. Wait a second, there is an ad outside my office with the most beautiful girl I've ever seen. **10:13**

的確可能會看不懂，等等，我辦公室外面的廣告上，有我所見過最漂亮的一個女孩。

                                                    SEND ⯈⯈

Let's Chat In English Via APP • ⏻ •

271

9:58

Ralph

The name of the movie is "Twilight". Have you heard of it? `10:14`

電影片名是《暮光之城》，你聽過這部電影嗎？

聽過啊，你看到的是女主角貝拉，那是一部奇幻類的系列電影，內容與吸血鬼和狼人有關。

Yeah, that girl is the heroine₄, Bella. It's a fantasy series about vampires and werewolves. `10:16`

Kevin

我記得票房也很不錯。

Tip the box-office為票房之意，用法延伸自「劇院的售票口」。

I know it has done well at the box-office, too. `10:17`

Kevin

Okay, how about you rent it and we have an indescribable "Twilight" night? `10:19`

好，那你去借，我們就來一個美妙的「暮光之城」之夜吧！

Ralph

或許我們可以租整個系列，然後一個晚上全部看完。

Maybe we could even rent the whole series, and watch them all in one night. `10:21`

Kevin

Now get a hold of yourself. We still have to work tomorrow. `10:23`

冷靜一點，我們明天還得上班呢。

Tip get a hold of yourself是在叫對方克制，核心意義來自hold。

Ralph

說的也是，我可不想帶著黑眼圈見人。

Tip dark circles表示因熬夜等因素造成的「熊貓眼、黑眼圈」。

You are right. I don't want to end up with dark circles in the morning. `10:24`

Kevin

 SEND ≫

 Let's Chat In English Via APP

12:10 📶 ⏹

我必須說,《暮光之城》沒有我想的那麼恐怖。

I must say, "Twilight" was not as horrible as I expected. `12:10`

Ralph

我原本以為電影裡面會有很多吸血鬼吸人血的畫面之類的。

Tip stuff like that適合用在口語聊天,有「之類的、…等等」之意。

I thought there would be a lot of bloody scenes with vampires sucking people's blood. Stuff like that. `12:13`

Ralph

Kevin

I am glad "Twilight" was about a love triangle between Bella the human girl, Edward the vampire, and Jacob the werewolf⑤. `12:16`

很高興《暮光之城》這部片是描寫人類女孩貝拉、吸血鬼愛德華以及狼人雅各之間的三角戀。

凱文,如果你是貝拉,你會選擇誰呢?愛德華還是雅各?

So Kevin, if you were Bella, who would you choose, Edward or Jacob? `12:18`

Ralph

Kevin

I guess it would be Edward. Look at his vampire family: everyone is extremely good-looking. `12:22`

應該是愛德華吧,看看那吸血鬼家族:每個都好看到不行。

嗯,我比較喜歡雅各,他強壯的體魄足以在風雪之夜帶給貝拉溫暖。

Well, I would choose Jacob. He has that strong body that kept Bella warm during the blizzard⑥. `12:24`

Ralph

而且他健美的肌肉及陽光般的笑容和我一樣迷人!

And his perfect muscles and smile are as charming as mine! `12:25`

Ralph

SEND ≫

12:10

Kevin

Now that I can't agree with. Your smile is not charming; it scares away girls. 12:27

這我可不同意，你的笑容不迷人；它只會嚇跑女孩子。

Tip 原句為 can't agree with that now，變換單字順序之後，講法就更活潑。

老實說，是因為我一看到血就會昏倒，所以無法想像別人把它喝下去。

Honestly, the real reason is that I faint at the sight of blood, so I can't imagine watching someone drink it. 12:30

Ralph

Kevin

Haha, neither can I! 12:31

哈哈，我也不能！

你是說你看到血會暈倒，還是無法忍受別人喝血啊？

You mean you would faint over blood or you just can't bear to see people drink it? 12:33

Ralph

Kevin

Of course the second one. Do I look like the kind of person that faints at the sight of blood? 12:35

當然是指不能忍受有人喝血，我看起來像是看到血就暈倒的人嗎？

這個我就不知道了，畢竟人不可貌相嘛！

Tip 實用俚語，用書籍的「封面」與「內容」形容人的外在與內在。

Well, I don't know. You can never judge a book by its cover. 12:39

Ralph

  SEND »

3. 還是大螢幕好看

Kevin 2015/1/21

If I had to pick one thing that keeps me coming back to the movie theater, it's the "big screen". The popcorn, candy, audience, and atmosphere are all nice, but they are nothing compared to that screen. Watching a movie on it is magical. My television at home is 52", which is quite large, but it is nothing compared to the size of a theater screen. I'm talking about a normal theater screen, too. An I-MAX screen is so big that it is breathtaking. In fact, if I had the chance, I would only watch movies on an I-MAX screen.

如果要我講一件能把我拉回電影院看電影的原因，那絕對是「大螢幕」，爆米花、糖果、觀眾，以及氣氛當然都很棒，但一和大螢幕相比，這些就顯得很次要了，在大螢幕上觀看電影的效果實在太不可思議了，我家裡的電視螢幕是五十二吋，已經算是相當大的，但和電影院的大螢幕根本沒得比，而且我說的還只是戲院普通尺寸的螢幕，如果是I-MAX的話，螢幕可是大到能讓人倒抽一口氣的呢！老實說，如果有機會的話，我只想在I-MAX的螢幕上看電影。

For me, movies really only come alive at the theater. I thought buying a big television and a nice stereo system would emulate that feeling, but I was wrong. The only way to experience a movie is to have your field of vision consumed by it. It is only then that you can lose yourself and be absorbed by the movie.

對我來說，只有在戲院裡觀看，電影才顯得栩栩如生，我原本以為買了大螢幕電視和不錯的音響設備後，就能仿效那種感覺，但是我錯了，體驗電影的唯一方式，就是讓畫面佔滿你的視野，只有在那個時刻，才可能讓人忘我地沉浸在電影的劇情當中。

17:21

4. 氣氛才是最重要的

Ralph 2015/1/24

I appreciate a giant movie screen, a booming audio system, and a bag of popcorn in my lap just like anyone else. They are fundamental❶ to enjoying a movie at the theater. However, they are not what make the movie-going experience so memorable. No, that honor goes to the people sitting in front of me, behind me, and next to me.

就像其他人一樣，我喜愛劇院裡的大螢幕、隆隆作響的音響系統、和放在我大腿上的一袋爆米花，那是享受電影的基本配備，然而，那卻不是到電影院看電影之所以叫人難忘的原因，不，看電影之所以令人難以忘懷，得歸功於坐在我前後左右的人們。

Audiences make everything better, not just movies. They make listening to music, watching sports, or sitting in a lecture❷ more interesting and enjoyable. I like to think it is because I am sharing the experience – whatever it may be – with others. To continue with movies, I know when there is something funny, everyone laughs together; when there is something sad, everyone cries; and when there is something scary, everyone jumps at once. I will always believe that watching a movie with others is better than watching it at home alone.

觀眾的反應能使所有事物變得更美好，不僅僅是電影而已，不管是聽音樂、觀看體育競賽、或聆聽演講，只要有觀眾在，這些事情就能變得更有趣、令人愉快，我相信這是因為與其他人共享了經驗的關係（不管那是什麼樣的經驗）。回到電影這個話題，當劇情好笑的時候，大家會一同放聲大笑；發生令人悲傷的事情時，我們會跟著流淚；突然出現可怕的畫面，每個人也都會跟著嚇一大跳，我永遠都相信，和別人同享一部電影比單獨在家觀賞要好多了。

Word 單字	Meaning 字義	Usage 常見用法
1 romance [roˋmæns]	名 愛情小說；戀愛	an air of romance 浪漫氣氛 a girl full of romance 十分浪漫的少女
2 affectionate [əˋfɛkʃənɪt]	形 充滿深情的； 溫柔親切的	an affectionate kiss 一個深情的吻 be affectionate to sb. 對某人充滿深情
3 fiction [ˋfɪkʃən]	名 小說；虛構的事； 捏造；謊言	sth. be a pure fiction 純屬虛構 science fiction 科幻小說
4 heroine [ˋhɛro͵ɪn]	名 女英雄；女主角	play the part of heroine 擔任女主角 identify with the heroine 同情女主角
5 werewolf [ˋwɪr͵wulf]	名 (神話中)狼人； 殘忍狡詐的人	a werewolf legend 狼人傳說 to be bitten by a werewolf 被狼人咬傷
6 blizzard [ˋblɪzəd]	名 暴風雪；大量	a blizzard of paperwork 大量文書工作 during the blizzard 暴風雪肆虐期間
7 atmosphere [ˋætməs͵fɪr]	名 大氣層；氣氛	in a cordial atmosphere 在好氣氛中 a bracing atmosphere 涼爽的空氣
8 compare [kəmˋpɛr]	動 比較；對照；比喻為	compare A to B 把A比喻為B compare with 與…比較；相匹敵
9 breathtaking [ˋbrɛθ͵tekɪŋ]	形 驚人的	a breathtaking action 驚人的舉動 be truly breathtaking 實在令人屏息
10 consume [kənˋsjum]	動 消耗；吃完；揮霍； 使全神貫注；著迷	consume away with grief 抑鬱而死 be consumed with 對…著迷的
11 fundamental [͵fʌndəˋmɛntl̩]	名 基本原則；綱要 形 基礎的；根本的	the fundamentals of sth. …的基本原理 be fundamental to sth. 對…十分重要
12 lecture [ˋlɛktʃə]	名 授課；演講 動 講課；訓斥	a lecture hall 講堂 lecture on modern drama 講授現代戲劇

Part 5

生活型態

原來每個人都不一樣

學會了基本說法，想要展現更多的個人性格嗎？
本章將藉由特殊角色，介紹更具特色的生活英語。
窩在家裡的宅男宅女、喜歡接觸大自然的戶外派、
埋首於辦公桌的工作狂、遨遊天下的背包客，
現在就跳脫教室英語，聊出屬於你的心情與想法吧！

Let's Chat In English
Via APP

APP CHAT!

宅女的日常
A Homebody～上篇

🔒 ✏️   13:16 📶 ▂▁

◀ APP CHAT **1** 就是喜歡窩在家

Diane, one of the local radio stations is holding a cycling event this Saturday morning. Let's join it! `13:16`

Eric

黛安，這個禮拜六早上，有家電台要舉辦騎自行車的活動，我們去參加吧！

艾瑞克，我們都已經認識那麼多年了。

Tip have known each other for years最後加上now，強調「從認識到現在」。

Eric, we've known each other for years now. `13:17`

Diane

你應該知道我不是那種喜歡出門的女生，更別說是外出運動了。

You should know that I'm not the kind of girl who likes to go out of the house for anything, let alone to exercise. `13:19`

Diane

Come on, it's just cycling. You just go and ride around on a bicycle for a few hours. It will be easy. `13:22`

Eric

拜託，就只去騎幾個小時的單車而已，很輕鬆的。

對你來說，或許是很輕鬆，但我即便是走一趟我家附近的雜貨店都會累。

For you, maybe. I get tired just from the short walk to and from the grocery store near my house. `13:24`

Diane

Don't you think that you should get some exercise and some sun? You know, for your health. `13:26`

Eric

為了你的健康著想，你不認為你應該多運動、多曬點太陽嗎？

說實話，我寧願待在家裡吹冷氣。

Tip with the air conditioning on的on強調空調的「開啓狀態」。

Honestly, I'd rather stay at home with the air conditioning on. `13:27`

Diane

  **SEND ▶▶**

Eric

Diane, I really hope that someday you can join me and have fun outdoors for a change. `13:29`

黛安，我真的希望有一天你能改變一下，和我一起享受戶外活動。

艾瑞克，我很感激你那麼貼心，但我對運動就是沒有興趣。

I appreciate your thoughtfulness, Eric, but I'm just not interested. `13:30`

Diane

Eric

Now...what about bowling? That's something we can do indoors. `13:32`

那打保齡球怎麼樣？它是室內運動。

Tip what about後面接提議的內容，詢問對方想法，口語常用。

嗯，打保齡球是可以…但保齡球館總是擠滿了人！

Umm, bowling is okay...it's just that the bowling alley is always so crowded₂! `13:34`

Diane

Eric

Great! Then let's go bowling this Sunday morning. There should be less people then. `13:37`

太好了！那麼我們這個星期天早上一起去打保齡球吧，那時候的人應該會比較少。

好吧，我只希望保齡球館裡的冷氣夠強。

Fine. I just hope the air conditioning in the bowling alley is strong enough. `13:39`

Diane

  SEND »

16:22 📶

真不知道該拿黛安怎麼辦，她太離群索居了。

I don't know what I am supposed to do with Diane. She has secluded₃ herself from the rest of society. `16:22`

Eric

Well, you know what I think? I think she just needs a man! `16:25`

這個嘛…你知道我是怎麼想的嗎？我覺得她只是需要一個男人。

Lynn

琳，我是認真的，不要開玩笑。

Tip joke around為口語表達，意指「鬧著玩」。

Lynn, I'm serious. Don't joke around. `16:26`

Eric

I AM serious! If she fell in love, she'd be willing to listen to her significant₄ other and open up more. `16:30`

我很認真啊！如果她談戀愛的話，她就會願意聽她另一半的話，並打開心扉。

Lynn

Maybe try new things, maybe go outside for a change. `16:31`

也許她就會願意嘗試一些新事物，或許就會走出戶外？

Lynn

我還是不認為替她找個男朋友就能解決問題。

Tip get her a boyfriend所強調的是「我們做的安排」。

I still don't think getting her a boyfriend would solve the problem. `16:33`

Eric

況且，什麼男人會對像黛安這樣的宅女有興趣呢？

Besides, what man would be interested in a homebody₅ like Diane? `16:34`

Eric

  SEND ≫

16:22

Lynn

What I mean is...we make Diane fall in love with somebody. Okay? `16:36`

我的意思是，我們讓黛安愛上某人，懂嗎？

是可以試試看，但你要怎麼介紹男人給她呢？

I guess we can try. But how do you plan to introduce a man to her? `16:38`

Eric

Lynn

That's easy. You'll help me organize a small party at her place. `16:39`

這簡單，你幫我在她住的地方舉辦一個小型派對。

什麼？這怎麼會簡單呢？我們要怎麼讓她同意在她的住所開派對啊？

Tip 口語英文，當說話者一點都不覺得簡單的時候，才會這樣反問。

Huh? How is that easy? How do we get her to agree to have a party at her place? `16:41`

Eric

Lynn

Simple. You tell her we are coming over to watch a movie, and we surprise her by bringing some people with us. `16:44`

簡單，你就告訴她，我們要過去看電影，再帶些人一起去，給她個驚喜就好啦。

你還真是會出餿主意啊，琳。

You are quite the schemer⑧, Lynn. `16:45`

Eric

Lynn

Haha, I thought you already knew that! `16:46`

哈哈，我還以為你早就知道這一點了！

  SEND »

1. 出門不如窩在家

📖 Diane 2015/1/27

11:25

I really believe that there's nothing for me outside. The weather, the people, the noises, the smells, I hate them all. It's always too hot or too cold, too sunny or too dark. If I go out, I need to put on make-up⑦ and dress up – it's a real hassle. I am not used to wearing make-up, so when I do wear it, I always feel awkward⑧. I'd much rather stay at home and read a book, watch a movie, or browse⑨ the Internet.

我真的覺得外出毫無樂趣，天氣、人群、噪音、味道，沒有一項是我喜歡的，外面的天氣對我來說，不是太熱就是太冷，陽光不是太強就是太暗，如果要外出的話，還得化妝和打扮，這真的很麻煩，我不習慣化妝，每次化了妝，都會覺得很彆扭，相較之下，我寧願留在家裡看書、看電影、或是上網。

I wish my friends would realize that I am happy. I like being indoors with the air conditioning on. I like wearing sweat pants and a T-shirt. I like being alone with my thoughts and my books and movies. I don't need a boyfriend or a husband (or anyone, in fact) to give me self-worth. When my friends express concern about me, I always tell them I am alone but not lonely and not to worry about me. It never works, though. Oh well, c'est la vie. (c'est la vie = such is life)

我希望朋友們能了解的是，我很喜歡這樣的生活，我喜歡待在室內吹冷氣，喜歡穿運動褲和短袖汗衫，我喜歡在家獨自思考一些事情，或者看書和影片，而且，我不需要由男朋友、老公（或任何人）來肯定我的價值，當朋友表達對我的關心時，我都會告訴他們，雖然我一個人生活，但並不寂寞，根本就不需要擔心我，但是，不管說了幾次，都沒有效果，不過，這就是人生囉。

🔒 ⚠ ✏   11:25 📶 ▮▮▮ 🔋

  2. 宅性堅強的好友

📖 Eric 2015/1/28

I really believe, deep down at the bottom of my heart, that Diane needs to change her habits and get outside. She needs to get some fresh air. She needs to use her body, to run and jump and swim and walk. Our bodies are made to move, not to sit in a chair or lie on a sofa all day. I have told her too many times that her sedentary lifestyle⑩ is both unhealthy and unnatural! I wish she would listen, for her own good.

我打從心底認為黛安需要改變她的生活習慣,她需要走出戶外,呼吸外面新鮮的空氣,她得多活動身體,跑跑步、跳一跳、游泳、或是多走路,身體生來就需要活動,而不是整天坐在椅子上或是躺在沙發裡,我已經告訴她很多次,她久坐不動的生活方式不僅不健康,也違反了自然法則!為了她的健康著想,我很希望她能把這些話聽進去。

Every year, I see Diane getting bigger and bigger. If she is not careful, she will turn into an old spinster⑪ with no husband and no children. She says she doesn't care and is happy to be alone, but I think she is either lying or in a phase⑫. Unfortunately, I don't know what more I can do to change her mind. My sister suggested that I introduce a boy to Diane, but I am not sure if that will work. However, if there is a chance to get her out of the house, then I guess it is at least worth trying.

我看著黛安年年增胖,如果她再不注意,就會變成一個沒有老公和孩子的老處女,她說她不在意這種事,而且也樂得一個人生活,但我覺得這不是在自欺欺人,就是一個暫時的想法而已,遺憾的是,我已經不知道還能做什麼來改變她的想法了,我姊建議我介紹男生給她,說實在話,我不知道這麼做是否會有用,但如果有機會讓黛安走出家門,那不管是什麼方法,都值得一試。

Word 單字	Meaning 字義	Usage 常見用法
1 **grocery** [`ɡrosərɪ]	名 食品雜貨	groceries in stock 現存的雜貨 at a grocery store 在雜貨店
2 **crowd** [kraʊd]	名 人群；大眾 動 擠滿；催促	push aside the crowd 推開人群 crowd sb. for an answer 催促某人回答
3 **seclude** [sɪ`klud]	動 使隔離；使獨立	seclude sth. from 隔離某物 a secluded valley 獨立的山谷
4 **significant** [sɪɡ`nɪfəkənt]	形 有意義的；重要的； 顯著的	a significant difference 顯著的差異 play a significant role in 有重要的地位
5 **homebody** [`hom͵bɑdɪ]	名 愛待在家裡的人； 宅男、宅女	a homebody personality 宅男(女)特質 a homebody at heart 典型的居家一族
6 **schemer** [`skimɚ]	名 策劃計謀的人； 操弄陰謀的人	a sly schemer 狡猾的陰謀者 a political schemer 操弄政治的人
7 **make-up** [`mek͵ʌp]	名 化妝品；補考	take a make-up exam 參加補考 put on one's make-up 化妝
8 **awkward** [`ɔkwəd]	形 笨拙的；不熟練的； 尷尬的	be awkward with 對⋯不熟練 be awkward in one's manner 樣子笨拙
9 **browse** [braʊz]	名 (牲畜吃的)嫩葉 動 瀏覽；隨便翻閱	browse by chapter 隨章節瀏覽 browse about the bookshop 逛書店
10 **lifestyle** [`laɪf͵staɪl]	名 生活方式	the low-carbon lifestyle 低碳生活方式 live a lavish lifestyle 過著揮霍的生活
11 **spinster** [`spɪnstɚ]	名 未婚女子；老處女	a forty-year-old spinster 四十歲的老處女 to be termed a spinster 被稱作老處女
12 **phase** [fez]	名 階段；時期 動 分階段前進	in an early phase 在早期 phase in 逐步引入

宅女的日常
A Homebody～下篇

 APP CHAT **3** 一起出門看球賽

10:12 📶 ▮▮▮▮

真是個陽光普照的週末，
黛安，別只是待在家裡，
浪費這樣的好天氣，我們
出去走走吧，就你跟我。

What a sunny weekend. Don't just stay at home and waste this weather, Diane. Let's go out, the two of us. `10:12`

Eric

No, it's too hot out for me. I don't want to get all sweaty and uncomfortable. `10:14`

不了，這種天氣對我來說太熱，我
不喜歡流汗的感覺，很不舒服。

Diane

別這麼說！我們去看棒球
比賽，可以吃熱狗、和球
迷一起大喊加油，可不准
你說「不」。

Come on! Let's go watch a baseball game. We can eat hotdogs and yell with the other fans. I am not taking "no" for an answer! `10:17`

Eric

Can't we watch the baseball game on TV? We can eat and yell inside where there is air conditioning. `10:20`

不能看電視轉播嗎？在
家一樣可以吃東西和大
喊，又有冷氣可吹。

Diane

那和現場看比賽的感覺不一樣，黛安。

Tip at the game能表示「在現場觀看比賽」的意思。

It's not the same as being at the game, Diane. `10:21`

Eric

棒球場的氛圍比在家更讓人振奮。

Tip vibe為俚語，意指「無形的氣氛、感受」。

The vibe$_①$ of sitting in a stadium is so much more exciting than sitting at home. `10:23`

Eric

Well, I don't see how you can be excited about watching a slow, boring sport like baseball. `10:26`

這個嘛，我不明白觀看
緩慢、無聊的棒球賽有
什麼好振奮的。

Diane

  SEND ≫

Let's Chat In English Via APP

287

Eric

緩慢的比賽步調才是重點，那能建立起觀眾的參與感，讓你期待每一球。

The slow pace of the game is the point. It builds anticipation and makes every pitch₂ exciting. 10:29

Diane

But isn't it boring to always be waiting for something? 10:30

但是，總是在等待不是很無聊嗎？

那種等待才是棒球最棒的地方，一旦你體驗過一次，你就會愛上它的。

Tip the beauty of sth. 所指的是「某事中最棒的部份」，指抽象的好。

The waiting is the beauty of baseball! Once you experience it, you'll love it. 10:33

Eric

Diane

I doubt that. I know I'm impatient₃. Watching baseball is not for me. 10:35

我很懷疑這一點，我這個人沒有耐心，不適合看棒球比賽。

Tip 口語會話常用，not for me 表示「不適合我」之意。

跟我去一趟就對了，我保證你一定會愛上棒球比賽的。

Just come with me. I promise you will love it. 10:36

Eric

Fine. I'll go this once if you promise not to ask again. 10:38

好吧，如果你承諾以後不再找我，我這次就和你去。

Diane

What day is the game? Where are we going to meet? 10:40

比賽是在星期幾？我們要在哪裡碰面呢？

Diane

  SEND ≫

Let's Chat In English Via APP

288

17:42 🛜 ࢸ 🔋

Eric

Lynn, it really is true that a leopard cannot change its spots. `17:42`

琳,「牛牽到北京還是牛」這句話說得一點都沒錯。

什麼意思,艾瑞克?發生什麼事了?

What do you mean, Eric? What happened? `17:43`

Lynn

Eric

Well, last weekend, I finally got Diane out of her apartment. I got her to go see a baseball game with me. `17:46`

上個週末,我終於把黛安從她的公寓拉出門,一起去看了棒球比賽。

哇!那可是天大的好消息!她總算出門了?

Tip 這裡的news並非新聞,而是代表「從他人那裡得知的消息」。

Wow, that's great news! She finally went outside④, huh? `17:47`

Lynn

Eric

Yeah, but after we got to our seats, all she did was immerse herself in her iPad. `17:49`

是啊,但是在我們坐定位後,她就完全沉浸在她的iPad裡。

Tip immerse oneself in意指「沉浸在」。

呃,換個正面一點的角度想:至少你讓她變成在戶外玩iPad。

Well, look on the bright side: at least you got her to play with her iPad outdoors. `17:52`

Lynn

Eric

That wasn't the point. The point was that I wanted her to interact with people, not just go out with me. `17:56`

那不是重點,重點是,我希望她可以和人互動,而不只是出門而已。

SEND ≫

Let's Chat In English Via APP ● ⏻ ●

289

17:42 🔋 📶 🔋

那你最好想個比棒球比賽更能引起她興趣的東西。

Then you'd better think of something that will interest her more than a baseball game.　17:59

Lynn

Maybe you're right. Any ideas?　18:00

你說的對，有什麼好主意嗎？

Tip 會話中常會省略 do you have，但這種表達只適合用在口語當中。

Eric

你知道她用iPad的時候，通常都在做什麼嗎？

Do you know what she usually does with her iPad?　18:01

Lynn

Yeah. She spends a lot of time browsing artwork online.　18:03

知道，她大部分時間都在網路上瀏覽藝術作品。

Eric

那麼你應該帶她去參觀一些畫廊或是博物館。

Then you should take her to some art galleries⑤ or the museums.　18:05

Lynn

那雖然不是在戶外，但她至少不是待在家裡。

They may not be outdoors, but they are at least places other than her house.　18:08

Lynn

SEND ≫

Let's Chat In English Via APP • ⏻ •

微網誌 🔖 3. 球迷的熱情

📖 Diane 2015/2/4

After being nagged₆ for so long, I finally gave up and agreed to go see a baseball game with Eric. It was my first time in a stadium₇ and my first baseball game. I thought the game would be boring, having to wait so long between each pitch. Much to my surprise, though, it wasn't so bad. I liked that the fans cheered₈, chanted, and shouted any time there was a pause. I was playing with my iPad during a lot of the game, but I was still interested and paying attention to what was happening on the field.

在被叨念了這麼久之後,我終於投降,同意和艾瑞克一起去看場棒球比賽,這是我第一次去棒球場,也是我第一次觀看比賽,我原本以為比賽會很無聊,得一直等待投手投球,出乎我意料之外的是,比賽還滿有趣的,一有空檔,球迷們就會歡呼、唱歌、叫囂,我很喜歡這一點,雖然大部分的時間我都在玩iPad,但我也很好奇比賽的情況,並注意著整個過程。

I think watching the game at home would have been better, though. I could have enjoyed it in the comfort of my air-conditioned apartment instead of under the hot, mid-summer sun. During the entire game, I felt like I was being enveloped in a wave of heat. It was just too hot! I am glad Eric introduced baseball to me, but I think in the future, the stadium will have to come to me!

然而,我還是認為在家裡看轉播比較好,這樣就不用在這種炎炎夏日待在太陽底下,而能舒服地在開著空調的公寓裡觀賞比賽。待在球場的時候,我真的有種被熱浪籠罩的感覺,實在是太熱了!我很高興艾瑞克介紹棒球這個運動給我,但如果以後還要看棒球,還是在我家客廳裡看就好了!

Let's Chat In English Via APP

4. 難以置信的宅性

Eric 2015/2/5

I thought getting Diane out of the house to see a baseball game was a big accomplishment. After all, I spent a lot of time and effort convincing her. When she finally said yes, I thought I had finally made progress with Diane and got her to change her lifestyle. I knew she would hate it at first, but I was confident she would quickly realize how much fun being outside and watching a baseball game can be. Watching it on television just can't compare.

我認為把黛安帶出戶外去看棒球比賽是個很大的成就，畢竟，我花了很多時間努力地說服她，當她終於答應時，我感覺自己在改變黛安生活型態的這一塊，終於有所進展了，我知道她一開始會討厭，但我相信她很快就會意識到，待在戶外看棒球比賽是多麼地有趣，看電視轉播根本就比不上現場的感覺。

Now, after the game, I think all my effort was pointless. I am not sure Diane saw anything other than the screen of her iPad the entire game! From the moment we sat down until the game was over, she had her iPad in her lap and her face glued to the screen. I only saw her raise her head when there was a home run. Maybe I should give up and stop asking her to leave her house. If she is happy alone in her apartment, then she is happy.

但是，比賽結束後的現在，我覺得這些努力都毫無意義，整場比賽下來，我不確定黛安除了iPad的螢幕以外，還看見什麼，從我們坐下來的那一刻起，到比賽結束，她都把iPad放在膝蓋上，臉根本緊貼著螢幕，只有出現全壘打時，她才會抬個頭看一下，也許我應該放棄，別再要求她到戶外了，如果她認為一個人待在公寓裡是快樂的，那麼，她就是快樂的。

Word 單字	Meaning 字義	Usage 常見用法
1 vibe [vaɪb]	名 氣氛；氛圍；氣息	a nostalgic vibe 思鄉的氛圍 have a bad vibe about 有不好的感覺
2 pitch [pɪtʃ]	名 投球；程度 動 投擲；把…定在	fly a high pitch 飛到高空；野心勃勃 pitch into 扔進；拋進
3 impatient [ɪm`peʃənt]	形 沒耐心的； 不耐煩的	be impatient with sth./sb. 對…沒耐心 be impatient to 切盼於
4 outside [`aut`saɪd]	名 外面；外部 形 外面的；極限的	judge sb. from one's outside 以貌取人 at the outside 至多；充其量
5 gallery [`gælərɪ]	名 畫廊；美術館； 旁聽席	the public gallery 大眾旁聽席 bring down the gallery 博得滿場喝采
6 nag [næg]	名 嘮叨的人 動 嘮叨；糾纏不休	nag at 數落(某人) nag about sth. 抱怨某事
7 stadium [`stedɪəm]	名 體育場；運動場	crowd into the stadium 湧進體育場 a stadium gig 露天搖滾音樂會
8 cheer [tʃɪr]	名 歡呼；鼓勵 動 歡呼；使振奮	a round of cheers 一陣歡呼聲 cheer up 使愉快起來
9 accomplish [ə`kamplɪʃ]	動 完成；實現	accomplish sth. by effort 經努力完成 a sense of accomplishment 成就感
10 progress [`pragrɛs]	名 前進；進步	make great progress 取得很大的進步 the progress in sth. 某事的進展情形
11 confident [`kɑnfədənt]	形 確信的；自信的	be confident of 對…有信心 with confidence 自信地
12 glue [glu]	名 膠水；黏著劑 動 黏牢；緊附	stick like glue to sb. 與某人形影不離 glue one's eyes on 盯著…看

UNIT 2
走出戶外露營去
Go Camping～上篇

153 MP3

Diane

Eric, do you have any places to recommend for a weekend trip?
15:20

艾瑞克，週末渡假的話，你會推薦哪些地點啊？

Tip 實用口語英文a weekend trip，表達「週末的假期」。

推薦的地點？等一下，你是說戶外郊遊之類的嗎？

Places to recommend? Hold on a second. Are you talking about going on some kind of outdoor excursion[1]?
15:24

Eric

Is that a problem? You are the one who always encourages me to get out more.
15:27

Diane

有什麼問題嗎？是你一直鼓勵我多到戶外走走的。

Tip 不是真的在問什麼，只是表達說話者感到奇怪。

沒什麼，只是沒想到妳會問這樣的問題，太讓我意外了。

No, it's nothing. I'm just surprised to hear you ask that.
15:28

Eric

既然最近天氣都這麼好，我會建議去健行或去海邊。

Well, since the weather has been pretty good recently, I'd recommend going hiking or going to the beach.
15:31

Eric

You know I'm not an athletic[2] girl. Tell me somewhere I can just go for leisure.
15:33

Diane

你知道我不是運動型的女孩，推薦能讓我悠閒放鬆的活動吧。

噢！琳說很久沒去露營了，如果我們這個週末去的話，你要不要參加啊？

Oh! Lynn said we haven't been camping in a long time. If we go this weekend, do you want to come?
15:37

Eric

 SEND »

15:20

Diane

Camping...sunshine...fresh air. Alright, that sounds okay. `15:38`

露營…陽光…新鮮空氣，好啊，聽起來滿不賴的。

你不擔心沒冷氣吹，也沒電視可以看嗎？

You aren't worried about having no air conditioning or television? `15:40`

Eric

Diane

Not really. I'm actually₃ excited about the idea of camping with you two. `15:42`

不會啊，事實上，要跟你們一起去露營，我感到很興奮呢！

Tip not really的程度介於yes與no之間，語氣沒有no那麼強烈。

真的嗎？好，我會準備吃的，你只要帶飲料就好，可以吧？

Wow, really? Okay, I will prepare the food. You just need to bring some drinks, okay? `15:45`

Eric

Diane

I want to prepare the food. Let me do it! `15:46`

我想準備吃的東西，讓我負責這部份吧！

不行！你只懂得準備薯條和洋芋片。

Tip no way意指「想都別想」，帶有強烈的拒絕口吻。

No way. The only foods you know about are French fries and potato chips. `15:48`

Eric

SEND ⟩⟩

9:32

Eric

Diane, where are you? You're already thirty minutes late! 9:32

黛安，你在哪裡？你已經遲到半小時了！

Tip thirty minutes late 表示「遲到半小時」，Eric 為了強調語氣，所以加上 already。

我在路上，但我好像迷路了。

Tip on the way 這個片語強調「已經在路上，只是還沒到」。

I'm on the way, but I think I've gotten lost. 9:39

Diane

Eric

Oh god! How can you get lost in a city you've lived in for eight years? 9:40

我的天啊！你怎麼有辦法在住了八年的城市裡迷路啊？

我上次出遠門已經是很久以前的事了，街道看起來都好陌生。

It's been a long time since I went somewhere this far away from my house. The streets all look unfamiliar. 9:43

Diane

Eric

OK! Just stay where you are and tell me what is nearby you. We will come find you. 9:46

好吧！待在原地不要動，告訴我附近有什麼，我們過去找你。

好，但是我不知道要怎麼說明我現在的位置。

Okay, but I don't know how to tell you where I am. 9:47

Diane

Eric

Just find some kind of landmark. A road sign, a store, a building…is there anything near you that stands out? 9:50

去找個地標，路標、店家、建築物…你的位置能看到的特殊地標，有嗎？

   SEND »

Let's Chat In English Via APP

296

9:32

嗯,我看到路邊有一棟綠色的大樓。

Well, I see a tall green building beside the road.
9:51

Diane

Diane, be specific! That is too vague₆.
9:52

Eric

黛安,講明確一點!你的描述太模糊了。

Tip 覺得對方說話太模糊,很難理解時,就可以用be specific。

我看到一個戶外劇場的路標;上面說沿著這條路走,就會看到劇場。

I see a sign for an amphitheater₇; the sign says that it's right down the road from where I am.
9:55

Diane

Actually, you are not that far from our original meeting point. It's really impressive that you could get lost there.
10:00

Eric

其實你離集合地點並不遠,真佩服你能在那裡迷路。

我又不是故意的,這些街道看起來都差不多啊。

I didn't do it on purpose. All the roads look the same.
10:01

Diane

Just stay right there. We'll come pick you up in about five minutes.
10:04

Eric

你就待在原地,大約五分鐘後,我們會過去接你。

Tip stay right there所強調的是「待在你現在站的地點」,語氣更強烈。

好!待會兒見了。

OK! See you in a little bit.
10:05

Diane

SEND ≫

Let's Chat In English Via APP • ⏻ •

微網誌

1. 賭上iPad的假期

Diane 2015/2/8

I can't stop thinking about that baseball game. The more I think about it, the more fun it becomes. I have started to think that maybe lots of things are not as bad as I have imagined. I asked myself: "Have I been missing out on other opportunities? What other fun things have I mistakenly thought were a waste of time just because they were outside my house?"

我一直在想那天看的棒球比賽,想得越多,就越覺得比賽有趣,我開始覺得,也許很多事情並沒有我想像的那麼糟,所以我反問自己:「我是不是一直都錯過了類似的機會啊?還有什麼其他有趣的事,只因為是在戶外,我就誤以為那些活動只是在浪費時間呢?」

I talked to my brother the other day and made a bet with him. I told him that I would be spending this weekend camping with my friends, away from my apartment, my TV, my iPad, and everything else. If I don't go, or I come back early, or even if I bring any of my electronics with me, I have to give him my brand-new iPad. The bet is not about forcing myself to go camping. No, the bet is to show my brother – and everyone else – that I am so serious about changing my lifestyle that I am willing to risk losing my $15,000 iPad!

我前幾天和我哥哥說了這件事,並和他打了一個賭,我跟他說,這個週末,我會遠離我的公寓、電視、iPad,以及其他東西,和朋友去露營,如果我根本沒去、去了卻提早回來、或是攜帶任何電子產品,我就把全新的iPad拱手送他。我不是為了強迫自己去露營才和他打賭,不,這個賭注是要讓我哥哥和其他人知道,我很認真地要改變自己的生活方式,就算冒著失去價值一萬五千元iPad的風險,我也在所不惜!

2. 她竟然想出門？！

Eric 2015/2/11

I don't know what has come over Diane. Without any coaxing⑩ from me, she asked me about outdoor things to do this weekend. Her interest in doing something outside was surprising, but what really shocked me was when she agreed to go camping with Lynn and me! Somehow, she went from being a girl who spent all her time at home to a girl who wants to spend an entire weekend camping in the mountains! The only thing I can think of that could have had this effect was the baseball game we went to recently. But then I remember she spent the whole time playing with her iPad, paying no attention to the actual game!

我不知道是什麼改變了黛安，我都還沒有勸誘，她就問我這個週末要做什麼戶外活動，她對戶外活動有興趣已經很令人驚訝，更讓我吃驚的是，她竟然答應和琳與我去露營！不知怎麼回事，她從一個整天窩在家的宅女，轉變成想要整個週末待在山上露營的女孩！對於她的改變，我唯一能想到的原因，就是最近我們去看的那場棒球比賽，不過，我記得她都在玩iPad，完全沒有在注意比賽！

Anyway, I am happy to hear she willingly⑪ wants to get out of her house. I plan to invite a friend to join us on our camping trip. If it's too awkward for Diane, I can spend more time with my friend and Diane can talk to my sister. I think this won't be a stressful⑫ experience for Diane. I just hope that she won't run away when she sees my friend, though…

總之，我很高興聽到她自發性地想走出戶外，我準備約我的朋友加入我們的露營之旅，如果冷場的話，可以換成我陪我朋友，黛安就跟我姐一起，這對黛安來說應該不會有壓力，我只希望當她看到我的朋友時，不會拔腿就跑掉…

Word 單字	Meaning 字義	Usage 常見用法
1 excursion [ɪk`skɝʒən]	名 短期旅遊；郊遊	an excursion to 去…郊遊 a one-day excursion 單日的旅遊
2 athletic [æθ`lɛtɪk]	形 運動的；體育的； 體格健壯的	an athletic meet 運動會 athletic supporter (運)下部護套
3 actual [`æktʃʊəl]	形 實際的；事實上的	the actual cost 實際成本 in actual practice 在實踐上
4 unfamiliar [ˌʌnfə`mɪljə]	形 不熟悉的；不熟知的	be unfamiliar with 不熟悉 an unfamiliar city 陌生的城市
5 landmark [`lænd͵mɑrk]	名 地標；里程碑	a landmark in art 藝術的里程碑 a scenic landmark 風景名勝
6 vague [veg]	形 模糊不清的； 不明確的	a vague promise 模糊不清的承諾 be vague on sth. 在某事上含糊
7 amphitheater [ˌæmfɪ`θɪətə͵]	名 戶外劇場；露天劇場	in an amphitheater 在露天劇場 Roman amphitheater 羅馬競技場
8 opportunity [͵ɑpə`tjunətɪ]	名 機會；良緣	seize an opportunity 抓住機會 at the earliest opportunity 一有機會
9 electronics [ɪlɛk`trɑnɪks]	名 電子學；電子設備	the electronics industry 電子業 the electronics publishing 電子出版
10 coax [koks]	動 勸誘；哄騙	coax a smile from sb. 逗某人笑 coax sb. out of (V-ing) 勸誘不要做
11 willing [`wɪlɪŋ]	形 願意的；樂意的； 心甘情願的	be willing to 願意 the willing cooperation 自願合作
12 stressful [`strɛsfəl]	形 緊張的；壓力重的	live a stressful life 活得很緊張 a stressful discussion 沉重的懇談

UNIT 2 走出戶外露營去
Go Camping～下篇

🔒 ⟁ ✎　　　　　　　　　　21:42 📶 📊 🔋

◀ APP CHAT **3** 第一次的盲目約會

Diane

I'm so embarrassed! I had no idea that you would set me up on a blind date. `21:42`

好尷尬喔！我不知道你會幫我安排一場盲目約會。

Tip set sb. up為「設計某人」之意，依情境不同，也有「陷害」的意思。

這個嘛，就把它當作陪我去看棒球比賽的獎勵吧！

Well, think of it as a little reward for going to the baseball game with me. `21:44`

Eric

But you could have at least told me in advance! I could have dressed up before meeting you. `21:47`

Diane

但是你至少應該事先告訴我！那麼我就可以穿得漂亮一點了。

穿得漂亮一點？你不一直都是「隨性派」的嗎？

Tip 出席正式場合、勸人穿衣服多注意，都可以用dress up。

Dressed up? Aren't you a "casual only" kind of girl? `21:48`

Eric

Diane

That's when I go out with you. It's different for other guys, okay? `21:50`

那是和你出去的時候，和其他異性出門不一樣好嗎？

哇！看起來有人對某人一見鍾情了。

Tip get a crush在口語中很常聽到，指的是戀愛方面的吸引。

Wow, why do I get the feeling someone's got a crush? `21:51`

Eric

Diane

Eric, stop teasing❶ me! I am worried I acted clumsy❷ around Cody. `21:53`

艾瑞克，別取笑我了，我很擔心我在柯迪面前表現得笨手笨腳。

  　　　SEND »

Let's Chat In English Via APP • ⏻ •

301

別擔心，男人喜歡有點笨拙的女人，他們覺得那樣子很可愛。

Don't worry. Guys like women to be a little bit clumsy; they think it is cute. `21:56`

 Eric

Really? Do you think that Cody thinks I'm cute? `21:57`

真的嗎？你覺得柯迪會認為我很可愛嗎？

 Diane

老實說，我不知道，因為我不是柯迪，但你們露營時玩得很愉快，不是嗎？

Honestly, I have no idea. I'm not Cody. But you two did have a good time camping, right? `22:00`

 Eric

Actually, I'm not articulate$_3$ when I chat with guys, but he was gentle and made me feel comfortable. `22:04`

事實上，我不知道要怎麼和男性聊天，但是他很紳士，讓我覺得很自在。

 Diane

那麼，你對他的印象不錯囉？

Tip make a good impression on 表示「留下好印象」。

So he made a good impression on you, then? `22:05`

 Eric

Yeah, he did. I hope that I also made a good impression. `22:06`

是啊！我也希望給他留下了好的印象。

 Diane

別擔心，我了解柯迪，那傢伙不會和一個他不喜歡的人聊那麼多的。

Don't worry. I know Cody. He won't talk that much if he doesn't like the person he is with. `22:09`

 Eric

         SEND ≫

14:35 📶 🔋

Eric

Diane, what's new between you and Cody? `14:35`

黛安,你和柯迪之間有什麼新進展嗎?

Tip 與朋友聊天常見的口語英文,問對方新進展、新消息時用。

沒什麼特別的,我們每天互傳APP訊息,而且也約了幾次會。

Well, nothing special yet. We send APP messages to each other every day and we've been on a few dates. `14:39`

Diane

Eric

That's great news. Tell me, how do you feel about him? `14:41`

那很棒啊,告訴我,你覺得他怎麼樣?

我不太確定,但我們有很多共通點,我們喜歡的電影和音樂,有很多都一樣。

I am not sure. But we have so much in common. We like a lot of the same movies and music. `14:45`

Diane

Eric

That's a good start, isn't it? `14:46`

那真是個好的開始,不是嗎?

Tip 實用表達,帶有正面的肯定意味,不管是公事還是私事都可以用。

而且我們每天晚上互傳二小時的訊息,我的拇指都因此開始痛了。

Also, we message each other for two hours every night. My thumbs have started to ache from all the typing! `14:51`

Diane

Eric

You two should go out together more often, not just text back and forth. `14:55`

你們兩個應該多出門約會,而不是互傳訊息。

Tip back and forth強調的是「來回」的方向。

SEND ≫

Let's Chat In English Via APP ⏻

有啊，艾瑞克，你多心了，我們每個週末都碰面，通常會去看電影或溜冰。

We do, Eric, don't worry. We meet up every weekend. Usually, we watch a movie or go skating. 15:00

Diane

不過有時候，我們就只是在公園裡散步、聊聊天。

Sometimes, though, we just walk in the park and chat. 15:01

Diane

Skating! Really? Is this the same Diane I am friends with? 15:03

Eric

溜冰！真的假的？你還是我那個超宅的朋友黛安嗎？

Tip 這句話在口語上很實用，有指對方「判若兩人」之意。

是柯迪推薦我去溜冰的，我發現溜冰很有趣，不像其他運動那麼累人。

Well, Cody introduced₆ me to it and I found that skating is interesting and not as tiring as other sports. 15:07

Diane

嘿，也許你和琳改天可以加入我們。

Hey, maybe you and Lynn can join us sometime. 15:08

Diane

And be a third wheel on your date with Cody? Let me think… 15:11

Eric

讓我們兩個去當電燈泡嗎？讓我想想…

Tip a third wheel延伸自腳踏車多裝的一個輪子，比喻情侶間多餘的電燈泡。

I know Cody wouldn't mind, but I don't want to get in the way of you two lovebirds! 15:15

Eric

雖然柯迪肯定不會介意，但我可不想被情侶檔閃呢！

🔊 ✂️ [   ] **SEND ≫**

微網誌

3. 盲目約會的對象

Diane 2015/2/13

When I saw Eric's car and noticed a third person in the backseat, I was shocked©. I was even more shocked when I got in the car and saw that the strange person I didn't know was a cute guy! Eric introduced him as his friend and told me his name was Cody. I shook his hand and asked him if he was joining us on our camping trip. I was absolutely mortified❼ when he said that he was. What was Eric thinking, setting me up on a blind date?!

當我看到艾瑞克的車子，發現後座還有其他人時，我被嚇到了，而當我坐進車裡，看到我不認識的陌生人居然是個可愛的男性時，我更震驚！艾瑞克介紹時說那是他的朋友，名字叫柯迪，我和他握手，問他是否會加入我們的露營之旅，當他說是的時候，我害羞得不得了，艾瑞克是什麼意思啊？居然給我安排了一場盲目約會嗎？！

Fortunately, Cody turned out to be a nice guy. He talked to me a lot and seemed very interested in everything I had to say. Whenever there was a moment of awkward silence❽, Cody would make a joke or say something to continue the conversation. He was really talkative❾, and I felt comfortable being with him. We exchanged phone numbers. I hope that we will still get on well together in the future. Now that I think about it, I guess I should be thanking Eric for introducing us.

可喜的是，科迪人很好，他跟了我聊了很多，而且似乎對我說的事都很感興趣，每當出現無話可說的尷尬場面時，柯迪都會開個玩笑，或說些什麼來打破沉默，他真的很健談，和他在一起，我感到很自在，我們交換了手機號碼，希望之後我們依然能相處愉快，這麼說來，也許我應該感謝艾瑞克介紹我們認識才對。

Let's Chat In English Via APP

305

20:28

4. 身心舒暢的露營

Eric 2015/2/17

Camping in the mountains this weekend was exactly what I needed. I have been spending a lot of time at the office recently. When I do have free time, I go running, playing tennis, hiking, or bicycling. Needless to say, with both the stress from work and the energy I use exercising, I am always exhausted. I have to say that it is my own fault because I love the outdoors too much. And when I am too tired, I don't want to do something that requires⑩ a lot of energy. That's why the camping this weekend was so great for me.

這個週末在山上的露營正是我所需要的，我最近花了很多的時間在工作上，一有空閒，我就去跑步、打網球、健行，和騎腳踏車，不用說，因為工作壓力和運動時所耗費的體力，我總是感到精疲力盡，不過，要我說的話，那是因為我太熱愛戶外運動了，而我在疲倦的時候，就不想做太耗費體能的活動，所以，這次的露營對我來說就很棒。

Our camping trip last weekend gave me the chance I needed to rest while still enjoying the outdoors. It really was a perfect combination⑪. If I had stayed inside and watched TV, I would have gotten some rest, but I would have also been bored to death. It's strange to say this, but I have to thank Diane for asking me to recommend a leisurely⑫ outdoor activity. Had she not asked me, I am not sure I would have thought to go camping.

上週末的露營不僅給了我好好休息的機會，也讓我享受到戶外的感覺，這的確是個完美的組合，如果我待在家裡看電視，當然也會得到一些休息，但我會無聊到死的，雖然這樣說很奇怪，但我真該謝謝黛安要我推薦悠閒的戶外活動給她，要是她當時沒問我的意見，我不一定會想到要去露營。

Word 單字	Meaning 字義	Usage 常見用法
1 **tease** [tiz]	動 取笑；揶揄	tease sb. about sth. 取笑某人某事 tease sb. with jest 用俏皮話取笑
2 **clumsy** [`klʌmzɪ]	形 笨拙的；笨重的	one's clumsy behavior 笨拙的行為 a piece of clumsy baggage 笨重的行李
3 **articulate** [ɑr`tɪkjəlɪt]	形 善於表達的； 口才好的	an articulate point 清楚的觀點 be articulate about 直言不諱
4 **ache** [ek]	動 酸痛；疼痛	get a toothache 牙痛 an ache in one's head 頭痛
5 **introduce** [ˌɪntrə`djus]	動 介紹；引薦	introduce sth. to sb. 介紹某物給某人 introduce into 引入；引進
6 **shock** [ʃɑk]	名 衝擊；震驚；電擊 動 使震驚；使電擊	culture shock 文化衝擊 be shocked by 因⋯感到震驚
7 **mortify** [`mɔrtə‚faɪ]	動 使屈辱；使羞愧； 克制(情慾等)	be mortified by 因⋯感到屈辱 mortify the flesh (宗)禁慾苦修
8 **silence** [`saɪləns]	名 無聲；寂靜； 默不作聲	break the silence 打破沉默 a man of silence 沉默寡言的人
9 **talkative** [`tɔkətɪv]	形 健談的；多嘴的； 喜歡說話的	a talkative man 健談的男人 be too talkative to 話太多以致於
10 **require** [rɪ`kwaɪr]	動 需要；要求	require sth. from sb. 從某人那得到 require a special offer 要求特殊報價
11 **combination** [ˌkɑmbə`neʃən]	名 結合；團體；聯盟	in combination with 與⋯結合 the color combination 顏色搭配
12 **leisurely** [`liʒəlɪ]	形 悠閒的；慢慢的 副 從容不迫地	a leisurely stroll 慢步 with a leisurely pace 以悠閒的步調

工作狂與背包客
Work And Journey～上篇

◀ APP CHAT 忙於工作的生活

嘿，喬伊，我昨天剛從歐洲回來。

Hey, Joey, I just got back from Europe yesterday. **13:10**

Renee

Joey

Renee! How was your trip? **13:11**

芮妮！旅行好玩嗎？

很棒啊，我去環遊歐洲，最喜歡的國家有英國、德國和瑞士。

It was great. I traveled around Europe: the U.K., Germany, and Switzerland were my favorite countries. **13:14**

Renee

Joey

Renee, sorry, but I have an appointment❶ with a client in half-an-hour. Talk to you later? **13:18**

芮妮，抱歉，半小時候後我跟客戶有約，晚點再聊，可以嗎？

沒問題，去忙吧！

Tip go ahead有「鼓勵、催促對方做某事」之意。

Yeah, sure. Go ahead. **13:19**

Renee

Joey

Later! **13:19**

那就晚點再聊了！

Tip 口語用法，意思等同於see you，「暫時離開，晚點見」的道別語。

Joey

Sorry about that. I have been freaking busy recently. **15:45**

剛剛很抱歉，我最近實在忙得不可開交。

Tip freaking強調語氣，表示「極度」。注意，這個字不文雅，請不要隨便使用。

  **SEND ≫**

Joey

I communicate with about ten clients on average₂ every day. I also have to attend tons of meetings. `15:47`

我每天平均要聯絡十個客戶，除此之外，還得出席一大堆的會議。

That sounds like a nightmare. You should take some time off and enjoy yourself. `15:50`

聽起來像場噩夢，你應該找時間休假，好好地慰勞自己。

Renee

I mean, I feel amazing after my trip in Europe. `15:51`

我的意思是，像我到歐洲旅行一趟回來之後，整個人都感到神清氣爽。

Renee

Joey

I know it's important to relax, but even when I am relaxing, I am thinking about work. `15:53`

我知道適時地放鬆很重要，但我連休息的時候，也會想工作的事。

Yeah, you are a typical workaholic₃. I am not asking you to quit your job or anything. Just treat yourself nice sometimes. `15:57`

是啊，你是標準的工作狂，我又不是要你辭職之類的，只是希望你有時候能善待自己。

Renee

Joey

Alright, alright. Anyway, when are you going on your next trip? `16:00`

好啦、好啦，對了，你下次的旅行會安排在什麼時候呢？

I'm planning a trip to India in six months. How about going with me, Mr. Workaholic? `16:03`

半年之後，我計劃到印度走走，要不要跟我一起去啊，工作狂先生？

Renee

SEND »

Let's Chat In English Via APP

◀ APP CHAT **2** 想找不一樣的工作

19:10 📶

Renee

Hey Joey, can you do me a favor? `19:10`

嗨，喬伊，你能不能幫我一個忙呢？

Tip 實用片語 do sb. a favor，意思等同於 help，但語氣上比較禮貌。

當然沒問題，是什麼樣的忙呢？

Tip what's up 的口吻很隨性，說話對象一般為熟悉的朋友。

Sure, what's up? `19:11`

Joey

You know, I've been working at home as an independent translator for a long time, but lately, I've been thinking of getting a full-time job. `19:16`

我在家當接案譯者已有很長一段時間，但我最近一直想找份正式的全職工作。

Renee

你的意思是，你想到公司上班嗎？在辦公室裡工作的那種嗎？

You mean...you want to work for a company? Like an office job? `19:18`

Joey

Yeah, I kind of want to work with others. I am tired of always working at home. `19:20`

是啊，我有點想跟團體一起工作，不想在家接案了。

Tip kind of 的作用在弱化動詞的強度、或者緩和語氣。

Renee

你確定已經做好成為團隊中一份子的準備了嗎？畢竟你長久以來都是一個人獨立作業…

Are you sure you are ready to be a part of a team? You've been working independently for so long... `19:23`

Joey

I think I am. The problem is that it's hard to find a similar job to the one I do at home. `19:25`

我想我已經準備好了，麻煩的是，要找到性質類似目前的工作，似乎很困難。

Renee

SEND ▶▶

19:10

現在找工作很競爭，話說回來，你那麼熱愛旅行，還是目前的生活比較適合你吧？

It is very competitive₅ out there. Anyway, you love to travel, yeah? Doesn't your current lifestyle suit you better? 19:28

Joey

Sure it does. But I want some different experiences now. Besides, aren't you always telling me how important work is? 19:31

這是當然，但我想增加一些不同的經驗，你不是老跟我說工作很重要嗎？

Renee

我的確是這樣說過，那你希望我怎麼幫你呢？

I did, yeah. So what can I do to help you? 19:32

Joey

If you happen to know people who could use my expertise₆, let me know, okay? You have a lot of connections. 19:35

如果你恰好碰到能用到我專業的人，通知我一聲，好嗎？你的人脈比較廣。

Renee

沒問題，有些老闆會將你在國外多年的經驗視為寶貴的資產。

Absolutely. You have lots of experience abroad, which some employers will see as a great asset. 19:37

Joey

如果有任何消息，我會盡快通知你的。

Tip ASAP為as soon as possible的縮寫，書信當中也可以用。

If anything comes up, I will let you know ASAP. 19:38

Joey

SEND ⟫

Let's Chat In English Via APP

311

1. 從旅行認識自我

📖 Renee 2015/2/21

I read somewhere before that traveling₀ is the best way to learn about yourself. I agree wholeheartedly with that statement. In fact, I agree with it so much that traveling the world has been my goal in life for almost a decade! I try to take two or three trips a year. Each trip is usually between two to three weeks, depending on how expensive the plane ticket is and how much money I have saved up.

我讀過一篇文章，說旅行是探尋自我的最佳方式，我完全同意這種說法，事實上，我真的非常認同這句話，所以近十年來，環遊世界一直都是我的人生目標！我每年盡可能安排兩或三次的旅行，每趟旅程的時間通常是兩到三個星期不等，要看當時的機票價格以及我存了多少錢而定。

I have traveled all over Asia, Europe, and the USA. I have met some wonderful people, both locals and fellow travelers, and felt welcome wherever I went. My plan for the future is to continue traveling around Asia and to begin exploring Africa. My friends all say my love of traveling is an addiction₈. I always tell them that, unlike drugs or gambling, traveling is a positive₉ addiction. Every time I travel, I both learn more about the world and more about myself. Traveling really is a fascinating experience!

我已經去過亞洲、歐洲，和美國，也遇見一些很棒的人（包括在地人和同行的夥伴），而且無論到哪裡，我都能感受到人們的熱情，我未來計劃繼續在亞洲各地旅行，並開始去非洲探索。我朋友都說，我對旅遊的喜愛只能用上癮來形容，我都會跟他們說，旅遊不像毒品或賭博，它可是能帶來益處的癮呢！藉由每一次的旅行，我不僅更了解這個世界，也更理解自我，旅行的經驗確實令人著迷！

微網誌

2. 拜訪潛在客戶群

Joey 2015/2/22

One of the most important parts of my job is meeting potential‚ clients face-to-face. We always begin our correspondence‚ through e-mails. Aside from discussing business, we often share jokes and make small talk. It's quite casual, really. When I go visit them at their companies, however, the mood is always way more serious.

我最重要的工作之一，是與潛在客戶面對面會談，我們都會先透過電子郵件聯繫，除了洽談業務之外，我們時常會分享一些笑話、或是閒聊，相當不拘小節，不過，每當我要去他們公司拜訪時，心情上總是嚴肅得多。

This week, I need to visit a new client. I have a ritual‚ I do every time to prepare: I get a haircut, have my best suit dry-cleaned and pressed, and buy a new bottle of cologne. I try hard to present myself in the best way as possible. Everyone says not to judge a book by its cover, but I have been doing this too long not to know that the first impression is very important. I also don't waste time talking much in the initial meeting. I believe my clients appreciate my professionalism as well as the clean-cut image I present. In fact, I am confident they appreciate it because I am now the sole person in my company responsible for meeting potential clients!

這星期，我必須去拜訪一個新客戶，我有一套自己的準備習慣：剪個頭髮、將我最好的西裝送乾洗、燙過、再買一瓶新的古龍水，我認真地呈現自己最好的一面，大家都說人不可貌相，但我做這一行很久了，所以深知第一印象很重要的道理，此外，初次與客戶碰面時，我不會長篇大論地講個不停，我相信客戶們會欣賞我所展現的專業和整齊外表，事實上，我在這方面可是充滿自信的，因為現在的我是公司裡唯一負責與潛在客戶面談的人！

Word 單字	Meaning 字義	Usage 常見用法
1 **appointment** [əˋpɔɪntmənt]	名 約會；任命； 職位；委派	make an appointment 訂下約定 hold an appointment 擔任職務
2 **average** [ˋævərɪdʒ]	名 平均；普通 形 平均的；一般的	on average 按平均值；通常 above the average 超過平均水準
3 **workaholic** [ˌwɜkəˋhɔlɪk]	名 工作狂 形 醉心於工作的	a workaholic personality 工作狂特質 turn into a workaholic 變成工作狂
4 **independent** [ˌɪndɪˋpɛndənt]	形 獨立的；單獨的； 無黨派的	be independent of 與⋯無關 be financially independent 經濟獨立
5 **competitive** [kəmˋpɛtətɪv]	形 競爭的	a competitive examination 答辯考試 be highly competitive 高度競爭的
6 **expertise** [ˌɛkspɚˋtiz]	名 專門知識、技術	expertise in economics 經濟學專業 one's field of expertise 某人的專業
7 **travel** [ˋtrævl̩]	名 旅行；遊歷 動 旅行；移動	an air travel 航空旅行 travel on half ticket 買半票旅行
8 **addiction** [əˋdɪkʃən]	名 沉溺；上癮；入迷	break one's addiction to 戒除⋯的癮 drug addiction 毒癮
9 **positive** [ˋpɑzətɪv]	形 確定的；積極的； 真實的	the positive reaction 積極的反應 be positive of 確信；確知
10 **potential** [pəˋtɛnʃəl]	名 可能性；潛能 形 潛在的；可能的	sb. with great potential 潛力很大 have potential in 在⋯方面有潛力
11 **correspondence** [ˌkɔrəˋspɑndəns]	名 一致；符合； 通信聯繫	teach by correspondence 函授教學 in correspondence with 與⋯一致
12 **ritual** [ˋrɪtʃʊəl]	名 儀式；老規矩 形 儀式的；典禮的	insistence on ritual 拘泥於儀式 a religious ritual 宗教儀式

UNIT 3 工作狂與背包客
Work And Journey～下篇

🔒 ⬙ ✎   11:21 📶 ⏹ 🔋

◀ APP CHAT **3** 最佳工作代言人

Renee

Joey, you really do work all the time, don't you? When was the last time you went traveling? `11:21`

喬伊，你一直都在工作耶，你上一次旅行是什麼時候的事情呢？

就兩個禮拜前的事，我去雅加達出席一場業務會議。

Two weeks ago, actually. I went to Jakarta for a business meeting. `11:23`

Joey

Renee

Joey, I'm talking about traveling for leisure, not business. `11:24`

喬伊，我講的是悠閒的旅行，不是出差。

Tip travel for leisure意指「以放鬆身心為目的的旅遊」。

一邊旅行一邊賺錢有什麼不對嗎？

What's wrong with traveling and making money at the same time? `11:26`

Joey

Renee

I think it is okay if you're doing some kind of long working holiday❶. Six months or a year, something like that. `11:29`

如果是長時間的打工渡假，那就沒問題，比如六個月或一年的那種。

Renee

Your business trip was, what, a few days? You probably didn't have even a moment to enjoy Jakarta. `11:32`

但是你那種出差只有幾天，不是嗎？你可能根本沒時間享受雅加達的美景。

老實說，完成工作後的成就感對我而言就很足夠了。

Seriously, the sense of accomplishment I got after finishing my work there was rewarding❷ enough. `11:36`

Joey

  [   ]   SEND »

Let's Chat In English Via APP • ⏻ •

315

Renee

I guess that you haven't been on a vacation since your graduation trip. `11:38`

我猜你從畢業旅行後,就沒有再去渡假了。

Tip be on a vacation強調「渡假的狀態」;go on則強調「動作」。

對啊,但那對我來說不是問題,我熱愛工作。

Yep, but it's not a problem for me at all. I love working. `11:39`

Joey

Renee

If I were your boss, I would appreciate you. But I would also make you take a break sometimes. You will exhaust yourself otherwise. `11:44`

如果我是你的老闆,我會感謝你如此地熱愛工作,但也會要你適時休息,否則你會精疲力盡的。

說真的,芮妮,我一點都不覺得累,工作讓我覺得很滿足。

Seriously, Renee, I don't feel tired at all. I feel content to work. `11:45`

Joey

Renee

Wow, Joey. Entrepreneurs and bosses should all hire you to be their spokesperson③. `11:48`

我的天啊!喬伊,企業家與老闆都該找你去當代言人才是。

沒錯,我可是完美員工呢!

Tip yes的口語表達,一般是和朋友聊天時會出現的用法。

Yep, I am the ideal employee. `11:49`

Joey

SEND ≫

Let's Chat In English Via APP ● ⏻ ●

316

22:39 📶 🔋

如果可以,我想一輩子都去旅行。

If I can, I want to travel until I die.
22:39

Renee

Joey

Well, if I can, I will keep working. Actually, what am I talking about... I can! And I will.
22:41

如果可以,我會選擇一直工作,等等,我在說什麼呢?實際上我真的可以!我會這麼做的。

所以你永遠不退休嗎?

Tip never強調語氣,Renee用誇張的說法反問,在告訴對方「總會退休」。

You will never retire?
22:42

Renee

Joey

Just imaging retired life makes me feel bored. So no, I don't think I will.
22:44

光是想像退休生活,我就感到很無聊了,所以我不認為我會有退休的一天。

你真是個怪胎,喬伊,有很多人年輕時努力工作,就是為了能早點退休。

You're a weirdo₄, Joey. So many people work hard when they are young so they can retire early.
22:47

Renee

Joey

I'm curious as to why people want to retire. Don't they like working?
22:49

我很好奇為什麼有人會想要退休,難道他們不喜歡工作嗎?

一般人都會想要早點退休,如此一來,他們就可以去完成他們真正想做的事,而不只是工作而已。

People want to retire early so they can do things they really want to do and not just work.
22:52

Renee

Renee

 SEND ≫

22:39

比方說去旅行、學畫畫、彈鋼琴、或者搬到鄉下住等等。

Things like traveling, learning how to paint or play the piano, maybe moving to the countryside. `22:54`

Renee

Then I don't need to retire because I am already doing what I really want to do: working. `22:56`

那我不用退休，因為我已經在做我想做的事了，那就是工作。

Joey

除了工作之外，你一定有什麼其他想做的事。

There must be something you want to achieve⑤ unrelated⑥ to your job. `22:58`

Renee

There was once, but not anymore. I guess you could call it my childhood dream. `23:00`

曾經有，但後來就沒有了，我認為那只能算是孩童時期的夢想。

Tip 後面用not anymore表示「事情不再存在」之意。

Joey

那就是我要講的，喬伊，一個終身的夢想。

Tip 口語英文，當對方講到自己想表達的意思時用。

That's what I am talking about, Joey, a lifelong⑦ dream. `23:01`

Renee

It wasn't a lifelong dream, though. Once I started working, I set that dream aside. `23:03`

那並不是什麼終身的夢想，當我踏入職場後，我就把那個想法擺到一邊了。

Joey

Now that I am an adult, it is more practical for me to focus on work and not something I dreamed about as a kid. `23:06`

我都已經是成年人了，與其像小孩一樣做白日夢，還不如專注在工作上比較實在。

Joey

Let's Chat In English Via APP

🔒 ✉ ✏   21:26 📶 ▮▮▮

3. 熱愛工作不行嗎？

📖 Joey 2015/2/26

Honestly, I have grown tired of explaining to my friends and family that I love my job. You might think after years of hearing the same thing, they would all take a hint and accept this fact, but oh no, they persist in doubting me. I wonder, how many more times I will need to tell them I am happy before they believe me? Renee told me that, apart from their jobs, most people have other interests. I of course acknowledged her point. However, if my job is the thing I want to do, how is that not a good thing?

老實說，我已經厭倦向我朋友和家人解釋我有多麼熱愛工作，你可能會認為，在聽了這麼多年同樣的話之後，他們就真能聽進去，並接受這個事實，但實際上並非如此，他們仍然懷疑我的說法，在他們相信之前，我究竟還得強調幾次「我很快樂」呢？芮妮跟我說，一般人除了工作，都會有其他想做的事，這點我認同，不過，如果工作就是自己想做的事，那不是很好嗎？

I think it is a good, positive attribute⑥ to love your job. If more people had my attitude⑨, companies would have fewer problems, food would taste better, shopping would be more pleasant, and the list goes on. Everywhere I look, I see people who hate their jobs. They only work to make money. I am proud to be different, to be someone who loves his job. I feel like I am lucky to have found a job I love.

就我看來，熱愛工作是個積極正面的良好特質，如果有更多人的態度和我一樣，公司的問題就能漸少、食物嚐起來的味道會更好、逛起街來也更加愉快，能帶來的正面影響不勝枚舉，不管到哪裡，都能看到討厭工作的人，因為他們工作的目的只是為了賺錢，能跟這樣的大眾不同，並熱愛工作，我感到很自豪，也很慶幸能找到一份自己喜愛的工作。

Let's Chat In English Via APP • •

4. 整理出書的相片

Renee 2015/3/8

20:52

I guess all the traveling I have done is going to pay off financially⑩. Yesterday, I had a meeting with a publishing company. They told me they want me to write a book about my travels abroad. I was full of doubt at first because I didn't know why they were offering me this deal. They said someone in the company discovered my blog and pitched the idea of turning that into a book. Apparently, they enjoyed both my writing and my photography⑪ and are interested in using both for the book.

我想我過去所有的旅遊經歷,可能就要成為我的經濟來源了,昨天,我與一家出版社的人碰面,他們希望我能寫一本有關我在海外旅遊的書,起初我感到很疑惑,因為我完全不清楚出版社為什麼會找上我,他們告訴我,公司的一位員工有天看到我部落格的文章,便提出旅遊書的構想,並極力地推薦我寫這本書,很顯然,他們喜歡我的文章和攝影,也有興趣將這兩項納入書中。

I am more than a little surprised by this opportunity. My work experience is all in translating, not writing. My blog is something I write just for fun. Before being called by the publishing company, I had no intention of trying to make money off my traveling. However, after our meeting, travel writing seems like an easy job that incorporates⑫ what I love most in life. So, why not try it? I have got nothing to lose.

有這樣的機會,我感到非常驚訝,我的工作經驗都與翻譯有關,而非寫作,我寫部落格純粹是好玩而已,在出版社打電話給我之前,我從來沒想過將旅遊經歷轉變成收入來源,但與他們談過之後,旅遊寫作似乎是個能結合我興趣的好方法,既然如此,我何不試試呢?反正我也沒什麼好損失的。

Word 單字	Meaning 字義	Usage 常見用法
1 **holiday** [`hɑlə‚de]	名 節日；假日	take a month's holiday 休假一個月 be away on holiday 外出渡假
2 **reward** [rɪ`wɔrd]	名 報答；酬金 動 報答；報償	in reward for 為酬答… reward sb. for one's help 答謝…的幫助
3 **spokesperson** [`spoks‚pɜsn]	名 發言人	as a spokesperson 作為發言人 the spokesperson for …的代言人
4 **weirdo** [`wɪrdo]	名 怪人；怪物	a bunch of real weirdoes 一群怪人 view sb. as a weirdo 視…為怪人
5 **achieve** [ə`tʃiv]	動 達到目的；贏得； 完成；實現	achieve one's ends 達到目的 the substantial achievement 重大成就
6 **unrelated** [‚ʌnrɪ`letɪd]	形 無關的	an unrelated rumor 無關的傳言 be unrelated to 與…無關
7 **lifelong** [`laɪf‚lɔŋ]	形 終身的；一輩子的	lifelong insurance 終身保險 a lifelong struggle 窮盡一生的奮鬥
8 **attribute** [`ætrə‚bjut]	名 屬性；特質	an attribute of a product 產品屬性 one's greatest attribute …最大的特點
9 **attitude** [`ætətjud]	名 態度；意見	the attitude towards 對…的態度 give attitude 要脾氣
10 **financial** [faɪ`nænʃəl]	形 財政的；金融的	apply for financial aid 申請助學金 in financial difficulties 陷入財政困境
11 **photography** [fə`tɑgrəfɪ]	名 照相術；攝影術	go in for photography 酷愛攝影 a photography album 攝影專集
12 **incorporate** [ɪn`kɔrpə‚ret]	動 合併；混合；包含	incorporate A with B 混合；合併 incorporate sth. in 將某事納入…

海外假期
Travel Overseas～上篇

20:06 📶 ▫️▫️▫️

◀ APP CHAT **1** 年假旅遊邀約

嘿，你今年有幾天的假呢？

Hey, how many days are you getting off this year for the holidays? `20:06`

Renee

Joey

Believe it or not, my boss gave me ten days off. `20:07`

信不信由你，我的老闆給了我十天假。

Tip believe it or not放在重點句之前，有引起注意的效果。

是嗎？！聽著，我正計劃到泰國旅遊，我認為你應該一起去，時間是一個星期。

Oh yeah?! Listen, I am planning a trip to Thailand, and I think you should come. It'll be for a week. `20:10`

Renee

有美麗的海灘以及美味的食物，是最完美的假期享受喔！

There will be beautiful beaches and great food. It'll be the perfect way for you to enjoy your time off. `20:12`

Renee

Joey

Sounds tempting, but I was actually thinking of writing a proposal at home. `20:15`

聽起來很誘人，但我其實打算在家裡寫企劃案。

哦不，又來了！你得好好休息一下，這個企劃案什麼時候要交啊？

Tip not again語氣上較強烈，且能看出情況沒有順著說話者的心意。

Oh, come on, not again! You have to take a break. When is this proposal due? `20:17`

Renee

Joey

Two weeks after the New Year. I have only started writing the rough draft. `20:20`

過完新年的兩個星期後要交，我才開始寫草稿而已。

  SEND »

Let's Chat In English Via APP • ⏻ •

322

旅行回來之後，你會有足夠的時間完成，一起去吧，你會玩得很開心的，而且，現在機票便宜到不行。

You'll have plenty of time to work on it after the trip. Come on, you'll have a great time. Also, plane tickets are dirt-cheap right now. 　20:24

Renee

Okay. Count me in, I guess. Are you going to plan the whole trip? 　20:25

Joey

好吧，加我一個，你要計劃全部的行程嗎？

Tip 和朋友出遊等情形常用，口氣隨性。

當然了！我已經有一些屬意的地點了，我們肯定要去普吉島看看。

Of course! I already have some places in mind. We will definitely go to Phuket. 　20:27

Renee

那座島嶼以寬敞的沙灘和宜人的熱帶氣候聞名。

It's an island that is famous for the spacious❷ beaches and tropical climate. 　20:29

Renee

What about Bangkok? Ever since I watched "The Hangover II", I've wanted to go there. 　20:32

Joey

那曼谷呢？自從看了《醉後大丈夫2》之後，我就一直想去那裡。

當然了，曼谷絕對會在行程中的，小心了，那可是一座瘋狂的城市。

Of course. Bangkok is absolutely on the itinerary❸. Be warned, though, it is a crazy city. 　20:35

Renee

Haha, thanks. I'll try to remember. Okay, I will start packing tomorrow. 　20:38

Joey

哈哈，謝謝你的提醒，我會謹記在心的，好吧，我明天要開始整理行李了。

 　　 SEND ▸▸

Let's Chat In English Via APP ● ⏻ ●

11:25 🛜 📶 🔋

Renee

Hey, Joey! I am planning to go to Australia next year. `11:25`

嗨，喬伊！我明年打算去澳洲。

所以今年去泰國，明年是澳洲？你不是去過澳洲了嗎？

Tip 口語英文the next，因為前面出現過this year，所以這裡簡化。

So it's Thailand this year and Australia the next? Haven't you already been to Australia? `11:31`

Joey

Renee

I have, yes, but I only had a chance to visit Melbourne. This time, I am going to visit Sydney and maybe Perth. `11:35`

是去過，但那時只有機會參觀墨爾本，這次，我打算去雪梨，也許也會去柏斯看看。

聽起來很棒，你真的很熱愛旅遊，這次也打算一個人去吧？

Sounds awesome. You really do love traveling, huh? You're going alone this time, too, right? `11:38`

Joey

Renee

Well, ever since that crappy❹ group tour experience in Korea, I swore to always travel by myself. `11:40`

自從那次糟透的韓國旅行團經驗之後，我就發誓，以後都要自助旅行。

你說的話是什麼意思啊？

What do you mean? `11:41`

Joey

Renee

If you are on an organized tour, you have to stick to a predefined❺ itinerary and schedule. `11:46`

如果參加旅行團，就必須受限於預定的行程和時間表。

Tip stick to有「堅持」之意，這裡表達「嚴守行程的呆板」。

  **SEND ≫**

But if you are led by a tour guide, you won't have any difficulty figuring out where to go and what to do. `11:48`

不過，如果有導遊帶領，就不用煩惱要去哪裡參觀、該做什麼活動了。

Joey

Renee

I know, but I don't like feeling confined₆ when I travel. `11:49`

我知道，但旅遊的時候，我不喜歡被限制住的感覺。

Renee

Plus, if you do some research before you leave, you can find out some cool places to visit on your own. `11:52`

再說，如果你出發前做足功課，就能找到一些很酷的景點。

那麼說，旅行團是屬於老人家的旅遊方式囉？對他們來說，一切都要事先安排好。

So group tours must be an old people thing, then. For them, everything has to be arranged well in advance. `11:55`

Joey

Renee

Exactly. But we are young. We should be out there experiencing how exciting life can be. That's the fun of traveling alone! `11:59`

沒錯，但我們是年輕人，應該到處走走，盡情體驗刺激的生活，那就是自助旅行的樂趣！

小心點，好嗎？安全還是第一優先的。

Tip priority本身就有「優先」之意，加上number one以強調最重要。

Well, be careful, okay? Safety should be your number one priority₇. `12:03`

Joey

1. 旅遊打包真累人

Joey 2015/3/10

Getting ready for this trip to Thailand has been exhausting! To be honest, I am not sure if I am bringing too much or too little with me. I think I spent four or five hours packing last week, and I have probably spent an hour everyday since then repacking, usually adding things I think I will need.

準備到泰國的行李真是讓我筋疲力盡！說實話，我不確定我帶的東西是太多還是太少，我上星期花了四、五個小時整理行李，從那之後，每天大概又花一個小時重新打包，通常是為了增加一些我認為會用到的東西。

I have never really been on a vacation like this before. The longest vacation I took was a three-day trip to Hualien for graduating university. For that trip, I packed one small bag and ran out of clean clothes on the third day. I wore a dirty shirt and dirty socks that last day and felt uncomfortable the entire time. This time, because I am going out of the country for a week, I have decided to over-pack just to be safe. For most things, I packed twice what I needed. For example: fourteen shirts, pairs of shorts, and underwear instead of seven. I also packed two toothbrushes, two soap bottles, and two chargers⑤ for my phone. Better to be safe than sorry, right?

我之前從來沒有真正像這樣去渡假，我最長的一次假期，是到花蓮三天的大學畢業旅行，那趟旅行，我只打包了一小袋行李，然後第三天就沒乾淨的衣服可穿了，所以在最後一天，我只好穿著髒衣服和髒襪子，那一整天我都覺得很不舒服。因為這次要出國一個星期，為了安全起見，我決定要多帶一點行李，大多數的東西，我都帶了一倍的量，比方說，我打包了十四件襯衫、短褲、內衣，而不是七件，我還帶了兩支牙刷，兩罐沐浴乳，和兩個手機充電器，小心一點總比到時後悔好，是吧？

2. 想走就走的旅程

📖 Renee 2015/3/10

The beauty of traveling alone is that there are no set plans. It's all up to me. That's why, to be as free as possible, the only thing I reserve in advance is my plane ticket. My entire plan for each trip is a departure❾ date and an arrival date. That's it. I don't book hotels in advance because I want to have the freedom to stay in one city or resort❿ longer if I want. Of course, I always do some research before traveling to see what is cool or interesting, but I don't reserve anything because I want to be able to adjust my trip.

　　自助旅行最棒的地方是，沒有既定的行程，一切都由自己決定，為了能盡可能地自由觀光，我唯一會事先預訂好的就只有機票，每次旅行，我花時間先計劃妥當的，就只有出發與抵達的日期，除此之外就沒其他的了。我不會事先預訂飯店，因為我希望能自由決定在一個城市或遊憩區的停留時間，當然了，我一定會在出發前做足功課，看看有哪些很酷或有趣的景點，但我不會作任何預約，以維持行程上的彈性。

I really think every trip I have taken has been more fun because I keep everything open. The first thing I do when I land in a new country is to find a taxi and get the driver to take me to a cheap, popular⓫ hostel. Without fail, I meet other travelers at the hostel and hear from them what is interesting and, more importantly, worthwhile⓬ to do, see, and eat.

　　我打從心底覺得，就是因為我保留了旅程上的彈性，才讓每次的旅行更加有趣，每當我抵達一個新的國家，我會做的第一件事，就是雇一輛計程車，請司機載我到便宜又大眾化的旅舍，我總會在旅舍遇到其他旅客，聽到他們談起有趣的事，更重要的是，他們會推薦值得做的活動、該看的景點、以及一定要品嚐的美食給我。

Let's Chat In English Via APP

Word 單字	Meaning 字義	Usage 常見用法
1 **tempt** [tɛmp]	動 引誘;吸引;冒…險	a field tempting to sb. 感興趣的領域 tempt one's fortune 碰運氣
2 **spacious** [`speʃəs]	形 寬敞的;廣闊的;無邊無際的	a spacious dining-room 寬敞的餐廳 live in a spacious villa 住在寬敞的別墅
3 **itinerary** [aɪ`tɪnə͵rɛrɪ]	名 旅行計畫 形 旅程的;路線的	on one's itinerary 在某人的行程上 agree on the itinerary 商定行程
4 **crappy** [`kræpɪ]	形 (俚)糟糕的	a crappy project 糟糕的企劃 sb. feel crappy 感覺糟透了
5 **predefined** [prɪdɪ`faɪnd]	形 預先確定的	a predefined schedule 確定的時間表 the predefined settings 預設的設定值
6 **confine** [kən`faɪn]	動 限制;使侷限	confine oneself to the subject 針對話題 be confined in jail 被關在牢房裡
7 **priority** [praɪ`ɔrətɪ]	名 在先;居前	a top priority 第一優先 enjoy priority in 在…方面享有優先權
8 **charge** [tʃɑrdʒ]	動 索價;控告;充電;指責	a voice charged with anger 憤怒的聲音 charge the battery 替電池充電
9 **departure** [dɪ`partʃɚ]	名 離開;出發	at one's departure 出發時 a new departure 新起點;新方針
10 **resort** [rɪ`zɔrt]	名 渡假勝地 動 訴諸;憑藉	stay at a summer resort 避暑 resort to 訴諸;求助於
11 **popular** [`papjələ]	形 民眾的;受歡迎的	be popular with 受…歡迎 at a popular price 廉價
12 **worthwhile** [`wɝθ`hwaɪl]	形 值得做的;有真實價值的	a worthwhile task 有價值的差事 be worthwhile to do sth. 值得做…

海外假期
Travel Overseas～下篇

◀ APP CHAT **3** 海外旅遊真好玩！

這趟假期真的太短了，我還不想回台灣。

This vacation was too short. I don't want to go back to Taiwan yet.
23:26

Renee

Joey

Tell me about it. I don't even want to think about that proposal I need to present in two weeks.
23:29

説得沒錯，我甚至不想去思考我兩個禮拜後要交的企劃案。

Joey

I already miss the sunshine and beautiful beaches on Phuket, not to mention[1] the beautiful women!
23:32

我已經開始想念普吉島美麗的陽光和沙灘，更別説那裡的美女了。

你怎麼能確定那些是貨真價實的女人，而不是人妖呢？

How do you know they were women and not ladyboys[2]?
23:33

Renee

Joey

Shut up. Don't ruin my beautiful memories.
23:34

住口，不要破壞我美好的回憶。

Tip 只有面對經得起玩笑的朋友才適用，否則很容易留下無禮的印象。

你應該停止做夢，回歸現實了，那些女孩當中，有一些可能真的是人妖。

Well, you should stop dreaming and be real. Some of those girls were probably ladyboys.
23:37

Renee

Joey

Well then, don't wake me up yet. I still want to dream about being on the beach surrounded by those angels.
23:40

那麼先別叫醒我，我還想夢見在沙灘上被那些天使圍繞著的畫面呢！

SEND ≫

Let's Chat In English Via APP

23:26

好吧，沙灘的確很舒服，但我比較喜歡高山和瀑布的景色。

Alright. I agree that the beach was relaxing, but I preferred the mountains and the waterfalls⑧. `23:42`

Renee

The waterfalls were awesome, I agree, but the highlight for me had to be lying on the beach getting a tan. `23:46`

Joey

我同意，瀑布的確令人嘆為觀止，但我最喜歡的還是躺在沙灘上做日光浴。

然後看著那些美麗的人妖，對吧？

And watching those beautiful ladyboys, right? `23:47`

Renee

You know it. They were much prettier than you – real feminine ladyboys. `23:49`

Joey

是啊，而且還是比你還漂亮、更像女人的人妖。

Tip 在這裡，只需將you know it當作接話的句子即可。

…就為了你這句話，我希望你無法準時完成那份企劃。

Tip on time為「準時」之意；in time則是「即時」。

…Just for that, I hope you don't finish your proposal on time! `23:50`

Renee

Hey, don't say that. Relax, I was just joking. `23:51`

Joey

嘿，別那樣說，放輕鬆一點，我只是在開玩笑罷了。

SEND ≫

Let's Chat In English Via APP

13:54

Renee: Joey, guess what? I've finally got a real job. 13:54

喬伊,你知道嗎?我終於找到一份正職的工作了。

Joey: Really? That's great! What kind of job is it? 13:55

真的嗎?真是太好了!是什麼樣的工作呢?

Renee: I'm going to be a columnist for a travel magazine. 13:56

我即將成為一家旅遊雜誌的專欄作家了。

Joey: Wow. A travel magazine? Is it a renowned④ one? 13:57

哇,旅遊雜誌嗎?是有名氣的雜誌社嗎?

Renee: I think so, yeah. I am just amazed I got the job when there are so many other good writers out there. 14:01

我想是吧!有那麼多優秀的作家,我還能雀屏中選,這真的讓我很驚訝。

Joey: Don't underestimate⑤ yourself. There are a lot of good writers, yes, but I doubt any of them have traveled to as many places as you. 14:04

別低估你自己,好作家是有很多沒錯,但我懷疑他們之中有人和你一樣,去過那麼多的地方旅行。

Renee: Thanks. I am actually a little worried I will lose my passion for traveling because of this job. 14:07

謝謝你,我其實還滿擔心自己會因為這份工作而失去對旅遊的熱情。

SEND >>

什麼？你做的會是你最喜
歡的事情耶，我認為你不
會有問題的。

What? You'll be writing about your favorite thing in the world. I think you won't have a problem. `14:10`

Joey

Well, I am concerned with the amount of work they are giving me. `14:12`

Renee

我是在擔心他們給我的工作量。

Tip 和worry相比，be concerned with
隱含說話者的擔憂與深思。

I need to think of several new topics every week and submit₆ two articles every month. `14:14`

Renee

我每個禮拜必須想出幾個新
主題，而且，每個月得交出
兩篇文章。

喔，聽起來的確很有壓力，必
須持續想有趣的新鮮事來寫。

Tip do/does能強調說話者所要
表達的內容。

Oh, that does sound stressful, constantly having to think of exciting new things to write about. `14:16`

Joey

Yeah. I am trying to be optimistic₇ right now and look at it as a challenge and a chance to grow. `14:19`

Renee

是啊，但我會試著樂觀
一點，當它是個挑戰與
成長的機會。

這種態度就對了，改天我請你
吃頓晚餐，慶祝一下吧。

Tip buy you (dinner)這種句型
在口語英文中常出現。

That's the right attitude. Let me buy you dinner sometime to celebrate. `14:21`

Joey

🔊 🥁 [_____] **SEND ≫**

18:20

  3. 增長見聞的旅遊

📖 Joey 2015/3/18

Thailand was an eye-opening experience. From the hectic[6] streets of Bangkok to the beautiful beaches of Phuket to the gorgeous waterfalls, I enjoyed every minute of my vacation. I am so glad Renee kept pushing me to go with her. It was my first true vacation since my graduation trip. Now that I know how fun traveling can be, I think I will try to make it an annual thing. I still love my job and don't want to stay away from it too often, so anything more than once a year is probably too much.

去泰國玩真是令我大開眼界,從曼谷繁忙的街道,到普吉島美麗的海灘,還有美麗的瀑布,這次假期的每一刻,我都感到非常享受。很高興芮妮之前一直不死心地勸我去,這可是我從大學畢業旅行以來,第一次體驗到真正的假期,既然我現在已經體驗到旅遊的樂趣,我會盡量將它變成每年的例行事項,我仍然熱愛自己的工作,不想太常離開工作崗位,所以,若是一年內旅遊超過一次的話,對我來說似乎就太多了。

I originally agreed to go only because I thought that if I went with Renee on one trip, she would stop pestering[6] me to go with her every time she traveled. After only a day in Bangkok, however, the trip stopped being about making Renee happy and started being about having fun. Man, did we have fun. I can honestly say I have never had that much fun in my life!

我本來之所以會答應去,是因為我覺得如果和芮妮出國一趟,那麼她以後要旅行時,就不會再一直糾纏我了。然而,在曼谷停留了一天之後,這趟旅程就不再是為了敷衍芮妮,而是我自己放鬆享受的一段經歷,天啊,真是太好玩了,我可以老實地說,我這一生從未有過這麼多的歡樂!

Let's Chat In English Via APP

333

微網誌

4. 人人都有適合的工作

📖 Renee 2015/3/21

After being hired to both write a travel book and a travel magazine column⑩, I have come to believe that there is a job out there that is perfect for each person. The key is keeping your options open. To be honest, though, I got lucky because both jobs found me. Last month, I would have never thought I could earn money traveling. It has always been my passion, never my job. It was only after I was hired by the two companies that I realized there are opportunities to make money doing what I love to do.

在受聘寫旅遊書和負責旅遊雜誌的專欄後，我開始相信，這世界上的每個人，都有最適合自己的完美工作，關鍵是保持開放的心態，別侷限選擇。說實話，我真的很幸運，因為這兩份工作都是自己找上我的，換作上個月的我，絕對想不到自己可以透過旅遊謀生，那一直是我熱衷的興趣，與工作無關，直到我被這兩家公司錄用，我才知道這世界上還有這樣的機會，能讓我在從事自己興趣的同時賺錢。

I think it is safe to say there are opportunities like that out there for everyone. If you are not doing whatever it is you are passionate⑪ about as a profession, I think you should look for a different job. If I am honest, I am concerned my new jobs will take some of the passion out of traveling with the stress and deadlines⑫ it will bring, but I can't think of a better job. It's the definition of my dream job: to get paid to travel.

應該可以這麼說，對每個人來說，類似這樣的機會是一定存在的，如果你從事的職業不是你所熱愛的，那麼也許應該另謀出路。要我老實說的話，我其實會擔心這兩份新工作所帶來的壓力，還有伴隨而來的交稿期限將減弱我對旅遊的熱情，但我想不出有更好的工作，這絕對是我夢想的職業：藉著旅遊賺錢。

Let's Chat In English Via APP

334

Word 單字	Meaning 字義	Usage 常見用法
1 mention [`mɛnʃən]	名 提及 動 提到;說起	not to mention 更不必說 mention sth. to sb. 對某人提起某事
2 ladyboy [`ledɪbɔɪ]	名 人妖	a beautiful ladyboy 美艷的人妖 to become a ladyboy 成為人妖
3 waterfall [`wɔtɚ‚fɔl]	名 瀑布	an artificial waterfall 人造瀑布 by the waterfall 在瀑布旁邊
4 renowned [rɪ`naʊnd]	形 聞名的;有名的	be renowned for 以…而聞名 sth. be world-renowned 舉世聞名
5 underestimate [`ʌndɚ`ɛstə‚met]	動 低估	underestimate oneself 低估自己 underestimate the value of 低估價值
6 submit [səb`mɪt]	動 使服從;提交; (律)建議	submit to one's fate 聽天由命 submit a case to the court 向法院起訴
7 optimistic [‚ɑptə`mɪstɪk]	形 客觀的	be optimistic about 對…樂觀 of an optimistic cast of mind 生性樂觀
8 hectic [`hɛktɪk]	形 忙亂的; 鬧哄哄的	the hectic pace of life 忙亂的生活步調 be hectic at work 工作忙亂
9 pester [`pɛstɚ]	動 煩擾;糾纏	pester sb. with sth. 以…煩擾某人 pester sb. for money 纏著某人要錢
10 column [`kɑləm]	名 專欄;圓柱	read the sports column 讀體育專欄 a newspaper columnist 報紙專欄作家
11 passionate [`pæʃənɪt]	形 熱情的;熱烈的	make a passionate speech 激昂地演說 be passionate about 對…充滿熱情
12 deadline [`dɛd‚laɪn]	名 截止期限	an approaching deadline 接近截止日 extend a deadline 延長截止期限

科技與人性
As Technology Develops～上篇

APP CHAT **1** 科技依賴症

20:08

Leo: My iPad is slow and old now. I have to buy the newest one. 20:08

我的iPad又慢又舊，我得買台最新的才行。

Ben: You're a technology addict, you know that? You already have an iPad, two smartphones, and a laptop. How are you not satisfied? 20:14

你真是個科技狂，你知道嗎？你已經有了一台iPad、兩支智慧型手機，還有一台筆電，這樣還不滿足啊？

Leo: It's just what I do and who I am. These gadgets are like fresh air to me; I can't live without them. 20:17

我就是會這樣，這些科技產品對我來說就像新鮮空氣，生活中不能沒有它們。

Ben: You sound like a drug addict. 20:18

你聽起來活像個犯了毒癮的人。

Tip addict意指「有癮、入迷的人」，前面加上沉迷的對象。

Leo: Come on, we are living in a world where technology is everywhere. 20:19

得了吧，科技在我們的生活裡隨處可見。

Leo: I can't imagine a day or even an hour without checking my phone or Facebook. 20:20

我不能想像自己有一天、或甚至一個小時沒查看手機或臉書。

Ben: My god! You are the textbook definition of an addict! 20:21

天啊！你根本就是教科書裡「上癮」兩個字的典型定義耶！

Tip the textbook definition所強調的是教科書，隱含「最典型」之意。

SEND »

Let's Chat In English Via APP

336

And how is that bad? With all my devices, I have access to comprehensive₁ and current information at all times. 20:24

那有什麼不好？有了這些科技產品，我隨時都可以獲得最全面、最即時的消息。

Leo

即便是知名科技公司的執行長，都承認「關機」的重要性。

Even the executives₂ at many notable₃ technology companies advocate₄ the importance of "logging off". 20:28

Ben

Yeah, well, that's easier said than done. 20:29

是啊，用說的當然比做的容易。

Leo

這些外界的資訊刺激可能會妨礙我們的人際交往與創造力。

The lure of constant stimulation₅ may get in the way of your relationships and personal creativity. 20:31

Ben

舉例來說，你與安妮最近的關係怎麼樣呢？

For example, how is your relationship with Anne? 20:32

Ben

Now that you mention it, not that good. She always complains that I don't pay enough attention to her. 20:35

既然你提到了，不是很好，她總抱怨我不夠重視她。

Leo

Hmm, maybe I do need to reevaluate my priorities... 20:36

嗯，也許我是該重新檢視生活的重心了。

Tip priority搭配reevaluate，有重新排序之意。

Leo

  SEND >>

8:45 📶 📶 🔋

Ben

Don't you hate GPS?

8:45

你不討厭GPS嗎？

Tip 注意用否定語開頭的語氣，可以看出Ben希望聽到的答案是「討厭」。

怎麼了？可別告訴我GPS害你迷路了？

Tip get you lost強調「GPS的主動性」，而非人本身。

Why? Don't tell me your car's GPS gets you lost.

8:46

Leo

Ben

How did you know? I went to Tainan yesterday for a meeting, and, thanks to my "smart" GPS, I was an hour late.

8:49

你怎麼知道？昨天我去台南開會，拜我「聰明的」GPS之賜，我遲到了一個小時。

真的嗎？是發生什麼事了啊？

Tip 詢問過程，what's up也有同樣的意思，但後者有時純粹為打招呼用語。

Really? What happened?

8:49

Leo

Ben

Well, my meeting was at this university on a hill outside the city. There were a lot of hills in the area, all with windy roads.

8:53

會議的場所位於市郊山上的一所大學，那個地區有很多小山丘，全都是蜿蜒的小路。

Ben

And I guess my GPS got confused and told me to drive up the wrong one.

8:55

我猜GPS因此無法判斷，所以帶我走了錯誤的路線。

是啊，GPS指引的方向有時會是錯誤的，尤其是在鄉下或路線崎嶇的地方，這種情形更常見。

Yeah. GPS directions are sometimes wrong, especially in rural or rugged areas.

8:58

Leo

SEND ≫

8:45

Ben

It would have been nice to know that before yesterday! Man, I was pissed off. 9:00

要是在昨天以前知道這件事就好了！真是氣死我了！

Tip 口語英文 piss off，表達「氣瘋了」，強調生氣程度時可用。

老實說，儘管我是個科技癡，但我車上並沒有加裝GPS或任何導航系統。

To be honest, although I am a tech geek, I actually don't use GPS or any other navigation⑥ systems in my car. 9:02

Leo

Ben

Really... you? You don't use GPS?! I am shocked! But you have a point. 9:05

真的假的…你？你不使用GPS嗎？！這太讓我驚訝了！但你的作法的確有道理。

Ben

If you depend on GPS entirely, you won't have any idea where you are while driving. 9:08

如果完全依賴GPS，開車時就不會注意身在何處。

沒錯，嘿，你何不下載一個地圖應用程式到智慧型手機裡呢？

Yep. Hey, why don't you download a map app on your smartphone? 9:10

Leo

Ben

If I use a map app, then I am still depending too much on technology. I will go buy a map later today. 9:14

如果我使用地圖應用程式，那我還是太依賴科技了，我晚一點再去買份地圖。

我還是搞不懂你的「不信任科技症」是為了什麼，畢竟，APP的路線會持續更新。

I still don't understand your total distrust of technology. After all, a map app will be updated⑦ continually. 9:18

Leo

SEND ≫

Let's Chat In English Via APP

339

1. 隨處可見的低頭族

📖 Ben 2015/3/20

Hate is a strong word, I know that. So when I say I hate that no matter where I go, I see too many people with their heads buried in their smartphones, I mean it. It is an epidemic❽, in my opinion. People don't talk to each other anymore. And I don't mean strangers making small talk while waiting for a bus. I mean husbands and wives, boyfriends and girlfriends, children and their parents. Interactions❾ between people have broken down. We no longer have conversations face-to-face but phone-to-phone.

我知道討厭是一個很強烈的字眼,所以,當我說我討厭無論到哪裡,都有一堆人將頭埋在自己的智慧型手機裡時,我就是認真的。在我看來,這簡直是一種流行病,人們不再相互交談了,我說的可不是陌生人等公車時的閒聊,而是夫妻、男女朋友、孩子和父母之間的對話,人際間的互動已經瓦解,大家不再面對面地交談,而是用機械的電話取代。

If I go to a restaurant, I see people playing with their phones. If I go to the movie theater, I see people playing with their phones during the movie. Even if I go on a vacation, I see people around me playing with their phones. It really is too much. I can understand using your smartphone while waiting for the MRT or something mundane❿, but I think it is a tragedy when I see a couple out on a date and both of them are staring at their phones.

到餐廳吃飯,周圍的人在玩手機;去電影院,觀眾邊看電影邊玩手機;即便是去渡假,我還是看到周遭的人們沉迷在手機裡,這真的太誇張了吧!我可以理解在等捷運或其他無聊的時候玩智慧型手機,但當我看到情侶約會,兩個人都盯著自己的手機看時,我就感到很悲哀。

2. 掌握全世界的資訊

📖 Leo 2015/3/23

Thanks to modern technology, work is no longer limited by time and place. For one, I can read or write e-mails twenty-four hours a day, wherever I am. For another, I can handle unexpected situations at my office in Taiwan even when I am abroad on business. Without access⓪ to my e-mail, I wouldn't be able to connect with my overseas customers or partners, and I am afraid my business would suffer. I remember when I forgot to charge my phone last week before I went to sleep. I almost had a heart attack when my phone died during lunch.

　　拜科技之賜，工作不用再被時間與地點侷限了。第一，無論我人在哪哩，都能全天二十四小時收發我的電子郵件；其次，當台灣的公司有突發狀況時，就算我人在國外出差，都能及時處理，如果沒有電子郵件，我就無法與海外的客戶或夥伴聯繫，業務可能就會有麻煩了，上星期，我睡前忘了幫手機充電，當我隔天用午餐，發現手機突然沒電時，我差一點就心臟病發了。

The amount of information I have access to when I have my phone or laptop with me is staggering⓫! I can check airplane ticket prices, stock quotes, or get news from around the world. If I don't know the name of a song or an actor, I can just take out my phone and check. Work, information, entertainment...it goes without saying that technology really helps me a lot!

　　當我有手機或筆記型電腦在身邊時，能處理的信息量是相當驚人的！我可以查機票價格、股票報價、獲得世界各地的新聞，如果我不知道一首歌或是演員的名字，只要拿出我的手機來查詢就沒問題了，工作、資訊、娛樂…不用說，科技對我的幫助實在太大了！

Word 單字	Meaning 字義	Usage 常見用法
1 comprehensive [ˌkɑmprɪˋhɛnsɪv]	名 專業綜合測驗 形 廣泛的；綜合的	a comprehensive insurance 全險 a comprehensive mind 理解力
2 executive [ɪgˋzɛkjʊtɪv]	名 執行官；業務主管 形 執行的；行政的	the chief executive 最高行政官 one's executive staff …的執行人員
3 notable [ˋnotəb!]	名 名人 形 顯著的；著名的	to be notable for sth. 以…知名 a notable difference 明顯的差異
4 advocate [ˋædvəˌket]	動 擁護；提倡	advocate a policy of 擁護…政策 advocate a tax on 提倡徵收…稅
5 stimulation [ˌstɪmjəˋleʃən]	名 刺激；興奮；激勵	in need of stimulation 需要刺激 receive stimulation from 得到刺激
6 navigation [ˌnævəˋgeʃən]	名 航行；航行術； 航運	an instrument of navigation 導航儀器 be adapted for navigation 適用於導航
7 update [ʌpˋdet]	動 提供最新訊息； 更新	the updated information 最新資訊 keep sb. updated 讓…隨時掌握狀況
8 epidemic [ˌɛpɪˋdɛmɪk]	名 流行病；傳染病 形 流行的；傳染的	an epidemic of hepatitis 肝炎的流行 stem the epidemic 遏止傳染病
9 interaction [ˌɪntəˋrækʃən]	名 互動；互相影響	the chemical interactions 化學反應 an interaction between …的相互作用
10 mundane [ˋmʌnden]	形 世俗的；世界的； 平凡的；無趣的	on the mundane level 就世俗上而言 the mundane chores 日常瑣事
11 access [ˋæksɛs]	名 通道；入口 動 接近	cut off the access to 切斷通路 in an access of fury 勃然大怒
12 stagger [ˋstægɚ]	動 蹣跚而行；猶豫； 使吃驚	stagger to one's feet 搖晃地站起來 be staggered at the price 對價錢猶豫

UNIT 5

科技與人性
As Technology Develops～下篇

12:24 📶 🔋

看看這張照片，你看我幫你買了什麼了，潔西。

Tip 口語英文check sth. out，表示要對方看一下某物。

Check this picture out. Look what I got for you, Jessy.　12:24

Ben

A new iPad?! Thanks, Ben! But isn't it expensive? I remember seeing somewhere that it was just released.　12:28

Jessica

一台新的iPad？！謝謝你，班！可是這不是很貴嗎？我記得這台才剛出來而已。

里歐帶我去電腦展，幫我找到了一台便宜的。

Tip expo為exposition（展覽會）的縮寫。

Leo took me to a computer expo and helped me find a cheap one.　12:30

Ben

Your friend Leo, the tech geek❶? You got the right guy to help you out, then.　12:32

Jessica

你那個科技癡朋友里歐嗎？你還真找對人幫忙了。

Tip 在名字後面加上特質描述，口語常見。

還用你說！他一進到會場，就好像虎入羊群一樣。

Tell me about it. He was just like a lion stalking his prey❷ when he got into that exhibition hall.　12:35

Ben

他很清楚要往哪邊走，如果我不是他朋友，絕對會以為他是展場的工作人員。

He knew exactly where to go. If I wasn't his friend, I would have thought he was a worker at the expo.　12:37

Ben

He must have gotten some new toys for himself, huh?　12:38

Jessica

他肯定替自己買了些新玩具，對吧？

SEND ▶▶

沒錯，他買了一台iPad 跟Macbook Air，他不 僅是科技怪胎，還是個 蘋果信徒。

Yeah, he bought an iPad and a Macbook Air. He's not only a tech geek but also a member of the Apple cult. `12:41`

Ben

Then we shouldn't call him a geek because Apple is so fashionable. `12:42`

那麼我們不應該再 叫他科技怪胎了， 因為蘋果很時尚。

Jessica

得了吧，就算用蘋果的產 品，怪胎還是怪胎，蘋果 也無法改變這個事實。

Come on, a geek using Apple products is still a geek. That doesn't change anything. `12:44`

Ben

Haha, you're so mean, Ben. Be nicer to your friend. He helped you get an inexpensive iPad for me. `12:47`

哈哈，你真的很壞，班，對 你朋友好一點，他幫你找到 了一台便宜的iPad送我耶。

Jessica

好啦，我要回去上班 了，我晚上六點去你那 裡，可以嗎？

Yeah, alright. I got to get back to work. I'll go to your place at 18:00, okay? `12:49`

Ben

Great! Don't forget my new iPad. `12:50`

太好了！可別忘了帶我的新 iPad喔！

Jessica

   SEND »

Let's Chat In English Via APP

344

14:48 🛜 ᵄ 🔋

Ben

Leo, I have started to regret asking you to help me buy a new iPad for Jessy. 14:48

里歐，我開始後悔請你幫忙挑新iPad給潔西的這件事了。

Why? What happened? Doesn't she like it? 14:49

怎麼這麼說？發生什麼事了？難道她不喜歡嗎？

Leo

Ben

No, it's quite the opposite₄, in fact. She loves it! She takes it with her everywhere. 14:51

不，事實上，正好相反，她愛死那台iPad了！到哪裡都帶著它。

Ben

She spends all her time with it, even when we are out at a nice restaurant. 14:53

她所有的時間都花在那東西上面，連我們到氣氛佳的餐廳約會，她也還是只注意那台iPad。

那也是會發生的，她現在就像一個五歲小孩沉迷於新玩具一樣。

Tip 口語常用，用來安撫對方的心情。

That happens sometimes. She's like a five-year-old kid obsessed with a new toy. 14:56

Leo

Ben

But she is an adult! And it's a tablet₅ computer, not a toy. 14:57

但她是個成年人！而且那是台平板電腦，不是玩具。

如果你這麼介意的話，何不用你的iPhone和她聊天呢？

If you mind so much, why don't you just chat with her using your iPhone? 14:59

Leo

SEND ≫

Let's Chat In English Via APP • ⏻ •

345

Ben

You're sick, Leo. What's the point of going out on dates, then, if we are both going to sit quietly and stare at different computer screens? `15:03`

真病態,里歐,如果我們都要靜靜地坐著,盯著各自的電腦螢幕,那又何必外出約會啊?

好吧,我了解你的意思,那你打算怎麼處理這個情況呢?

Yeah, I get your point. So…how are you going to deal with the situation? `15:04`

Leo

Ben

I made her promise me not to bring any tech devices on dates. `15:06`

我和她做了約定,她約會時不帶科技產品。

Tip I make sb. promise強調「我」,sb.較為被動,make帶有些許的強迫意味。

連智慧型手機也不能帶嗎?

Tip 在聊天時,若所聊內容很明確時,會省略部分資訊。

Including her smartphone? `15:06`

Leo

Ben

She can have her smartphone with her, but, when we are out together, she has to turn it off. `15:09`

她可以帶智慧手機,但是,當我們約會時,她得關機才行。

噢,老兄,那對我來説是種折磨,要是安妮要求我這樣做,我們肯定會大吵一架的。

Oh, man, that sounds like torture⑥ to me. If Anne asked me to do that, I think we would have a big fight. `15:12`

Leo

 [   ] **SEND ≫**

Let's Chat In English Via APP •   •

346

3. 眼花撩亂的資訊展

Ben 2015/3/27

Without Leo, I would have been lost at the computer expo, lost in a sea of electronics, people and showgirls. All of the booths overwhelmed$_7$ me; I didn't know where to even begin looking for a gift for my girlfriend. Leo led me past all of the smaller tents to the giant Apple one in the middle of the exhibition hall. He told me the new iPad was not the best tablet at the expo, but it was the one I should buy. What could I do but trust him? I wasn't about to go around to every booth and try to find one myself. I wouldn't know the first question to ask!

沒有里歐的話，我肯定會迷失在電腦展裡，會在一堆電子產品、人群還有秀場正妹中不知所措，所有的攤位都讓我驚嘆不已，根本不知道該從何處尋找要送給女朋友的禮物，里歐帶著我穿過所有的小攤位，來到展場中間的蘋果電腦展覽館，他告訴我，在這個展場中，新的iPad並非最好的平板電腦，但卻是我應該要買的一台，除了相信他，我還能怎麼做呢？我才不打算自己到每個攤位尋找產品，我根本連問都不知道該怎麼問！

I didn't realize how perfect the new iPad was for Jessica until I gave it to her. She doesn't know anything about processors or screen resolution$_8$. Trying to find the best tablet would have been silly. She loves pretty and fashionable things, so of course she would love the iPad. That must be why Leo took me straight to the Apple booth.

直到我將這台新iPad送給潔西卡，我才理解它對她來說有多麼的完美，她一點都不了解處理器或螢幕解析度這些事情，所以試圖買最好的平板電腦給她會有點蠢，她喜歡漂亮且時尚的東西，所以她當然會喜歡iPad，這肯定是里歐之所以直接帶我到蘋果攤位上的原因了。

4. 與人聯絡零距離

微網誌

Leo 2015/3/29

The great thing about phones today is how versatile they are. I can talk to my friends and family the old-fashioned way, text them with any of my chat apps, use Skype to video chat with them, play video games, watch videos, listen to music, and I can do all of these on one small, compact device. Phones today are, in a word, amazing.

現在手機最棒的地方,就在於多功能,我可以用傳統的撥電話方式跟我的朋友和家人聊天,也可以使用聊天軟體發簡訊、用Skype開視訊聊天、一起玩遊戲,觀看影片、和聽音樂,只要有一台小手機,我就能做到上面所提的事情,簡單來說,現代的手機實在令人驚嘆。

The problem, though, is that I have grown used to having all of these available anytime, anywhere. It's usually good because it keeps me connected to friends all over the world. But because I have gotten used to this ease of connectivity, when my phone has no power or, god forbid, I leave it at home, I feel naked and lost. I know others would say that is unnatural. They would say I should be able to enjoy life without a phone in my pocket. I don't know, I guess I just love enjoying such an intimate level of connection with my loved ones, regardless of how far away they are.

然而問題是,我已經習慣了這種不受限於時間與地點的便利性,這通常是一件好事,因為它能讓我與世界各地的朋友聯絡,但因為我已經習慣這種連繫上的便利,一旦我的手機沒電,或者(拜託千萬不要)當我把它忘在家裡時,我感覺就像裸體般困窘,六神無主,我知道其他人會覺得這很不自然,他們會說,我應該要能享受口袋裡沒有手機的生活,我不知道,但我也許就是喜愛這種無論距離多遠,都能與我所愛的人維持緊密連繫的感覺吧。

Word 單字	Meaning 字義	Usage 常見用法
1 **geek** [gik]	名 怪胎；雜耍演員	a computer geek 電腦迷 consider oneself a geek 視己為怪胎
2 **prey** [pre]	名 獵物；犧牲品	swoop down on the prey 俯衝撲擊獵物 fall prey to one's charms 被…迷倒
3 **cult** [kʌlt]	名 信徒；信眾；擁護者；狂熱	a cult of celebrity 名人的擁護者 the cult of physical fitness 健身熱
4 **opposite** [`ɑpəzɪt]	名 相反物；對立物 形 相反的；對立的	my direct opposite 與我截然相反的人 be opposite to 與…相反
5 **tablet** [`tæblɪt]	名 平板；藥丸；便箋簿	a tablet computer 平板電腦 take a tablet 吃顆藥丸
6 **torture** [`tɔrtʃɚ]	名 折磨；酷刑 動 折磨；拷問	put sb. to torture 拷問某人 be tortured with anxiety 為焦慮所苦
7 **overwhelm** [ˌovɚ`hwɛlm]	動 戰勝；征服；壓倒	overwhelm one's enemy 戰勝敵人 be overwhelmed by 被…打敗、淹沒
8 **resolution** [ˌrɛzə`luʃən]	名 決心；決定；解決；解析	adhere to one's resolution 堅持決定 a resolution on a matter 某事的決議
9 **versatile** [`vɝsətl]	形 多功能的；活動的；多才多藝的	a versatile material 用途廣泛的原料 a versatile artist 多才多藝的藝術家
10 **unnatural** [ʌn`nætʃərəl]	形 不自然的；奇怪的；不近人情的	have an unnatural smile 做作的笑容 in an unnatural manner 態度奇怪
11 **intimate** [`ɪntəmɪt]	名 至交；密友 形 親密的；精通的	be intimate with sb. 和…熟悉、曖昧 have an intimate knowledge 精通知識
12 **regardless** [rɪ`gɑrdlɪs]	形 不注意的 副 不顧一切地	regardless of danger 不顧危險 to work regardless 不顧後果地工作

Note

國家圖書館出版品預行編目資料

搶救英文失語症!照著學就能説的超簡單國民英語 / 張
翔、賴素如英語教學團隊 編著. -- 初版. -- 新北市：華
文網, 2015.04
　　面；　公分. -- (Excellent ; 76)
ISBN 978-986-271-594-9 (平裝)

1. 英語　　2. 會話

805.188　　　　　　　　　　　　　104004032

知識工場‧Excellent 76

搶救英文失語症！
照著學就能說的超簡單國民英語

出 版 者／全球華文聯合出版平台‧知識工場
作　　者／張翔、賴素如英語教學團隊　　　印 行 者／知識工場
出版總監／王寶玲　　　　　　　　　　　　英文編輯／何牧蓉
總 編 輯／歐綾纖　　　　　　　　　　　　美術設計／吳佩真

郵撥帳號／50017206 采舍國際有限公司（郵撥購買，請另付一成郵資）
台灣出版中心／新北市中和區中山路2段366巷10號10樓
電　　話／（02）2248-7896
傳　　真／（02）2248-7758
ISBN-13／978-986-271-594-9
出版日期／2015年4月初版

全球華文市場總代理／采舍國際
地　　址／新北市中和區中山路2段366巷10號3樓
電　　話／（02）8245-8786
傳　　真／（02）8245-8718

港澳地區總經銷／和平圖書
地　　址／香港柴灣嘉業街12號百樂門大廈17樓
電　　話／（852）2804-6687
傳　　真／（852）2804-6409

全系列書系特約展示
新絲路網路書店
地　　址／新北市中和區中山路2段366巷10號10樓
電　　話／（02）8245-9896
傳　　真／（02）8245-8819
網　　址／www.silkbook.com

本書為名師張翔、賴素如英語教學團隊等及出版社編輯小組精心編著覆核，如仍有疏漏，請各位先進不吝指正。來函請寄mujung@mail.book4u.com.tw，若經查證無誤，我們將有精美小禮物贈送！

Knowledge is everything！

知識工場

Knowledge is everything !

知識工場
Knowledge is everything！